demons

book 2 of the seers trilogy

demons

heather frost

sweetwater books
an imprint of cedar fort. inc.
springville. utah

This one is dedicated to you, Dad.
You've taught me so much—
the least of which is the answer to everything: 42.

© 2012 Heather Frost

ISBN 13: 978-1-4621-1034-6

Published by Sweetwater Books, an imprint of Cedar Fort, Inc.
2373 W. 700 S., Springville, UT 84663
Distributed by Cedar Fort, Inc., www.cedarfort.com

LIBRARY OF CONGRESS CATALOGING-IN-PUBLICATION DATA

Frost, Heather (Heather Marlene), 1989-, author.
  Demons / Heather Frost.
     pages cm. -- (The Seers Trilogy ; book 2)
  Summary: Things become dangerous for Kate as she is hunted by the Demon Lord.
  ISBN 978-1-4621-1034-6 (alk. paper)
  1. Clairvoyants--Fiction. 2. Immortality--Fiction. I. Title.

  PS3606.R646D46 2012
  813'.6--dc23

                          2012024499

Cover design by Erica Dixon
Cover design © 2012 by Lyle Mortimer
Edited and typeset by Melissa J. Caldwell

Printed in the United States of America

10 9 8 7 6 5 4 3 2 1

Printed on acid-free paper

prologue

Patrick O'Donnell
May 10, 1797
Wexford County, Ireland

My lower back was beginning to ache. I'd been hunched over far too long, but I wasn't about to move just yet. I was finally getting it right. The shading wasn't too dark around her eyes, and the gentle planes of her small face were sloped almost to perfection.

This in itself would have been reason enough for me not to move. I was a painter—sketching had never come easily to me. When I worked with paints, it required no thought. The canvas called to me, guiding my strokes. The art of drawing was an entirely different experience, however. I would agonize over every line, second-guess every mark I tried to make. Sometimes I enjoyed the challenge, while at other times I had to force myself through every second. Today was surely a mixture of both.

There was another reason I refused to acknowledge the muscles screaming in my body, the reason for my taking up the sketch at all, even though I would have rather spent the day working on the painting of my mother's garden—a painting I'd started a few days ago. I'd recently finished a painting of my father's cherished church, where he was the local pastor, and my mother loved it so much that she insisted I immortalize her flowers.

• • • ❖ | ❖ • • •

That is how I would have spent the day, had I not remembered the dream.

It was simple, as dreams go. Just a face. At first, I believed it to be pretty, though upon further staring I realized the deeper beauty. Small, delicate, and perhaps more rounded than most people would consider attractive. But there was something so warm, so real about that face. She had a small smile playing about her lips, and her hair was long—a combination of blonde and brown. It looked so soft, and I remember wanting to reach out and touch the subtly waving locks, though I couldn't. In my dream, I stood frozen. I simply watched her, and although she didn't seem to notice me, I had a feeling that she knew she was being watched. Her eyes were green at first glance, yet a deeper look revealed thin flecks of gold.

It felt like I stared at her all night. Her image was burned into my mind, and I was sure that it would be forever. Still, I was working feverishly to finish this unjust portrayal of her unique beauty. And though it did not capture her completely, my drawing was one of the best sketches I'd ever managed to create.

"My brother, the genius!" a boisterous voice called suddenly, breaking into my thoughts.

I glanced up quickly, my pencil pausing instinctively against the paper. I smiled as I watched my younger brother approach. He had just celebrated his sixteenth birthday two days ago. I would be eighteen soon, but I knew he would still take pleasure in the fact that he was "gaining" on me.

Sean strolled across the yard, stepping through the long green grass with full, leisurely strides. He looked a great deal like me, though many claimed he had inherited more of my mother's attractive looks. He was certainly the stronger personality between us. Where I was often seen as shy and studious, Sean was always smiling and thoroughly involved. He was the first to begin a dance, and the last to leave any social event. Many praised his quick wit, and he was acutely aware of this admiration.

Though I had plenty of reasons to be jealous, I was not. He was my brother, and I loved him. As he loved me.

"Your dedication amazes me," Sean continued, his hands deep in his pockets. It was the characteristic pose the men of our family took, except he always made it seem natural rather than nervous. "I've never finished a thing in my life," he said with an oddly satisfied grin, jumping easily over the small stream that trickled through our back pasture.

Our modest home of gray stone and brown wood dominated my view, a dirt lane and rolling hills the only other things in sight. It was a backdrop I loved, and one that I often called upon to help fuel my creativity. The old stump that I sat on was at the back edge of our land, though it wasn't close enough to the rudimentary fence for me to recline against. Nevertheless, sitting here afforded me the most inspirational view, so I suffered through the slight discomfort.

I watched Sean close the remainder of the distance between us, and I finally spoke. "You've never regretted that before."

"Ah, but I don't regret it now. I merely state fact." He stooped before me, and I quickly lifted my pencil as he snatched my unfinished drawing away. He brought it closer to his face, so he could inspect it critically.

While he did, I stretched my knotted back muscles and flexed my stiff fingers. I didn't stand, though. I didn't rush him to speak—I knew he would give his opinion with minimal urging, once he was finished appraising the piece.

I expected a jibe of some kind, but instead his voice was mildly surprised. "This is good, Patrick." He paused, then added playfully, "What is it supposed to be?"

I frowned at him, and he laughed as he caught sight of my face. "Merely teasing you, big brother. Really, it's quite good. Who is she?"

He returned the thin book that held my drawings, and as I took it back I quickly ran my eyes analytically over the sketch. "I don't know. I saw her face in a dream."

"She's pretty."

"Yes," I whispered, gazing into her eyes. "She is."

He cocked his head, coming around me to look at the sketch over my shoulder. "You know, she's almost familiar."

I glanced over at him, interested. "Are you sure?"

His brow furrowed in thought, eyes drawn to her face. "Yes. Still,

I can't imagine where I might have seen her. Surely not your dreams, though."

We shared a quick laugh at the absurdity of that thought, and then Sean slapped a hand against my shoulder, pulling me out of my thoughts before I could become submerged again.

He knew me well.

"Mother wishes you to come inside." His blue eyes—an exact repetition of mine—grew knowing. "Sarah McKenna came to call on her, and we're to entertain her until mother can finish listening to Father's preparatory sermon."

I hesitated, my eyes darting back to the page in front of me. "I'm nearly done."

Sean sighed loudly. "Patrick, you are the epitome of hopeless. You are aware that Mother arranged this for your benefit, surely?"

My brow furrowed in confusion. "But Sarah called on mother."

"Diabolical, isn't she?"

"Who? Mother or Sarah?"

Sean shrugged. "Both?"

I chuckled with him, scooping up my work under one arm so we could walk together back to the house.

Sarah McKenna waited in the small parlor. She was wearing a nice dress of pleasant blue, and her red curly hair caught my artistic eye as it always did. The color was just so bright, so vivid. It was piled carefully on her head, in a way only a woman could accomplish. She was sitting near the window, thumbing through one of Father's philosophy books. She looked up as we entered, and a smile spread across her face.

She was my same age, our birthdays mere weeks apart. We had played together as children, and she had teased me through adolescence. And now as we approached adulthood, she always seemed to find an excuse to visit my parents. Her eyes were a beautiful blue, and her face was pale and lightly freckled. Her face was very feminine, and somehow managed to be smoothly angular.

She was perhaps the most beautiful woman in the province; she knew this, sometimes to her detriment. Still, though her quick tongue could often get her into trouble, her dazzling eyes always seemed to repair any damage.

She laid the book aside and stood. "The O'Donnell brothers. What a pleasure."

"The pleasure is strictly ours," Sean rejoined at once, offering a quick bow.

I added my own nod and a not so graceful, "Good day, Miss McKenna."

She smiled at me and then noticed the brown leather book under my arm. "Your drawings. Have I interrupted the master at work?"

"You flatter me," I said honestly, following her glance to my book.

"May I see your newest masterpiece?"

"If you wish."

She smiled. "I do."

I shifted the book to her hands, and she opened it to the last drawing in the sketchbook—almost in the exact middle. I watched her face as she studied my drawing, and I felt my stomach tighten when she frowned.

Sean stood next to me, silently watching this exchange. I was grateful that he didn't leave, because I knew that I'd soon run out of things to say to her; his wit would come into play beautifully, as it always did.

Finally, Sarah looked up at me, her eyes impressed. "You've improved. The last sketch of yours I saw was . . ."

"Horrible beyond comprehension?" Sean supplied, his tone exceedingly helpful.

I sent a warning glance toward him, but Sarah was laughing lightly.

"It wasn't like your paintings," she admitted. "However, this . . . You have captured emotion. Except it is almost a nameless one. Who is she? And what is she thinking that creates that smile and so captures your attention?" She shook her head lightly. "Whatever it is, I would certainly like to learn it."

I nearly blushed but somehow managed to keep calm. "I don't know who she is. And what she is thinking . . ." I shrugged slowly. "Perhaps I'll never know."

Sarah smiled at me. "Why, Patrick, you speak so mysteriously."

"I don't mean to."

Sean grunted. "Of course he does. Miss McKenna, he is just so supe-rior, isn't he?"

"Yes, he is." Watching the way her eyes drifted back toward me—so intently, so easily—I suddenly realized a startling truth. Sarah McKenna was genuinely taken with me.

Perhaps even more startling, I realized in that moment that I might genuinely be taken with her.

❉

Fear Dearg
Present Day—Midnight
New Mexico, United States

I waited. There had been so much waiting the past few weeks. But it was nearly over now.

I stood in a small city park, just beside the pool of yellow light cast by the lone street lamp. It was a quiet night—no cars could be seen, and even the sounds from the highway were distant, as if muffled by the dark. Humans were asleep in their homes, unsuspecting of the evil that lurked in their midst. Unaware of me.

All at once I heard a car approaching down the otherwise quiet street. I straightened, angling my long body toward the sound. In seconds a pair of headlights flashed across me as the car came out of a side street and pulled toward the park, coming to rest against the curb. The lights switched off, but the car continued to run. I heard the power locks disengage, and I stepped up to the passenger door in front of me. I pulled it open before ducking smoothly inside.

There was no illumination in the car, yet from the glowing light out-side I could see the scarred face of the driver. A man I'd seen many times but never really spoken to. Takao Kiyota was his name.

He was reaching into his jacket, pulling out a thin spray bottle. It appeared to be innocent perfume, though I knew differently.

He handed it over sleekly, skipping a greeting and moving on to the warn-ing. "There isn't much. Only one guaranteed potent dose. You cannot fail."

I took the bottle and stuffed it into my own pocket without bothering to study it. "I never do."

Kiyota's head dipped once, allowing that, before he continued. "The Demon Lord assures me your target will be susceptible. Romero reported as much when his Seer saw him at the club last week."

"I'm sorry I missed O'Donnell. I was in the area."

The Demon Lord's personal Seer smiled, but it was completely chilling. It was a smile I knew well, for it was identical to mine. "Yes, that was a pity, wasn't it?"

I glanced out the windshield, my words firm. "I will be doing this differently than originally discussed."

"How differently?"

"I'm unwilling to approach O'Donnell so directly. This situation requires a bit more finesse."

"Are you sure that's wise?"

My nonanswer was answer enough.

The Demon Lord's Seer spoke deeply. "Very well. But you must not forget the stakes. There is more than the Demon Lord's fury to risk."

"I'm perfectly aware of the risks. That's the reason I'm here. I would not entrust this Seer to anyone else. Kate Bennett is mine."

The Seer seemed to consider his words carefully. When he spoke, his voice was low. "You're sure she's the one?"

"I'm positive."

His lips compressed into a thin line. "If you're right, she's worth more than the Demon Lord first imagined."

Again, I didn't bother to comment. Instead, I got right to the point. "I could use your talents, if you can spare a couple of days."

Kiyota's answer was immediate. "My orders were to see that you have everything you need."

I smiled darkly, fingering the bottle in my pocket. "Excellent."

one

Kate Bennett
New Mexico, United States

knocked loudly on the bathroom door, surely bruising my knuckles. "Josie!" I yelled. "You've been in there for forty-five minutes!"

My other sister, Jenna, stood behind me, and she grunted when her twin didn't answer. "She's going to take all the hot water."

"Forget hot water," I muttered, glaring at the closed door. "We're not even going to get to brush our teeth before Christmas."

Jenna pushed past me and began banging on the door with both hands. "Josie, get out right now!"

The running water continued, however, and I knew we were being punished for something.

This was a perfect example of Josie behavior, and I shouldn't have been surprised. Both of my little sisters were devious when they wanted to be, but only Josie would do something this ridiculous. I was guessing this treatment came because she hadn't eaten the last cookie.

Eleven-year-old girls could be so annoying.

I turned away from the door, giving up. I walked back to my room and heard Jenna start yelling again before I closed my door, effectively muffling the pounding and screaming. I sat on the edge of my bed and pulled my makeup bag closer to my knee. Luckily I stored all my cosmetics in my room, where the twins wouldn't try using them, so at least I could freshen up before school started.

The right side of my face had some light cuts, which I tried to cover with my foundation. They were constant reminders of a fight I'd been in about a week ago. Because even though I had normal problems with normal sisters, my life wasn't exactly normal.

I was a Seer—a human caught between two worlds, the regular world and a supernatural one, where immortal beings, called Guardians, fought to protect the human race from the evil influences of Demons. It was all a little confusing because I hadn't been immersed in it for long. Sometimes I wondered if I'd ever understand it all.

I'd been seeing auras since my parents died a few months ago, but still tried to live a normal life, despite seeing people's emotions. And then I started seeing invisible people, with no mood auras— just a thread of silver outlining them. These invisible people eventually became my Guardians, helping to protect me when a group of Demons began haunting me. A dangerous couple of weeks followed, bringing me to a final climactic moment when my sisters had been kidnapped by their Demon teacher. Luckily they'd been drugged, so they had no memory of the terrifying experience. The Demons had wanted me, though I still wasn't sure why they'd wanted me so badly. The leader, Quin Romero, had mentioned it was the Demon Lord who was interested in me. I knew that revelation bothered my Guardians. Sheesh, it bothered me! And of course I was freaked out because I didn't understand *why*. I was a new Seer, and though Demons depended on Seers to help protect them from Guardians, it seemed pretty far-fetched that the Demon Lord himself would want me. But he must. According to Romero, the Demon Lord wanted me so badly he'd sent his personal Guardian/Seer hunter after me—the mysterious *Fear Dearg*, or Far Darrig. That thought still kept me up at night.

It had been a week since I'd narrowly escaped Romero's people— primarily the beautiful and evil Demon Selena Avalos. Honestly, I think I had more nightmares about her than anything else. She absolutely terrified me.

But here it was, a sunny Monday morning—seven days since I'd last seen her. I shouldn't still be so shaken by my encounter with her, but I was. I don't think people got over someone like Selena very easily.

I finished brushing on my makeup, grabbed my backpack, and moved for the stairs. I glanced back down the hall to see Jenna had finally managed to get into the bathroom, and she was brushing her hair into a messy ponytail.

My own ponytail swished from side to side as I moved quickly down the stairs, heading for the kitchen. I'd already had breakfast, but I hoped to talk to my grandpa for a moment before school. He was one of the only people who knew what was really going on in my life—at least the Demon-stalkers part. That was mostly because he was a Seer himself, though he considered himself retired at this point. I'd learned this just a week ago, though I still wasn't quite used to the fact. I mean, how is anyone supposed to react when they find out their grandfather used to battle Demons alongside immortal Guardians? Except, even though it was hard to visualize, at least I had someone to talk to. Aside from my Guardians, the only other person that knew a fraction of the truth was my best friend, Lee—and she only thought I was psychic or something, and able to see auras. I hadn't exactly taken the time to update her on the whole Seer and Demon thing.

I entered the kitchen and Grandpa Bennett looked up from the morning paper, lowering it slightly. "Good morning," he greeted me, sounding distracted.

"Hey." I moved to sit in the chair next to him, running my eyes quickly over the paper. "Any more news on the Death Train?"

He shook his head. "No more accidents attributed to it so far. But Far Darrig is still out there—I'm sure of it."

The mysterious and seemingly accidental deaths had begun in Santa Fe weeks ago. Recently I'd learned it was the Demon Far Darrig, making a trail that would eventually lead to his target— me. Understandably, I was trying to keep tabs on his movements. Admittedly, for a week now, there had been nothing. I knew the tension was wearing on my grandpa, and my Guardians weren't exactly relaxing either. Personally, I tried not to think about it too much. I had a big algebra test coming up, which was enough of a scare for me.

Grandpa sighed and lowered the paper to the table, rubbing a hand across his eyes, forcing his reading glasses up as he did so. "I don't know, Kate. This silence can't be good."

"Maybe it is," I offered slowly. "I mean, maybe the Demon Lord's decided I'm not worth it? Maybe Patrick and Toni were more of a force than he imagined they'd be."

Grandpa shook his head. "No. That's not how the Demon Lord operates. A couple of Guardians won't stop him."

I reached over to grab his hand lying helpless on the table. "Grandpa, it's okay. Everything's going to be fine. Toni and Patrick are working on it."

"Maybe I should get more involved in the search," he muttered, practically to himself.

"Absolutely not," I insisted. "You're happily retired, remember?"

"I don't want to go back to the life of a Seer. At least, not permanently. But I want to be there for you."

"You're doing enough, really." I released his hand and changed the subject. "Where's Grandma?"

"The store. She's worried about dinner tonight."

Though I knew the answer, I asked the question anyway. "Why?"

He sighed, one old hand scratching the side of his head. "I don't understand exactly why she's still so upset about your breakup with Aaron, but she is. The thought of having another boy over scares her. Aaron was a great kid—she doesn't want to be disappointed."

Grandma hadn't actually met my new boyfriend, though everyone else in my family had. Patrick O'Donnell was my Guardian, and we'd been officially together for a week now. It had been a really weird but wonderful week. I'd hardly talked to Aaron, and though I regretted that, I wasn't sure how to change things. He'd been a part of my life for so long; it was strange not having him around now. True, things hadn't been great between us since the accident, but he'd been the best boyfriend a girl could wish for. A great friend.

In the end, it just couldn't work between us. It wasn't him; it was me. And though I regretted breaking up with him, it had been the right thing to do. In all honesty, I should have had that conversation with him a long time ago.

Still, school got a little awkward sometimes. But despite the uneasiness of the past week, the wonderful stuff outweighed the bad.

Patrick was everything I'd ever wanted, and he was everything I needed. When I'd finally realized that I was falling in love with him, I broke up with Aaron and went to see Patrick the same night. We'd kissed and talked until late into the night and early morning. Our relationship was beautiful, albeit unique. He was two hundred and thirty, and I was eighteen. He was immortal, and I wasn't. He'd been born in the greenest spot on Earth, and I lived in a desert. But we fit together perfectly, despite our differences. True, I knew we'd run into problems—it was inevitable, considering everything. But for now, things were great. We didn't think too far into the future, which was fine by me. I was content to just enjoy the blissful moments we had together.

"You like him, don't you?" I asked my grandpa suddenly.

He glanced up at me, taken aback by the question. "He's a Guardian," he finally stated. "There must be something good about him."

I frowned, sensing the deeper meaning in his words. "That's not an answer at all."

He straightened in his chair, pushing the paper down against the table. He was uneasy, and it made me all the more curious to know what he was thinking. "He cares about you deeply," he hedged. "Anyone can see that. It's just that . . ."

"What?"

"I would have chosen differently for you."

I stared at him, unsure I'd heard him right. "We *are* talking about the same person, right?"

His expression turned wary. "Patrick O'Donnell is a fine man and a great Guardian. I trust him with your safety, which is a hard thing for a grandpa to admit. But as far as him being your boyfriend . . ." He sighed, and then it was his turn to take my hand. "Kate, you're going to get sick of this life. Trust me. No matter how thrilling it is at first, you won't want this forever. I did it for fourteen years, and that's longer than most manage to hold out. And when you finally decide to cut yourself off from them—once your safety is assured and the Demons have moved on to someone else—you *will* want out. And where will that leave you and Patrick? I just don't want you to get hurt. And I don't want Patrick to get hurt either."

I continued to look at him, barely believing he was saying these things—thinking these things. "I love him," I said, saying the words out loud for the first time.

Grandpa's lips pressed tightly together, and I could see in his aura he was going to stop pressing me—for now. Nevertheless, his green uneasiness remained; a thick tendril of emotion surrounded his body. "It's your life. I understand that. And I'm not going to get all preachy and difficult. I just wanted to give you a dose of reality. As harsh as it may seem, it's only because I love you."

I heard someone coming down the stairs, and I knew this conversation needed to end. "Thanks, Grandpa. But don't worry—I know what I'm doing."

Josie entered the kitchen, her wet hair pulled back into one huge braid. She moved for the toaster, grabbing the nearby loaf of bread. She pulled out two slices and plopped them into the waiting slots, then pressed the button.

"Still upset about those cookies, huh?"

Though Josie was obviously avoiding me, she turned around after hearing Grandpa's question.

"The last one was supposed to be mine," she said loudly, resolutely keeping her eyes away from me, though I was sitting right next to him. "*Some* people don't understand how calling things works."

I wasn't going to fight with her, but Jenna had just come in. "Only because *some* people are dumb enough to call the last cookie. I mean, how is that fair? You ate like half of them."

"Did not."

"Did too."

"I did not!"

"Yes you did! And Grandma said me and Kate could finish them, so there! It's not my fault you were at a stupid soccer game."

"Now, now," Grandpa said loudly, his deep voice cutting through their high-pitched arguing. "You girls need to stop this. The cookies are gone, Josie, so there's no point crying."

"I am *not* crying!" Josie snapped heatedly.

"And Jenna," Grandpa said, ignoring Josie's protest. "Didn't you call the last cinnamon roll when Grandma made them last week?"

"Yes," she muttered, sounding angry.

"And didn't Josie honor that call?"

"Yes I did!" Josie grunted.

"Jenna?" Grandpa pressed.

Jenna sighed. "Yeah. But Kate helped eat the cookies too—why isn't anyone yelling at her?"

Grandpa Bennett sighed. "You two fight more than anyone else I know. And no one's yelling at Kate because she's not carrying on about this."

"But she's as guilty as me, and that's not—"

Jenna's haughty words were cut off by Josie, who insisted it was time to go now that her toast had popped. She was infamous for always having the last word. While she hurried to butter the toast and then cover it with an unhealthy mix of cinnamon and sugar, Jenna grumbled and dug in the pantry for the Pop-Tarts.

Once the twins had gathered something resembling a meal, I hugged my grandpa and slipped my bag onto my shoulder, leading the way out of the house. My sisters trailed behind me, still not speaking to each other as we walked. I opened the front door, stepped off the porch, and followed the short sidewalk around to the driveway, where my maroon Hyundai Elantra waited. I climbed into the driver's seat, hoisting my backpack into the backseat in the familiar routine. While I got my iPod plugged in, the twins pushed into the backseat and put on their seat belts. They were still too upset to speak to me, so I didn't bother to ask their opinion on the music. I started a Disney playlist, and seconds later we were on the street, leaving our house behind.

As I made the way toward my best friend's house, I could hear scattered muttering in the backseat. But since it wasn't directed toward me, I ignored it. I let them eat their breakfast, and I let myself wonder what the day would bring.

I never could be sure what would happen, now that I was a Seer. The days had been relatively quiet ever since Selena Avalos had disappeared, but I knew it wouldn't last. Still, even the brief reprieve from danger had been great. It had given me a chance to readjust to my new life and some time to explore my new relationship with Patrick.

I pulled up to Lee's house without thought. It was like the car knew where to take me each morning out of pure habit. I looked out the window, knowing that Lee would open her front door any second. She'd never kept me waiting.

She'd been my best friend since I'd first moved here, back in grade school. She was the funniest person I knew, and she had more spunk than most girls dared take with them to high school. Though she was probably the most secure-in-her-own-skin girl in the country, if not the entire world, she had this hilarious habit of completely changing her style every couple of months or so. Most recently she'd been strictly gothic. I'd grown so used to seeing her in black that I hardly recognized her when she opened her front door and stepped out onto her porch.

Gone was the black hair and attire I'd come to expect. Lee—if indeed it was her—was a walking Popsicle.

She was orange. And I mean, *orange*. From the flat shoes she walked in, to the orange, spiky 'do that was her hair, my best friend was orange. Orange shorts, orange shirt, orange bracelet, orange necklace, orange backpack. And as she crossed her yard and moved closer, I was able to make out the orange lipstick and eye color. Even her mascara was orange.

She was a walking explosion.

Before Lee reached the idling car, I heard Jenna mutter in wonder, "Nothing scares her, does it?"

Lee opened the passenger door and lowered herself into the car. She gave me a happy smile, and I said the first thing that came to my mind.

"You cut your hair."

"Locks of Love," she assured me.

"Was that before or after you dyed it?"

"Before. But only just. You like it?"

"Where's the radiation spill?"

She punched my arm good-naturedly. "I was going for happy, not post-apocalyptic."

"That's a fine line you've chosen to walk." I squinted closer, catching sight of her nose when she pulled her door closed and reached for her seat belt. "You kept the piercing?"

"Yeah—it killed to get it, so I may as well get some more use out of it. It's a cute orange jewel, isn't it? My mom says it's too much, but she hated it in the first place, so I didn't dare trust her opinion."

I settled back into my seat, watching as she clicked her buckle into place. "You know, Lee, not many people can pull off orange. What's the occasion?"

"Rainbow Days," she answered matter-of-factly. "It's a seven-week holiday I invented! I lived without color for so long, I decided to celebrate the rainbow. So each week I will honor a different color." She extended her painted fingernails for me to inspect. "The shade isn't quite right, but does it work with the shirt?"

"Surprisingly, yes." I shook my head at her. "You've done so many weird things; this actually seems perfectly normal."

Josie spoke up from the backseat. "At least you won't get lost if you go on a hike. A satellite could pick you up, no problem." She gestured with her hand, laying it in one place and then emphasizing the next. "The Great Wall of China, The Pyramids, Lee . . ."

Jenna giggled, and I shifted the car into first gear. Lee just grinned at the compliment, and we headed toward the elementary school. It was a typical morning.

Once we were clear of the subdivision and had merged onto the main road, Lee suddenly turned down the volume. I glanced over at her, noting her more serious expression. "Did you hear the news this morning?" she asked me. Her voice was quiet, but my sisters just leaned closer so they wouldn't miss a word.

"No—what?"

Lee bit her bottom lip, then spoke quickly. "Some park ranger found a body late yesterday. It was Ms. Rhodes."

I felt my body grow cold, despite the warm morning heat. I tried to keep my face impassive, but all I could think about was Selena Avalos, and my fingers curled tightly around the steering wheel. I knew Toni had been searching for the old elementary school teacher, and though I knew in a remote part of my mind she was most likely dead, the thought that Demons would kill someone harmless like Ms. Rhodes made me sick. She'd died because the Demon Lord had wanted me.

Jenna spoke up from the backseat, sounding scared. "Her body? She's dead?"

"Why do you sound so surprised? You're the one who told us all she was probably murdered," Josie reminded, but her voice was pretty small, revealing her own shock at the news.

Lee was still watching me, waiting for my response. I cleared my throat, grateful I had driving for an excuse to stall. "What happened? Did they say?"

"It looked like it was an accident. She was hiking and must have fallen off this cliff or something."

Josie's tone was confused, more than regretful. "Ms. Rhodes? Hiking? How stupid could the police be? She could barely walk from the cafeteria to the classroom."

"Yeah," Jenna agreed, her voice thoughtful. "She was too old to be out in the mountains alone."

Lee shrugged. "I'm just sharing what I heard, no matter how weird it sounds."

Jenna sighed. "Our class is cursed. First Ms. Rhodes went missing, then Miss Avalos . . . I pity our next replacement."

"Who's teaching you now?" Lee asked.

Josie answered. "Some cranky old woman. She wears more makeup than a roomful of models—only she can't pull it off."

"Her name is Ms. Pierce," Jenna cut in. "She's ornery, but at least she's better than the other sub we had. Mr. Burke smelled like old chili."

"True that," Josie agreed fervently, wrinkling her nose at the memory.

two

pulled into the parking lot of the elementary school and the twins scooted promptly out the door, gone without a wave. I shook my head a little as I pulled away from the sidewalk and followed the sluggish line of cars back out to the street.

Lee's voice broke through the softly playing music. "My mom's dating again."

I glanced her way, glad for the topic change even though my mind was still trying to take in Ms. Rhodes's death. "Really? Have you met him?"

She nodded slowly, eyes focused out her window so I couldn't see her face. "Yeah, once. He came over last night, after they'd gone out to dinner. We all watched a movie together."

"And?" I prompted, when she didn't continue right away.

She sighed. "And . . . I don't know. He's a little weird."

"Have you looked in a mirror, Lee?"

A smile tugged her lips, and she glanced toward me. "Yeah, I know. But it's different. She'd kind of stopped the dating game for a while, and I thought maybe she'd given up."

"What's his name?" I asked, sensing she wanted to keep to the facts for now.

"Peter Keegan."

"He sounds like a lawyer or something."

She grimaced. "Yeah, I know."

"So, did she meet him at work?"

"No, I'm not sure where they ran into each other. My mom just said they'd been seeing each other for about a week now, and she thought I should meet him."

"So, is he, like, a creep or something? Like Larry?"

She laughed. "Not even close. He's even better than Ray. He's just . . . weird."

"What does he do?"

"I'm not sure. I didn't put him through the Inquisition. I was more worried about my outfit coming together, to be honest."

"So what's so weird about him?" I asked, pulling into the crowded parking lot of the high school.

"It's hard to define," she answered cryptically. "I want you to meet him."

Her request wasn't uncommon to me—I'd been asked to meet all the guys Lee's mom brought home. I think she relied on me even more ever since I'd become "psychic."

I answered as I carefully guided my car into an available space. "Okay—I'd love to."

"Great. My mom's invited him to dinner this Friday. Does that work for you?"

"I'll clear my schedule," I promised lightly.

She smiled appreciatively. "Thanks, Kate. You're the best."

Once all the doors were locked, we walked together toward the front of the school. Class wouldn't start for another thirteen minutes or so, so we took our time. Lee's outrageous new look got many stares, but she didn't even seem to notice. She was absorbed in asking about me and Patrick.

I kept my answers concise, but the little smile I couldn't keep back made Lee laugh out loud. "He's that great, huh? I knew it. I'm glad you're happy together and that things are going good."

"He's perfect," I agreed. "Now you just need one like him."

She chuckled. "Yeah, you're right. 'Cuz all the guys love orange, huh?"

"I just want you to be happy."

"I am happy."

"Maybe your mom's right, and these extreme fashions you choose are actually your inner cries for help."

"Yeah, maybe." Her phone vibrated, and she pulled it from her pocket quickly. I was a little surprised to see it wasn't orange, but I guess even Lee had limits. She flipped it open, the sudden light in her eyes more telling than words.

"Toni?" I guessed easily, wondering how I should feel about an immortal Guardian showing interest in my best friend. Especially when that immortal Guardian was Toni.

"Yep." Lee answered with a smile. "He's such a funny guy . . ."

"Isn't he in class?" I asked, though of course I knew my Guardian didn't attend the community college like he claimed. He was probably at the warehouse he called home, lounging on the broken couch and killing time on the computer. Immortality seemed a bit wasted on him.

"Yeah—but since when did that stop anyone from having a decent conversation?"

"Are you guys getting serious?" I asked.

She rolled her eyes at me. "We've only hung out a couple times. It's no big deal."

"Are you okay with that?"

"Of course." It was time for us to part ways. "I'll see you in second hour," she called over her shoulder, fingers still tapping over her phone.

I shook my head fondly in her direction before continuing my walk toward the main entrance. A couple classmates sitting on the grass called out to me, and I gave them each a quick wave. I was ready to start up the stairs when I heard a deep voice speak up somewhere behind me.

"Kate, wait up a sec, huh?"

My legs stopped moving and I twisted around to face Jaxon, Aaron's best friend. He was a big guy—a star athlete. His white teeth gleamed brightly on his otherwise dark face. He was usually spouting jokes or laughing at someone else's. Today he was looking serious, his aura a combination of uneasiness and determination, accented with wisps of red anger. His face was firmly set, but he was trying to keep his eyes from looking too accusatory. It was in situations like these I really disliked my Sight: Seeing the full force of a person's emotions was intimidating, and that intimidation was only exaggerated when the person was putting on a relatively calm face.

I'd been hoping to avoid this conversation with Aaron's best friend and, after a week, I'd thought I was relatively safe.

I guess not.

I forced a smile. "Hey, Jaxon, what's up?"

He smiled just a little, his eyes still tight. "Nothing much. You?"

I shrugged, reaching up to grip the shoulder straps on my bag. "Nope."

He nodded, coming to a stop two steps away from me. A few clusters of students passed around us on their way into the school, but for the most part we were ignored.

I refused to shift my weight and appear awkward. I kept my smile firmly in place and waited for him to speak while my fingers circumspectly strangled my bag.

He blew out his breath, half wincing. "Look, I wasn't going to do this. Honestly. What you and Aaron do isn't my business. I respect you too much to lecture you or anything."

"Thanks. I appreciate that, Jax."

"But, Kate," he continued quickly, ignoring my words, "I don't think you understand what you're doing. What this looks like. I mean, you completely dumped him without any warning. He came to pick you up for a dance—after you stood him up all day. Then Monday morning comes around, and you're with O'Donnell, holding hands and smacking lips. Couldn't you have at least waited a week before moving on? Aaron's ego is completely shot. He's a wreck."

I swallowed hard and glanced at my feet, the guilt making my stomach twist. "Jaxon—"

"I know. Totally not my place, totally awkward—I get that." I looked up and our eyes locked. I'd never seen him so serious. "But Aaron's my best friend, Kate. And I think he needs some kind of explanation or something. I don't think he's going to get over this unless you talk to him about what happened. Why it happened."

"What on earth would I say?" I asked, honestly hoping he'd have some ideas.

"I don't know." He sighed. "But come on, you can't pretend that you don't feel guilty about all this. I know you too well not to see the signs. I know you cared about him a lot, and feelings don't just disappear like that."

"Jaxon, things between us were shaky at best since I lost my parents."

"I know. I saw that. I think everyone did. But Aaron was trying. I thought you were trying too. So did he. You didn't even give him a chance to talk this out with you."

"We talked," I argued.

He cut in firmly, the red in his aura flaring sharply. "No. *You* talked. He listened without a choice."

I pursed my lips and glanced away. His words hurt, but I knew that was only because they were true. After all Aaron had done for me . . . I hadn't treated him fairly at all.

Jaxon continued heavily. "Sorry. I don't mean to sound like a jerk. But he's my best friend. What would you do in my place?"

I didn't answer. I didn't have to. We both knew the answer. "I can't make any promises," I finally said. "But I'll try talking to him."

"Thanks. That's all I'm asking for. Just give him a chance to talk this out with you."

I narrowed my eyes, hoping to convey my seriousness. "This isn't going to change anything. You know that, right? Aaron and I . . . we're through."

"I know. But let him at least understand that before you stop talking to him forever."

"He's the one that's been avoiding me," I said defensively.

Jaxon's stare was unwavering. "And you blame him?"

He waited a moment—like I'd have a good rebuttal for that?—and then gave me a quick nod before moving around my still form and up the few stairs to the school doors.

I didn't follow right away, because I didn't want him to see how much his words had affected me. For the first time, I really started to see how all of this had looked to Aaron. And knowing how much I'd hurt him . . . the guilt was almost making me sick.

I let out a sigh and walked into the school.

Patrick was waiting for me in American Lit, like he always did, sitting in the prearranged circle. He was the first one in the room, which was usually the case. He was thumbing through a paperback—probably *The House of the Seven Gables*, the book he'd finished long before the rest of the class. We were going to be taking a test on it today, so maybe he was refreshing his memory. Or maybe he was just waiting for me to show up. Because as soon as I stepped into the room, he looked up, closing the book and laying it on his desk in the same motion.

He smiled over at me, and I felt my own smile mirror his without effort or thought. He was wearing the usual light jeans and button-up shirt, this one dark blue. The sleeves were rolled to just above the elbows and a thick black bracelet circled his left wrist, something Toni had filched for him years ago, though Patrick hadn't known it was stolen property initially. His well-defined face was lightly dusted in freckles, and his eyes were the clearest, brightest blue. Just the sight of him made my heart lurch. To know he cared for me made it hard to breathe.

I stepped into the room quickly, wanting to be at his side as soon as possible. He stood to meet me, taking the final step that brought us together. He kissed me gently and then pulled me close in a warm embrace. "Good morning," he whispered, his Irish accent obvious but not overpowering. "I feel like I haven't seen you for so long . . ."

"Saturday night, wasn't it?" I teased, pulling back so I could brush my fingers against the side of his face.

He grinned and caught my retreating fingers in his hand. "Too long," he insisted.

"For being immortal, you'd think you'd have a bit more patience."

"It's something to work on, I guess."

I mumbled an agreement and pressed my lips back to his. With his free hand, he rubbed my back and then moved it to rest against my cheek. His thumb stroked my sensitive skin, just below my closed eye, and I sighed in contentment.

"I've waited two centuries for you," he whispered against my mouth. "I think I've earned the right to be a little impatient."

I didn't bother to answer. I was too distracted by his deep kiss, his delicate fingers, the closeness of his body . . . I don't know how much time passed, but all too soon someone stepped into the room behind us and grunted loudly.

Worried that it might be Aaron, I pulled back quickly, turning to see the intruder. Patrick looked with me, his hand still holding mine tightly.

It was a fellow student named Andrea, probably the most jealous and judgmental person I'd ever encountered. She didn't talk a lot, but her aura—purple enough to join Lee's Rainbow Days—told her whole story.

I blushed a little, but I knew Patrick was inwardly laughing. "Sorry," he told her, though he didn't sound remotely apologetic.

Andrea gave us a withering look before stepping away from the open door. She sat across from us in the circle, and in seconds she was digging in her bag for her battered copy of *The House of the Seven Gables*.

I looked up at Patrick, pressing my lips tightly together to keep a laugh from escaping. He placed a long finger up to his mouth, his eyes wide as he pantomimed for me to stay quiet. That made it all the harder to keep my laugh from exploding out.

We took our usual seats side by side and I reached down to get my things, lips still twitching in amusement. After the bell rang, students began to amble into the classroom. Once everyone had taken their seats, and we weren't alone anymore, Patrick spoke.

"So, are you still planning on dinner tonight?"

"You don't seem that nervous," I commented, a bit wryly.

He shrugged a single shoulder. "Why should I be nervous? I already know your grandfather, your sisters love me, and your grandmother sounds like an amazing woman."

"What about me? Don't I make you nervous?"

He ducked his brown head slightly, his eyes deeply amused. "Extremely nervous. You're the only person I really worry about scaring off."

"Pretty sure you don't need to worry about that." He grinned at my almost blushing response. "What? Are you nervous about tonight?"

"Nope," I lied quickly. He cocked his head to the side in question, but I changed the subject quickly, my voice subdued. "I heard about Ms. Rhodes."

His eyes tightened, the shift in his mood almost tangible. "I was going to tell you after school," he explained slowly.

"Did Toni find her?"

Patrick nodded once. "The little sneak is quite the tracker, actually. We're not sure if it was Avalos or Romero, but . . . the accident was no accident."

I bobbed my head, showing I understood. "I know. I just . . . It's hard to know she died because of me."

Patrick reached for my hand, and I surrendered it to him with a sigh. "It wasn't your fault, Kate. The Demons are to blame. And Toni and I . . . we should have been paying closer attention. There just aren't enough Guardians to be everywhere at once."

"I know. And I don't blame you—not at all."

One corner of his mouth lifted into a tentative smile, though it was clear he didn't fully believe my words.

Over his shoulder I caught sight of Aaron, stepping into the classroom. Patrick followed my glance, and we watched while my old boyfriend took a seat beside Andrea, not looking in our direction even once.

I sighed without thinking, and Patrick's gaze settled against my face. But Patrick was wise enough not to say anything, even though I knew he wanted to.

Class started a minute later, and gradually Patrick relaxed beside me. We focused on Mr. Benson's instructions, and then we concentrated on the essay-form test with the rest of the class. Regardless, it surprised me—like it always did—how hard it was to keep my eyes from wandering across the circle to steal a glance at Aaron.

Jaxon was right—we needed to talk. Things hadn't ended well, and until they did, both of us were going to have a hard time moving on.

three

Patrick and I had every class together. Originally, choir was the only one he wasn't technically in, but that was only because he'd stood there the whole period, completely invisible. Since we'd become a couple, he'd started participating in the last hour of the day. His tenor voice was amazing, and Mr. Hyer was more than happy to welcome him in. Attending class invisible for weeks had also given him a great handle on all the music, so he looked even more like a show-off—something I pointed out often, much to Patrick's delight.

The only problem with being together all day: there wasn't a great chance to talk to Aaron. But then, I guess stealing a couple minutes with him in the hall probably wasn't the best way to communicate. And so I made a resolution to stop by his house sometime—maybe tomorrow, once tonight was over with.

Lunch found us with Lee and the special-needs kids. Trent called out several hellos, as was his custom, and he begged for spaghetti, just like always. (He liked mac and cheese too, though, luckily.) Bianca's long, somewhat flat face was twisted in a strange mix of fear and pleasure at seeing Lee's new look. Bianca's favorite color had always been purple, but after Lee had assured her she wasn't some kind of freaky orange alien, Bianca assured us all she really liked orange too. Mark was hunched over his lunch tray, and he scratched distractedly at a sore on the side of his face as he talked about a new game he'd received for his birthday. Jason—a larger kid—was listening intently, though he hardly spoke a word. Sitting right next to him was the bright-blue-eyed Landen. He was even quieter than Jason, but his aura was definitely the brightest of the bunch. I didn't quite understand how Landen's yellow aura could be so much happier than the others at the table, since all of the special-needs kids were noticeably happier than anyone else in the cafeteria, but it was. Sometimes I wondered if the answer was in his smile. It was like he knew something we didn't—knew a kind of joy the rest of us could only guess at.

David was listening in on our conversation, inserting his thoughts occasionally while pushing his glasses further up his nose in a nervous habit. Olivia sat next to me, eating her cookie before even thinking about eating her sandwich. She liked her dessert and refused to get distracted by substantial food. She'd grown attached to me despite the little time we'd spent together, and she sat next to me every day. Patrick was on my other side, sitting closer to the other boys.

These teenagers were, in a word, awesome. They weren't judgmental, and their quirkiness was something I'd come to really appreciate. Their auras were childlike, as was their behavior. Sometimes they could be very perceptive. Most of the time they talked about favorite toys, their families, or nothing at all. And all still firmly believed in the power of cooties, ergo the split of boys and girls at the table.

There was a time Aaron and Jaxon had joined us here, but that was before I'd ended things between us. Trent had mentioned their absence every day last week, but today he said nothing. I was grateful for that, because I didn't need another reason to feel the guilt return.

"I already won the hardest level," Mark was bragging.

"You couldn't have," David protested nasally, fiddling with his glasses. "You just got it yesterday."

"I played all night," Mark said.

David just shook his head. "Your mom wouldn't have let you."

"Yes she did. It was my birthday."

"She wouldn't let you stay up all night."

"Yeah she would."

"Patrick," David whined, hoping for back up.

Patrick just shook his head, swallowing his bite of chicken sandwich quickly. "Nope, I'm not getting in this, guys." He then spoke to Landen, asking if he could steal one of his apple slices.

Landen blinked at him, appalled my boyfriend would even ask such a question.

I smiled at the simple rejection and quietly sipped my water.

Bianca spoke from across the table. "Stop fighting, boys," she told Mark and David.

Lee grinned beside the larger girl. "Yeah, boys—knock it off."

David grunted at her. "Why are you orange?"

"Because I like orange. Don't you?"

"No. It's a stupid color."

"Orange was my favorite color," Mark confided. "Then I chose blue instead."

"Blue?" Trent asked, lifting his head quickly. "Blue?"

"I thought you said it was green," David said to Mark.

"No fighting," Bianca reminded sternly.

Patrick cleared his throat and looked to Lee. "So, Rainbow Days, huh?"

She smiled happily. "Like it?"

"I love it."

"Want to participate?"

"I think I'll pass," he said casually.

She shrugged. "Your loss. But I think you'd look great in all orange. Or pink."

"Purple," Bianca added.

I chuckled. "That I'd like to see," I admitted.

He grimaced. "I'm afraid you'll be waiting an extremely long time for that one."

"That's okay. Unlike some people, I'm really good at the whole patience thing."

Lee laughed along with me, and then the others slowly joined in, whether they understood the light scowl on Patrick's face or not. Landen even reached over and poked Patrick's arm, causing Patrick to grin and Landen to laugh more loudly.

Amid the laughter, Trent gave a toothy grin and asked knowingly, "Spaghetti?" Which of course only made us laugh harder.

When lunch ended Patrick took my hand, and we told everyone a quick good-bye. Lee promised to meet me at my car after school, and then my boyfriend and I left the cafeteria and headed to our next class. While we walked in the crowded halls, I asked him what he really thought of Lee's newest transformation.

"I was a bit shocked at first," he admitted with a smile. "And though it's a little blinding, it's uniquely Lee."

"My thoughts exactly." I paused, wondering if I should continue, then decided I had nothing to lose. "What do you think Toni would think of it?"

"Toni?" Patrick asked, looking surprised.

"Yeah. Toni. I mean, you knew, right? That they're sort of seeing each other?"

"Really?"

I gave him a weird look. "You honestly didn't know?"

"Toni and I don't usually bare our souls to one another," he explained. "I had no idea he was interested in Lee. Poor girl."

"I don't know—she's definitely a force to be reckoned with."

Patrick allowed that with a nod, but his brow was furrowed, and I knew he was thinking about something else.

"What is it?" I asked. "What's bothering you?"

But his fingers just tightened around mine, and he offered a reassuring smile that didn't quite reach his eyes. "Nothing. Really."

Of course I didn't believe him, but we were walking into the classroom now, and the conversation was dropped.

The last classes of the day moved by rather quickly, and I knew that was only because I was so concerned about tonight. Time was rushing, speeding me toward that fateful moment when my grandma would pass judgment on my new boyfriend. My feelings of anxiety needed no more of an explanation than that.

When choir ended, Patrick walked me toward my car. As was usually the case, we saw Trent in the hall, and he waved to us with excitement. We returned a greeting/farewell that wasn't quite as energetic, and then we were outside, walking the crowded sidewalks as students flocked toward their cars or the waiting buses.

"So, dinner's at six, right?" Patrick clarified.

"Yep—and you'd better not be late. Or too early. My grandma has always been pretty strict about punctuality."

"Are you *trying* to frighten me?"

"I don't want to be the only one biting my nails."

He shook his head disapprovingly. "That's a nasty habit, Kate. It destroys your nails, and your teeth—"

"I've heard all this before," I assured him. "But that's why I call it a nervous habit—as in, I can't control it."

"Not the best excuse I've ever heard, but . . ."

We reached the parking lot, and now that people weren't swarming directly around us, I felt free asking the question I'd been avoiding all day. "Any news on Far Darrig?"

I could tell from his abbreviated silence that he didn't want to discuss this, but he answered me. "No. Jack is still trying to track him, but so far he hasn't found anything. It's like the Demon just disappeared."

"But he hasn't."

Patrick sighed. "No, probably not. But now that Ms. Rhodes has been found . . . Toni is going to start focusing on locating Far Darrig. Hopefully the two of them can find something Jack couldn't see alone." Thinking of the somewhat eccentric Guardian from Australia—my grandfather's old Guardian—I knew that wherever Far Darrig was hiding, he couldn't elude the tenacious Jack forever.

Lee was already waiting at the car, leaning against the passenger door. One hand was raised over her eyes, shielding them from the sun; the other was cradling her phone, thumb working feverishly to complete a message.

"Hey, Lee!" I called out as we got closer.

She glanced up, though her thumb kept moving. "Hey."

Patrick continued to hold my hand as he stepped around the back of the car, and with my free hand I dug in my pocket for the keys. I bent to unlock the door, and Patrick released my hand to pull it open for me. He held the door as I shrugged out of my backpack and chucked it into the backseat. I ducked into the car and stretched to unlock Lee's door and then dragged myself back out. Lee moved nonchalantly into the car, still texting, and I turned to face Patrick.

"I'll see you tonight then," he said, his eyes bright.

I smiled. "Yeah. Don't be late."

He leaned in to kiss me good-bye, and I rested my hands against his chest as our lips met. His fingers lingered on my skin, framing my face. Reluctantly he pulled his mouth away to let his forehead rest against mine. I sighed happily, squeezing my eyes closed briefly. He put his arms around my shoulders and pulled me close before lightly tugging on my ponytail. "Lee's waiting," he reminded in a whisper, lips shifting to brush against my forehead.

Who's Lee? I wanted to mumble. Instead, I just sighed again.

He laughed evenly, then pulled his head back. "I'll see you soon," he promised, hands sliding up to rest on my shoulders.

I kissed him a last time, my fingers moving up to push his longish hair back behind his ears. I felt him shiver, and his warm lips begged me to stay. Grudgingly I pulled back, offering him a small smile. "Six o'clock," I reminded.

He nodded surely. "I'll be there."

I turned away and climbed into the car, glancing up to see that he was holding the door, waiting to close it. He looked past me, focusing on Lee. "See you tomorrow," he said.

She looked up from her phone to nod. "See ya, Patrick."

My seat belt was locked into place by now, and Patrick gave me a last smile before closing the door carefully. I put my keys into the ignition and watched from my peripheral vision as Patrick stepped away from the car, waiting for me to pull away.

My life might be pretty crazy right now, but at least I had something amazing to hold on to—even if I had to wait until tonight to see him again.

❋

I offered to help Grandma with dinner, but she insisted she was fine. Already she was making the sauce for the chicken enchiladas, and there wasn't a whole lot I could do. I stuck around for a few minutes, hoping she might talk with me. I wanted to know what she was thinking—what she was most nervous about. But her straight face gave away nothing, and as she meticulously cut up the chicken breasts I decided she didn't really want to discuss things. I was sort of grateful, but at the same time I wished she'd just tell me exactly what was bothering her. Her forced calm was making me antsy.

The twins were really excited that Patrick was coming over. They'd fallen in love with him the first time we'd watched movies together, a couple weeks ago. They thought he was the funniest person to walk the planet, and so they were cleaning the bathroom without any complaints—a major feat. I don't think the end of the world could have made them cooperate any better.

Grandpa Bennett had been sent to the store to pick up something for dessert, and so I was left to entertain myself for a couple hours. I played with the idea of going to visit Aaron but eventually decided against it. It didn't seem right for me to go over there right before a night with Patrick. So I stretched out on my bed and tried to focus on a novel I'd been wanting to read for weeks.

I had just started chapter two when my phone vibrated loudly against my desk. I reluctantly set the book aside, making a mental note of the page number since I hadn't grabbed a bookmark. I swung off the bed and moved for my phone. I glanced at the caller ID, but I didn't recognize the number. Frowning a little, I flipped the phone open.

"Hello?"

I don't know what I expected to hear, but the out-of-breath voice certainly took me by surprise. "Hello. Is this Kate Bennett?"

"Um, yeah," I said, wondering after the words were out if I should have made something up. "Who is this?" I asked, turning around so I could lean back against my desk.

"I'm sorry—my name is Terence Blank."

The muscles that had been tensing in my body suddenly relaxed. "Oh." I wasn't sure what else to say. Could I technically say it was nice to meet him, even if we were only talking on the phone? I didn't know a lot about the Guardian named Terence, only that he was the one who supplied Patrick and Toni with money and information. I guess he was the supervisor or overseer for Guardians in the area. Luckily, I was too nervous about dinner to worry about why the boss would be calling me.

"I hope I'm not interrupting anything," Terence continued quickly.

"No, I'm not doing anything."

"Good. I won't take too much of your time."

My brow furrowed. "Are you . . . running?"

He laughed, though it was a heavy, breathless sound. "No. Just using the stairs. The elevator is out in my building."

"Oh." I blushed, but he was kind and didn't linger over the potentially embarrassing comment.

"I was hoping I could call before dinner. Patrick isn't there yet, is he?"

"Um, no." It felt weird that he knew about our evening plans, but he was speaking quickly now.

"Good. I know this must be strange for you, since we've never spoken before, but I would like to set up a time that I could meet with you in person. Without the knowledge of your Guardians."

"What?" I was so surprised by his words that I didn't know what else to say.

"I know it's a strange request, but I assure you it's for your own protection."

"What are you talking about?"

"Please, the last thing I want to do is alarm you. I'm wary to say much over the phone, but there are some things I must speak with you about. There is a reason he's after you, and I need to meet with you in order to find out why."

Of course I knew who he was referring to. Far Darrig. Or, ultimately, the Demon Lord. Either one made sense.

Terence continued quickly, his voice growing anxious. "Please, Kate, I don't mean to alarm you. But there are some things I must ask you and only you."

"Why does it have to be a secret?" I asked, finally finding my voice.

"Trust me, it's for your own safety."

"I'm sorry, but you'll have to do better than that . . . sir," I added quickly, worried I'd gone too far.

There was a limited silence, and all I could hear was his distant panting. Finally he spoke. "I know you have reasons to doubt the goodness of people. However, I promise that I'm telling you the truth. Keeping our meeting private could potentially save your life—and your family."

I opened my mouth, unsure of what I was going to say exactly, but he was speaking again.

"I'm planning a visit to New Mexico very soon. I will ensure that while I'm there, you can formally meet me with your Guardians present. Before I leave the area, I will arrange a place for us to privately meet and talk. We can discuss everything then, once you are sure of your safety with me. Until then, please don't tell anyone that I have made contact with you."

"But, why?"

"Please, Kate. As hard as this is, I need you to trust me. Some secrets are necessary to protect the ones we care about."

I pinched the bridge of my nose in frustration. "How do I know that you're who you say you are?"

"That's why I'm asking you to meet me with your Guardians first. I realize how unsettling this is for you. Until then, I ask only that you keep this call to yourself."

"Why even bother to call me, then? Why not just talk to me when you stop by to visit?"

"Because I will need your cooperation. If I'm right about you, Kate, you're in more danger than you realize." His voice changed— became lighter. "If you need me, feel free to call this number at any time, night or day."

I could tell he was winding things up, ready to end the call, whereas I still had so many questions. The only problem was, I wasn't sure how to ask them. "Mr. Blank, how can I just—"

"Someone's on the other line. I have to go. Good-bye, and good luck, Kate."

"But—"

He hung up. I stared at my phone, seriously considering calling him back. Instead I just saved the number as a new contact, wondering if my life could get any weirder.

four

Ten minutes to six, the doorbell rang. I could hear Josie and Jenna both running, fighting to get to it first. I was in my bedroom, debating whether I should put on a necklace or not. The deliberation was a ruse, though. Honestly, all I could think about was the strange call I'd received from Terence. The weirdest part about the whole thing was his demand for secrecy. That, of course, made me want to tell Patrick about it. The only thing that had kept me from calling Patrick was Terence's vague reference to the importance of my silence—that somehow it would protect my family.

The biggest reason I'd decided to comply was that keeping it a secret didn't necessarily seem like a bad idea. It wouldn't hurt anyone to keep quiet, and if indeed Terence was right about the silence being warranted, I would learn everything when he came here.

I heard the front door open downstairs and the rumble of Grandpa's voice amid the giggles of the twins. Patrick's lilting accent could also be easily distinguished, though I couldn't make out the individual words.

I decided on no necklace, and I left my phone on my desk. It was symbolic of me leaving the Terence mystery up here, where it belonged.

I closed my door behind me and stepped down the short hall to the stairs leading to the entryway. On my way down, I had a clear view of the door, which was just closing. One hand slid easily down the railing, and I tried to keep my smile natural as I moved to join the small group gathered by the front door.

Patrick was laughing at something Jenna had just said, and so his eyes seemed brighter than usual as they lifted to watch me. His laugh dimmed to a smile, and his eyes didn't leave my face as I hurried down the stairs.

Josie was tugging on his arm, but his lack of reaction had her casting a look over her shoulder. "Oh," she muttered. "It's you."

"About time," Jenna grunted to me. "It's not polite to keep your *boyfriend* waiting."

"Yeah," Josie chimed in, still tugging his arm. "It's not like his coming was a surprise or anything." She switched to her best mocking voice. "*Oh! It's six o'clock and the doorbell just rang. Who in the world could that be?*"

I stepped off the last stair but didn't move directly to his side—that would have been weird with my sisters and Grandpa looking on. So I stopped next to Josie and patted her head. "Thanks for the tips, sis."

She ducked out from under my palm, still hanging on Patrick's wrist. "Ugh, get off me." She straightened in front of Patrick, still jerking his arm. She was leaning her whole weight into the tug, but Patrick didn't budge. His feet remained firmly planted, and his eyes remained on me.

"Kate. How was your afternoon?"

I shrugged. "Pretty good. Yours?"

He nodded once. "It was good."

Grandpa cleared his throat a bit loudly. "Why don't we wander back to the kitchen, before Josie takes off your arm?"

Patrick allowed himself to be pulled by Josie while Jenna followed alongside him, talking about her upcoming piano recital. Grandpa led the way down the entryway toward the kitchen, and I followed just behind the group. I was close enough to Patrick that I placed a hand against his back, my way of silently thanking him for coming.

He cast me a quick smile, but his closest hand was turning white in Josie's grip so he couldn't return any other gesture.

Jenna was still talking quickly. "I hate my recital piece, but I don't really have a choice. My teacher says it will show off my pedal work. Like I care about that . . ."

"You're coming to my soccer tournament this Saturday, right?" Josie cut in urgently, walking backwards so she could continue strangling his hand while keeping eye contact.

"Um, maybe," he hedged artfully. "I would like that very much."

"Are you coming to my recital?" Jenna pressed.

I rolled my eyes at the both of them. "Come on, guys. Let him breathe for a minute, okay?"

"Why should we?" Josie asked, one eyebrow cocked. "He didn't let us breathe last time he was over." She was referring to the movie night that had ended with most of us dying of laughter on the floor.

Patrick chuckled lightly. "Hey, that wasn't my fault. It was your hyena laugh that kept us going."

"Was not!" Josie protested, though her shining eyes contradicted the fierceness of her tone.

"Was so," Jenna interjected. "You were snorting and everything."

"What about Kate?" Josie reminded everyone.

Patrick nodded thoughtfully. "Yeah, Kate was pretty funny."

I smacked his arm with the back of my hand. "Are we all forgetting the fact that Patrick moved the couch?"

The twins laughed together as we entered the kitchen. Grandpa was filling up a pitcher of water at the sink, and Grandma was just taking the cheesy chicken enchiladas out of the oven. She placed the pan on the stove and closed the oven door deliberately. She then tossed the oven mitts onto the counter and turned to face us, a thin smile on her face.

Her aura was complicated. It always had been, but tonight—when I wanted to read it so badly—I found it hard to interpret. Which emotions were associated with tonight, and which ones had nothing to do with Patrick? I noticed immediately that the yellow in her aura was virtually absent. She wasn't happy. The blue was also being rapidly replaced by green uneasiness, and there were the usual stains of brown regret and gray sadness. The pain I saw was small, though, so I knew Patrick's presence wasn't the cause of it. And that was a relief. There was also another color mixed in with the rest that I'd never seen around her before—red. In my experience I'd come to think that red signified anger, or competition. Seeing it around Grandma left me more confused than enlightened, and I sort of wished that I hadn't searched her aura in the first place.

If I hadn't been nervous before, I was now. Was she angry at me? Or Patrick?

Jenna skipped around us to help Grandpa get some ice, while Josie continued to grip Patrick's wrist. I stepped forward and waved to Patrick, trying to swallow back any fear I felt. "Grandma, this is Patrick. Patrick, this is my Grandma Bennett."

He nodded politely to her, extending his free hand. "Ma'am, it's a pleasure to meet you. Kate's told me a lot about you."

Grandma took his hand and shook it once. "Patrick. I've heard a lot about you too." She nodded toward dinner. "I hope you like enchiladas."

"They smell wonderful. Thank you for letting me join you tonight."

Her head dipped in appreciation, though the colors in her aura remained rigid. "You're welcome. Josie, please stop hanging on him like a monkey and help Kate set the table."

I took my indirect order in stride, leading the way to the cupboard that held the plates. I lifted a small stack down and handed them to my grumbling sister. She hefted them over to the wooden table in the corner, where Grandpa was just setting down the water pitcher. Jenna was putting cups at each place setting, so I moved for the silverware drawer. I felt Patrick following behind me, fully aware of my grandmother turning her back on us to focus on the enchiladas.

I opened the long drawer, and Patrick set his hands on my waist from behind. His head ducked next to my ear, his whisper barely audible. "Maybe I should have been more nervous. She really doesn't like me at all, does she?"

I just shook my head noncommittally, hoping it would somehow make him feel better, but I didn't dare speak. He shifted to stand beside me, and while I counted out forks, he pulled out a small handful of knives.

When I pushed the drawer closed, he leaned in for a last quick comment. "I can't imagine being a Seer—she's scary enough without actually *Seeing* her disgust. Good luck."

The drawer thumped closed, and I sent him a small scowl. He smiled deftly, then led the way across the kitchen, back to the table. The twins continued to badger him about soccer games and piano recitals as he laid a knife beside each plate, and I was grateful for the distraction they caused. I passed off the handful of forks to Jenna and wandered over to the fridge, where Grandpa was looking for the salsa and sour cream.

"She's more upset than I thought she'd be," Grandpa admitted quietly, stooping lower behind the door.

I sighed thinly. "Yeah. I've never seen her with red."

He chuckled very dimly. "It's not her best color," he agreed. He pulled out the sour cream and handed the carton to me. I took that as my dismissal and crossed back across the room to get a serving spoon.

Things got a little better after we were all seated and Grandma got some food in her. I watched as the red in her aura lazily retreated; still, I knew we weren't out of the woods yet. Grandpa's aura grew more relaxed as Grandma's became less defensive, and slowly dinner became more natural. Not for the first time, I wished I could catch even a glimpse of Patrick's emotions, but he hid his aura like most every other immortal person did. All I saw was the silver thread that outlined him, marking him as a Guardian.

He seemed at ease, though. We sat side by side, facing my grandparents. The twins sat at either end, more focused on food than the slow and stilted conversation.

Grandpa asked Patrick a few questions about Ireland, and luckily he kept away from the sort of discussion that would betray the fact that Patrick hadn't been in the country for over two hundred years. Roads and buildings might have changed, but the vegetation probably hadn't altered much over the centuries, so green grass was definitely a safe topic.

Grandma was the one who asked the hardest questions, but in the end I shouldn't have panicked. Patrick was a good liar.

"So," she asked suddenly, "how are your parents adjusting to the change of scenery?"

Patrick chewed quickly and then answered promptly after swallowing. "Pretty well. We lived back East for a couple of years, so at least it wasn't a direct move—that would have been much harder."

"I can imagine," Grandma said, setting down her glass of water. "New Mexico is quite the opposite of Ireland." She straightened in her chair. "What is it your parents do for a living?"

My fingers curled tightly around my fork, and I forced my eyes to stay away from him. This was exactly the sort of thing I'd dreaded about tonight.

Patrick's fluent answer betrayed nothing. "My father works for the church. My mother's jobs include parenting, cleaning, and helping my father. She's the perfect homemaker."

Grandma nodded, and I could see in her aura that she approved of the occupation. "Do you have any brothers and sisters?"

I thought I was prepared for this answer, but he surprised me. "No. I'm an only child."

I sent a quick glance toward him, but he was concentrating on taking a drink, and he didn't seem to notice my reaction.

Grandma gave the twins pointed looks. "Well, hopefully all the noise and attention hasn't scared you off. Little girls can be a little overwhelming."

Patrick shook his head, smiling for a quick moment at each of my sisters. "Not at all. They're very welcoming." He then turned his clear eyes to my grandma, and no one could doubt the sincerity in his words. "You're doing very well with them, Mrs. Bennett."

I watched in amazement as her aura transformed before my eyes. The pain and gray depression that had been so present for so long dimmed. The change was slight, but the overall result was staggering. It was like his few words had the power to release her from a good portion of the worry and grief she'd been feeling ever since her son's death. The responsibility that had been so heavy on her shoulders was slightly eased—if only for a moment—and she gave him her first genuine smile.

"Thank you, Patrick. That's a very kind thing to say."

I sent my Grandpa a look, but he seemed as surprised as I was. He offered a thin shrug and then turned back to his food. I watched as Grandma followed his lead, a new thread of yellow widening around her body.

I felt Patrick's eyes on the side of my face, and I turned to meet his gaze. Our eyes locked, and I saw the question in his eyes. He'd seen the exchange between Grandpa and me and was silently asking for an explanation. His blue eyes were tinged with worry, and I realized he wondered if he'd said something wrong.

I just shook my head, letting my pleasure show in my small smile.

Reassured, though still confused, Patrick returned my smile.

Jenna brought up school and their newest sub. Josie thought he was "okay," but Jenna loved him.

"Will he become permanent?" Grandma asked.

Jenna shrugged. "I don't know. But I hope so."

Josie blew out her breath in a deep sigh. "Until the curse gets him too, I guess."

Grandpa spoke for really the first time. "I'd like to meet him. Aren't parent-teacher conferences coming up?"

Grandma blinked at him. "Henry, you've never wanted to go to those. Not once."

"You saying I don't have a right to meet the guy that's teaching my granddaughters?"

"Of course not. I'm just confused as to why you *want* to."

I knew perfectly well why he wanted to go. He wanted to make sure the new teacher wasn't some kind of Demon, like the last sub the twins had. And I was way ahead of him. I was going to make checking on this sub a new assignment for me and Patrick. The sooner the better.

After everyone was done eating, Patrick thanked my grandmother for the wonderful dinner and even offered to do the dishes. She waved his offer away, though, and enlisted Grandpa instead. He frowned in Patrick's direction but started to gather the dishes without a word. The twins left to go pick a movie, and I volunteered to prepare dessert.

While I got out the root beer Grandpa had bought earlier, Patrick opened the freezer and pulled out the vanilla ice cream. Together we stood at the counter and made root beer floats—he scooped and I poured.

We listened to the sounds of my grandparents in the background clearing off the table—his affable jibes, her precise comebacks. It was a comforting back noise, and it reminded me of my parents.

Beside me, Patrick spoke thinly. "Did I pass?"

I watched the ice cream fall out of the scoop and into the glass before I looked up at him and smiled. "I think you excelled."

"Excelled, huh?"

"Don't let it go to your head." I nudged my elbow into his ribs, and he leaned away in mock pain.

I just shook my head at him, wondering as I often did what it would be like to be immortal. He'd seen so much—experienced so much. Yet here he was, standing in my kitchen, serving root beer floats to my family.

"You're kind of amazing, you know," I whispered, lifting the bottle of soda to fill the next glass. The foam rose faster than the liquid, and I had to stop and allow the fizz to fall back down.

"Are you *trying* to inflate my ego?" he asked lowly. "I'm getting mixed signals . . ."

I glanced over my shoulder and saw that my grandparents were still hovering around the table. We still had a moment alone. I looked back up at Patrick, regarding him seriously. "What's the most incredible thing you've ever seen? I mean, you've lived for so long, seen so many advances in technology . . . what's the coolest thing to you?"

He glanced away from me with pursed lips, working to lever out another scoop of ice cream from the frozen box. "The most amazing thing," he mused, to himself. He stole a quick look at my face. "That would have to be you, Kate Bennett."

I rolled my eyes and started to pour more root beer. "Come on, Patrick, be serious."

"I am."

"I said some*thing*, not some*one*."

"Oh . . ." His eyes sparkled mischievously. He then turned to watch as he pulled the scoop out the carton and plopped the rough ball of ice cream into the waiting glass. "I don't know . . . root beer floats. They're pretty cool."

I shook my head at him.

"What?" he asked. "Root beer is a relatively new thing. Just because you've had it your whole life doesn't mean it was always around."

"What about computers? Cars? Phones? Indoor plumbing? I guess I thought you'd say something along those lines."

We worked in silence for a significant moment, and I thought that would be the end of the conversation. Then he suddenly spoke, and his voice was serious. "Cameras."

I looked up to catch his expression; he seemed completely focused on the task of scooping ice cream. He moved meticulously, and I wished once again that I could see his aura. To understand the warmth of his words, the longing in his voice. He must have sensed my silent prompting, because he started to elaborate. "You're very lucky to have them. The power to freeze time, capture a moment, an emotion . . . a person. That's the most amazing thing to me."

I finished filling the glass before setting the root beer aside and turning to face him. He pushed the ice cream scoop back into the box, but before he could fill it again, I placed my hand over his cold fingers.

He glanced up at me and my lips twisted into a delicate smile. "That's a good one," I whispered. "And I agree. Cameras are pretty amazing."

His eyes searched mine, his jaw flexed with an emotion I couldn't name, and then he was smiling. "Thank you, Kate."

Jenna came quickly around the corner, gripping the doorway to stop her thin body from sailing too far into the room. "Kate, can we watch it Patrick-style? Josie wants to know."

"It's named after me, huh?" Patrick asked, his voice sounding light and carefree once more. Still, the mood of our brief conversation lingered, and I regretfully retracted my hand from his.

Jenna was nodding. "Yep. So can we or not?"

"Ask Grandma," I told her, and she darted across the kitchen at once, leaving us to finish with dessert.

In the end, Grandma gave in to watching a movie Patrick-style, though at first she was hesitant. Resisting the twins was easier said than done, so soon we were all gathered in the family room with our root beer floats, watching an action movie with the radio taking the place of the actual movie's audio. Watching a shootout to classical music was just as hilarious as the twins had remembered, and the grandparents weren't exempt from the gasping. Grandma had this really deep laugh that seemed to rumble the whole room, and she wasn't shy about using it.

When the movie was over and our laughter finally eased, Grandpa laboriously came to his feet and shut off the TV and stereo. "Phew—I haven't laughed like that for a long time."

Grandma snorted. "It may bring on a heart attack. . ."

The twins spoke at the same time, both turning pleading looks toward their grandfather. "Can we please have another one?" And, "It's not too late yet; there's still time."

Grandma was already shaking her head. "Nope. It's a school night, and it's off to bed with the both of you."

Patrick had been holding my hand, but he released it now to stand. "I should be going. Thank you for a wonderful time, Mr. and Mrs. Bennett."

My grandmother nodded up at him. "Thank *you* for coming over, Patrick. It was nice to finally meet you."

Patrick said his good-byes to the twins, and I stood while he stretched to shake Grandpa's hand across the coffee table. They seemed to exchange a deep look, one I didn't think anyone else noticed besides me. Then Grandpa released Patrick's hand, and the moment ended before I could really make sense of what had been expressed.

We stepped out of the family room together, since I'd excused myself to walk him to his car. He took my hand again as we wandered through the house, back to the front door.

Once in the entryway, I spoke softly. "You did great tonight."

He paused and reached to open the door, pulling it wide and holding it for me. "You have a wonderful family, Kate."

I nodded, taking the first step into the night. I waited on the porch as he closed the door behind us, our hands still joined. "I wish you could have known my parents. They were a lot like my grandma and grandpa . . ." I didn't finish the thought, and he didn't press for more.

We walked leisurely down the porch stairs and followed the trailing sidewalk that wrapped to meet the driveway. His car was parked at the curb, the blue paint gleaming in the night. A few scattered lamps made the street feel safe, despite the darkness.

I glanced up at him while we crossed the length of the driveway. "So—an only child, huh?" I regretted my more severe tone when I saw the slight grimace twist his face.

"It was the safest thing to say," he explained quietly. "If I admitted to having a brother, there's more of a chance someone would ask to meet him. Parents are hard enough to fake when all I have is Toni."

"It makes sense—it just took me off guard."

"Lying can get pretty complicated."

"You do it well. No offense," I added hastily, realizing only after I'd spoken that there could be a negative connotation to my words.

A thin smile tugged at the corner of his mouth. "None taken. As long as you realize that I would never lie to you."

My brain chose this moment to remember the phone call from Terence, and the sudden urge I had to tell Patrick the secret took me by surprise. "Um, yeah. I know you wouldn't. I wouldn't either."

As we stepped onto the street, he glanced over at me. Instead of the skeptical or even mocking look I sort of expected to see, I saw his bright eyes and pure smile. He twisted to face me completely, walking the last steps backward and pulling me tenderly with him.

He stopped at the driver's door, his fingers winding with mine as his free hand came up to cup the left side of my face. His fingertips traced against my skin, his head ducking closer to kiss me. Our lips met perfectly, and I closed my eyes instinctively. I shifted closer to him, my thumb drawing circles on the back of his hand. I felt him relax around me, and his palm smoothed against my cheek briefly before sliding to support the back of my neck. I wished my hair was loose and not bunched up in the ponytail, though his trailing fingers still managed to make my scalp prickle with just touching the few strands that had escaped throughout the day.

He pulled back and sighed deeply, his lips moving fondly against the corner of my mouth. "I love you, Kate Bennett." He kissed my cheek once, then delicately pressed his lips to my forehead. "I will love you always."

He squeezed my hand casually before slipping his fingers free so he could wrap both arms around my waist. I stepped closer into his embrace, saving him the trouble of pulling me in. I wrapped my arms around his shoulders, keeping his head near mine. His hair lightly grazed my ear, and I could feel his breath through my shirt as he buried his face in my shoulder.

"I just thought you should know that," he mumbled, and my already pounding heart went wild.

"That's not fair," I whispered, relishing the feel of his arms so tight around me.

"Hmm?"

I sighed. "How can I compete with that? A simple 'I love you' won't be enough now."

He drew back at once. I let my hands slide down to his waist. I stared up into his serious face, and my whole body shivered when I saw the depth of emotion burning in his eyes. He lifted a single finger to trace my lips, his own tugging into an effortless smile. "Your love will always be enough," he assured me.

I let out a shaky breath, laughing weakly. "See what I mean? You're a lot better at this than I am."

He tapped the tip of my nose, shook his head once with a bit of regret, then affectionately grasped my shoulders, forcing me back a step. "If I don't go now . . ." His voice trailed off, and his smile was shaky. He released my arms, pushing his hands deep into his pockets. He rocked back on his heels, grinning widely now. My stomach flipped.

"Your grandma's probably watching out the window, so . . . I better go."

I bit my lower lip and scratched absently at one eyebrow. "Um, yeah. Good idea."

I took a second step back as he pulled the car door open, but before I could move any further, he turned back to face me, smile still in place. "I'll see you tomorrow."

"Good night, Patrick."

When I said his name, his eyes glowed happily, and he couldn't seem to resist the urge to lean forward and kiss me one last time.

"Sleep well, Kate," he whispered, a breath from my lips.

And then he was getting into the car, closing the door softly. I wandered back to the driveway, where I hesitated and turned back to watch him start the car, shift into gear, and ease away from the curb. His headlights sliced through the dark street, and I watched until I couldn't see his brake lights anymore.

five

My chance to check up on the new sub at the elementary school came sooner than expected.

I was dropping the twins off for school; Josie was just preparing to open the door when Lee—once again decked out in complete orange—whistled lowly. "No way," she breathed, almost to herself, though she'd managed to get the attention of everyone in the car. "Oh my Oreos, it *is* him."

"Huh?" Jenna asked, trying to peer over Josie's shoulder and catch sight of whatever Lee had found so shocking. All I saw was the school, a lot of students, and a few teachers milling about.

"It *is* him!" Lee repeated more firmly, voice growing louder as the initial shock wore off. "Peter Keegan—the guy who's dating my mom!"

"Mr. K?" Josie asked, sounding more than a little disgusted. "Our sub?"

That got my attention. I jerked the gearshift into neutral, pulled on the emergency brake, and then took my feet off the clutch and brake. I twisted in my seat and leaned closer to Lee, staring through her window.

"Which one?" I asked quickly.

Lee's finger jabbed against the glass. "There—the one in the geeky brown suit."

"He's almost to the doors," Jenna added, but her help wasn't necessary. I could see him now.

The good news—he wasn't a Demon. He wasn't even a Guardian. I had to squint hard to be sure of the gold thread outlining him, but the colors swimming around his body were most definitely not hidden. So he was human. That was a major relief, obviously. But something still seemed a little off about him. Maybe it was just the coincidence of him dating my best friend's mom *and* teaching my little sisters.

Even though he was too far away to get a good read on his aura, I could see a whole lot of green; that couldn't be a good sign, right? Or maybe he was just a nervous person? Was I becoming paranoid?

I knew the answer to that question.

Josie was making a gagging sound. "Your mom's dating our teacher? Gross!"

Jenna looked a little pale, but her voice was perfectly normal. "He's a really nice teacher." She paused, and we all thought she was going to say something else. But she couldn't seem to think of anything to add, so she closed her mouth.

Lee's orange lips were twisted in something like revulsion. "A grade-school teacher? Really, mom? *Really?*"

"You said he was pretty cool," I reminded her, settling back into my seat as Mr. Keegan reached the door, held it for a group of young girls, and then disappeared inside.

The door swung closed and Lee turned to face me, grimacing a little. "Yeah. I thought he was."

Josie remained confused. "How did your mom meet him? He told us he hadn't been in town long."

"Yeah," Jenna agreed. "He said he was from California or something."

Lee just shook her head. "Guess I'll have to ask her. Wow, that's weird."

I didn't say anything—but I agreed completely.

Lee and I drove in silence to the high school. I knew she was trying to work everything out in her head, sort out her feelings concerning this new information. As for me, I spent the remainder of the drive trying to assure myself there wasn't anything to be worried about. Just because my whole life had been flipped upside down didn't mean that coincidences had stopped happening.

When I parked and shut off the car, Lee finally looked at me. "My mom's conferences. A lot of them happened in Southern California. Do you think she's . . . what if she lied, and they've been seeing each other for a lot longer than a week? What if this is serious?"

I just looked at her, not knowing what to say.

"Maybe that's why he was acting so weird. Maybe they've been together for a long time, and meeting me was . . . just an afterthought."

"Lee . . ."

She shook her head and reached down for her backpack, forcing out a thin laugh that held no humor. "And I thought him being a lawyer might be bad." She jerked the door handle, kicked the door open, and pushed her way out of the car. For the first time ever, she remembered to lock her door without my reminder.

I grabbed around in the backseat, found my bag, then hurried to follow her. She was already to the sidewalk, so I had to step fast. I watched her aura, though it was a little hard to focus on because of her bright orange-ness—it dimmed all the other colors surrounding her. But as I got closer the surging colors blended into something I could interpret.

The yellow that generally billowed around my best friend was gone. Red, minimal green, and a lot of gray and brown seethed in her aura. I'd never seen her so hurt, so upset. My heart ached for her as I jogged quickly to her side.

She was stepping with heavy purpose, her empty hands dangling at her sides. I got to her side at last, and though the backpack hanging on her one shoulder made it a little awkward, I wrapped an arm around her.

She didn't look at me, but I could feel some of the tenseness slip out of her body. We didn't speak until it came time for us to go to our separate classes. She finally slowed her walk and sent me a quick glance. "I know—you don't have to tell me what my aura looks like." She sighed deeply. "But can you pretend that you're not psychic for one minute, and let me lie and say I'm okay? Please?"

I pursed my lips, then dropped my arm. "Of course. Whatever you need, Lee. I'll see you in history."

She forced a small but grateful smile before stepping around me and toward the school. I shrugged my backpack on—something I hadn't taken the time to do yet—and continued to walk alone to the front of the school, wishing I had a way to comfort her.

I was the first person to step into the American Lit room, and I glanced around just to be sure that I hadn't somehow missed Patrick. He was always here first. Admittedly, I had enough to think about for now, so I just moved to my desk and lowered myself into the chair.

For a couple silent minutes I wondered what I could do to help Lee, but no magical answer revealed itself. In the end, I just found myself hoping her mom hadn't lied to her. Despite the fact Lee dared to try any fashion, I knew she was a really sensitive person. Her father had skipped out when she was only five so he could be with a younger woman he'd been secretly seeing for over a year. Lee's trust had been violated so early in life; I knew Lee's mom had made her young daughter a tearful promise that she would *never* keep anything from Lee.

Not that I was a fair judge when it came to keeping secrets. Aside from not having a good opportunity to tell Lee everything about Guardians, Demons, and Seers, I mostly hadn't gotten around to it because I didn't want her to accuse me of hiding the truth.

I couldn't decide if this would make a good time to tell her everything or if this thing with Mr. Keegan had just ruined my best chance.

"Hey, is everything all right?"

I looked quickly toward the uncertain voice and found myself staring at Aaron's guarded face. He was standing just inside the door, hesitating before finally stepping closer. He stopped when he reached the circle of desks but didn't move to take a seat or come closer to me.

"Yeah. Everything's good."

His fingers tightened around his bag's strap, pulling against his stiff shoulder. His eyes narrowed. "Are you sure?"

I nodded. "Yeah. It's, um . . . something with Lee."

"Is she okay?"

"Yeah, she's fine. It's just her mom. She's . . . dating again."

"Oh." Aaron's aura still sported a good amount of uneasiness, but his hard face relaxed a little. "Lee doesn't like the guy?"

"It's complicated," I said, trying to force myself to believe that this conversation wasn't awkward at all.

He nodded once, seemed to search for something meaningful to say, then settled for another, "Oh."

He twisted and moved around the circle, sitting in the desk opposite me. We both pretended to be really occupied with getting out notebooks and pencils, but finally I had to break the silence.

"How are you doing?"

I winced inwardly as soon as the words were out.

He forced a smile. "Great. Good."

"I heard about the swim team—your win in the meet last weekend."

"Yeah. It was close, but we pulled it off."

A vivid break, and then we both spoke at once.

"How're your sisters?"

"What did you think of this book?"

His lips tugged into a strained smile, and I tapped my fingers against the cover of *The House of Seven Gables*.

"Um, my sisters are good. Josie's got a big soccer tournament coming up."

"Yeah, I remember. Isn't Jenna's piano recital sometime this week?"

"Next Monday."

"Oh. Right." His hand slid into his hair nervously, and he stretched out the muscles in his neck. "Uh, yeah—this book was pretty good. I liked the ending, even if there were some slow parts in the middle. And beginning. And end."

The warning bell sounded, and I glanced away from him, turning to thumb open my notes as the rest of the class moved into the room.

When class started and the seat next to me remained empty, I started to worry. Patrick had never been this late. I surreptitiously checked my phone: no new messages, no missed calls.

Before I could start really panicking or begin imagining all the horrible things that might have happened to keep him away, the door opened and Patrick hurried inside.

Mr. Benson cut off his words to throw Patrick a meaningful look before steadily continuing his lecture, trying to start up exactly where he'd left off. I tuned out his voice to better focus on Patrick. He didn't look hurt or worried—just tired. His hair was more untidy than usual, and as he slid into his seat beside me I noticed the deep sleep line that sliced across his cheek. He settled into his chair and pushed his bag to the floor before finally sneaking a look at me.

I questioned him with my eyes, and he mouthed one maddening word: *Later.*

I tried to make my eyes more insistent, but he was already turning away, trying to dig out his notes and look like he was paying attention.

Though I was burning with curiosity, I tried to act like I was listening too. I could feel Aaron glancing between us, and though I wanted to look at his eyes and guess what he was thinking, I didn't dare risk meeting his stare.

I sighed and waited for class to end.

six

The bell finally rang, and students hurried to grab their things, dump them in bags, and be first to reach the seething hallway.

Patrick and I moved a little slower. I followed his lead as he took his time putting first his notebook, then pencil, then pen into his open bag. Only then did he stand, and I quickly copied him. Aaron was already gone, and Mr. Benson was too preoccupied with a student asking a question to bother reprimanding Patrick for his tardiness.

I reached for Patrick's hand, needing the contact, and he wordlessly twisted his fingers with mine. As soon as we stepped into the busy hall, my patience ran out.

"What's wrong?" I spoke mildly, hoping that no one would overhear us amid all the noise and clamor of the hall.

Patrick glanced down at me and his hand tightened around mine. "Jack called last night, just after I got back to the warehouse."

I instantly assumed the worst. "Far Darrig?"

He shook his head, and his thumb rubbed my skin comfortingly. "No. It was something else."

I knew he was reluctant to keep talking, but no one seemed aware of us, let alone interested in what we were discussing. "What then?" I pressed stubbornly.

He glanced around us and seemed to reach my same

conclusion—it was safe to continue. He spoke quickly, his eyes on mine as we walked the familiar path to second hour. "He and Jason were out scouting for Far Darrig, following a few narrow leads. They found someone else: a Guardian."

I could feel the confusion on my face. Why was he hesitating? What was so awful about finding a fellow Guardian?

"And?" I prompted, when it seemed like he wouldn't continue.

His clear blue eyes were tense. "Jack stepped forward to offer assistance, like any Guardian would. He couldn't see him very clearly—they were in a narrow alley. The Guardian told them not to come any closer."

He hesitated again and I tried to picture the scene in the momentary pause—guess what would happen next. Whatever I was imagining, it wasn't what really happened. Patrick's voice was flat and unbroken, hardly any emotion in the words. "He told them that he was dying, and that they needed to stay away from him. And then he turned and ran."

"What? Dying? But that's not possible," I protested. "You're immortal. You can't die."

Patrick nodded slowly. "Yes. But why would a Guardian lie to another Guardian?"

"Did Jack go after him?"

"Of course. You know Jack. According to Jason, the Guardian's aura was exposed, and he could see the overwhelming fear and pain the Guardian was feeling."

"He could see his aura? Did Jack catch him?"

"No. He seemed to vanish. Jack called me and Toni, and we drove out to help them search. We couldn't find any sign of him. We gave up around six this morning. Jack reported the incident to Terence, who told us that he'd come as soon as he could—Sunday, tentatively. I'm sorry if I worried you. I fell asleep on the couch and woke up just as school was starting."

"No, don't be silly. You could have just called me. You should go back to bed."

He shook his head. "I'll be fine. I don't want to miss my time with you."

I squeezed his hand. "So what now? Are you going to go out looking for him again?"

Patrick's smooth face revealed nothing, so I wasn't sure what answer to expect. "Terence told us not to."

I slowed my walk, and he hung back with me. The door to history was open a few small steps away, but I completely ignored that as I gazed up at him. "You aren't going to listen to him, are you?" I guessed.

Patrick swallowed hard. "Kate, we can't just abandon a Guardian. Whoever he is—no matter what's wrong with him, or what's got him so scared—he needs help. Jack and Toni are already back out there, and Jason and I are going to take over the search tonight."

"What about what Terence said?"

"I need to know what's wrong with this Guardian. We all do. Maybe he's just snapped from the stress of being a Guardian for too long, and he thinks he's dying. It's happened to some of the older Guardians—they've gone a little crazy. But what if he's not? What if . . . what if we're not as invincible as we've always thought?"

The bell rang and I jumped. We were alone in the hallway, and Patrick's ominous words hung heavily between us.

I could feel the fear on my face, and I tried to push it back—even as Patrick's brow pulled down with worry. It was clear he regretted telling me any of this.

✺

Patrick got a call from Toni during lunch. He quickly excused himself and headed outside to answer it.

I wanted to follow him, but Lee still looked so sullen that I didn't dare leave her. Trent kept asking Lee what was wrong, and Lee kept forcing a smile and telling him that everything was fine. The other kids didn't seem to notice anything, other than Patrick's absence. I helped Jason open his water bottle—something Patrick normally did—and Landen kept looking around, searching for his missing buddy. I tried to tell them that he'd be here soon, and then I focused my attention on Lee.

"Are you okay?"

She snorted, but at least her aura didn't seem as tumultuous as before. It had calmed a lot since second hour. "Yeah. But I can't concentrate on anything. I'm really tempted just to skip out and drop by my mom's office—ask her some questions. I mean, what if Peter Keegan's teaching at the elementary school *because* he and my mom are really serious? What if he moved from California just so they could be closer? That's pretty serious, right?"

I reached out and touched her hand, trying to offer comfort. "You need to stop overthinking this. No matter what the truth is, you're making it worse by agonizing over it."

"How can I not?"

I gave her a thin smile. "Do you want me to take you to your mom's office?"

"No. Thanks, though." She sighed loudly. "No, I think I'll wallow a little bit longer. I don't do it near enough, you know?" She pulled her hand away and started eating her lunch. I followed Olivia's example and ate my dessert first—I needed a sugar boost.

The bell rang, signifying the end of lunch. I stood, wondering if I should wait for Patrick here or just go on to our next class. Before I could decide, he came up behind me, trying to act alert and normal despite his hard mouth and weary eyes.

"Where were you?" Lee demanded loosely, slinging her backpack over her shoulder.

"Just some, um, parent troubles," he lied—not quite as lithely as usual.

Lee snorted. "Yeah, I hear you on that one," she mumbled, before turning to walk away.

Patrick watched her retreat, before turning a worried look to me. "Is something wrong? Did I say something?"

"No it's, um . . . nothing. Lee's mom, and . . . stuff."

Landen and Jason nodded as one to Patrick, and he nodded promptly in return as the kids began to stand. Patrick stooped to snatch up his bag and waved to Trent (who refused to follow the helping aide until Patrick said good-bye), and then we were walking out of the cafeteria.

"So?" I asked, impatient to know what Toni had said.

"They haven't found anything. They're taking a break."

"Are you still going out there tonight?"

His head bowed affirmatively.

I sighed. "I guess I can make something up—I probably shouldn't even talk to my Grandpa, 'cuz he'll know I'm lying from my aura. But I can tell my grandma something."

"Why?" Patrick asked, honestly looking confused.

"I'm coming with you."

He shook his head emphatically. "No, you're not. The unknown variables constitute a very real risk that I'm—"

"I'm coming. You need a Seer."

"I'm taking Jason with me."

"Patrick—"

"No, Kate. There's no reason for you to go along. Not this time."

I stared into his eyes, and I knew there would be no budging him. Trying to stifle my hurt and displeasure, I focused on where we were walking.

We didn't speak again until after school. Patrick walked me to my car quickly—we'd beaten Lee today—and though he was distracted, he leaned down to kiss me briefly.

"I'm going to hurry back to the warehouse—try to get some sleep before tonight. But if you need anything, feel free to call."

I turned to unlock my car and pulled the door open before he could lean in and grab the handle. He held on to the door as I pushed my backpack inside. I tried to keep my emotions in check as I twisted back to face him.

I felt a little guilty for my obstinate behavior when I saw the flicker of hurt in his eyes. I sighed quickly and then gave in and embraced him. "Just promise me you'll be careful," I whispered fiercely, my arms tight around his neck.

His arms flexed around me, and he nodded into my shoulder. "I will." He pulled back, smiling dimly. "I love you."

"I love you," I whispered, before leaning in to lay my lips against his. He responded with a tenderness that made my stomach flip, and for a very brief moment, I forgot to be upset with him, and even my twinge of fear was gone. For one fervent moment.

He ended the kiss much too soon and gave me a last smile. It was meant to be reassuring, but he was so tired it was more worrying than anything else. And then he turned and walked away, heading further into the parking lot.

I rolled down the window in an attempt to let some cool air in while I waited inside the car for Lee and was distantly annoyed by an intrusive vibrating sound.

It took me a long second to realize it was my phone, which I'd stashed in my backpack earlier. I twisted around so I could drag my bag up from the floor of the backseat, but by the time I tugged on the zipper and jerked the bag open, the vibrating had stopped.

My searching fingers finally brushed the flat device, and I snatched the phone out. As I settled back into my seat I flipped it open. Toni had tried to call me.

I redialed and waited a bit impatiently for him to answer. For someone who had just barely tried calling me, he took his sweet time to pick up.

"Kate, glad you called me back. What's up?" His joking voice was a little less enthusiastic than usual.

"According to Patrick, there's nothing worth worrying about, if you get my drift."

"So, he shot you down, huh? No hunting trip for you."

"Did you call to taunt? Because if that's all, give it a rest. Lee will be here any—"

"Trust me, I'd love to rest. But Jason just called, and he won't be able to go on the hunt tonight—something about some huge group project due. Like that matters, right?" I couldn't help but roll my eyes at Toni. I for one looked up to Jason, who not only supported Jack as a full-time Seer but was attending college at the same time. Toni continued easily, not missing a beat. "So anyway, I was going to just take his place and Patrick and I would go out again to look for this guy, but we really have no idea what he looks like. Jack's already been working for over two days straight, so we need a Seer to help pick him out. Want the job?"

I could hardly believe it. "Yes. Of course I would."

"You sound a mite eager there, chica. I thought these Guardian activities were too exciting for you."

"This is different. No Demons. Besides, this is why I'm here, right? To help?"

"And spend time with your *boyfriend?*"

I could picture his eyebrows wiggling from here. "You sound like my eleven-year-old sisters," I told him calmly.

"Yeah, well, just be at the warehouse around eight. Does that work for you?"

"I'll make it work."

"Then we'll try to get you back before school tomorrow."

"Maybe I should go take a nap."

"Good idea. I think I'll do something similar. Oh, and Kate?"

"Yeah?" I could see Lee, just a few cars away.

"Don't tell Patrick I invited you. Wait by the car when you get here, and I'll break it to him on the way down."

"Be gentle," I told him.

He sounded offended. "When am I ever otherwise?"

I hung up on him just as Lee opened her door. I hid my phone between my legs, hoping she wouldn't notice and ask questions. She didn't.

We drove in silence to the elementary school, and I tried to mentally prepare for my next Seer assignment.

seven

Patrick O'Donnell
New Mexico, United States

I was completely exhausted. Driving from the school back to the warehouse was hard, my burning eyes begging to close and relieve the sting if only for a second. But one second turned too easily into two, then three, and then I would jerk awake, grateful that the roads I traveled weren't busy. The couple cars around me honked at my unexpected lane changes or sudden slowing, and for a second I would feel alert. But too soon my body would relax, and I became a danger to everyone on the road once more. Some kind of Guardian I was being today.

Luckily the warehouse wasn't far. Within ten minutes, I was pulling into the alley that led back to the somewhat-hidden building that had become my temporary home. I drove around the abandoned warehouse, back to a small shed currently serving as our garage. I twisted the key slowly, and the purr of the idling engine died. I seriously considered falling asleep right there, but somehow I managed to drag myself out of the car. I pulled my backpack up onto my shoulder, closed the door, and stepped out of the shed.

I didn't bother to close the large doors because I knew I'd be back out here in a few hours anyway. My heavy feet trudged to the building as I crossed the main factory floor, which was covered in dirt and dust, littered with debris and broken machinary. Climbing the large staircase that would take me to the second floor, I decided to focus on something other than my aching limbs.

Kate's face came immediately to mind, and I relived last night in the next long thirty seconds it would take to get my tired body upstairs.

Despite what Kate thought, I had been more than a little nervous to meet her grandmother. I knew she was a wonderful, loving woman. It wasn't her character that frightened me. It was the approval I knew she'd felt toward Aaron that had me worrying. The worst part was, I agreed with the older woman I'd never met: Kate's previous boyfriend had been a great person. He treated her well and was respectful. So I could understand why Mrs. Bennett would be worried about meeting me. In her eyes, I'd ended a beautiful relationship, and I'd done it in record time.

But as I'd left the Bennett house that night, I felt that I'd passed. She wasn't completely sure of me, that was clear. She was wary, and with good reason. But she no longer believed I was a bad person, a manipulative person. She was resigned to the fact that I loved her granddaughter, and that fact alone was more than I could have hoped for.

Thinking of this brought back more emotions from that night, the most poignant being my feelings for Kate. Standing next to my car, holding her in my arms, having her kiss me in the moonlight—they were images I knew I'd carry with me for the rest of my existence. In the end, nothing else mattered to me more than her. After being a Guardian for so long, wondering if I'd ever feel even a tenth of the happiness I'd felt while I was alive and living with my family, I'd found her.

I'd chosen this life to save my brother—to preserve him as he fought in a bloody revolution. I had watched over him like I'd promised I would, and though I was invisible to him, I felt that he could sense my presence. I'd protected my family when they were forced to flee Ireland for France, but the pain of watching them grow older, moving on with their lives, was too much for me to bear. I left them when Sean turned twenty-one, and though I'd been tempted to return and check on them, I never had. I focused on the life I would have to lead—alone.

It's not uncommon for Guardians to have brief fits of depression. Mine was an ever-present thing, haunting me just below the surface. I wasn't incapacitated by it—only scarred. A slight wound always in my distant thoughts. I tried to do the work of a Guardian. This was the price I would have to pay for saving my brother's life. That's the way I approached my eternity. It was all a payment. A way for Sean to live.

But in the ensuing years—after everyone I knew must long-since be dead—I began to question my own choices. I didn't regret becoming a Guardian and saving my brother. But I found myself wondering what my life would be like now if I hadn't chosen this life. What if I had gone on to heaven? Sean may have died. My parents would have eventually died. But then we would have been together again. Forever.

Put bluntly, I believed that I'd ruined my only chance for happiness.

Some days were darker than others. Coming west had been my best decision in years, for it put me under the care and supervision of Terence. He'd introduced me to Toni, and though for years I had been working alone (as many Guardians choose to do), I accepted my new partner quite eagerly.

Toni's lighthearted spirit helped bring me back from the depression I'd been slipping into, and having someone to teach and protect was almost like having Sean back. Though Toni could be an annoying little creep, he was the closest I'd come to finding a family again. I think he felt that too. That's why we stuck together, though we'd had many opportunities to separate.

Still, the pain and regret was present. Lurking, these feelings would suddenly rear up to stab me, then retreat back into the far reaches of my mind. And they would probably remain a part of me for all eternity. But for now—for this moment in time—they were suspended. Because of her.

Kate's presence in my life had been unexpected. Life-altering. Wonderful. Heart-rending. Something about her gave me a new sense of purpose—a second chance at happiness. And when she chose me, admitted to loving me, for a brief moment I *was* in heaven. Perhaps not the one I'd been pining after, but that was because I hadn't known this one existed. Kate's love was the sanctuary I'd been yearning for. The destination I'd been hungering after. The only heaven I needed.

For now, being with her, loving her—being loved by her—was enough. More than enough. Of course it wouldn't last forever. In my experience, nothing truly wonderful ever lasted. I would never die, and she would. She would go to heaven, and I would remain here. There was no middle ground. No way around it. That fate was unavoidable. One day—far too soon for me—she would be taken away.

In the beginning, before she'd admitted any feelings for me, I'd imagined what it would be like to love her. What it would be like for her to fall in love with me. Ultimately, I found myself wondering what it would be like when she was gone. The glimpses of that darkest future had shaken me to the core, leaving me almost glad she didn't return any of my feelings. Losing her friendship would be enough to bring me to my knees in despair. To lose her love . . . I could think of no worse fate. I would be ruined by that blow. Completely destroyed.

Over time would I heal? Possibly. I had managed as much after losing my family.

Would I ever stop aching for her? Never. The mere thought was absurd. My already mixed feelings concerning regrets would become insanely complicated.

In becoming a Guardian, I had found her. Living as a Guardian, I had lost her.

I had never encountered a more paradoxical tragedy.

Whenever these thoughts plagued my mind, I tried to force them back. One day, I would have to face this pain. But I swore to myself it would be a distant day. I would continue to protect her and keep her safe.

These deep thoughts were draining on a normal day, but in my current exhausted state, they were crippling. And so I pushed them away by summoning up the memory of Kate's hands on my face, and let all future doubts slide away. They didn't exist for me. Not here, not now.

Climbing these stairs had never taken me so long. I nearly stumbled as I reached the second floor and tread on the worn floor down the hall. I reached the closed door, pulled it open, and stepped into the living space.

I thought of crashing on the couch but decided my bed wasn't much farther. It was worth the extra effort. I entered my room, closed the door, and fell onto my bed. The mattress was hard, but I was too out of it to complain.

Lying on my stomach, I pinched my eyes closed, loving the instant relief from the burning sensation that had been torturing me for hours now. I considered changing into pajamas, but I didn't want to move.

My room was pretty nondescript. Most Guardians didn't live lavish lives; still, even by Guardian standards, Toni and I lived pretty meanly. This was mostly an attempt to teach Toni that stealing wasn't necessary, because *stuff* wasn't necessary. Sometimes I wondered if my plan had backfired, but at least it kept things simple. All Guardians had to stay under the radar, and having nothing made that easy.

The old mattress, a hard-backed chair, a battered desk with a small lamp—that made up my personal furniture. Oh, and the threadbare rug, of course.

It wasn't much, but it was enough. There was only one thing in this room that mattered to me, and it was something I wasn't supposed to have at all. Guardians weren't supposed to take things from their old life, and that was the first rule I promptly broke.

I would have preferred to have one of my paintings, such as my mother's beautiful garden, captured on a warm spring morning. But

I knew that my memento would need to be small—easy to transport at a moment's notice. And so the small leather-bound book sat perched on my desk, resting in an abandoned warehouse, thousands of miles away from where it had been made. Sketching was not my favorite form of artistic expression, but it was something to hold on to. Something tangible that proved I once lived a normal life with a loving family.

I used to open my sketchbook often—especially during the years after leaving my family in France. In the last hundred years, I'd probably looked at it twice. And I never got past the first few pages—it was just too painful. The drawing I'd tried to do of my brother, Sean. A sketch depicting my parents, my home . . . even Sarah McKenna, the girl I thought of often right after my death. I wondered if I would have married her, since my mother had most obviously been trying to push us together.

These memories were like painful stabs to my heart. Maybe someday I would look at them without hurting. I hadn't seen that day yet. Still I kept the book. I never thought of throwing the old, worn book away. There were empty pages, yellowed with age, but I didn't intend to ever use them. The book was unfinished, just like my life had been.

I wasn't sure when these thoughts merged into my dreams, but I had fallen asleep at some point—because in my mind Sean and I were sitting together on my bed, and he was talking to me. Just talking. He was teasing me about my drawings, subtly praising my paintings. I elbowed him, and we laughed together.

We both knew our time together was short—it always was in these dreams. We refused to admit it was only sleeping thoughts that had reunited us, and we never discussed anything serious. Our time was too precious to waste.

And so I brought up the last village dance, mocking him with my words, and communicating my love through my eyes. He flirted outrageously with all the young women, and it was an easy thing for me to target.

Sean smiled and told me about Sarah McKenna, and how her eyes had wandered to me more than once during father's last sermon . . .

Soon the dream faded, and there was only blackness. I was asleep, and Sean was gone.

⁂

Time had passed. I couldn't tell how much. My head was still heavy, but my mind was less clouded. My eyes were no longer burning. I rolled onto my back and stared up at the ceiling. I pulled in a deep breath, then threw a glance to the digital clock poised on the edge of my battered desk.

7:37 p.m.

I didn't want to get up, though I knew the few hours I'd stolen were going to have to do. It wasn't so much the thought of working now that made me reluctant to rise—it was knowing I'd probably be up all night and then have to make it through school without a break.

I swallowed hard and reached into my pocket, where the hard lump of my phone pressed uncomfortably against my leg. I tugged it free, checking to make sure I hadn't missed any calls or messages. A quick text from Jack had come in a couple minutes ago—that must have been what stirred me out of my deep sleep.

Jus a frndly rmndr—duty calls. G'night.

I shook my head at his too-positive Australian vernacular while double-checking I hadn't missed anything from Kate. Seeing nothing, a part of me relaxed that I hadn't even realized was tensed. But it was always that way, until I knew she was safe.

There was a single knock on the door, and Toni pushed his way inside. His hair was a disaster.

"Hey, man, how'd you sleep?"

"Pretty good. What are you doing up? It's not your shift."

Toni yawned hugely then shrugged. "Jason's got some dumb group project at a stupid library. He can't miss it. So I'll tag along with you."

I grunted and pushed myself into a sitting position, the heels of my hands rubbing fiercely against my closed eyes. "Great. So we're looking for something neither of us has ever seen. This ought to be fun."

Toni didn't answer with some quirky line, which mildly surprised me. I guess he was too tired to crack jokes. I should try to wear him out more often.

"Well," I continued, dropping my hands and regarding him thoughtfully. "Guess we can do this without a Seer. A delusional Guardian should stand out in a deserted industrial area."

"If he's still hanging around there. Jack's beginning to think he might have completely left the area."

"Only one way to find out." I heaved myself off the bed and started to get ready for a night out on the town—that included a lot of hidden knives.

Toni left to get himself ready, but he was faster and returned to stand in the doorway, watching me fasten on the last of my holsters—one on my right leg, one on my left forearm.

"Sooo," Toni said, breaking the quiet. "Things got so crazy I forgot to ask how meeting the fam went. So—how'd meeting the fam go?"

I shook my head at him, foot balanced on the edge of my bed as I cinched the strap tighter to hold the knife exactly in place. "Better than expected. Thanks for asking."

"Sure, no problem-o. I am your buddy after all, right?"

"Right." I jerked the pant leg down, so it would cover the weapon, then pushed up my left sleeve, baring my arm.

"So things with you and Kate," Toni continued slackly. "They good?"

I glanced up at him, then focused on securing the last blade to my arm. "Yeah. Things are great."

"Good. I'm happy to hear that."

There was a brief pause, but it spoke volumes.

My eyebrows drew gingerly together. "Toni, is something on your mind?"

He snorted and leaned back against the doorframe. "Nah, not at all. I mean, it's perfectly natural for me to talk about your girlfriend, right? Even if she is our Seer. Yeah, it's a little weird, but that's life."

My head cocked slightly. "Are you trying to tell me you don't approve? I thought you encouraged this relationship." I straightened and tugged my sleeve down to my wrist, turning to regard him fully.

He looked decidedly awkward. "Look, man, I'm totally happy for you. And Kate. And I know it's not my place and all that, but . . . something's been bugging me."

I waited, but he didn't elaborate immediately.

"And?" I finally prompted.

He pushed away from the doorframe and took a step toward me, and in the dim light his eyes were hard to read. "I just want to know if you've told her yet," he said, his voice meeker than before. "That's all. About what happens when her time runs out."

I hated that he said the words out loud. It made them seem more real. I flinched but hoped he wouldn't be able to see it in the semi-darkness. "No, I haven't. The time hasn't been right."

When *would* the time be right to tell her that she wouldn't get the choice when she died? She'd be sent to heaven, end of story. A good thing for her and her family. A tragedy for me. It wasn't exactly a light subject.

Toni was speaking again. "Don't you think she should enter this relationship fully informed? I mean, hate me for saying it, but there's a reason Seers and Guardians don't do this very often—if at all." He held up his hands defensively. "I'm not saying you two shouldn't be together—I'm freaking glad you've finally found someone to be happy with. I'm just worried about what it's going to do to you both when she finds out it can't be a forever kind of deal. And maybe that's not what she's after in the end—but you . . . I know you, Patrick."

"I know," I broke in. "I know, Toni. You don't have to lecture me."

"Yeah, I think I do," he argued easily. "This isn't like you. You're supposed to be the responsible one. You need to tell her. I kind of assumed you already had." He shivered. "Look, I don't want to be the adult here. It's giving me the heebie-jeebies. So I'll make this fast. I'm happy for you. She makes you happy. And I don't want to see this end badly. But it will end eventually, one way or another. She's going to learn the truth at some point, so I just think it should come from you—before you completely enchant her with your Irish charm and make her unable to live without you and all that romantic junk. Not just because you're her friend, or her Guardian, but because I think you're genuinely in love with her. Capiche?"

I knew he was right. That didn't make the words any easier to hear. What if I told her the truth, and she got scared and decided to end things? Maybe I was insecure and shallow, or maybe I was just a man who'd lived so long he'd steadily lost everything he'd ever loved. Perhaps I was selfish. I preferred the term *fatalistic*.

I sighed and nodded—hoping that if I looked really sincere he wouldn't bring this up again. "Thanks, Toni. I appreciate you looking out for me—and for Kate. But I'm handling things the best way I know how. I'll tell her, I promise. But right now we need to focus on finding this Guardian. You with me?"

He still looked a bit uneasy. But he forced that away. "Of course I'm with you." He clapped his hands together, wrecking the previous mood. "Let's go find us a loony!" At my dark look, he added meekly, "And I say that with the deepest sensitivity."

I rolled my eyes, slipped my phone back into my pocket, and led the way out the door. It was time to focus on the job. My personal problems could wait.

✺

We walked down the stairs together, neither of us saying a word. I knew he was still thinking about our conversation, but I didn't want to dwell on that. Instead I thought about this Guardian and what it would mean if we didn't find him—again. Obviously he was in some kind of trouble, though it must all be in his head. But that wouldn't make it any less real for him, and so I was determined to find him, help him.

Terence didn't want us going after him, but that was only because he was worried about the effects of us seeing a Guardian driven insane by the lifestyle we led. It wasn't exactly a morale booster, so I understood his fear. But it was beyond my capabilities to ignore someone who needed help. There was a time I might have been more wary, but I'd never felt as at peace with my life as I did right now. Kate made peace possible; I knew seeing a crazy Guardian wasn't going to drive me insane. Terence had nothing to fear from me. And since Toni had never once regretted his decision to become a Guardian, I felt pretty confident Terence wouldn't be upset with us if he found out we'd disobeyed him.

We crossed the large factory floor, headed for the side exit. I pushed it open, and Toni followed close behind me as we entered the darkened alley. We turned and started walking together toward the car, but after a couple of steps, I froze—There was someone standing in the open shed, next to the car.

I heard Toni sigh loudly behind me. "Oops," he muttered. "My bad."

"What?" I glanced at him, but then the figure in our shed flipped on a flashlight, pointing it toward the ground to avoid blinding us.

"Hi," she called, sounding much too happy.

"Kate?" I asked, taking a single dubious step forward. "What are you doing here?"

I began walking in earnest now, and Toni came beside me as my steps suddenly quickened. The two of us crossed the short distance rapidly, but not quickly enough. My stupid heart was beating an uneven rhythm, and I wished it would stop. I shouldn't be happy to see her, because she shouldn't be here. Why was she here?

When we got close enough that I could see her face, I was surprised by the sour look she was directing at my partner. Not that I should have been surprised, of course.

"Toni—" she began, her eyes narrowing.

"I forgot," he cut in with a warning tone. "Can't a guy make a mistake anymore? Sheesh." He turned to face me, waving a hand in her direction. "I invited her. Sorry I forgot to mention this before." He stopped in front of her, offering a mock bow. "Are we happy now?"

"No, we're not," I said, frowning deeply at her dimly lit face. "Kate, I thought I made it clear that your assistance would be unnecessary."

"Unnecessary?" Her eyebrows rose dramatically. "You need a Seer. At least, that's what Toni told me."

"Quite true," Toni nodded. "So let's all get into the car and start—"

"What about your family?" I demanded, still focused solely on her.

"I told my grandma I'd be staying at Lee's."

"Did your grandfather believe that?"

"I don't know—I avoided him."

I shook my head at her. "Kate, you're not trained for this."

"Patrick, we're dealing with a Guardian who thinks he's dying. It's not exactly the kind of mission anyone's completely prepared for."

Toni grinned at me. "She's got a point. Can I drive?"

"No."

Toni frowned, though I wasn't directing my words at him. I tried to relax my tone in an effort to sound more reasonable. "Kate, there's no reason for you to come."

"It's not going to be dangerous. We're looking for a Guardian— one that you guys won't be able to pick out without me. I think I'll be just fine. Besides, don't you think I want to know what's going on too?"

"Are we going to do this tonight?" Toni complained.

I stared at Kate, wanting so badly to come up with a reasonable excuse to make her stay behind. I know it was stupid. She was right— we could use her help. But she was wrong in assuming it wouldn't be dangerous. There was really no way to know what a crazy immortal would do—how he'd react to being approached. Still, there would be no dissuading her. So I sighed and gave in.

"All right. You can come. But please, *please* follow my lead."

She smiled, and my stomach twisted at the sight. "Yes, sir." She mock saluted.

I sighed again, and Toni asked if he could drive—again.

It was going to be a long night.

eight

Patrick O'Donnell
New Mexico, United States

I drove, and Kate sat in the passenger seat—looking much too satisfied with herself. I held in a groan. She was learning too quickly that she could get me to do anything, and since I was her Guardian, that wasn't the best position for me to be in.

To an outside observer, my overprotectiveness might seem extreme. Except keeping the woman I loved safe wasn't the only reason I was reluctant for her to come along on this particular mission. I suppose, in the end, it was a way to protect myself. I know it's absurd—she had no way of knowing I'd once lived in such despair. She had no way of knowing I'd once believed I would be driven insane. But just because she didn't know it didn't mean I wanted her to see what I might have become. What I would probably become once she was gone. She didn't need that image haunting her.

As for me, I didn't really want to see my fate. But some sort of sick fascination had me unable to stay away. That, almost more than the desire to help the poor Guardian, had me burning to find him. I needed to see what was in store for me, when a life without Kate became too much to bear.

Toni sat in the backseat, looking at satellite images of our destination. The areas we'd already searched were clearly marked, making it easy to see we were running out of places to look. Maybe the Guardian had moved on. There was no way of knowing.

Once we were on the highway, I glanced over at Kate, her profile clearly defined from the dim dashboard lights. She was staring out the windshield, looking lost in thought. I saw the backpack resting between her legs and asked about it.

She smiled at me, her eyes bright. "I came prepared," she said simply. She patted her left leg. "I've even brought that knife you gave me."

My lips twitched into a smile, and I forgot I was still slightly exasperated with her. "Now I just need to teach you how to use it."

"I've seen a lot of movies," she assured me.

Toni chuckled from the backseat. "Honestly, Kate, I can't even picture it—you jumping all around a room, waving a knife, and executing some flips. It's so not you."

She twisted around the edge of her seat to look at him. "Are you making fun of me?"

"Yeah. But I make fun of everyone."

"You're saying I couldn't learn how to defend myself?"

"Of *course* not," he mocked soothingly. "I'm sure you'll save my life someday and everything." He paused, and I could picture the thoughtful expression crossing his face. "But then, probably not, because I can't die."

She rolled her eyes as she turned back around, and I tried to keep a straight face. It was true—the thought of Kate holding a knife threateningly just didn't seem possible.

"What are you smiling at?" she asked suddenly.

I pushed my smile down and concentrated firmly on the road. "Nothing. Nothing at all."

There was a fleeting moment of silence before Toni spoke—his voice serious. Well, as serious as Toni could ever get. "Maybe we should start back where Jack first saw him. We'll recheck those old offices, and maybe we'll get lucky and find something they missed in the initial sweep."

I nodded, agreeing with his plan.

Kate waited, hesitating before finally asking the question that was obviously lying heavily on her mind. "So when Guardians get really old . . . they can go insane?"

Toni answered before I could. "Nah. I mean, it's not like we're all destined to go crazy or anything. But sometimes living forever isn't so great. There's not a lot to look forward to when you're a Guardian— just more of the same. Some people, like me, are totally fine with that. Others . . . sometimes they regret the choice that brought them here."

"You mean, some Guardians wish they'd chosen heaven instead?"

Though I wasn't looking at her, I knew she was fighting to keep from glancing at me. She was wondering which type I was.

"Yep," Toni continued. "Sometimes that regret turns into some sort of delusion that there's nothing else to live for, and so the depression drives them a little mad. Sometimes they recover. Sometimes they don't. Usually someone like Terence—an overseer of a district— will step in, and sometimes they just keep their distance for a while. It depends on the situation."

"So you've never regretted your decision?" she asked him.

"Nope. Never. I mean, sometimes I *wonder* what it would have been like to go to heaven and meet my parents. But I was raised in an orphanage, left to fend for myself. It's not like I have a lot to miss, you know? I don't like to brag or anything, but, I'm a prime example of the most successful Guardian."

"Except for the greediness, compulsive lying, and chronic kleptomania," I said.

"Minor setbacks," Toni assured the car in general.

I knew the question Kate was going to ask next, and I worried how to answer her.

Surprising me, she didn't ask. At least, not right then. Maybe she wanted to wait until we were alone. Nevertheless, I knew she would ask me someday. She would want to know if I had any regrets. And how was I supposed to answer that? With the truth? What if I repelled her with my dark days?

Forty minutes later, I was shutting off the car and we were staring up at the hulking, long-deserted office complex. It had been built decades ago—perhaps a full century. It was a brick structure and in need of a bulldozer. It was on the outskirts of a quiet city with only a few homeless people in sight. They looked old and tired lying in the alleys, wrapped in frayed material and old newspapers.

I watched Kate scan them briefly. "They're all human," she virtually whispered at last. "We have nothing to fear from them. They're all tired, and I don't think they even realize we're here."

"You can tell all that by their aura?" Toni shook his head. "Good thing I hide mine, I guess."

I took charge. "This is where Jack saw him. Toni, why don't you ask these people if they've seen anything. Kate and I will start looking around inside."

He nodded. "Sure. You got any money on you?"

Before I could open my mouth to reprimand him for spending all of his allowance again, Kate was pulling out her wallet from the front pocket of her backpack. She handed him the whole thing, which I thought was a little too trusting of her, since he'd stolen it once before.

"Use whatever you need," she said. "There's not much, but it should be enough to thank them for their time."

Toni snatched it away from her, pulling it open, and plucking out her driver's license. He squinted deeply at it. "You're not too photogenic, are you?"

"Toni," I warned.

"Right. I'm gone. Don't have too much fun without me." He left the map on the seat as he pushed his way out of the car, wallet in hand.

"He won't really steal that, will he?" she asked as soon as Toni closed the door.

"I'll make sure you get it back," I promised. I pointed to her backpack. "Want me to carry that?"

"Nope, I got it." She grabbed up one strap, then opened the door and stepped out, slinging the backpack over one shoulder with a graceful, practiced motion.

I followed quickly, locking all the doors and then pushing the keys deep in my pocket. I skirted around the hood of the car and met Kate, watching as she zipped up a thin blue jacket. I took her hand when she was done, and we walked side by side across the narrow street and up toward the six-story building. I glanced over my shoulder and saw Toni standing near a dumpster, talking with two homeless men. I saw money exchange hands, but then I focused on my own task.

The sidewalk up to the building was wide, and Kate nearly tripped over a large tangle of weeds growing out of a crack. I steadied her and we continued walking without a word. I could feel the eyes of the homeless on us, though no one challenged our approach.

The doors and windows of the first floor had been boarded up, but the front door had been broken into before. I jerked it open, and it groaned heavily, a protesting screech echoing down the dark hall.

We stepped inside, and as the door swung closed, Kate moved her backpack around and retrieved her flashlight. She switched it on and swept the beam of light across the hall. There were closed doors on either side of us, and at the end of the long hall were two elevators.

"Stay close," I told her needlessly, leading her toward the first door on our left. Jack had assured us he'd searched the area, but he'd admitted to Toni that the search probably hadn't been as in-depth as in other buildings, simply because it had been the first place he and Jason had frantically scanned. I knew if we didn't find a sign of the Guardian soon, we'd have to give up. Tonight might be my last chance to find him.

Kate held the flashlight, swinging it back and forth across the deserted office. The carpet had been ripped out, leaving a hard cement floor. I could hear mice scrambling out of the corners to avoid the light. I wondered if Kate heard them, but she didn't seem to react to the sound. Some walls had also been kicked out, leaving the wood and steel supports exposed. It was a pretty creepy place, even by my standards.

Kate didn't seem bothered. Either she was a lot more resilient than I'd given her credit for, or my presence was somehow enough to keep her at ease. I liked to think it was the latter, mostly because her faith in me gave me extra courage.

We walked through the room, and I even took a good look in the walls. It was easy to imagine this had been some type of legal office or even a dentist's waiting room. There were three smaller rooms connected to this one, like smaller offices or cubicles. A fourth door led to a large storage-like space, which was marginally longer than the other small rooms. There was a considerable amount of dust and pieces of crumbled drywall, but not much else.

We moved back into the hall, searching the office space behind the door opposite us. Similar rooms, similar findings: absolutely nothing. We searched the entire first floor, and the small hope I'd been harboring slowly died. We would search the other floors, of course, but the main floor had made the most sense for a hiding place. It was easy to access, easy to escape from. The perfect place for someone who was paranoid.

We were at the end of the hall when the front door was pulled open and Toni stepped inside. Kate shined the light right at him, and he froze and flinched. "Wow, thanks a lot. It's not like I was attached to my retinas or anything . . ."

"Sorry. I wanted to make sure it was you," she apologized, flicking the flashlight down and out of his eyes.

"Learn anything?" I asked him as he made his way toward us.

He shook his head. "Not much. One guy said he'd know if anyone new was hanging around the area, because he's an alien from the planet Kiljoth, or something, and has psychic abilities. For obvious reasons, I really didn't believe anything else that came out of his mouth. Then there was an older woman who claimed she saw a ghost up in one of these upper windows last night. She said he looked 'frantic' and 'creepy.' Personally, that was what I thought *she* looked like."

Kate's voice was excited. "That might have been him, right?"

Toni shrugged and stopped in front of us. "Every other person

I talked to calls the old lady Scary Amy. She thought the dumpster was haunted too. No one else claims to have seen this person." He handed Kate her wallet. "You'll need to stop by an ATM sometime. You're completely out."

She tucked it back in her backpack, muttering a somewhat sarcastic "thanks."

"Anything on your end?" Toni asked me. "Though of course, if there had been, you probably wouldn't have asked me first."

I shot him a disparaging look. "Toni, your brilliance amazes me."

"We each do what we can." He grinned with mock humility. "So—next floor?"

"We'll split up," I said. "You take the basement, Kate and I will take the second floor."

"Thanks, give me the creepy cellar," he muttered. "Give me the keys and I'll go back for some flashlights."

"No need." Kate still had her backpack off after returning the wallet and was now pulling out two more flashlights, smaller than the one she held firmly. "I came prepared," she repeated.

Toni took one, and Kate held the other one out to me. I took it, a somewhat confused look on my face.

She hurried to explain her logic while shrugging her bag back over her shoulders. "We'll cover more ground if we all split up. I'll take the second floor."

"I'd feel better if you were with me," I argued quickly.

She just grinned. "You don't need to worry so much. I've got a loud scream. Besides, I have my knife, remember? I can always just pull off a few ninja moves."

"You seem a bit too happy tonight," Toni commented.

She shrugged. "Living in the moment is all."

"Fine. Do you want the scary basement?"

She half grimaced. "Um, I think I'll let you keep that one."

"Kate," I started, but she was already moving toward the closed door with a somewhat faded sign that depicted stairs.

Toni wiped a fake tear. "She's growing right up," he mourned.

I frowned at him and then hurried to follow her before she could get too far.

The stairwell was dark, and our footsteps echoed loudly. It was very musty—more so than the rest of the building. Toni moved down, and Kate and I climbed up.

When we reached the second-floor landing—despite my better judgment—I sighed and held the door open for her. "Scream loud," I begged her, only partly joking.

She smiled leaning in to give me a fast peck on the lips. "I'm still sort of hoping for no screaming, personally."

"Just be careful."

"You too."

She released my hand, and in seconds she'd disappeared into the dark hall. I let the door slowly close. I felt like I was betraying her, not living up to my Guardian duties by leaving her behind, but I didn't know what else to do. She could be so stubborn. I blew out my breath before proceeding on to the next floor alone, hoping she wouldn't find anything bigger than a rat.

The third floor was identical to the first. The stairs deposited me right where the front door would have led, so I just followed the same search pattern I'd used on the lower floor. The door on the right, then the one across the hall . . .

When I opened the fourth door—second one on the left—I immediately knew I'd found something. A horrible smell assaulted my nose, and I fought the initial reaction to gag. I habitually pulled out the dagger from my belt, just in case, and inched my way into the room.

It was the larger room, the one like a lobby or waiting area. Several holes dotted the walls, some large enough that I could have stood inside. I debated about switching off the flashlight—minimal moonlight was able to creep between the boards on the windows—but I decided to leave it on. Keeping the light aimed at the floor, I swept it across the dark space, finding nothing out of the ordinary. Still, it smelled like someone had been violently sick somewhere close by, perhaps in one of the smaller offices.

Feeling the first tug of fear, I hesitated. Call it common sense or some deeper premonition, but I was suddenly worried about what I'd find if I searched any further. I was sure the smell was caused by a homeless vagrant, because Guardians never got sick. It was one of the bonuses of living forever. We could get tired, we could sometimes get headaches, but we never heaved or got a cold.

I overrode my instinct to turn back, mostly because this is what I did. I was a Guardian—I helped people. It didn't matter who needed my help, whether it was a homeless beggar or a somewhat crazy Guardian.

I stepped into the room, crossed it tentatively, and pushed open the first door. The smell hit me again, stronger this time. A musty smell mixed with the bile, and the combination turned my stomach. There were other smells too—decaying flesh, body odor, and the strong stench of urine. I lifted the beam of my flashlight, wishing I had a spare hand to cover my nose and mouth.

I took a single step into the small room, and the yellow light fell on a body in the far corner.

It was a large form, not scrawny as I would have imagined a sick beggar to appear. He was rolled up in some dusty old carpet, but despite that he was shivering—shuddering. His body rose and fell with rasping breaths. I pushed the beam of light up to his face and saw that he was sleeping.

Correction, he was pinching his eyes closed, blearily trying to see me through the sudden light. He groaned, and the sound was weak and full of pain.

"No," the surely dying man croaked. "No."

I moved the light to his chest, taking the strain off of his eyes. My heart went out to such misery, and I had to move closer, though I did so cautiously. I slid the knife into my belt, hoping that he hadn't seen it in the first place. He sounded distressed enough just by my appearance. "It's all right, sir. I'm going to take you to a hospital."

"No!" He wheezed desperately, his voice incredibly dry. "Don't come any closer!" He struggled against the carpet, but he'd wrapped himself well.

I paused, then crouched to the ground, thinking if I didn't tower over him he would be less likely to perceive me as a threat. "I mean you no harm," I assured him soothingly.

He finally pushed free of the constricting cocoon, and the carpet fell away from him. His clothes were worn and soiled, stained with dirt and sweat—and spattered with some blood, as if his nose had been recently bleeding.

It was strange. He acted so frail—yet his body looked fit and strong. He couldn't have been much older than forty, and yet his shaking hands marked him as an old man.

"No closer," he gasped, pushing up into a sitting position. He nearly crumpled over, and he grabbed his head and groaned.

"Please," I said, endeavoring to sound calm. "I can help you. Trust me."

His back slumped against the wall, and he slowly raised his head. Blood was trickling out of his nose, but he didn't seem to notice. His next words stole my breath. "You're a Guardian. You can see me. I told the other Guardian to stay away."

My face had frozen. I stared at him, uncomprehending. It was him. The Guardian we'd been searching for, for two straight days. But that couldn't be possible. My mind rejected the thought. This man was dying—the room reeked of his painful passing. It couldn't be true. This couldn't be a Guardian.

Yet it was. His eyes—though filled with agony—were clear and sharp. He was telling the truth. Why would a dying man lie?

"What happened to you?" I breathed at last, every hair on my body rising in trepidation.

His body convulsed, and his eyes shut tightly. His face contorted in gut-wrenching pain, and his arms abjectly snaked around his stomach, as if that could stop his torment. When the spasm faded, he turned tearful eyes to me. "They did this," he roughly sobbed. "They must be stopped. There is no way to stop them. I'm going to die." He closed his eyes, his cries tremulous now. "For years I've wanted it to happen, but now . . ."

I stared at him, horror on my face. I couldn't help it—I'd never seen anything this frightening. He was obviously going insane from the pain. He was rambling, muttering fiercely one second, whimpering like a small child the next.

I had to do something. I knew that. Yet I hesitated. This moment seemed eternal.

How was this possible?

Suddenly he opened his eyes, and his gaze cut into my soul. "You must go," he hissed, breathing fast, shallow breaths. "Leave me. Get out of here!" He choked, coughed—his body shook with the torment.

I did the only thing I could think of doing. I sank to my knees and raised my hands carefully. "I can get you help," I said calmly. "We can figure this out, if you come with me."

He shook his head. "No . . ."

I reached out my hands, but the movement alarmed him. He pushed off from the floor in an effort to crouch away from me, but couldn't maintain his balance. He tipped forward, my arms instinctively lashing out to catch him. One palm slapped under his shoulder, the other slipped down his arm and brushed the back of his cold hand.

Something terrible happened in that split second of contact.

I could feel beads of sweat, but there was something else against his skin—and now I could feel it on mine. An irritation. An itch. I drew back my hand in quick surprise, flipping it over so I could view my palm. I moved my fingers quickly, seeing nothing—but the irritation remained. Almost a burn now.

I wiped my hand on my pant leg quickly, trying to scrape off whatever it was.

I glanced up when I heard the Guardian cry out, a late reaction. He jerked back, and I wasn't opposed to the small distance between us. "No!" he burst, sounding stronger than ever. "Don't touch me!"

His sudden surge of energy surprised me, and—already off balance—I fell back, my hands darting back to stop my fall. The skin on my hand was twitching, and the sensation spread from my fingertips down across my palm, rushing up my arm next. My skin prickled, and I drew in a fast breath of shock and dread. Soon every inch of my skin was enveloped by the strange sensation. Not really pain, but certainly not comfortable.

Already, though, the sensation was fleeing my fingertips and dying down across my hand. It felt normal again. My arm, shoulder, chest . . . slowly, every section that had tingled now throbbed with normality. I shuddered from the rapid change, and my mind wondered if the experience had even happened.

I noticed distantly the Guardian was moving, scrambling in the carpet for something. I tried to ignore what had just happened to me, so I could focus on him. He was agitated, and I knew I needed to calm him down. I needed him to trust me so I could get him to Terence.

Before I could speak, he found what he'd been groping for.

Gasping, he sat up and pointed a small pistol at my chest. "Don't touch me!" He groaned, his desperate eyes already knowing it was too late. But there was something else there—a grim hope that maybe he'd imagined my touch.

I lifted a reassuring hand in an attempt to keep him calm, though my own heart was pounding.

He panicked and pinched his eyes closed. "I'm sorry," he whispered, then he squeezed the trigger.

There was a loud explosion of sound, and I felt the bullet plunge into my body. I was thrown back violently, the back of my head cracking painfully against the cement.

I gasped in pain, the sound ending in a painful groan. I pulled in a shuddering breath and blinked rapidly, feeling the blood escaping from the back of my head, wetting my hair. The bullet was lodged inside my chest—I could feel it. I wouldn't heal until it was removed. I couldn't die, but the injury was enough to slow me down—that must have been his point. He was going to run. He was going to leave me.

"Help me," I gasped at him. The pain was intense and familiar. I had died like this. My whole body felt cold and then suddenly hot.

"I'm sorry," the Guardian's husky voice repeated. I heard him struggling to stand. "No one can touch me. No one can find me. No one. I'm sorry." He was rambling again, muttering insanely.

The gash on the back of my head was already healed—my head was still pounding in pain, but the bleeding had stopped. I squinted at my chest, saw the blood blossoming out from the bullet hole. It burned and throbbed.

I felt dizzy. I heard the Guardian rise and stumble past me, still holding the gun defensively. He was almost to the door when I heard a distant door slam, followed by unsure footsteps.

"Patrick?" Kate called, her voice overcome with worry.

The Guardian moaned, fingering the gun nervously. "You're not alone?" He pushed through the open doorway without another word and hobbled out, gaining speed and surety with each step.

"No," I rasped, trying to make my voice louder. "Please. She's not a Guardian!"

He didn't stop. Maybe he hadn't even heard me.

Kate advanced down the corridor, still calling for me.

I groaned and rolled onto my stomach, a cry of agony escaping before I could lock my jaw, my lips tightly compressed. Sweat beaded on my forehead, and I pushed myself unsteadily to my knees. I swallowed back the pain and tried to stand.

I had to stop him. He was going to kill her.

Seconds later I heard a gunshot, and my blood ran cold when I heard Kate scream.

nine

Kate Bennett
New Mexico, United States

I hadn't actually thought to ask Toni over the phone what a Seer should bring when hunting for a Guardian who may or may not be insane, so I just stuck to some basics. A light jacket, a few assorted flashlights, a couple water bottles, a small first aid kit, some paper, and a pencil. (Not really sure why on the last two, but it didn't seem like a *bad* idea, per se.) I'd also dug around in my closet until I found the small dagger and black leg holster that Patrick had given to me when we'd gone to rescue the twins from Romero and Avalos. I'd dumped it in there and buried it behind a couple totes, somewhat hoping I wouldn't need it again for a while. Still, I was going for preparedness, so I slapped it on my left leg and artfully rearranged my flared pant leg to cover it.

I hadn't actually thought I'd ever need any of these things, other than the flashlights and maybe some water. But then I heard the gunshot.

I was searching the second floor of the abandoned office building by myself when the quiet that pervaded the building was shattered. The shot sounded like an explosion, and though it echoed loudly I knew it had come from above.

Patrick.

Knowing he couldn't die was only a small reassurance. I spun away from the room I was searching and darted up the stairs, disregarding my personal safety. It didn't even occur to me to be afraid for myself.

I reached the stairwell and screamed, "Toni!" but I didn't linger on the landing. I was pretty sure that—even in the basement—he would have heard the gunshot too. I grabbed the railing and leaped up the stairs, my backpack slamming against me with each huge step I took. I couldn't breathe—I couldn't think. I just needed to get to him.

I crashed into the third-story door and pulled it open. I stepped into the hall, suddenly hesitating, unsure of where to go. "Patrick?" I called out, not caring if anyone else heard me.

I took a step forward, moving for the first set of doors. I pulled the right door open and stuck my head inside, pushing the flashlight fiercely across the room. It was too quiet—this whole floor was too quiet. Had he already finished and moved on to the next floor?

"Patrick!" I called again, desperate for an answer. I darted back into the hall and checked the room opposite, somehow already certain he wouldn't be there.

"Patrick!"

I heard shuffling footsteps in the hall. I quickly turned around, stepping back into the hall, prepared to see Patrick. My flashlight lifted, and I let out a shaky breath and my insides tightened.

Now I felt fear for myself.

I was staring into the barrel of a gun. It was amazing how far away I was from the weapon and yet how large the hole seemed. It was held by a hunched man, and it was far from steady. He'd just emerged from the next door down the hallway and his eyes were focused right on me.

For an indefinite second, I thought he was going to say something. But his eyes revealed a lot. There was pain, despair, fear—a perfect match for his aura, which I could see. He wasn't hiding anything.

It was him—the Guardian. But why was he holding a gun? Why

was he pointing it at me? Was he the one who'd fired the weapon? Had he shot Patrick?

My heart constricted. My lips parted as his compressed.

The Guardian aimed for my stomach. He closed his eyes tightly, and I knew he was going to shoot me.

I fell back into the room I'd just come from and heard the bullet discharge loudly. I couldn't stop the scream of fear and shock from ripping through my throat. I slammed the door and sagged against it, glancing around wildly, wondering where I could hide. A crazy Guardian was shooting at me, trying to kill me. Running was the only natural thing to do. I could hear his slow and shuffling footsteps, steadily stalking me.

I pointed the beam of light toward the longish storage room each office space seemed to have, and then I clicked the flashlight off. I stumbled a little through the darkness, but at least I knew it would be that much harder for the insane Guardian to see me. I had just closed the storage room door, shutting myself completely in the dark, when I heard the outer door open.

I could hear rasping breaths, labored steps.

I didn't dare breathe.

I closed my eyes and bit my lower lip, hating the suspense of this moment and wishing I hadn't put myself in a corner. Now all I could do was wait and squirm.

I listened to the Guardian cross the room, feet scraping along the floor like a zombie's.

And then I heard a voice in the hall. "Guys!" It was Toni. I decided to chance it, hoping Toni could move with a lot more alacrity than this haunted Guardian.

"Toni!" I screamed loudly, hurting my own ears in the confined space.

I heard footsteps, the dragging, thumping ones. But they weren't coming toward me. They were moving for the hall, growing faster, gaining speed out of desperation. I heard the door open and close, then a gunshot—and another.

I opened the storage room door, running for the outer door that was once again closed. I pushed it open cautiously, and someone grasped the outside handle and yanked it open quickly, jerking me out into the hall. I let out a small, strangled scream, but it was only Toni.

I stumbled, and he wrapped a steadying arm around me. "Are you all right?" he demanded.

My eyes widened when I saw his arm—it was covered in blood. "He shot you!" I gasped.

Toni grunted, following my gaze. "Yeah—but the bullet went right through, I'm fine—already healed. Where's Patrick?"

I shook my head quickly, pulling away. "I don't know. That Guardian—"

"He shot me, then ran down the stairs. I'm going to go after him, once we find Patrick."

I opened my mouth, ready to tell him Patrick wasn't answering, that he might be on the next floor.

Then we both heard Patrick's wavering, pain-filled voice. "Kate!"

I pushed away from Toni and stepped further down the hall. "Patrick?" I stepped up to the open door the gun-crazy Guardian had come from and pushed myself inside. The smell nearly caused me to throw up, but I somehow ignored the uncomfortable tug on my stomach. Toni was right behind me, his flashlight slicing through the darkness.

My heart stopped when I saw him.

Patrick was lying just inside the lobby floor, gasping in pain, breathing shallowly into the cement. It looked like he'd been struggling to stand but had settled on dragging himself instead. One hand was groping for the door, and he lifted his head painfully, blinking into Toni's light.

"Patrick!" I darted across the floor, falling to my knees next to him. I was able to put a hand on his forehead before his head fell, which cushioned him from the cement floor. Toni came closer, his flashlight flickering over Patrick's prone body.

I touched the back of his head just before Toni cast light on the spot. My fingers were wet with blood; Patrick's hair was sticky with it. Again I fought the urge to retch.

"What happened?" I gasped. Toni knelt on his other side, and he pushed my hand away so he could get a better view of the wound.

"It's already healed," Toni stated evenly. My heart started beating again. "But he must have been shot somewhere—the bullet's probably lodged inside, or he would have already recovered. Help me roll him over."

I cradled his head and helped push his shoulder, although Toni did most of the lifting and shifting. Patrick groaned, and a huge grimace twisted his face. I reached for his hand, squeezing his fingers tightly. "Patrick? Patrick, you're going to be okay."

"Kate," he whispered blearily, his eyes unfocused.

Toni had picked up the flashlight he'd set aside while rolling Patrick over, and he now shined the light over Patrick's stomach, then up to his chest.

My breath caught in my throat when I saw all the blood.

"Kate," Toni asked, glancing up at me. "How prepared were you exactly? A first aid kit, maybe? I can dig with my fingers, but that's gonna hurt him pretty bad."

I pulled in a steadying breath and then gradually set Patrick's head back against the floor. I shrugged off my backpack, and with trembling fingers I jerked the zipper open. I fumbled around inside, finally finding the blue-and-white case with a red cross on top. I handed it to Toni, who opened it and began rummaging around inside. I pulled off my jacket, making a pillow for Patrick's head—I didn't care about bloodstains.

I brushed my fingers over his tense forehead, pushing his hair back. "Patrick, I'm here," I whispered. "It's all right. You're going to be all right."

His eyelids peeled back and his clear blue eyes found mine. "Kate," he stated thinly. He swallowed painfully. "Are you all right? I heard—I heard the gun, your scream . . ."

"No, I'm fine. He missed."

Toni found what he was looking for—some gauze and forceps.

I balked. "There's some anesthetic in there too." I almost choked on the words.

Toni just shook his head. "Medications don't work on us. It wouldn't do any good." He held out the flashlight. "Hold this."

I didn't take it right away. I could feel Patrick's weary eyes on my face, but the shock was wearing off, and I was beginning to realize what Toni was intending to do. "You can't take that bullet out. He needs a hospital."

"No hospitals," Toni protested. "We can't. Any damage I cause through inexperience will mend itself. That's the upside of being immortal."

"You can't just operate on him without medicine by flashlight!"

"Kate," Patrick whispered. "It's okay. Let him take it out."

I looked down at his face, saw the pain there, and tears pricked my eyes. I didn't want to give in. I wanted him to be all right. I didn't want to see this. He was supposed to be the strong one. He wasn't supposed to get hurt.

Despite all the suffering he was going through, his eyes were understanding. "You don't have to stay," he breathed. "I'll understand."

I was tempted. But I realized that was only because I didn't want this to happen. Leaving him in his moment of need would be far worse than witnessing his pain.

"I'm staying," I whispered.

Patrick smiled wearily, his feeble fingers twining with mine.

Toni held out the flashlight, and I took it with a trembling hand. I squeezed Patrick's fingers with my other hand, and I held the light for Toni while he unbuttoned Patrick's shirt. He pushed the folds back, and Patrick's body shuddered as Toni's cold fingertips searched for the bullet hole in the puddle of blood. When his fingers brushed over the wound Patrick groaned, his whole body tensing. I breathed in deeply and blinked back tears.

Toni also took a deep breath and then lifted the forceps. In seconds, he was pushing the instrument inside, digging around. Even a first-year medical student would have fainted from Toni's indelicacies.

Patrick moaned, and my eyes flickered up to his face. It was twisted in a lurid grimace, and his eyes were shut so tightly he must be seeing stars.

"Kate!" Toni called warningly, and I turned back and readjusted the light, which had faltered.

Patrick cried out and his fingers strangled mine. I bit my bottom lip and focused on keeping the light in place.

It was a long few minutes, agonizing for all of us.

And then—finally—Toni retracted the tightly clenched forceps, a bloody bullet pinched between the two metal arms. Patrick shivered violently, our joined hands clasped so tightly that my fingers felt numb.

I watched in sick amazement as the hole disappeared in front of my eyes. One second it was there—a hole in his shuddering body—and the next it had shrunk back to nothing. The blood remained, but the skin on his chest was completely unbroken.

I felt the tenseness leak out of him as the internal damage was repaired and his pain slowly lessened.

He let out a deep sigh, and his eyes opened. "Thanks, Toni," he croaked.

Toni let out a thin laugh. "Sure. No problem. I do this every day."

Patrick's eyes rolled up to mine, and he saw the tears on my face. "It's okay," he breathed. "Kate, I'm going to be fine. I'm just tired. And a little dizzy."

Toni dropped the blood-smeared bullet into the first aid kit, along with the stained forceps. "I'm going after that Guardian," he said by way of explanation. He handed me the gauze and plastic box. "Wipe up the blood. Help him down to the car when you're finished here. And don't listen to him—he needs help. I'm going after that guy."

I nodded, but Patrick interrupted weakly. "Toni, I don't know if that's a good idea. There's something seriously wrong with him. Do you smell that?"

"How could I not?" Toni grunted.

"Toni . . . as crazy as it sounds, I think he really is dying."

Toni's eyes tightened. "That's impossible, Patrick."

"He shot me to keep me from touching him," Patrick continued firmly. "There's no telling what he's capable of."

"So what do you suggest?"

"Call Jack. Tell him what's happened and ask his opinion. I think maybe we should take Terence's advice. Let him take care of it when he comes."

"What if he hurts someone else?" I asked.

Patrick glanced over at me. "He was afraid. He just wanted to be alone. I think he wants to be alone when he dies."

"Immortal people don't die," Toni inserted stubbornly, still defying the implication.

"Demons do," I offered thinly.

"That's different—they're Demons." Toni sighed. "I'll call Jack. See what he thinks. That Guardian couldn't have gotten far—he was really hobbling."

Toni stood, walking back into the smaller room Patrick had crawled from. He snatched up Patrick's dropped light, leaving us with the one I held. He pulled out his phone as he walked into the hall, quickly dialing Jack's number.

I blew out my breath through my mouth and released Patrick's hand so I could quickly swipe the back of my hand over my face, drying my tears. Using the gauze, I started sopping up the blood on his chest. I could feel Patrick's eyes on me, so I tried to keep a straight face. But when my finger slipped and blood smeared onto my skin, I felt myself go pale.

"Kate, I can do that," Patrick whispered. He struggled into a sitting position, and I was too worn out to stop him. We sat facing each other, the flashlight practically on the ground, my hand had slumped so low.

He touched the back of his head, wincing deeply.

"Does it hurt?" I asked softly, knowing it was the dumbest question I'd ever asked.

He forced a shaky smile. "A bit. We're not exempt from headaches after an injury. Here." He reached down, placing his hand over mine on his chest. "Let me do it. You've done enough."

"You were shot," I informed him.

"Says who?" he joked thinly. "I don't see any hole . . ."

"That's not funny."

"I'm not in any danger."

"It's still not funny."

He regarded me carefully, and finally I gave in and pulled my hand away, turning the task over to him. While he cleaned the blood off his chest, I found some more gauze and tried to clean the back of his head. But the blood was matted to his hair and not easy to get out. "You'll need a shower," I said.

He chuckled. "That sounds good."

"Do you guys even have a shower?"

"Sure. A hose, a bucket, and a sink. It works great." His voice still sounded fragile, but it was perceptibly stronger. I allowed myself to relax a little more.

He was rebuttoning his bloody shirt when Toni reentered the room, and I helped him to stand so we could face the grim-looking Guardian. I held Patrick's arm, and he leaned on me a bit more than I expected he would.

"Well?" Patrick asked eagerly.

Toni shrugged. "Jack agrees with you. Says we gave it our best shot, and the Guardian doesn't want to be helped. All we can really do is wait for Terence. Jack's afraid if we keep cornering him, he'll get more dangerous. He might try hurting a human."

Patrick's head drooped in a nod, but he regretted the movement instantly, if his deep wince was any indication.

Toni flinched sympathetically. "Dude, we need to get you home. You hit your head pretty hard."

Patrick wasn't arguing.

Toni gathered up the supplies I'd brought, stuffing them all in the open backpack. I helped balance Patrick, and Toni led the way out, holding my jacket gingerly by one hand.

Back out in the open air, we all seemed to breathe easier. Getting away from that stench had done us wonders. The homeless people gave us a few looks, but nothing more. It was probably too dark for them to see the blood, let alone the bullet hole in Patrick's shirt, which was good for all of us. Patrick handed Toni the keys, and Toni unlocked the doors. I helped Patrick slide into the backseat, following close behind him.

"Toni, hand me the jacket," I said, stopping him before he could chuck it into the dumpster. He passed it to me without a word, and I made a pillow for the back of Patrick's head to keep blood from smearing on the upholstery.

Patrick leaned back gratefully, and I pulled the door closed and turned back to face him. "Can I get you anything?" I asked, holding his hand tightly.

"Did you bring any water?" he asked.

"Sure."

Toni opened the driver's door and climbed inside, setting the backpack on the passenger seat. He started the car, and I asked him to pass me the bag. He handed it back, and I released Patrick's hand so I could unzip it and search inside. Toni shifted the car into gear, and we pulled back onto the narrow street, heading back for the more populated part of the city.

"So," I said, making thin conversation to distract us all. "Guardians get thirsty?"

Toni answered. "We can't die of thirst, if that's what you're getting at. We can't die, period. But our mouths get dry, just like a human. We don't get dehydrated or anything, but a cool glass of water is nice on a warm day."

I pulled out one of the water bottles and twisted it open. "Well, I don't know how cool it is at this point, but . . ." I handed it to Patrick, who took it gratefully. He sipped slowly and then leaned back against the seat, his head perched up on the jacket.

I took the bottle from him, putting the lid back on as I watched him carefully. He noticed my vulture-like stare, and the corner of his mouth twitched into a small smile. "Relax, Kate. I'm not dying. I just need some rest. I'll be fine tomorrow."

"You're not coming to school," I told him firmly, reaching for his hand once more. "You have some really good reasons to stay home and sleep." I glanced toward the front of the car. "Toni?"

"Right," he called from the front, meeting my eyes in the rearview mirror. "I won't let him leave. A day's rest will do you good after these past couple days, Patty."

Patrick sighed. "I guess I've been outvoted."

"Yep," I whispered, leaning in to lay a kiss on his temple. I curled up next to him, and he leaned wearily against me.

Toni turned on the radio softly and tried to give us some privacy. But his Peeping Tom glances every minute or so ruined the facade. Once we were back on the highway, Toni seemed to give up, and he focused completely on the road. I wanted to kiss Patrick—really kiss him—but he was lightly dozing at this point, his head slumped against my shoulder. And so I just held his hand and traced my fingers over his arm, grateful to know that no matter what happened, he'd always be safe.

ten

Morning came quickly. By the time we'd gotten back to the warehouse and helped Patrick inside, and I assured myself that everything was all right, it was well past midnight. Toni told me I could sleep on their couch if I didn't feel like driving home, but one look at that rickety thing reminded me why I wanted to say no to that offer. So I left Toni yawning in their living room and drove to my house.

Everything was quiet, and I was able to sneak inside with no one the wiser. Despite all the crazy, adrenaline-pumping things I'd gone through that night, sleep came instantly. Unfortunately, morning seemed to come just as quickly.

Grandma had made waffles, which the twins were making quick work of. Grandpa was reading his paper, and when he glanced up and saw me, I could tell from his aura and his gaze that he wasn't very happy.

Grandma turned around and gave me a smile. "Kate—I didn't know you were here. When did you get in?"

"After midnight," I said, moving for my seat at the table. "Lee was pretty bad, but she didn't need me to stay all night."

"The poor girl."

"Yeah," I agreed distractedly. "It's really bothering her this time."

Grandpa lifted his paper higher as if wanting to block out my lies. I grabbed a waffle, hoping my hurt wouldn't show on my face. I didn't realize my leaving would have offended him so—I would have told him if I'd known. So now I had to endure a torturous breakfast, knowing that behind his paper, he was almost seething.

Luckily, Grandpa couldn't confront me. Not with Grandma and the twins around. Hopefully having the day to cool off would do him good—calm him down. If not, I was in trouble.

We stopped to pick up Lee, as usual. She came out almost instantly, as usual. And she was wearing complete orange, her usual for now. Her aura, though, was decidedly different. I'd never seen such streaks of red anger and brown pain.

Her smile was fake, but the twins didn't notice. "Howdy, guys," she addressed them. "What's up?"

Josie gave her a weird look. "You never say hi to us."

"Not directly," Jenna corrected fairly.

Lee squinted at them. "What? You're like adopted sisters. Why wouldn't I say hi to you?"

"I don't have any money," Josie warned.

"I'm out of it too—so don't bother asking."

Lee frowned at me. "Can't a person be friendly anymore?"

I shrugged, and we were off.

Once the twins were out of the car, I cautiously broached the subject. "So . . . did you talk with your mom?"

She snorted. "Something like that. I was ruder than I should have been. But she wasn't exactly innocent either."

"And?"

"Yeah, they've been dating secretly for just about eight months now. How am I supposed to take that?"

"I'm sorry, Lee."

"I just wish she would have told me, you know? I mean seriously— would it have been that hard? 'Gee, Lee, by the way, I'm dating this guy in California.'"

"Am I still on to meet him?"

"Yep. Friday if you can make it. I'm supposed to spend some quality time with him first. Tomorrow night. Gag."

"Maybe he's not so bad."

"Why did they have to lie about it? Why do people always think lies are necessary?"

I didn't really want to answer that, so I was glad it was a general sort of question.

We drove to the high school, and soon we were going our separate ways. I let Lee pretend she wasn't quite as angry over this whole thing as her aura told me she was, and I think she was grateful for that.

In American Lit, it didn't surprise me to find Aaron already in his seat across the circle from my usual desk.

"Hey," he said, forcing a brightness his aura didn't quite support. "How're you?"

"Good," I lied. "A little tired, but . . ."

He nodded. "You look tired."

I sat in my seat and started pulling out my notes, hoping someone else would join us.

His voice broke through the stiff silence. "Kate, I miss you."

I looked up, and he started shaking his head. "Not like that. I'm fine about the breakup." His aura told a different story. "I just miss you. Talking to you. Seeing you. We were best friends once. It's hard to lose that so quickly."

"Aaron . . ." I decided I'd lied enough for the day, and I was abruptly truthful. "I miss you too. But I don't think we can just dive back into a friendship. Our relationship complicated all that."

"I know. I realize that. But don't you think a friendship is worth saving? We could try. That's all I'm asking for. Jaxon is having a party Saturday night, at his house. I just wanted to invite you. I already invited Lee. You can both bring whoever you want." That was his way of avoiding Patrick's name.

I fought back a sigh and instead forced a smile. "Sure. That sounds fun. What time is it?"

"Eight."

"I'll talk to Patrick."

Aaron nodded once, and the motion was a little stiff. Still, I had to hand it to him. He was a great guy. A wonderful friend. It would be nice if we could find some balance. Unfortunately, I didn't see that happening anytime soon. Maybe after he got a girlfriend. I prayed for the day.

❊

School passed slowly without Patrick. It was hard to concentrate on things, and the special needs kids really missed him. I told everyone he was sick, and no one pressed for more details—except for Trent, who just kept repeating Patrick's name over and over, an endless question.

Lee mentioned Jaxon's party and asked if Aaron had invited me too. When I'd given her a yes, she begged me to come. "I think I'm going to invite Toni, if he's not doing anything," she said. She suddenly blew out her breath. "I know the only reason I was invited to the party is because of you. It would be awkward without you. I'm sure Patrick will understand."

I gave her the same answer I'd given Aaron—I'd ask Patrick. Then she looked at me with those wide eyes, surrounded by orange, and I had to give in.

"It will be a way to unwind after Friday night, when you meet my future stepfather," she added sourly.

"They're that serious?"

"He moved here. That bespeaks some dedication."

I didn't know what to say to that, so I said nothing. When school ended I picked up the twins, drove Lee to her house, and then the twins and I proceeded home. It wasn't until we pulled in and I saw Grandpa sitting on the porch steps that I remembered he was upset with me. I didn't want this. I wanted to go inside and call Patrick and make sure he was fully recovered.

I sighed and shut off the car. The twins darted out, and I had to call them back so they'd remember to lock their doors. I locked my own door and slammed it closed. I trailed after the twins, walking much slower than their eager steps.

I paused on the sidewalk in front of my grandfather, and the twins closed the front door without realizing I'd stopped. I gripped the straps on my backpack and forced a thin smile. "Hi."

I could tell from his aura that he'd calmed down moderately since this morning. Still, his frown was deep, and the disapproval on his face was hurtful. "Kate, I know I'm retired. I realize that you don't have to report to me about Guardian business. But I just figured you'd tell me when you left on dangerous missions."

"I'm sorry. I didn't think you wanted to know."

"You're my granddaughter. Of course I want to know what you're doing." He sighed and ran a thumb under one of his overall straps. "You seem to forget that I know exactly what you're going through. Yes, there's excitement. But the danger is real too, Kate."

"Patrick and Toni were there—"

"Were you going after Far Darrig?" he demanded.

"No." I tried to turn my surprise into something more hard and defensive. "We were helping Jack."

He blew out his breath. "And that's supposed to comfort me? Kate . . . I just don't feel good about you doing all this when you have no training whatsoever. I realize that you and Patrick are distracted—but he is your Guardian first and your boyfriend second. This is your life we're talking about. I'm too old to train you in defensive fighting, but you need to learn how to defend yourself before you endanger your life some more. Is that understood?"

My head bowed once, duly reprimanded. I'm sure he could see that in my aura. "Yes, sir."

"Will you talk to Patrick about this? Or shall I?"

"I'll talk to him."

Grandpa nodded firmly, his aura still sporting some tense uneasiness despite the sudden subject change. "I was planning to visit an old friend today. I wondered if you'd like to tag along. It would be to your benefit to know him, I think."

I waited for more information, but he didn't say anything else. I nodded. "Sure. Just let me take my bag upstairs."

"I'll be waiting in the truck," he said.

Fifteen minutes later we were parking in front of a weathered building, a large and faded sign declaring the establishment as *Clyde's Pawnshop*. A little unimaginative, but the place didn't look to be all that amazing from the outside either. But that was usual for this side of town.

I got out of my dad's old truck, a white Chevy, and followed Grandpa to the front door. A little bell clanged as he pushed it open, and we went into the dingy room.

Stuff was everywhere. There didn't seem to be a lot of organization to the chaos—just the basic divisions. Some shelves were piled high with dusty VCRs, DVD players, and stereos. Televisions sat along the right side wall, all of them playing the same movie in sync—just the menu now, over and over. Books were stacked on the left side, along with a glass case holding DVDs, video games, and CDs. Scattered in different corners were some guitars, a slightly bent flute, and a stained weed-cutter. The place smelled old and of tobacco smoke. The carpet was dull orange and threadbare. While I hesitated to take in the sights, Grandpa continued walking to the counter, as if he'd been here a hundred times and knew exactly where to go.

I followed slowly, my eyes drawn to the locked cases behind the long counter, which were full of guns. I think they'd continue to give me the creeps for a while yet, but I suppose that was understandable. The counter itself was made of glass, containing more junk. One side held digital cameras, the other a wide assortment of jewelry.

We stepped up to the counter, and I cast a wondering look to my grandfather. He gave me a quick, reassuring smile, then looked through a beaded curtain that hung in a doorway, which presumably led further back into a storage room.

"Hello?" Grandpa called out, since the bell at the door hadn't seemed to make anyone appear.

"Just a second!" a gruff voice called out distantly. "Be right with ya!" There was a loud grunt, an unexpected thud, and a curse following rapidly behind. Then hurried footsteps. The beads parted, and a thickly built man of about forty-five lumbered out.

The first thing I noticed was his lack of aura. The second thing I noticed was the black thread surrounding him. He was a Demon.

The third thing I noticed was his huge grin as he saw Grandpa. "Henry! You look older every time I see you!"

I watched in mute fear and confusion as the Demon walked around the counter to shake my grandfather's hand. I quickly stepped back, too shocked to do anything else but stare.

Grandpa noticed my reaction, and he chuckled, tightly gripping the Demon's hand. "Kate. I'd like you to meet Clyde—a dear friend. Clyde—my granddaughter."

The Demon smiled at me and offered a somewhat-dirty hand. "Nice to meet ya, Kate."

I didn't offer my hand. "You're a Demon," I stated, sounding a lot calmer than I felt.

He lowered his hand and shot my Grandpa a glance. "A Seer? Interesting. Runs in the family genes, then?"

Grandpa tried to explain things to me, though his words made little sense. "Clyde here has been a friend of mine since . . . when was it?

"Summer of '81, I think," Clyde the Demon interjected.

"Something like that," Grandpa agreed. "Anyway, I was keeping my eye on him. Then I learned he could get me some really good deals. Some easy cash."

"So you didn't report him?" I asked, completely astounded. "*You* broke *rules?*"

Clyde sighed. "You're not one of them prim and proper girls, are you? Always following the rules?"

Grandpa laughed, the sound somehow hard and affectionate at the same time. "She's certainly not."

I couldn't believe this was happening. "But he's a Demon!" I protested.

Grandpa gave me a simple smile. "Clyde here's a special case. He's one of the few that actually reformed—most don't. I've found that he's great for getting information regarding the Demon world, and that help has been invaluable over the years."

"Aw, shucks." Clyde laughed loudly. "Henry, you're too kind. But if you *really* feel that way, I'm a bit short on cash, so maybe . . ."

Grandpa sighed. "You'll never change."

"Most likely not. So! What can I do you for?" He moved back around the counter, digging in an apron pocket as he did so.

"Well, I mostly wanted to introduce you to Kate. I want you to help her as you've helped me."

"Right. I won't forget the tight spots you've helped me out of, old chum. I'm completely grateful. I would like to see a little more green next time, but these are hard economic times, after all." He found what he was looking for in his pocket and pulled out a box of cigarettes. He slid one out and pushed the rest of the pack back into his apron. He lifted the lighter and lit up, his eyes going back to Grandpa. "So, what else did you come for?"

"Well, I was wondering if you've heard anything else about Far Darrig."

The Demon shook his head easily, smoke curling from the end of his cigarette. I cringed at the smell and tried not to breathe too deeply. "Not much, Henry, old boy. He's gone pretty quiet. Philippe says he heard that a strange Demon is still in the area, but that's Philippe for you—always trying to get everybody jumping at shadows."

Grandpa nodded thoughtfully as he distractedly reached over the counter and plucked the cigarette out from between Clyde's lips. The Demon frowned as Grandpa ground the end into a nearby ashtray and let it fall lifelessly into the small dish. "Not in front of my granddaughter, Clyde," he said simply. "Besides, smoking is a nasty habit."

The Demon grumbled and leaned against the counter. "It's not going to hurt me none. I'm immortal."

"It killed you once."

"Can't touch me now."

Grandpa shook his head, and I had a feeling they'd done this many times before.

I spoke at last, drawing them back into the conversation. "You've been keeping tabs on Far Darrig?"

Clyde laughed once. "Keeping tabs on him? He's not the ruddy circus. Do I hear things? Yeah. Do I have his itinerary? He—" He saw Grandpa's look and amended the curse word in the same breath. "Heavens no."

"So he's still in the area?" I shivered despite the heat.

Grandpa shrugged. "There've been no mysterious deaths reported, but . . . I think it's safe to assume he's here. Philippe's word doesn't mean much, but if there was anything he wouldn't lie about, it's something like Far Darrig."

"Any Demon with an ounce of sense is afraid of him," Clyde agreed with a grunt. "So mysterious and deadly. The Demon Lord's right hand and personal assassin. Many believe that the king wouldn't be this powerful without Far Darrig standing by him."

"How long has the Demon Lord ruled?" I asked, suddenly curious for these details Patrick had yet to tell me.

Clyde shrugged. "Not long, considering we live forever— Guardian blade willing, of course." He bit the inside of his cheek, considering briefly. "It's all happened in the last two hundred years or so, I'd say. Before that, there were just groups of Demons that would fight each other for more power and human dominion. I was alive during such times, and trust me—they were dark. The vilest, most evil of Demons divided up the earth like it was a pan of brownies— everyone vying for the centermost, gooiest piece. And then *he* came along. All persuasive and charismatic. If a powerful warlord didn't join him, he was killed. It was simple in a sick sort of way. Strange too. Everything seemed to fall into place for him. He knew who to ask first, who to avoid until the end. Some believe he has dark powers and can read minds. As for me, I just think he's ruddy smart. And so he came to command pretty much everything. With Far Darrig at his side."

"So the Demon Lord hasn't been a Demon for long?" I guessed.

Clyde shrugged. "Maybe. Or perhaps he's just been waiting a

long time for the perfect opportunity. Personally, I hope I never find out. I stay pretty well under the radar and that's how I like it."

My grandfather seemed absorbed in his own thoughts—only distantly aware of our conversation.

Clyde turned to him, trying to pull him back. "There's something else Philippe mentioned—something a bit odd. Some strange rumor he overheard in his bar."

Grandpa glanced up, still looking partially distracted. "Yes?"

Clyde shifted his weight uneasily. "Well, it seems so fantastical . . . so impossible in broad daylight. But according to the rumor, there have been some strange deaths along the West Coast."

"Far Darrig?" Grandpa asked quickly, the powerful Demon still clearly on his mind.

Clyde shook his head. "I don't know. Maybe. But they aren't just some random humans dropping like flies. They're Guardians."

My heart stopped beating, and the small electric fan in the corner suddenly seemed loud.

Grandpa's wrinkled face crinkled further in confusion. "What? That's not possible."

Clyde raised his hands defensively. "I know, I know. I'm just passing along what Philippe heard. Or what he said he heard."

"How did they die?" I asked, thinking of the insane Guardian who'd tried to kill me last night.

The Demon shrugged helplessly. "I'm sorry. I wish I knew more. But it's just a rumor. According to Philippe, several have been found dead. The higher-up Guardians have been hiding the bodies—and the truth—in order to stop panic from spreading among their ranks."

"But Guardians . . . they have no weaknesses," Grandpa muttered. "No soft spot, like the Demons. You can't kill a Guardian."

"Maybe it's a false story—most rumors are groundless. I'm just passing along the word."

It was obvious he wasn't hiding anything—he'd told us everything he knew. But I wanted more details—something definite. If Guardians were indeed dying . . . that would explain the crazy one.

But could it be true? And if so, what did that mean for Toni and Patrick?

Clyde suddenly straightened, waving a quick hand around the room. "Planning on buying anything, Henry?"

Grandpa wavered. "I'll scan the books," he finally said, before wandering in that direction.

Clyde looked to me, offering a wide, helpful smile. "What is it *you're* interested in? I assure you, I have it all. Instruments, computers, jewelry, movies . . . Whatever your heart desires."

I wanted to question him more about the rumor, but I knew that the conversation had been dropped—there was nothing further to explore on that front. And so I did the polite thing and glanced around the shop, before I focused down at the counter, peering into the glass case.

An idea slowly grew, and I quickly told him what I wanted. Then, as an afterthought, I asked, "Mind if I look through your movies?"

eleven

Our purchases were bagged and paid for. (Luckily he took a debit card, since all my cash was gone, courtesy of Toni.) Once back in the car, Grandpa spoke immediately. "Kate, I know you're going to be tempted to tell Patrick and Toni about Clyde, and the things we talked about. But I need you to promise me that you'll protect Clyde." I opened my mouth to protest, but he overrode me. "I know—what's the point of getting information if you can't share it with the Guardians? Now, if we'd learned something concrete, I'd let you call Patrick immediately. But Clyde rarely deals with solid facts. It's speculation—something I've used to steer my Guardians in the right direction."

"But what about that rumor? About Guardians dying?"

He shook his head. "A rumor. Nothing more. There is no evidence. The only thing that would come of your telling them is trouble for Clyde. Trust me on this. He's not a danger to anyone, but some Guardians would see things differently. They could end his business—disturb the easy life he's cultivated for himself. Besides, when Guardians start paying attention to a Demon, other Demons follow the gaze. If they learned what Clyde's been doing for me, there's a good chance he'd be killed. Do you understand what I'm saying?"

He kept glancing back and forth between the road and me, but I knew I had his full attention. "Grandpa, I need to tell them about this rumor. Last night—the mission I was on. We were searching for a Guardian Jack saw. This Guardian claimed he was dying."

Grandpa nodded. "It happens sometimes. Some Guardians buckle under the stress—"

"Patrick thinks he really was dying. "

"Guardians can't die."

"You sound like Toni."

"Kate, Demons have been afraid of Guardians for thousands of years, simply because they *cannot die*." He shook his head. "I don't think they've suddenly turned vulnerable. Unless you know something I don't. Patrick and Toni—their regenerative abilities still function?"

I nodded. "Yes. But—"

"Please, Kate. I'm asking you to save a man's life. Promise me you'll keep Clyde and his information a secret."

I knew I didn't have a choice—and a part of me recognized that he had a point—and so I agreed, though somewhat reluctantly.

Satisfied, he nodded, and that was the end of the discussion.

Back home, I carried my sack from the pawnshop up to my room and set it on my bed. I closed the door, then I pulled out my phone and made the call I'd been dying to make all day.

Patrick answered on the fifth ring. "Kate, I was hoping you'd call soon. I was getting worried."

I walked over to my bed and sat on the edge, a small smile on my face just from hearing his voice. "I wasn't the one who was shot last night," I reminded him. "*I'm* the one who's supposed to be worried. Did I wake you?"

"No. I was in the living room with Toni, and I left my phone on my desk."

"Are you feeling better?"

"Much. Still a small headache, but that's probably more from lack of sleep than anything else. How was school?"

"Good. Slow, without you."

"I'm the lucky one—I got to sleep through most of it. Still, I think even in my dreams I was missing you."

I fingered the plastic bag. "So . . . I was thinking that—if you're feeling better—maybe I could come over tonight."

"I'd like that."

"I know for a fact that Lee would love to hear from Toni. She could use some cheering up."

"You want Toni out of the house?" His voice was amused.

"Well, I don't know if I'd call the warehouse a house, but, yeah— that's the idea."

"Should I be scared?" There was a flirtatious air to his lilting accent, and I felt a grin stretching my face.

"Absolutely. Are you busy around seven?"

"I think I can clear my schedule for you. I'll make sure Toni knows the time."

"I can't wait to see you."

"I'll be counting the minutes," he promised.

We said our good-byes quickly, and I headed downstairs, hoping we had a cake mix in the pantry.

❋

Just before seven I pulled up to the warehouse. As soon as I shut off the car, I ran fingers through my hair, which I'd left down. I'd had a quick shower in an attempt to get the cigarette smoke off of me, and I hadn't been able to blow-dry it completely so it was still a little damp. I knew the heat would dry it soon, and hopefully he wouldn't notice before then.

I was wearing a nice pair of dark skinny jeans and a dark-blue top. A pair of black sandals wrapped around my feet, and a simple silver chain circled my neck. It wasn't an elaborate look, but it showed a little effort, which was just what I wanted.

It was hard juggling everything, but at least Grandma's cake pan had a lid, so I could stack the plastic container holding dinner and the two wrapped presents on top. I shouldered my purse and carefully closed the door with my foot.

It was a balancing act, trying to get the front door open, but by the time I'd crossed the floor to the large staircase, Patrick was coming down the stairs to meet me, his smile still tired but pleased nonetheless.

His eyes grew confused when he caught sight of everything I held, and he hurried the last of the way toward me. "What's all this?" he asked, taking everything but the cake from my arms.

I grinned up at him, standing two steps above me. "Happy birthday," I told him, my voice echoing in the deserted room.

His brow furrowed in confusion. It took him a split second to find his voice. "It's not my birthday. Not even close."

I shrugged. "I figure I've missed enough of them—it's time I threw you a little party."

He frowned, staring down at me. "You didn't have to do any of this, Kate."

"I want to." I glanced around him, further up the stairs. "Come on—I'm starving." We walked side by side up to the second floor, and I opened the door since I was holding fewer objects. He thanked me and walked into the room, depositing the stuff on the low, scuffed coffee table. I was right behind him, and I set the cake down. Through the plastic lid all I could see was a bunch of the blue frosting.

I turned toward him, seeing his eyes wandering over me. The blue in them was excessively bright tonight. "You look beautiful, Kate," he finally whispered, holding out his arms.

I embraced him carefully, worried about putting too much pressure on his chest. He held me tighter, proving that everything was fine. I sighed in a mixture of relief and happiness, then leaned up to receive his kiss.

We stood there holding each other for a warm moment, until my stomach grumbled loudly. Patrick broke his lips away, a small and breathless laugh escaping. "I'm sorry. I'm being rude."

"It's your honorary birthday—you can do anything you want," I told him.

"Hmm . . . you tempt me," he whispered, his lips brushing against my mouth, teasing my lips. Finally he pulled back and frowned at the coffee table. "Kate, you really shouldn't have—"

"Is Toni gone?"

Patrick sighed and reached up to run his fingertips against the side of my hair line. "Yes. He and Lee went out to eat, and then I believe he was going to take her bowling."

"Toni bowls?"

"There's not much of anything that Toni doesn't do."

"And you?"

"I'm not quite as adventurous . . . I'm pretty boring, actually." He kissed me again, and my verbal response was slower than it should have been.

"Absolutely boring," I agreed at last, my lips pressed easily against his, my hand sliding along his jaw.

He shivered at my touch, then reached up to grab my hand. He held it tightly and offered me a dazzling smile. "As it's my honorary birthday, I'd like you to eat something."

"Do you like grilled cheese sandwiches?"

"They certainly smell good," he answered. He squeezed my hand once and then released it. "I'll get some plates."

"You splurged and bought some, huh?" I teased, bending over to peel the plastic lid off the dish holding the warm sandwiches.

"You'd be surprised what good deals await those who shop discount stores and garage sales."

"That's what Lee tells me all the time."

He wandered back with two plates, then went back to get a couple water bottles. We sat on the couch, but before I handed out the sandwiches I reached out and plucked up the first present, which was thin and rectangular.

"Here—I can't wait anymore."

"You're more impatient than I am." He laughed lightly, taking the present from my hands. I watched as he carefully tore the paper, moving slowly just to torture me. Finally the wrappings fell away, and he was holding a Disney DVD—*Peter Pan*. He glanced up at me, his eyes shining. "You remembered," he stated simply.

I smiled and curled my legs up onto the couch. "Your favorite book. I thought maybe you'd want to watch it tonight."

He nodded. "I'd like that very much. Thank you."

I snatched up the next present—smallish and boxy. He sighed when he felt the weight of it. "Kate, you shouldn't have spent all this money on me."

"Patrick, stop complaining and open it already. If it makes you feel better, I got them used."

He looked somewhat appeased, and I watched his face as he intently unwrapped a plain, old cardboard box. He hesitated, and in that moment I knew that he'd guessed it. His fingers moved even more slowly than before, until finally he was lifting the corners of the flaps and reaching inside. He pulled out a silver digital camera and cradled it in the palm of one long hand, simply staring at it, unable to speak.

I filled the short silence. "There's a charger inside and an extra memory card. There wasn't an instruction manual included, so you'll just have to learn as you go. It looked fairly simple, though."

He glanced over at me, his brown hair falling into his eyes—eyes that seemed bluer and clearer than ever before. I'd never seen this depth of emotion on his face, and if I hadn't known him so well, I might have wondered if he was somehow upset by the gift. But he was overwhelmed—speechless.

"Thank you," he finally said. He placed the camera almost reverently on the coffee table then set the box aside as well. He reached for me, pulling me close in a tight embrace there on the lumpy couch. I wouldn't have wanted to be anywhere else.

"Thanks," he breathed into my ear. He rubbed my back lightly, then pulled away, the smile back on his face. "Let's get you something to eat, huh?"

I'd forgotten napkins, and I guess Guardians didn't really care about frivolous things like that—so we just ate quickly, ignoring the greasy fingers. We talked while we ate—avoiding the most obvious topics of Far Darrig and insane Guardians.

In my attempt to get to know him better, I asked Patrick some more questions about himself. I learned during this process that, as I'd rightly guessed, his favorite color was indeed blue. He also loved spring, the rain, and Sundays.

We swapped some silly childhood stories, and by the time our meal was over, we were both relaxed and amused. His eyes kept wandering to the camera, and I knew he was almost afraid to start using it. So I decided to help him break it in.

I set my dirty plate aside and opened up the cake. I'd forgotten candles, and that was another thing that Guardians didn't seem to stock up on. And so I made him pretend they were there anyway, and though he was reluctant to get his picture taken, I made him blow his imaginary candles out while I leaned back and snapped a few pictures.

He set the cake aside, but I kept taking pictures of him. He frowned and tried to snatch it away from me, but I just leaned further back, laughing and shaking the camera in the process of yet another picture.

Thus began the camera war. He eventually snagged it, after unfairly tickling me. Once it was in his hands, he darted from the couch and around the coffee table, taking picture after picture of me trying to steal it back from him.

We finally called a truce and set aside the camera, for the time being. We settled back on the couch, and Patrick turned on the laptop while I cut the cake. We ate his first birthday cake in over two hundred years and watched *Peter Pan* on the laptop from Terence, sitting contentedly side by side.

The sun went down, and Patrick reached to switch on a dim lamp. I cuddled next to him, and he put his arm around me, pulling me closer. He was completely absorbed in the movie, and I think he loved every minute of it. We were near the end when the door opened, and Toni walked in.

He ambled over, watched the screen for a moment, then straightened. "You guys are *so* cool," he muttered sarcastically.

"How was your date?" I asked, glancing up briefly.

He nodded. "Good. Lee is probably the funniest girl I've ever met." He leaned closer to the coffee table, squinting at the cake. "'appy Birday atrick.'" He read the two lines, or what remained of them. "Huh. I never knew. What is today, anyway?"

"It's not really my birthday," Patrick told him, his hold on me tightening infinitesimally, his eyes still glued to the screen.

"Oh. That of course makes *total* sense." Toni jerked a thumb at the cake. "Are you guys going to finish that?"

"You're not seriously thinking of eating the whole thing," I said, casting him a worried look.

He shrugged and scooped up the pan. "It can't hurt me," he reasoned simply, before turning and marching toward his bedroom.

"Bring that out before I leave!" I warned him.

He waved a hand but didn't even bother to turn around.

I sighed and settled closer to Patrick. He shifted his arm out from behind me, instead curling it around my knee, which was bent next to him, foot braced on the edge of the couch. I tipped my head against his shoulder and sighed easily. "I'm so happy right now," I confided in a whisper.

I could almost sense the smile that tugged against his lips. "You have that same effect on me, Kate."

I wrapped my arms around his arm that surrounded my knee, and we settled comfortably against the back of the couch.

A second later Toni reemerged from his room, and we glanced up at him. "Forgot a fork," he explained, walking toward the corner of the room that was their kitchen.

We focused back on the movie, and Patrick spontaneously craned his neck to place a kiss on the top of my head.

There was a flash of light, and Patrick and I blinked quickly.

Toni cheered triumphantly, standing on the other side of the coffee table, fork and camera in hand. He must have snatched it when he grabbed the cake. "That was perfect!" He fairly crooned. "I couldn't have planned that any better. I was hoping for vacant faces, but wait until I show your grandpa, Kate. He's going to love this intimate moment."

"Toni," Patrick said, voice level. "Leave the camera and get out."

The Hispanic Guardian sighed but did as he was told—surprisingly. He must have really wanted to eat that cake.

Patrick reached out to lift up the camera, and he quickly pushed a few buttons, finding the way to view the saved pictures.

I watched the display as the picture Toni had taken flicked into place, and I was surprised by how much I fell in love with the candid shot.

Patrick humphed beside me. "I was going to delete it, but . . . "

"It's beautiful," I finished for him.

He nodded once. It depicted us on the couch, holding each other. The lighting wasn't perfect, but it was sufficient. Patrick's lips were buried in my hair, and my face was angled toward him. Our arms were wrapped around each other, and the emotion of the moment was almost tangible.

"I would love to paint this," he whispered.

I rubbed his arm. "Maybe you'll get some canvas and paints for Christmas," I hinted.

He groaned. "Enough, Kate. You've done enough." He kissed me for real this time, and then we finished the movie without any other interruptions.

Once it was done, Patrick went to get the cake pan from Toni while I stacked up the dirty dishes. Patrick stopped my attempt at cleaning, and I obediently grabbed my purse. He walked me out to my car, and the night was so quiet and peaceful that the last thing I wanted to do was leave. But I knew Grandpa would be anxious until I got home.

Thinking of Grandpa reminded me of Clyde. Which in turn reminded me of the other secret I was keeping from Patrick—Terence's phone call.

He seemed to sense my mood change, and he rubbed his free hand against my arm. "Hey, what's wrong?"

I looked out at my car, which was only a few long steps away. I couldn't tell him the things I was honestly thinking about, so I decided to bring up the one thing I could. "Grandpa pulled me aside after school. He was pretty upset about my leaving last night," I hedged.

Patrick nodded silently, understanding perfectly.

I glanced up at my quiet Guardian. "He says he'd feel better if I had a little training before my next mission. He threatened to talk to you himself."

"He's completely right. I haven't been doing my duty."

We hesitated at the car, and I twisted to face Patrick. "It's not your fault—we've been busy. He's just paranoid."

Patrick bowed his head once, allowing that, but his ready words were no less compromising. "What are you doing tomorrow after school?"

I smiled a little. "Training with you?" I guessed.

"If you can fit it in," he agreed smoothly, reaching up to push my hair back behind my ear. His eyes tilted to mine, and I held his gaze easily. At first I simply enjoyed the peaceful moment. Then I noticed the tightness around his mouth, and I realized he was debating whether or not to say something.

"What is it?" I asked softly.

His head ducked and he seemed to consider his next words carefully. I felt my stomach tense, unsure if I wanted to hear what he was thinking, if it was this hard to say. But knowing was better than being in the dark, so I waited patiently for him to break the amplified silence.

I was surprised and rather relieved when he raised his head with a thin smile. "Nothing," he said simply. "Nothing important, anyway. I want to end the night on this note, right here." He leaned in, and I met his lips with mine, kissing deeply. After a long moment he pulled back, his voice incredibly gentle. "Thank you, Kate. For everything."

"I love you," I reminded him, one hand rubbing against his shoulder.

"I'm glad of that," he confided, before leaning in to kiss me affectionately one last time. "Go. I'll see you tomorrow."

We said our good-byes quietly, afraid of ruining the perfect air between us. He held my door while I climbed inside, and he handed me the empty cake pan once I was seat-belted in. I put it on the passenger seat and whispered a last good-bye. He closed the door and stepped back. I started the car, switched on the lights, and rolled slowly away from him, then shifted into gear and drove away—glancing at him through the rearview mirror, where he stood silently, watching me go.

twelve

Thursday promised to be a long day. Lee was in a bad mood because tonight she was supposed to go out to eat with Peter Keegan, her mother's boyfriend. Also, I had battle training to look forward to, and though it might sound silly, I was nervous. I didn't want to look stupid or mess up in front of Patrick. I didn't know anything about fighting—my dad had showed me a few defensive maneuvers, in case someone ever tried to grab me from behind or around my wrist. I'd never used them, though. Besides— Patrick was most likely going to teach me how to use knives—something a *little* bit different than squirming away from an enemy.

Aaron talked to me in American Lit again, but this time Patrick was present as well. It was a little awkward, though we all tried to make it seem natural. Aaron mentioned Jaxon's party Saturday night, and Patrick really had no choice but to agree. Saturday was also Josie's big soccer tournament, but it would end in plenty of time for the party.

At lunch, everyone was glad to have Patrick back. They treated him like he'd been gone a year. Mark and Trent both kept talking to him, trying to get his attention. I watched him interact with them, loving the fond way he dealt with them.

I noticed he kept stretching out the fingers on his left hand, and it seemed unconscious. He would curl them up, only to twist them back out again. It was as if his hand were numb, and he was trying to bring feeling back. The corner of his mouth was turned down in discomfort, and finally I leaned over to touch his flexing hand. "Are you okay?" I whispered, hoping no one else would notice the exchange.

He followed my gaze, and his fingers suddenly stopped moving. He forced a smile. "Yes. My hand just feels a little stiff. It's nothing."

I didn't press him, because it was obvious he didn't want to talk about it right now. But I kept a surreptitious eye on him the rest of the day. His fingers continued to twist around and that frown of discomfort remained in place. Sometimes he would catch himself, and his hand would be immobile for a couple minutes. But in the end, the fingers would start to twitch again.

After school Patrick walked me to the car, and I promised to meet him at the warehouse in an hour. He nodded his approval, we said our good-byes, and then he walked away—his hand still twisting, fingers stretching at his side.

Once the twins and I were home, I moved up to my room to work on some homework I'd been procrastinating. I didn't get everything done by the time I was ready to leave for the warehouse, but that was the beauty of history—it didn't change very often, so I knew it would still be there when I got back.

My lesson with Patrick was actually pretty short—at least it seemed like that to me. He'd laid out some large dusty rugs to stand on, and there on the main floor of the abandoned building he demonstrated some defensive stances. Balance was a big thing he stressed, and he told me to always keep my knees slightly bent in a fight. He also showed me how to throw a punch, though after seeing my paltry right hook, he smothered a laugh and told me I should probably only use my arm as a last resort. Like that built my confidence. He warned me never to fully extend my arm, and he had to demonstrate how to curl my fingers into a fist.

I'm not going to lie, I felt pretty stupid.

He also taught me how to hold a knife for the different kinds of thrusts, stabs, and swipes. Though I got the motions down, I couldn't imagine ever using them in real life.

In the beginning, I watched his hand, which was still flexing more often than normal. But then I became so absorbed in the lesson that I didn't think about keeping an eye on him.

Toni wandered down for the last few minutes of the lesson, and he offered a couple valid suggestions. When Patrick declared us finished for the day, Toni just sighed and folded his arms tightly across his chest. "I'm thinking we should just keep a really good eye on her. She's got a long way to go."

"Thanks," I muttered, tired and a little sore. "Some of us haven't been practicing for a hundred years."

"You're doing great," Patrick told me kindly.

"For a beginner," Toni added grudgingly.

"What time is it?" I asked, glancing at the tall windows to see the sky dimming.

"Later than you thought, by the look on your face," Toni commented helpfully.

"You should probably be getting home," Patrick said.

I nodded, blowing out my breath. "Thank you—for teaching me."

"I'm sorry I've taken so long to get to it."

Toni snorted. "Yeah, we're all horrible, lazy people. Now if you'll excuse us, Kate, I'm trying to expose our mutual friend Patrick to more quality entertainment tonight—if you don't mind. He's watching too much Disney these days. The man needs some solid TV shows in his repertoire."

Patrick sighed at him, but I just nodded.

"Maybe we can find time to train again this week," Patrick said.

"She needs all the help she can get," Toni agreed, talking about me like I wasn't there again.

Patrick rolled his eyes and walked me out to my car. While he kissed me good-bye, I considered asking about his hand again. But I knew, just from the way he held himself, that he was tired, so I decided against mentioning anything. The stiffness would probably be gone by tomorrow anyway.

As I stepped into my cool house, I could smell dinner cooking, but things were quiet. That told me the twins were probably out with friends, so the shower would be all mine. I shut the door and saw Grandma sitting alone in the front room on the couch, angled so her back was to me. I almost called out to her, since it was obvious she hadn't heard me return. But then I noticed her aura, and curiosity kept me from saying a word.

Normally Grandma's aura was jumbled and hard to read because there were so many emotions mixed together. But at this moment, her aura was calmer than I'd ever seen it. A thick blue band wavered around her, revealing the high level of peace she was feeling. Even more curious, I took an inaudible step closer, so I stood at the doorway, hoping to see what was absorbing her attention and eliciting such peace. I could see the edge of a photo album on her lap, and she was focused completely on the open page. I recognized the album as my mother's, something I'd spent hours holding after her death. I'd never seen Grandma take it out.

I stared once more at her aura, wishing that the blue and yellow I saw around her now would stay with her. I hated seeing her pain all the time. There was more blue than yellow at the moment, and I was glad she was feeling so content. The blue was so deep, almost hypnotic . . .

My stomach clenched suddenly, and I was immediately surrounded by an image. A crowded room, dimly lit, soft voices and even softer music. A familiar young man with glasses and a dark suit was grinning, standing beside a familiar, beautiful woman in a floor-length white gown. Together they held a knife wrapped with a wide maroon ribbon around the handle, and together they pushed the blade into a tall white cake while everyone clapped.

My gut twisted painfully and my knees buckled. "Kate?" Grandma twisted around at the sound of my falling to the floor. She pushed the open album onto the couch and hurriedly moved to crouch in front of me. My head was spinning, and I was exhausted—I felt like I might fall asleep. "Kate, what's wrong?" She clutched my shoulder and I wordlessly opened my mouth.

She helped lift me from the floor and we stumbled together into the front room. She slipped me down onto the couch and peered into my blinking eyes. "Were you working out? You're all sweaty . . . Do you have heat stroke?"

I didn't think she'd relax if I told her I was sweaty from training with Patrick, so I just half-shrugged.

What had just happened?

"Stay here," she commanded. "I'm getting you a glass of water."

I pressed a hand to my stomach as she retreated, surprised that the lurching feeling was completely gone. Not even a slight pang remained. The sleepiness was passing too, and I felt mostly like myself again. I closed my eyes tightly and worked on leveling out my breathing, because my heart was pounding with what must have been adrenaline. I'd been staring at auras for months, and I'd never experienced anything like this. The lifelike . . . *vision*—I suppose *vision* was the right word—and the sudden fatigue.

I could hear Grandma filling up a glass of water as I happened to look down at the photo album beside me—and my stomach dropped. The picture my grandma had been staring at—probably reliving, if her blue contentment was any indication—was a close-up picture of my parents on their wedding day, captured as they cut the cake.

My grandma had been looking at this picture, lost in the memory of that day, and I'd seen it by looking at her aura. I'd known what she was looking at just because I'd seen what she was feeling. It was almost like . . . I'd read her mind.

The front door opened and Grandpa's feet scuffed loudly on the entryway as he moved to close the door. Grandma was just coming back with the water, and she sounded relieved to see her husband. "Henry, Kate just collapsed."

His aura flared with concern and his head whipped around to follow Grandma's gaze. I met their stares, still feeling completely shocked by what had happened. Somehow, I'd seen my parents at their wedding. I hadn't been born until years afterwards, but somehow I'd been there, after looking at Grandma's aura.

They approached me together and Grandma was quick to offer me the tall glass of water, ice clinking against the sides as I took a sip.

"What happened?" Grandpa demanded roughly. "Have you been hurt?"

I shook my head quickly. "No. I don't think so . . ."

They debated awhile about taking me to the hospital, but I calmly tried to convince them I was fine, even though my mind was racing. Had I really just read my grandmother's thoughts? The idea was more than ludicrous. But seeing auras wasn't exactly in the realm of normality. I wanted to be alone with Grandpa. He'd been a Seer for years—he'd know what was going on, if anyone in the world did.

At last Grandma frowned deeply, but already her aura seemed to be calming down. "Were you and Lee working out? Honestly, it's too hot to be jogging outside. I want you to drink that whole glass, young lady."

Grandpa wasn't really relaxing. "Are you dizzy? Have you been feeling sick?"

"No. I was . . . but just for a second. Right before I fell . . ." He seemed to understand my hesitation—that I needed to discuss this with him alone.

He reached out to touch his wife's arm. "Charlotte, I think she's all right now. I'll sit with her for a bit. You go ahead and get back to what you were doing."

Grandma blew out her breath. "Kate, you nearly brought on my heart attack. Don't ever do anything like that again." She waved a long finger at me. "You drink every drop, and then go take a cool shower, all right?"

I quickly nodded, and with a last look at both of us, she slipped back into the kitchen.

Grandpa moved to sit next to me on the couch, pushing the album to the far side of the sofa. "What happened?" he asked seriously.

I tried to put the strange experience into words, but it was harder than I imagined it would be. The whole thing had happened too

quickly—a brisk flash into my grandmother's thoughts. Not to mention the fact that it all seemed so insane. I watched his firm face carefully as I relayed what I'd gone through, and he was silent for a full
minute afterward, his gaze shifting to focus on the opposite wall. I
tasted my cold water again and studied his aura, which was pretty
scrambled.

When my water was a fourth gone, I spoke quietly. "Grandpa,
can Seers read minds?"

My point-blank question sounded even more ridiculous out loud,
but he looked at me with complete attentiveness. "That's one way of
putting it, I suppose."

My eyebrows pushed together. "Why didn't you tell me? Why
didn't anyone tell me?" *Patrick, Toni . . . Were they keeping secrets
from me?*

My grandpa's next words nullified my worries on that count "It
isn't normal, Kate. I mean, it's not something Seers do, generally.
Most Seers don't experience this, and an even smaller number of
Guardians are aware of the . . . problem." He shook his head, eyes
back on the wall. "There are many unknowns in the world—especially in the world of Guardians, Demons, and Seers. This incident
you described sounds like something that happened to me once. I
can only tell you what was told to me by my Guardian overseer at the
time: keep it to yourself."

"But, wait—don't you know why it happened? What triggered it?"

He looked at me at last. "My working theory, based on my own
experience, is stress."

My voice was doubtful. "Stress?"

He nodded. "And I didn't think to warn you, because, for one,
it's a rare occurrence among Seers, and for another . . . well, I figured
if you made it through all the stressful situations you've faced over
the past few weeks, you wouldn't have to worry about these fainting
spells."

"But I didn't faint."

He patted my knee. "I'm glad."

"Grandpa, why do I get the feeling you're not telling me something?"

"Because there's nothing to tell. The simple fact is, no Seer I've talked to understands why this happens. Sometimes it does, and that's all there is to it."

"Did you ever tell your Guardians?"

"Nope. My supervisor advised me not to, and I agreed with him."

"So, you don't think I should tell Patrick and Toni?"

He hesitated. "If I were you, I wouldn't. But I can't tell you what to do."

I frowned. "I guess I don't understand why it would be an important secret to keep."

He shrugged. "It's not good tactics to let people know of your liabilities."

I could see what he meant, but at the same time, he wasn't quite making sense. Maybe my head was more muddled than I thought.

He spoke before I could. "Kate, it's up to you. Tell them if you'd like. But promise me you won't let it happen again."

"How can I stop it from happening? I didn't do anything. I mean, I was just looking at her aura—like I always do."

He pursed his lips, considering his next words carefully. "You felt that pull in your gut . . . I think that's what you need to resist."

I didn't understand exactly why he'd want me to resist reading a person's mind—other than for moral reasons, and of course the brief bout of nausea. And though a part of me was interested in trying to read a person's mind again sometime, I'd come close enough to passing out for one day. So I nodded.

He looked comforted. "I'd like you to try and take it easy for the next couple days," he said. "No Seer business, okay?"

I nodded again. "I think the Guardian schedule was pretty empty for the rest of the week, anyway."

"Good. Now go on and finish that water. It can't hurt, and it would make your grandmother feel better."

❊

After dinner I'd made my decision. Closed up in my room, I pulled out my cell and called Patrick. It took me only a few minutes to explain the weird mind-reading experience and to tell him about my grandpa's explanation. He sounded worried, of course—Patrick was a regular worrywart. But after all the small secrets I'd been keeping from him, I had to tell him at least one. And unlike my grandpa, I couldn't see the harm in telling my protector.

"Aside from the side effects, it was actually pretty cool," I finished.

His words formed slowly. "I'm grateful you chose to tell me. But I agree with your grandfather—promise me you won't try that again."

I rolled my eyes. "The two of you . . . honestly, it wasn't so bad. And it could be a really useful skill. I mean, what if I could practice, and get used to it? If I could see a person's aura, I could read their mind. That could be super useful on a mission."

"Demons don't show their auras, so I fail to see how it would be very useful. Besides, I'm sure you're not the first Seer to think of that. And if the Guardian Council thought it was valuable, they would be helping Seers master the ability. But I think your grandpa is right. It's a liability more than anything."

"Well, thanks."

"Of course I don't mean you're a liability. I just don't think mind reading is an asset."

"Uh-huh." I grinned when I heard his frustrated sigh. He was good at digging himself into holes, when he was nervous.

"You know what I mean, Kate. A Seer is valuable enough to a mission without stopping to read minds. And the resulting passing out sensation could be pretty problematic, if we were in a dangerous situation."

"I guess my grandpa did say that it's more of an accidental thing. I mean, it's the first time it's happened to me, and he made it sound like it had only happened to him once, in his whole career."

"And he did say that most Seers aren't susceptible."

I nodded, not that he could see. "Should we tell Toni?" I asked.

Patrick's answer was immediate. "Only if you want to be teased about fainting."

"Fair point. Let's not tell him."

"Agreed. If you'd like, though, you could discuss it with Terence when he comes. As a supervisor, I'm sure he knows of it. He may be able to answer some of our questions."

I blew out my breath. "Tell me something, Patrick. How much strange can you handle in a girlfriend? Because I just keep getting weirder and weirder."

"I think as long as you're my girlfriend, I can handle anything—regardless of how strange."

thirteen

I was grateful for Friday morning to arrive. After the long week, and most recently yesterday's mind reading, I was more than ready for a weekend. Both my grandpa and Patrick had urged me not to worry about the experience, so I was trying to follow their advice. But it was hard not to. I'd seen my parents, after all. True, they hadn't looked quite right because they were so much younger than I remembered. But still. It hadn't been until I was lying in bed, trying to find sleep, when my eyes had filled with tears. I'd seen my parents, and they'd looked so happy.

I wondered if I'd ever get over their loss.

As soon as we'd dropped the twins off at school, I asked Lee how her night had gone. I'd noticed that her aura was still tinged with brown and gray, but the red that had become so common in her had mostly disappeared—a few thin wisps were all that remained. I hoped that meant good news.

Lee cast me a level look, and her tone was even. "Kate, I know you already know."

"I can see some colors—I want you to tell me what happened."

She sighed, then shrugged once. "He was really polite. He tried to be understanding . . . I don't know. It went better than I expected. There was only one sort of weird thing that happened . . ."

I waited, sending her a couple glances while I drove.

Finally she spoke, eyes focused out the front window. "Sometimes when I talk to you, your eyes don't quite reach mine. I know you're looking at my aura. Well . . . Peter Keegan would do the same thing. It made me feel really weird." She turned to me, meeting my fast look. "I think maybe he's psychic too," she admitted.

✻

Patrick listened to every quick word I told him, and I kept glancing around to be sure we were still alone in the American Lit classroom.

When I finished, Patrick considered shortly before speaking. "Lee thinks he might be a Seer?"

"She used the term psychic."

He shook his head slowly. "Kate, I don't think you have anything to fear. According to Lee, her mother has been dating this man for several months. Their relationship can't be connected to you because you haven't been a Seer for that long."

I sighed and placed a hand over my eyes, rubbing wearily. "I know. You're right. I just . . . everything seems so complicated lately, and I feel like every stranger is working for the Demon Lord."

Patrick reached out a hand to kindly massage my shoulder. "It's all right. You've been through a lot, Kate. You're entitled to some paranoia."

I dropped my hand from my face to regard him. "I have an excuse to go crazy? Is that what you're telling me?"

His lips twisted into a small smile. "You're not crazy, Kate. You're being cautious. And I'm glad that you are. It makes my job easier."

I blew out my breath while straightening, and his hand fell back to his desk. "You're right. I'm being irrational. This man is a Seer—and maybe he's not even that. Lee couldn't be sure."

"Are you going to be all right at Lee's house tonight? If you want, I can come along—no one would see me."

"Unless Peter Keegan *is* a Seer."

"Then we'd know, I guess." He shrugged. "I'll call Terence if you'd like—see if he knows anything about this man."

I shook my head. "Don't worry about it. I overreacted. I'm going to treat tonight like it is—a chance to meet my best friend's mother's new boyfriend."

"Because that makes it so much less complicated," Patrick joked.

"I guess I could just try reading his mind . . . Kidding, of course," I added when I caught his stern look.

I noticed his left hand on the desk, stretching out again, as if fighting numbness. He saw my stare and quickly shifted his hand beneath the desk. "I'm fine, Kate. Just stiff."

Aaron walked in, and Patrick seemed grateful for the interruption. Normally, I don't think I would have been so concerned about his hand. But after hearing strange rumors and meeting a crazy Guardian, I was starting to feel the first twinges of worry. Not that Patrick was going to let me do anything about it, of course.

❄

Lee is nothing like her mother, Jeanette Pearson. While Lee is somewhat eccentric—all right, *really* eccentric—her mother is probably the calmest, most easygoing person on the planet. She never wore anything too bright, and she always dressed with class. A tee shirt and sneakers? Never. Black dress shirts, white blouses, and dressy slacks made up her wardrobe. Maybe it was because she worked so hard at the office, so she'd just grown comfortable in the fancier clothes. In any case, seeing them on the street you wouldn't think they were mother and daughter by the way they acted and dressed.

Jeanette Pearson kept a clean house. Or maybe I was just used to living with two younger sisters. She also liked things to be planned and executed perfectly, so I was sure to arrive ten minutes early for dinner.

I parked on the street, since there was already a car in the driveway. A new-looking Mini Cooper, red with white stripes and a black top. It wasn't exactly what I'd pictured Peter Keegan driving, but I wasn't really sure what I'd expected. The Batmobile? I had no reason to think that he was anything special or anyone to be worried about. I needed to stop jumping to dramatic conclusions. Patrick was right—even if he was a Seer, Peter Keegan didn't know about me. There was nothing to be nervous about.

Lee opened the front door for me, looking relieved that I was here. I could hear the sound of muted laughter coming from the back of the house, but Lee's clothes were so bright I could hardly squint a look behind her. "Hey, thanks for coming," she said, pulling the door wider.

I stepped into the small entryway and gave her a fast hug. "Happy to be here."

She patted my back once, then pulled away to close the door. "He's already been here for a half hour. Came early to help her cook."

"That's nice of him."

She frowned, her orange lips stretching. "Or devious. What if he only wants to *look* like a nice person?" she grabbed my hand. "I need you. Check out his aura. When I excuse myself to go to the bathroom, follow me one minute later."

"Yes, sir, major general," I mocked, letting her pull me across the room. I dropped my purse onto one of the huge pillows as we walked by the couch.

Lee dragged me back to the kitchen, where she gave me a last warning look to pay attention before pushing the swinging door open and stepping inside. I followed her, my eyes sweeping over the room, trying to take in everything at once.

Mrs. Pearson was standing over the stove, stirring around the taco meat that was nearly done. She was wearing black pants and high heels—big surprise—with a white, loose-fitting blouse. Her hair was a long bob that curled under about halfway down her long neck. It was dark blonde—similar to my own, only thicker.

Lee stepped to the side, and I got my first look at Peter Keegan.

He was human, as I'd established, the day I'd seen him at the school. The gold lining around his body was proof of that. There was no telling if he was a Seer or not. The colors around his body weren't threatening either, and I felt myself relaxing. Small yellow clouds surrounded him, connected with a thick strand of blue. I could see some gray depression—more than in the average person, but somehow that made sense. A middle-aged man, still single and alone. That could be explained. I saw no anger, nothing that screamed for me to confront him or run. A little green—the smallest hint of purple jealousy. (Maybe he was jealous of Lee? The attention she got? Who knew?)

In short, he looked like a completely normal person.

He was slicing olives on a white cutting board, and it looked like he'd just finished dicing some tomatoes. His back was to the room, and he was glancing out the back window while he worked. That didn't seem exactly safe, but stupidity wasn't exactly a crime.

He was wearing the brown suit he'd worn in the schoolyard, and I could just see the dark-purple tie he wore. It added a splash of color that marked him as someone who wanted to enjoy life, and I felt that my first instincts about him were right—he wasn't anyone to fear.

Lee's mom was just turning toward the door, and Mr. Keegan was only a second behind her. "Kate!" Jeanette cried happily, her mood still exuberant from whatever they'd been laughing at before Lee and I had intruded. "I'm so glad you could make it. Peter—" She threw him a glance and then waved toward me. "This is Kate Bennett— Lee's best friend. She's like a second daughter to me."

Mr. Keegan set the knife aside and reached for a towel lying on the table. He dried off his fingers, a smile on his surprisingly handsome face. There were laugh lines around his eyes, but he was probably barely forty. His hair was still dark black and thick, and his eyes were bright with life. Still holding the towel, he stepped toward me, holding out his free hand in the same motion.

"It's a pleasure to meet you, Kate."

I took his hand, shaking it firmly. "Mr. Keegan, it's good to meet you too."

"None of that—just Peter, please."

I nodded, and our hands fell apart mutually.

Jeanette was smiling widely, and the yellow of her aura was almost overwhelming. She was glowing as brightly as Lee's pants.

"Would you girls mind setting the table? We'll have this ready by the time you're done."

"Sure, Mom," Lee said, and we both crossed the kitchen to the cabinets. Peter Keegan retook up the story he'd been telling, at Jeanette Pearson's insistence, and soon they were both laughing again.

Lee and I gathered the appropriate dishes and carried them out to the dining room. Once the kitchen door fell closed behind us, Lee sent me a look. "Change of plans—forget the bathroom break. What does he look like to you?"

"Well, I don't think he's a murderer. At least, he's not planning on it anytime soon." I set down the stack of plates I carried, and Lee set down the glasses.

"You're saying he's perfectly harmless?"

I shrugged and started setting the plates around the table. "He looks fine, aura-wise. What did you expect me to find?"

"I don't know. I thought maybe . . . maybe he'd have a silver aura, like Patrick. Something different about him, you know?" I didn't say anything right away and finally Lee sighed. "He's pretty normal, huh?"

"I'm afraid so."

She just shook her head. "I guess I just wanted something to be wrong with him. That's dumb, huh?"

"Not at all."

She sighed. "I'm going to get some forks."

"I'm sorry, Lee."

"Don't be. I guess it's a good thing he's a good guy. Not a loser like everyone else she's dated. I'll be right back." She returned to the kitchen, and I continued to set the table alone, wondering what on earth I could say to make her feel better.

Dinner was great. The food was excellent, and Peter Keegan was entertaining. He didn't hog the conversation, but he put a lot of energy into everything he said. I helped him make the connection between me and my sisters, and he seemed to warm up to me even more after that.

"They're both great girls," he told me. "Josie can be a handful, but she's got spirit. And Jenna . . . she's easily the top of the class."

"She's always been really smart," I agreed.

Mrs. Pearson spoke from her side of the table. "Doesn't Josie have a soccer game tomorrow?"

I nodded. "A pretty big tournament, apparently. They're playing three different games—four if they win at least two of the first ones."

Jeanette Pearson smiled sadly. "I would love to come watch , but I have to go into work tomorrow. Computer problems—can't live with 'em, can't live without 'em."

"I'll cheer extra loud for you," Lee told her mother.

"Do you think I could tag along?" Peter asked. "I'm not doing anything else."

I wasn't sure who he was asking—me or Lee—but I answered for the both of us, hoping Lee wouldn't care. "If you don't mind sitting in the sun for a few hours, you're welcome to be there."

He cast me a grateful smile, and that's when I noticed his eyes flicker to the top of my head. I instinctively knew what he was looking for—my aura. Lee was right—Peter Keegan was very possibly a Seer.

I just wasn't sure if I should be worried, relieved, or even care at all.

If nothing else, Lee looked a lot more at ease with Peter by the time I was ready to leave. I hoped that she was. Because as far as I could tell, Peter Keegan was a great guy.

On the drive back to my house, I called Patrick to let him know that everything had gone great. I told him that Peter was most likely a Seer, but whatever he was, he was super friendly. Patrick sounded pleased but distracted, and when I asked him about it, he said he just had a headache. I told him to get some rest, and I know he could hear the worry in my voice. I wasn't trying to hide it. He assured me that everything was fine, and then he promised to meet me at the soccer field at nine the next morning. Reluctantly, I said good-bye, wishing I could tell him to take some aspirin or something.

fourteen

I rode in my grandparents' van with them to the elementary school, where Josie would to be playing. I'd considered calling Patrick when I woke up, just to check in and make sure he was feeling better. But in the end, I'd decided against placing the call. I was overreacting, and I knew he didn't appreciate it. So I decided to be the cool girlfriend and just see him at the field.

Josie was wearing her soccer uniform, looking as serious as she always did before a game. Jenna wasn't a big sports fan, so she'd brought her backpack with books, a notebook, and other miscellaneous things to keep her entertained. Pure habit forced me to snatch up a novel I'd been trying to forge through for weeks now, but I had little intention of actually opening it. Ever since I'd met Demons and Guardians, fiction had lost a lot of its appeal.

Grandpa was driving, and Grandma kept ordering him to slow down because he was speeding. He made some random excuses, mostly to distract her so he didn't have to let up on the gas. It was the same thing that always seemed to happen when we drove anywhere together, and we were all pretty used to it by now.

As soon as we parked, Josie slid open the long door, and Grandma wished her luck. My sister usually had a red streak in her aura—her competitive edge—but in anticipation of the important tournament, red was her dominant color. I imagined that most people would be overwhelmed by such intense emotions, but the blue and yellow that swirled around her assured me that Josie thrived on days like these.

She was a mystery to me and the rest of my family.

Josie was already across the parking lot by the time the rest of us had unloaded ourselves from the van, but she didn't seem to mind being alone. She was focused on the game already, which wouldn't start for at least another fifteen minutes.

Though it was still early in the morning, the day promised to be warm. Grandma was wearing a sun hat, and she was trying to force Grandpa to wear one too. Jenna and I walked behind them, and my younger sister yawned loudly beside me. She wasn't a morning person, and waking up at 7:30 a.m. on a Saturday hadn't been her definition of a good time.

We sat on the home side, halfway up the bleachers. I sat on the end, and we spaced out to save spaces for Lee, Peter Keegan, and Patrick. I pushed on some sunglasses and opened my book, trying to keep from worrying about Patrick and failing horribly.

A few minutes before the game started, I glanced up to see Lee and Peter Keegan climbing up the bleachers toward us. Lee was laughing at something Peter had said, and he looked both pleased and relieved that she was beginning to warm up to him.

Jenna glanced up and grimaced. "Wow, she's bright. Good thing I've got my shades, or I'd be blind right now. Is orange week over after today?" I nodded, and my sister sighed. "Good. Orange is just . . . too orange."

"She's going out with a bang," I agreed. She'd worn some bright pants up to this point, but these shorts were neon all the way.

It wasn't until they were almost to us that Jenna finally realized who was walking behind her. She blinked rapidly, her mouth hanging open. Peter was wearing khaki shorts that reached his knees and a white polo shirt. He was also in flip-flops and wearing sunglasses. He looked very un-teacher-like, so I understood how she'd missed him at first.

"Mr. K," she muttered, completely shocked and bordering on disturbed.

They were close enough to have heard that, and Lee laughed as they stepped up the last couple rows.

Peter Keegan just looked up at my sister and smiled kindly. "Hello, Jenna. How are you doing today?"

"Um, good," she stumbled out, a little awkwardly.

Grandma and Grandpa were looking this way now, and Peter Keegan leaned over me and Jenna to shake Grandpa's hand. "Hello, I'm Peter Keegan—I teach here at the elementary school."

I watched Grandpa's face closely, as his muscles relaxed into a warm smile—his handshake became more firm, more friendly once he realized there was nothing immortal about the school teacher. "Pleased to meet you, Mr. Keegan. I'm Henry Bennett."

"Kate's grandfather." Peter nodded with a warm smile. He glanced down at Jenna. "You have three beautiful granddaughters."

Grandpa released his hand, but before Peter could pull back, Grandma was stretching out her hand. "I'm Charlotte Bennett. I've heard some good things about you from Jenna and Josie, Mr. Keegan."

He laughed vaguely, the sound bordering on nervous. "Guess the blackmail I use is working, at least," he joked feebly. "They're good girls. Both of them."

He dropped Grandma's hand and straightened, and Grandpa Bennett cleared his throat, his aura clearly displaying his conclusions about this new teacher—skittish, and certainly not dangerous. "You here for the game, then?"

He nodded and threw a glance to Lee. "I had a free morning, and I thought it would be a good chance to spend a little time with Lee."

Grandma smiled knowingly. "That's right. How is Jeanette doing?"

Lee handled the potentially embarrassing question with fast reflexes. "She had to work."

Grandma grunted. "That woman does a bit too much of that."

Grandpa squinted at Lee's hair. "She's got to in order to pay for all that dye. Must've been black market—that stuff's bright enough to be some kind of military-grade weapon, Lee."

My best friend grinned. "Thanks, Mr. Bennett. That's the nicest compliment I've had all week."

While we talked, we easily scooted around so Mr. Keegan was soon sitting between Grandpa and Jenna—who kept sending him quick looks, as if she didn't believe it was really her teacher. Lee and I sat on her other side, with me still at the end.

After the initial greeting banter was over—my grandma asking a couple pointed questions about Lee's mom—Peter Keegan visited with my grandparents almost exclusively, leaving Jenna free to return to her book, and Lee and I were somewhat able to talk alone.

The first topic was, of course, her mom's new boyfriend.

"He picked me up this morning, and we went out to breakfast," Lee told me quietly. "Now that the secret's out, he doesn't seem quite as weird to me. He doesn't act as awkward around me, anyway. I still think he might be psychic like you, though."

I nodded my agreement. "I think you're right," I whispered.

"Do you think I should call him on it?"

I shrugged. "That's up to you, Lee."

She sighed. "Gee, thanks."

"You seem a lot more at ease with him."

"Yeah, I guess. He's pretty cool. It's just still a little weird."

I knew she wanted a subject change, so I easily asked about Wednesday night. "You never told me how your date with Toni went."

A small blush climbed her cheeks. "He kissed me."

I tried to keep my face straight. Inwardly, I wanted to scream. What in the world would have possessed Toni to do such a thing! I was fine with them being friends, but I didn't want my best friend getting all confused over an immortal boyfriend. I knew from experience how complicated that could get.

"Really?" I finally managed.

Lee clasped her hands together and twisted to face me full on. "Kate, I don't know what happened. I mean, he's a college guy. Why's he even interested? He's funny, and I like to think that we've got a good friendship going, but . . . kissing him was kind of weird."

"Then why did you let him?"

She shrugged. "It was fun?" She overrode my reply, lifting a single hand, palm out, to ward off my warnings. "I know. I was weak, blah blah blah. But can you blame me? He's so cute. There's only one problem."

"Which is?"

Her lips curled tightly, but the wall finally broke and the words poured out. "I think I might also like someone else. Maybe more than Toni. I didn't tell you, because I didn't want you to make fun of me."

Taken aback, I quickly shook my head. "Lee, I'd never make fun of you. Of your feelings," I amended, when she sent me a wry look.

She nodded once, satisfied with my revised sentiment.

"So who's this other lucky guy?" I asked, intrigued.

"Well, um . . . I've sort of had a crush on him forever."

I blinked. "Really? *Him?* I thought you were over him!"

"Shoosh!" she grabbed my arm, panicked, but no one had heard us. "Want the whole world to know? Yes, *him.*"

"Rodney Sommers." I smiled languidly. "You little liar. That's why you've been so focused on organizing the music library this semester!"

She frowned. "Kate, I'm facing a few dilemmas here—can we cut the jokes?"

"No, no, he's a good-looking kid. A little nerdy, but he's a band geek—it's to be expected."

"Thanks a lot, pal," she muttered sarcastically, dropping my arm.

The soccer game had started by now, but I couldn't focus on that, not after discovering my friend was still infatuated with her first crush. "It's really sweet, Lee. You two would make a cute couple."

Lee shook her head. "We've just been distant friends forever. I mean, we have band in common, but that's it. He makes fun of the clarinet to boot."

"Everyone makes fun of the clarinet. It's an easy target." I ignored her dark look. "Lee, I think you need to just ask him out already. If I'd known you still had it this bad, I would have forced you a long time ago."

"Exactly why I didn't say a word."

I shook my head at her. "You need to ask him out. Spending a couple hours in the music library doesn't count."

"But what about Toni? What if he's really interested?" She sighed. "Then I've got my mom to deal with. Her and her dating problems . . ."

"From what I can see, things seem to be going well on that front."

"For the moment." Lee's phone vibrated, and she pulled it out promptly. I knew it was Rodney just by the added color that washed over her face. Suddenly I wondered how many times I'd assumed it was Toni she was talking with, when really it had been Rodney all along.

She started tapping out a reply to his text, and I prompted her with an elbow jab and a unbroken chorus of, "Ask him out, ask him out . . ."

Once the message was sent, she closed her phone and sent me a look. "Where's your boyfriend, anyway? Wasn't he coming?"

Internally, I was instantly sobered. But I fought to keep my expression playful. "Yeah, he said he was planning on it."

"He missed the toss-up. Or the kickoff. Or whatever the heck this sport does at the beginning of a round."

"It's soccer," Jenna said, and we both twisted to look at her—the little eavesdropper. She was innocently turning one of the pages of her book, her eyes focused on the black words. "I think the orange has dulled your mind."

Lee looked ruffled. "What sort of brainiac are you, using words like *dulled*. Loser." She paused, then added evenly. "Speak of any of this to anyone, and you die."

"Ten dollars?"

"No way, you little snoop!"

Jenna's head bowed once, then she turned to look at her teacher, who was talking to Grandpa, laughing lightly. She opened her mouth to speak, but Lee was strangling her wrist in an instant.

"You little creep," she hissed. "Remind me not to get you a Christmas present!"

"Ten dollars," Jenna reminded smugly.

"Five," Lee bargained between her teeth.

The eleven-year-old thought about this, then agreed with a nod. "Fine. Five."

Lee growled something under her breath—it didn't sound like her usual "Oreos"—as she dug in her small purse, dragging out her wallet at last. The older people on the bench didn't seem to notice as the crinkled five-dollar bill switched hands.

Jenna looked extremely satisfied.

For a few minutes we all focused on the game—cheering loudly when Josie's team made the first goal.

The game was intense, for being peewee. Josie wasn't the most competitive player out there, I was able to see that, but even the less-committed girls began to play more seriously as the time ticked on. In the end, Josie's team won, but only barely.

Patrick was still conspicuously absent.

There was about a fifteen-minute break between the first and second game, so Peter Keegan stood, declaring he was ready for some nachos. Lee wanted a snow cone, and—once Jenna was sure she wouldn't be alone with her teacher—she hopped up too. I didn't really want anything, but Grandma asked if I could get her a water, and Grandpa wanted a Coke. And so I followed the group to the concessions stand, somewhat grateful for the distraction.

This was the second time in a week that Patrick had been late, and it made me nervous. It wasn't like him—especially without some kind of warning or phone call. He wasn't an early riser, and if he still had a headache, then there was a chance he was still asleep. I shouldn't leap to any conclusions. But what if something had happened? Maybe Jack had called, and Toni and Patrick had left on a mission without me. I know they didn't report to me, but I was the Seer. That meant something, didn't it? If nothing else, I was Patrick's girlfriend. He shouldn't keep me hanging like this.

But I wasn't going to call. I wasn't. I'd already made that commitment. I just hoped I heard something soon. My resolve was fading as quickly as my worry was escalating.

While we walked, Peter suddenly spoke to Jenna. "So, you like to read?"

She looked surprised by the question. She was used to answering questions in a classroom, but out on a soccer field, on a Saturday, was a different story. "Um, yeah . . . It's my favorite thing to do. That and play the piano."

"You play the piano? My mother made me take lessons when I was a kid." He smiled at some distant, amusing memory. "She made me quit after I broke a vase."

Jenna's forehead creased. "You broke a vase while playing the piano?"

"I was trying to avoid the piano, actually. I threw my theory book across the room and it knocked the vase over."

Jenna giggled despite herself. "I've done that. But I didn't break anything. How old were you?"

"Ten or so." He shrugged a single shoulder. "A long time ago."

"Do you still play?" Lee asked.

He nodded, grinning. "On my CD player, most every day."

"That doesn't count," Jenna scoffed.

"I wish I did. But I haven't touched a piano for so long . . . I'd probably murder 'Chopsticks.' No, I'll stick to reading books. That's a fairly safe way to spend some time."

We reached the wooden snack shack and had to wait in a short line. Lee ordered first, getting her snow cone, and Jenna went next. She got a Popsicle, but while she was reaching into her pocket for the money, she ended up dropping the frozen stick to the dirty ground. Without a word Peter stepped forward and ordered another, and by the time Jenna had picked up the dirt covered Popsicle, her teacher was handing her a replacement.

I gave Lee a pointed look, and she sort of rolled her eyes and took a small bite of flavored ice. Yes, I'd made my point—he was a nice guy. Seer or not. I'd already guessed that he wasn't an active Seer, if he was a Seer at all. Still, Terence might know something about him. I made a mental note to ask him when we finally met.

I bought the drinks for my grandparents, and I got my snow cone. Peter got his nachos, and then we walked back to the bleachers. By the time we were settled, the second game had started.

Josie's team played hard, but the other team was good. Josie was mad when they lost, but she looked only more resolved to win the next game. If they didn't, this would be the end. If they won, they'd get to play the fourth game.

Peter got a phone call just after the third game started. He spoke laconically and seriously, his expression hard to read. His aura was easier but still confusing. Green uneasiness—a lot of it— was billowing out around him, overtaking the yellow. The red flared up too, as if he were angry. He didn't look it, though. Just serious. I could see Grandpa watching him from the corner of his eye, prob- ably just from habit. I wondered what he made of the severe color change.

Peter ended the call after a concise minute, before he sighed and handed Jenna the rest of his nachos, which they'd been sharing for the past few minutes. "I've got to run," he apologized to the row in general. "My landlord didn't get my last payment, and he's threaten- ing to call the cops on me if I don't get over there now." He looked to Lee. "Do you want me to take you home?"

She shook her head. "Nah, I'm fine here. That is, if I can get a ride home after?" She glanced at Grandma, who was nodding and already turning back to watch the game.

Peter excused himself again, sounding apologetic. Lee and I watched him until he was out of the bleachers and out of sight, disap- pearing toward the parking lot.

"I don't know why he's so worried," Jenna said, following our gaze. "His landlord sounded like a wimpy girl over the phone. Mr. K could take him."

I didn't reply, because my phone was finally vibrating. I reached for it a bit too eagerly, earning a snort from Lee, but that didn't matter to me—it was Patrick.

"Hey," I answered quickly, reminding myself that I'd need to speak carefully. "Where are you? Is everything okay?"

There was a sound in the background—a car running. His apologetic voice punctured the sound. "I'm sorry, Kate. I slept in—Toni didn't wake me up, and I didn't hear the alarm. Are you still at the school?"

"Yeah, the third game just started."

The tired edge that I'd come to expect in his voice was now extremely heavy. "I'm so sorry. I would have left sooner, but then Terence called, trying to set up a meeting time for tomorrow. I just barely left."

"Um . . ." I was aware of Lee's eyes on my face. "When will that be?" I finally asked.

Patrick didn't seem to find my slight hesitation odd. Maybe he realized someone was listening. "He'll be at the warehouse around five. I wouldn't ask you to leave your family during Sunday dinner, but Terence would like to meet you. If you can make it."

"Of course. I'll see you soon, then?"

"Just a few more minutes."

"Okay. But if you aren't feeling well . . ."

"I'm fine. Besides, we have a party to attend tonight, don't we?"

Jaxon's party. I'd nearly forgotten. "Not if you don't want to," I said.

"Really, Kate, I'm fine. Don't worry about me. I'm feeling a lot better today."

I wonder why I didn't believe him.

We said our good-byes and I hung up the phone, glancing at Lee, who looked concerned. "Is he still feeling sick?"

"A little," I admitted. "I told him he didn't have to come, but he was already in the car."

"The flu?" she asked sympathetically.

"Um . . . yeah."

"That stinks. Are you guys still coming to Jaxon's party?"

I shrugged. "Probably."

She sighed and scrolled through a long message on her phone. "I was thinking about inviting Toni, but . . . Rodney just dropped the hint that he's not doing anything tonight. What should I do?"

"Are you serious? You even have to ask? Invite him!"

"What about Toni?"

"Did you already ask him?"

"No, but . . ."

"Ask Rodney. Now."

She sighed loudly, but obediently started to text. "If I do this, there's no turning back. Things with Rodney will be weird. He'll know I like him."

"Lee, the guy's been helping you sort old band music for weeks. I don't think a party is going to scare him off."

I made sure she actually sent the text, and then I focused back on the game.

fifteen

Patrick arrived during halftime, coming up so fast that I didn't really see him until he was already stepping up the bleachers a few rows away from us. He gave me a smile and nodded a quick hello to my grandparents and Jenna. I pushed closer to Lee, and Patrick took the seat on the end.

Before we could really greet each other, Lee was leaning over me. "Patrick, Kate says you're still not feeling good. Ever heard of a doctor?"

He smiled calmly. "Actually, yes. Thanks for your concern, Lee, but I'm feeling much better."

"No problem. Just thought I'd say something. You're driving Kate crazy, by the way. Her nails are completely gone."

"Thanks a lot," I shot at her through thin lips.

She positively beamed. "No problem."

When she focused back on the game, I turned to Patrick, keeping my voice low even though I knew Lee was listening to every word. "She's blowing it out of proportion. I was a little worried—that's all."

He forced a smile, and I noticed that his right hand was rubbing his left arm—as if trying to return circulation to the limb. "You worry too much."

"You're not taking this seriously," I whispered. "You've been worn out since Tuesday night."

He let out a mild laugh. "I guess I'm getting too old for running on no sleep."

I wasn't going to let this slide. "What about your head?"

"It doesn't feel great," he admitted at last, though I could tell he didn't want to be having this conversation. "But it feels a lot better." His right hand was still moving in unconscious smoothing motions against his arm, and I didn't know what to say. I couldn't argue with him, not if he wasn't even admitting something was wrong. Especially with Lee sitting right next to me.

Patrick's eyes revealed a sympathy with my plight, and I knew he didn't want me to agonize over this. He scooped up my hand and squeezed it tightly. "What have I missed?" he asked.

The crowd suddenly exploded with a cheer, and Grandpa jumped to his feet, yelling, "Go Josie! Go, go, go!"

We all watched as Josie ran with the ball, kicking it expertly across the field. She'd stolen it, or so I gathered, and was now booking it with her round prisoner toward the goal. Other teammates clamored for the ball, and for a pointed second I worried she wasn't going to pass it. But at the last moment she did, and another girl took the ball the rest of the way. She kicked it, and it sailed into the net.

The opposing spectators groaned, jibed, and criticized. The rest of us cheered, shouted, and congratulated. There was still a good portion of the game remaining, but Josie's team was ahead again.

Patrick was wincing at the loud screams of the crowd and the shrill whistles of the refs, and Jenna laughed at his face. "You look like you hate sports as much as I do, Patrick."

He smiled slightly, his face still twisted. "I'm just not used to this much noise," he admitted.

And while that might be true, I knew his headache was still present, despite his many assurances. Our eyes met, and I knew he knew that I knew. The headache was worse than ever before. Sleep wasn't helping, and apparently neither was more time. I hated to even consider the idea, but something had happened when he'd been shot. He hadn't been the same since. And if he wouldn't admit it, I would need to talk to Toni, Jack, or even Grandpa.

He pressed his lips together tightly as he read these thoughts and emotions in my eyes, and his hand twisted around mine, twining our fingers together in response. His thumb immediately began tracing comforting circles on the back of my hand in an effort to calm me down. I sighed, and he focused back on the game, his jaw tight.

I watched him, growing more and more worried but unable to say a single thing with Lee and my family so close. So I just held his hand, hoping the game would be over soon and we could get some time alone.

Josie's team lost the game, meaning that the tournament was over for us. Jenna bounced down the bleachers lithely, pulling her backpack on while she skipped. My grandparents followed close behind, leaving Patrick, Lee, and me to take up the rear. We reached the field before turning toward the parking lot, knowing Josie would join us at the van.

Patrick continued to hold my hand as we entered the parking lot, but I got the feeling he wasn't really aware of any of us. He seemed lost in thought, deep and distant, and I had to squeeze his hand to break his concentration so my Grandma could repeat her question. "Would you like to join us for lunch? We're just going to stop at the malt shop, if you want to come along."

Patrick smiled gratefully, but I already knew he was going to decline before he opened his mouth. "I would love to, Mrs. Bennett. But I'm afraid I'm helping my father with the yard today. I could barely get away for the game."

She nodded her understanding, but she seemed genuinely sorry. "Oh well. Maybe another time, then. You'll hang around to see Josie, though?"

He nodded carefully, as though afraid his head was going to explode if he moved it too quickly.

We reached the van, and Grandpa unlocked the doors with the quick touch of a button. Jenna pulled the van's sliding door open and climbed into the backseat without a word. Grandpa was still sipping his soda, which had to be warm by now, but I think he was drawing it out just to annoy Grandma, who didn't want him drinking it in the first place.

Lee, Patrick, and I made a little half circle of our own, and my best friend broke the immediate silence. "So, Patrick, do you feel up to Jaxon's party tonight?"

His hand flexed around mine, and he shot me a tired smile. "I think so. If Kate still wants to go."

Lee answered for me. "Of course she does. She needs to support me on my date."

"Who are you going with?" Patrick asked.

"A kid from school. Do you know Rodney Sommers?"

He hesitated, then shook his head. "I can't picture a face."

"He's a drummer, and we've been in band together forever." Her voice was very dismissive, but her dim blush told a different story. I wondered if Patrick noticed or not.

"I look forward to meeting him," he said at once. He didn't seem to think it was strange that she hadn't asked Toni, since I'd just recently brought them to his attention. But since he'd never actually "met" the Toni that Lee knew, he couldn't very well ask her about him.

If Lee picked up on any of this, she didn't have a chance to ask. Josie was walking the last few yards to the van, and her flushed face spoke almost more volumes than her aura.

"I can't believe we lost," she fumed. "I mean, really! The girls from North Park? Really? Their team sucks."

"Didn't look like that to me," Grandpa stated firmly, stepping forward to give her a side hug. He squeezed her shoulders and then took a step back.

Grandma embraced her next, her deep voice soothing. "You played great, Josie. I'm so proud of you." After a long moment, she pulled back and said with a smile, "Who's ready for some lunch?"

Grandpa patted his stomach and took Grandma's arm, leading her around to the other side of the van. "I'm starving, even after all that Coke."

Grandma began to gently scold him, but then they rounded the back of the van and their voices faded.

Josie was still just standing there, breathing heavily. Her fists clenched and unclenched at her sides, and she looked completely miserable. Her uniform was dirty, and hair was escaping from her ponytail. Her crooked nose had a smudge of black on the side of it, and I knew without looking that it had come from her hands. I hoped she wouldn't get it on me, because I knew in that moment that I needed to hug her.

I released Patrick's hand and stepped forward, my hug somewhat awkward because she was still so upset about losing that she didn't really hug me back. I was preparing to pull away, thinking I was embarrassing her even more, when I realized she was crying. Hot tears dripped onto my shirt, and I was so shocked that I couldn't let her go.

I bent over her ducked head, pulling her closer against my body. I could feel Lee and Patrick watching us, but I wasn't self-conscious. "Hey, Josie, it's okay. You can't win every time."

She sniffed loudly, and suddenly her arms were around my waist, pulling tighter and tighter. In that instant I was back at my parent's funeral. Josie and I hadn't hugged like this since that horrible day.

Her voice shook dangerously, and her next words caused me to wonder if she could somehow read my mind. "I was going to win for Mom and Dad. But I couldn't do it. I couldn't—" Her voice broke, and she buried her head against my chest, her tears falling faster, her ragged breathing becoming louder.

I bit my lower lip, swallowed hard, and began to rub her back. Unshed tears stung my eyes as I felt a small girl's heartbreak along with a lethal dose of my own. "Josie, it's okay. Mom and Dad . . . they understand. I know they do."

Without looking I knew Lee was staring at the ground, feeling out of place and unsure. But Patrick . . . his eyes were burning against my back.

Josie's voice was so subdued, I barely heard the words. Somehow,

I knew that Patrick was catching every word. "Why did they have to die? Why couldn't all of us have been in the car with them? Why did I ride home with Grandma and Grandpa? Why couldn't they have made me and Jenna come with you guys? Why did they die and you didn't? Kate, why does it have to hurt so bad?"

It felt like a huge weight was pressing down on my chest, forcing the air out of my lungs and surrounding my heart with a painful pressure. I tried to blink back my tears, but they fell on her head anyway. I tried not to shake, but I couldn't help it—no matter how tightly I held my sister, we both trembled from the pain.

"I don't know," I whispered into her hair. "I don't know why it has to hurt like this. But it isn't over. They're not gone forever. We'll see them again. I promise." My voice hitched painfully, and I had to stop the flow of words or reveal how badly I was losing it.

"How do you know that?" she demanded quietly, her loss and anger mixing into overwhelming grief. "Sometimes I wake up and I'm so mad at them. And every night I tell them I'm sorry, and I ask them to come back. But they don't. If they're still out there somewhere, why can't we see them? Why do we have to wait until we die too?"

"I don't know," I repeated in a slow whisper.

She suddenly pushed away, and she wiped quickly at her eyes. She avoided looking anyone in the eye, including me. "It was just a stupid game," she muttered. "A stupid soccer game." She stepped quickly around me, past our grandfather, who was standing near the back of the van. She jumped through the open door and pushed her way to the back, where she sat heavily next to a silent Jenna.

I twisted around to watch her escape to the car, and I continued to watch her for a second through the tinted window. But once she was seated, she didn't move. Neither did Jenna. They were both frozen. My eyes flickered to meet my grandpa's stare, which was intense.

The pain in his aura was overpowering, and I imagined that mine couldn't look much better. I could see him debating, wondering if he should approach me. But he and I both knew that Josie hated displaying emotion and that making a bigger production out of her outburst would only hurt her more.

Grandpa moved for the driver's door, and luckily his action seemed to break the trance. Lee stepped past me, a hand brushing my arm comfortingly as she made her way to the open door.

I blew out my breath slowly, rubbing my wet eyes and face with both hands, trying to get rid of the emotional evidence.

Patrick was watching me carefully, the pain on his face not for himself. He was hanging back, following my grandpa's lead, and it was killing him to do it.

I swallowed hard and tried to force a believable smile.

He didn't buy it.

His arms were around me in the next second, one arm hooked fiercely around my waist, the other hand cradling the back of my head. I leaned against him, placing my forehead against his hard shoulder. I tried to breathe evenly, tried to keep from shaking. His fingers stroked my hair, his lips were soothing against my neck, kissing me before he lifted his chin and balanced it on my shoulder.

He didn't say anything, and he didn't have to. I knew what he was feeling—I knew what he was thinking.

Somehow, I didn't shed any tears while he comforted me. They burned in my eyes but didn't spill. Being violently thrust back into the memory of my parent's death was one of the hardest things about their passing, because it happened so unexpectedly. Like yesterday's mind reading, and the emotions I'd continued to feel long into the night. The sudden rush of emotion, of grief . . . and glimpsing Josie's pain and then seeing Grandfather's . . .

I was so grateful to have Patrick's steadying arms around my suddenly weak body.

I knew everyone was watching—they had to be. I knew this moment had to end. It would be best for the twins to just think their older sister was saying good-bye to her boyfriend, rather than the truth. I needed to be strong for them. I couldn't let them see how much I was still affected by the loss of the two most important people in my life. They couldn't see me break down any more than I already had.

I lifted my head, placing my mouth against his ear. "Thank you." The faintly spoken words were sincere but insufficient. I hoped he was able to read me as clearly as I was reading him. I wanted him to understand how much he meant to me right now.

His voice was surprisingly rough, and I was almost stunned by the depth of his empathy. "You *will* see them again, Kate. I promise. Someday, you'll be reunited, and you'll never have to leave them again."

A deeper emotion seemed to throb beneath his words, but I didn't have the time or the emotional strength to question him about it. I only nodded gratefully, kissed him briefly, and then pulled away.

His hands dropped, and his blue eyes were shining with clarity. "I'll pick you up tonight, if you'd like."

"Thank you, Patrick," I breathed. And I wasn't just referring to his offer to drive.

I moved quickly, knowing the sooner I left, the sooner I could push my way into a new conversation, new surroundings. The sooner I could escape from this moment, the sooner I could abandon this pain.

I sat next to Lee in the middle seat and dragged the sliding door closed. While I put on my seat belt, I stared out the window, watching as Patrick pushed his hands into his pockets and stepped back to watch us pull away.

If anyone thought that was creepy or weird, they didn't say anything. But then no one was talking, period.

Lee reached out for my hand, and I sent her a grateful look as we backed up and headed for the road.

I didn't look back.

sixteen

I wasn't sure what to wear that night. In the end, I decided to wear the outfit I'd worn to Patrick's honorary birthday party. It had worked great once before.

I wasn't exactly in a party mood, but Patrick would soon pick me up, so I couldn't put off getting ready. I was no longer drowning in the depression that had overtaken me after Josie's game, but those thoughts were still understandably near the surface. No, mostly I didn't want to go to the party because I didn't want to listen to Patrick deny that anything was wrong again. Because obviously something wasn't right. I'd tried calling Toni, but he wasn't answering my calls. I assumed he was off being weird again, probably being a little invisible thief.

Josie hadn't mentioned her traumatic breakdown, and none of us were going to bring it up. We ate lunch together, and Jenna pulled Lee into the conversation about Peter Keegan. Josie made a few jokes about having her teacher watch her play soccer and how embarrassing that was. Grandpa was closely watching her aura, but it was drifting back to normal. He slowly began to relax, and I eventually did too.

When we dropped Lee off at her house, I told her I'd see her at the party—with Rodney. She blushed a little but assured me they'd both be there. And then we'd driven home, and we'd all separated to do our own things. Josie was in her room, Jenna sat at the piano, and I went up to my room. I pretended to do homework for a while, but

I couldn't keep fooling myself, so I went through my email, which I hadn't checked for days.

And then—hours later and with not much to show for it—it was time to get ready. I put on the blue shirt, the same silver necklace, and the long dark jeans. I pulled my hair into a half ponytail, keeping most of the light locks bouncing over my shoulders. Once I'd freshened up my makeup, I went downstairs to eat a quick dinner with my family.

We ate with minimal conversation. It was pretty obvious by the auras in the room that we were all thinking about what had happened in the parking lot, and we were each dealing with our own personal emotions. Grandpa and I shared a few looks, but mostly we just watched the colors of our family.

When Grandma finished, she started packing up the leftovers, and Grandpa rose to help her.

I was loading the dishwasher when the doorbell rang, signifying Patrick's arrival. It was as if his coming broke some spell. Both girls went running out of the kitchen, the dishes they were tasked with clearing left abandoned on the table.

"I'll get it!" Jenna shouted.

"Let me!" Josie argued hotly.

Their feet pounded on the wooden floor of the entry hall, and then slammed rapidly to a skidding halt at the door. A grunt or two, and then—

"Hey Patrick!"

"Patrick!"

"Hello." His lilting voice was surprised by the energetic reception, but he sounded pleased too. And tired. "Do you answer the door like this for everyone?"

"No," Jenna admitted with a laugh, but Josie overrode her.

"Of course we do! You're nothing special. Just our sister's *boyfriend.*"

I shook off the excess water on the plate I was rinsing, and then I placed it carefully in the bottom rack of the dishwasher. "Patrick!"

I called loudly, hoping to save him from further embarrassment. "I'm in the kitchen!"

I heard the footsteps coming, accompanied by teasing girlish voices. I rolled my eyes, grateful that he'd had to deal with far worse over his years. They could annoy just about anyone.

The silverware clinked into the dishwasher, and when I straightened and turned, Patrick was walking into the kitchen, a sister on each arm. He smiled across the room, and I smiled back. But as I watched him pull against the twins, I noticed the set of his mouth—the small furrow between his eyebrows that fought to grow deeper. His headache hadn't gone. If anything, it was worse. How could it be worse?

Grandma twisted awkwardly as she dug around in a cupboard, craning her head over her shoulder to view the commotion. She sighed. "Jenna, Josie, let go of him, please. I'm sorry, Patrick."

He shook his head minutely, his smile genuine but careful. "It's all right, Mrs. Bennett. They're perfectly all right."

But Grandma's stern look persisted, so the twins finally released him and returned to the table to gather their dishes. As soon as he'd been released, Patrick rubbed at his wrists. It was impossible to know if it was his strange new habit or reflexive after being strangled by four small hands. Still, it was disconcerting to me.

I snatched up a towel lying listless nearby and quickly wiped my hands dry. I leaned back against the counter and turned to watch him as he walked toward me. I was still holding the towel when he reached me, but that didn't stop me from wrapping my arms around his neck. His hands slid around my waist, and he pulled me close, murmuring a low greeting against my hair.

My sisters made gagging sounds behind us, but I wasn't really paying attention. Being held by Patrick did that to me.

His hand rubbed my back gently, then he pulled away to face my grandparents, one hand still linking us together. "We won't be out late," he promised.

Grandma shrugged, still searching the white cupboard for a lid to match the plastic container she'd already taken out. "It's a Saturday night, and we're not Nazis—take your time."

"No later than midnight." Grandpa spoke for the first time, and the way he looked at Patrick made me wonder if he sensed something was wrong. But watching his aura, I think he was less worried about Patrick and more concerned about the possibility that we were going on another mission.

Patrick only nodded, his hand tightening around mine. His blue eyes clearly conveyed to my grandfather that everything was fine. "No problem, sir."

"Well, have a good time," Grandma told us, finally finding the object of her searching. She brandished the lid proudly, and we said our good-byes.

The twins walked us to the door, two steps behind us, demanding if we were going to kiss in the car, at the party, or as soon as the door was closed.

We made no comment.

I hesitated at the door, patting my pocket to be sure I had my phone. I considered running up for my purse, but then I decided that there probably wouldn't be a need for it.

Patrick had the door open by now, and he held it for me as I stepped out onto the porch. He gave the twins a last smile, then firmly closed the door on their grinning faces.

I sighed and shook my head. "I'm sorry about them."

He reached for my hand, which I surrendered at once. He gave me an unconcerned grin. "Kate—relax. I happen to think they're adorable."

I chuckled ruefully. "Can I get that in writing?"

He shook his head at me, a reluctant smile pulling at the corner of his mouth. He tugged me toward the stairs and walked leisurely toward the street, where his car was parked and waiting for us. "So, where does Jaxon live?"

"It's about fifteen minutes from here, on the east side of town. We don't have to stay long, I promise."

"Can I ask why you're so nervous?"

I shrugged a single shoulder and watched the driveway pass beneath my feet. "I'm worried it could get pretty awkward. Especially for you."

There was an acute silence, then he tried to speak glibly. "Oh. I thought you were worried about that side of town. It's not as dangerous as *my* side, but it's more populated. But don't worry—I'm your Guardian, remember?"

His sorry attempt at a joke made me roll my eyes. "You're hopeless."

He opened my door for me, and in minutes we were pulling out of the subdivision. Once we'd successfully merged onto the larger street, I shifted in my seat so my back leaned almost completely on the door.

"Patrick, what's going on? Why haven't you recovered since Toni took that bullet out?"

His eyes flickered toward me, but his head remained forward, focused on the traffic. "The honest answer?" he finally asked, reaching out to twist the volume down.

"I'd prefer that over a lie."

His lips pressed tightly together. He deftly switched lanes and flicked off the blinker; in the same second, he glanced my way. "I don't know," he admitted quietly, and I knew his honesty cost him. He didn't want to tell me this. He concentrated on the road. "Was it a combination of age, exhaustion, and then getting shot? I don't know. But any damage the bullet caused . . . I can feel that it healed just fine."

"What about a doctor?"

He flashed me a quick smile, trying to lighten the air. "Right. Because I'm perfectly normal and able to see a doctor."

"No, I mean—you have to have someone to consult with. You Guardians seem to have everything else covered."

"Kate, Guardians don't get sick. That's just a fact." He shrugged. "I'm planning to discuss it with Terence when he comes. Toni wanted me to keep our indiscretion private, since we were told to stay away from that Guardian. But I think it would be prudent to see if Terence has any idea of why I have this persistent headache. It's not normal."

I bit my lower lip, unsure of what to say. In the end, I was just relieved that he planned on talking to someone. I told him so, and he smiled and stretched out his hand, seeking for my fingers.

"You worry too much, Kate. I'm the immortal one, remember?"

I shook my head at him. "Does that mean your headache's eternal too?"

He grimaced. "I certainly hope not."

I had been to Jaxon's house a few times, when Aaron and I were together. Most of those parties had been football related, and as we pulled up and I saw all the familiar pickup trucks, I knew that this one was no different. Not that I should have been surprised. Jaxon usually didn't host anything but sports celebrations. The team had had a home game the night before, so I assumed this party was directly related to that.

As if we could be any more out of place. All of Aaron's friends and old teammates would be here, and we'd stick out like sore thumbs. I wondered if Patrick had ever even attended a football game. Was Aaron *trying* to embarrass us?

I felt bad just thinking it. Aaron wouldn't have deliberately put us in this situation. He may not have even realized it was a football team get-together. Jaxon was having a party . . . Aaron just hadn't thought about how weird it would be for me and Patrick—and Lee and Rodney too. But I'd been stupid not to realize this was exactly what we were in for. It was the football season, after all.

Aaron and I had gone to parties like this all the time, though I never really enjoyed them. A bunch of egotistical jocks all thinking they were on top of the world after a big win. It wasn't uncommon for someone to smuggle in a pack of beers, but that had always been mine and Aaron's cue to leave, since neither of us were comfortable around alcohol. (Honestly, I just didn't understand the appeal. Where was the fun in losing control, suffering memory loss, and enduring massive hangovers?) Bottom line, it was the sort of party a parent wouldn't approve of, and it was the last place I wanted to go with Patrick. A bad situation had just gotten a lot worse.

We parked on the narrow street, near Jaxon's neighbor's mailbox. The music was loud enough inside the house that we could hear it from the car, and Patrick winced at the pounding bass as he shut off the engine.

"Ow," he muttered.

Concerned, I squeezed his hand. "We don't have to stay," I said, trying not to sound too eager to leave—after all, it had been my great idea to drag him here.

He laughed once. "So quick to abandon Lee?"

"I have a feeling none of us will be staying long," I tried to assure him.

"Let's at least go inside and tell her that. Don't worry about me."

Easier said than done. But I gave in with a sigh and obediently waited for him to come around and get my door. I held his hand as we walked on the cracked sidewalk, toward the small old house. I asked Aaron once why the parties were always held at Jaxon's, since Jaxon lived in one of the poorest sections of town. His simple answer had been that Jaxon's parents were out of town a lot. The longer one was that he lived on the border of our school district, and playing pranks was an easy way to liven up a party.

The neighborhood was dark, and even with Patrick I felt a little anxious. If Lee hadn't been around, I probably wouldn't have even gone inside at all. But Patrick was right—I couldn't abandon Lee. And then there was Aaron. I promised Jaxon I would make an effort, and I wanted to try and help Aaron any way I could. I said I would show up, and I knew I wouldn't forgive myself if I turned around now. And so Patrick led me up the driveway and to the small porch, where a football player I recognized but couldn't name was making out with a red-headed cheerleader.

The front door was open, so we stepped almost cautiously inside, the thin hallway flashing drastically from the effects of a strobe light in the adjoining living room. The music was obnoxiously loud, and the house was full of people laughing, dancing, and kissing. Just stepping inside made me feel uneasy. The atmosphere was dark and dangerous. Thrilling, maybe, unless you knew enough to be afraid of the thrill.

Patrick stopped walking, unsure of where to go. He cast me a silent look that spoke volumes. He was obviously uncomfortable and out of his depth here. I couldn't blame him—so was I. Without Aaron, this felt a lot different. But I tried to look reassuring as I took the lead, guiding him down the narrow hall and toward the kitchen. We had to step around a couple sitting on the floor making out, but once we got to where the light wasn't blinking spastically, it was easier to see. The kitchen was dimly lit—everything but the main light was on. The light over the stove, a tall lamp in the other corner . . . it was enough to see that the room was filled with more people kissing or swaying to the music while they sipped some punch. Patrick and I backed up against the far wall, and I made a note to myself: don't drink anything.

I was about to pull out my phone and find Lee via text when a small group of people burst in through the back door. They were laughing boisterously, their arms wrapped all around each other as they stumbled into the kitchen, leaving the door wide open to the backyard.

I was shocked to realize I knew the person in the middle.

"Aaron?" I gaped, the music drowning me out. Patrick's eyes were narrowed—against the pain or in an effort to see better, I wasn't sure.

Aaron lifted his head, and in the scarce light I could see how flushed he looked, like he'd just run a mile. Or gotten drunk for the first time. He had a girl on each side, their bodies tangled together. Jaxon was on one end, laughing hugely. The guy on the other end was the quarterback, an arrogant blond named Micah Grimshaw. He hit on every girl in the school, but while most girls reveled in his attention, or were at least mildly flattered, he just plain gave me the creeps. Luckily, I hadn't ever had to share a lunch hour with him, and since I was in mostly AP classes at this point, we really didn't run into each other much at school. And ever since Aaron had quit football, there hadn't been a reason for me to even think about Micah, because I never saw him anymore.

I hadn't realized how lucky I'd been until right this moment.

"That was great!" Jaxon hooted over the music. "This is going to be awesome."

The girls laughed, and Aaron nodded his agreement. "I can't believe we just did that . . ."

Micah snorted and reached past one of the girls to thump Aaron on the back. "See what you've been missing? You sissy swimmer."

I stood silently next to Patrick, wondering what I could say. Apologize? Tell him I was ready to leave? Call out to Aaron? Knock some sense in to him? All of their auras matched the rest of those I'd seen in this house—tinges of gray from the alcohol, large patches of red competition and passion, and swirls of blue contentment. But it wasn't a natural blue. It looked faded to me—hardly blue at all. It was hard to tell what was blue and what was gray.

Before I could decide what to do, Jaxon spotted me, just a few dark steps away now. "Kate!" he called happily, nudging the tipsy group toward us. I hoped they staggered like that because they were standing so closely together and not because they were already that drunk.

As they moved closer, I was relieved to see that Aaron's eyes were unglazed. Maybe he wasn't drunk after all. Maybe he was just caught up in the party atmosphere. I hoped that was the case.

Micah's eyes, however, were dull. Jaxon's weren't entirely normal either.

In that moment, I was tempted to call the cops, just to keep them from rubbing off on Aaron. He was still one of my great friends, and he would always have a special place in my heart. I didn't want him turning into them.

"Hey there," Micah said to me, leaning in a little too close. I got a whiff of his repulsive breath and I grimaced reflexively. "Haven't seen you for a while, beautiful."

Patrick was tense beside me, so I tried to keep my face as easy and calm as possible. "A little wasted, aren't we?"

Micah shrugged a bulky shoulder and his aura suddenly contained a spark of yellow happiness. "The night's young." He grinned.

Aaron tried to push forward, but the girls weren't releasing him. He was rather embarrassed, and it was hard to see where his blush ended and his flushed aura began. "Kate . . . I'm, uh, glad you could make it."

His eyes communicated the words he wouldn't say—he'd had no idea it would be this kind of party. And I think I believed him, mostly. It was hard to say, while I was standing here in Jaxon's kitchen, surrounded by people I barely knew.

"Yeah, we can't stay long," I said loudly but just barely making myself heard.

"Oh, come on," Jaxon moaned. "You guys can't leave yet. Have you tried the punch? I could get you some, if you'd like."

"No, thank you," Patrick said. Somehow he found the perfect volume to use. He was heard but able to retain the flat, almost menacing edge. He wasn't happy, and I think Micah's open admiring of me wasn't helping.

Micah's eyes jumped to Patrick, his lips twisting into an amused smirk. "No, *thank you,*" he mimicked. "What an accent. Do you practice that, or what?"

"Micah, lay off—he's cool." Aaron's defensive words were welcome, but I worried that they'd only serve to egg Micah on.

Surprisingly, the quarterback raised his hands in surrender and then pulled a giggling brunette out into the hall. I didn't know where they were going, and I didn't care—as long as it was away from us.

I relaxed once he was gone, and I thought Patrick might have too. But only a little. I knew without looking or asking that the music and strange lighting was hurting his head, and I wanted to get him out of here as quickly as possible. His hand was growing clammy in mine, and I knew his head was hurting more than he let on.

I turned to Aaron and kept my voice loud enough to be heard. "Aaron, have you seen Lee?"

He shook his head. "No. But we've been . . . out. I might have missed her."

Jaxon and the girls laughed at Aaron's word choice. "Out?" Jaxon grunted, his grin exposing essentially all of his white teeth. "Nice, man. Nice . . ."

Aaron seemed to remember that his arms were wrapped around two girls, and he quickly shrugged them off. They seemed mildly disappointed, making pouty faces before wandering to the front of the house.

One girl remained, her arm slung around Jaxon's thick waist. Her dark skin glowed strangely under the weird lights, and the effect was almost hypnotic. I had to pull my eyes back to Aaron, before I could grow dizzy staring.

"So . . . this is quite the party."

Aaron still looked embarrassed, but Jaxon answered quickly. "I know, right? One of my best. The team deserves it though, after losing to stupid cheaters . . . You weren't at the game, were you?"

I shook my head. "No. Sorry I missed it."

"Something was up with those refs," Jaxon muttered angrily. "They kept calling us on everything, and we got more penalties than probably any team in the entire state's ever got. And ours were in one night."

I tried to look sympathetic, and I think I was doing a pretty good job. Patrick suddenly dropped my hand, and I looked to him in surprise. His face was sallow, and there was a sudden sheen of sweat on his forehead. But he wasn't looking at me—he was looking at Jaxon. "Where's your bathroom?" he asked quickly, voice tight.

Jaxon blinked, then pointed. "Uh, down that hall, second door on the left. So you *did* get some of the pun—?" But Patrick was already moving, dodging a slow-dancing couple and disappearing down the dark hall, which was lit sporadically by the strobe light.

I realized my mouth was slack, and a new wave of fear washed over me. Patrick looked . . . *sick*. Like, puke-your-guts-out sick. Something was terribly wrong. This went beyond simple tiredness or an annoying headache that wouldn't leave.

I didn't realize I was moving to follow him until Aaron reached out for my wrist, snagging it midstride. I looked to him and saw that his aura was changing—I could see his guilt for inviting me, his uneasiness for being caught in the midst of all this, and his worry that maybe I was thinking badly of him now . . .

"Um, Kate?" He offered a thin smile. "Trust me, a guy doesn't want his girlfriend walking in on something like this. I'll check on him for you."

"Aaron, you don't have to—"

"Kate, I don't mind. He wouldn't have forced himself out here if it weren't for me pressing you, so I owe you both. Please . . . allow me."

Reluctantly, I dropped my hand in acquiescence, and Aaron traced Patrick's footsteps, moving more leisurely into the hall than my Guardian had just seconds before.

I appreciated Aaron's concern. But at the same time, I wished he would have just let me go. Now what was I supposed to do?

I was alone with Jaxon and his girl standing opposite me. There was an awkward second, and then I decided to call Toni. There wasn't much he could do, since we had their car here, but maybe he could tell me something Patrick hadn't. It was a thin hope, but it would be something to do.

I knew I wouldn't have a prayer of hearing him in here, where we were drowning in heavy rock, and so I told Jaxon I was going outside to make a call. He promised to tell Aaron and Patrick where I'd gone, though not in that many words, and then I made my way to the open back door.

It was still warm outside, but the air was almost a shock of cold after being in the heavily crowded house. The dark sky was oddly comforting. Even though the sound of the loud bass thudded through the walls and flowed from the open door, the backyard was a lot quieter. Not peaceful, exactly, but I could breathe out there.

I wasn't the only one enjoying the outdoors. The yard was small and overgrown with weeds. There was a single large tree in the center of the ground, and it was the least populated area. Quiet laughter drifted from behind a run-down shed, and several couples were making out at different intervals around the chain-link fence.

I stepped off the single step that served as a back porch, headed for the tree. While I walked, I reached for my phone—but it went off before I could slip my fingers into my pocket. I pulled it out quickly while it vibrated sharply, and in a cursory glance of the top display I saw that it was an incoming call from Lee. Not exactly the person I wanted to talk to right now, but I *did* want to make sure she wasn't trapped somewhere in this "party."

"Lee, where are you?" I answered quickly, still wandering toward the tree. I spoke quietly, but I don't think the kissing couples would have been disturbed, even if I was screaming.

"Whoa, nice to hear from you too," Lee said. "Is it enough to say that I'm in a car, or do I have to give you the mile marker too, *Mom?*"

"Sorry—I just . . . I think Patrick's sick, and this party isn't exactly like I imagined it would be."

"You sound stressed."

"I am stressed, a little."

"Well, I'm glad to hear the party's a bummer, because we probably aren't going to make it. Rodney's tire went flat, and it took longer changing it than I thought it would. Two people don't always make a job easier, remember that." Someone made a comment I couldn't quite pick up on her side, and Lee laughed. I waited for her to remember my existence, and eventually she did. "So *now* we're heading back to his house, and I think we'll just stay there and watch a movie."

"Good plan," I encouraged. "You won't be missing anything."

"Yeah, I keep telling Rodney he got a flat on purpose—the rivalry between jocks and geeks, you know . . . yes, I'm calling you a geek," she teased him.

"Well, I want details later," I told her.

"Yeah, yeah . . . oh my Oreos! Let's get some ice cream! . . . No, you can turn up here and go back. Please? . . . I'll pay you a buck for gas. Come on . . ."

She must have won, because in seconds she told me she had to run and freeze her brain. I rolled my eyes and wished her luck.

seventeen

After I ended the call with Lee, I started looking through my contact list, searching for Toni. I'd been so absorbed in my call to Lee that I hadn't noticed someone come up behind the tree, until Micah slipped around the trunk to stand beside me.

"Hey," he said, looking pleased with himself for finding me. It was all over his face, his aura, his words. "You ditch your date already? Can't blame you. I just did the same thing. I hate clingy women."

I looked up from my phone, taking an instinctual step back when I realized just how close he was to me—and leaning closer. "Um, Micah?"

He grinned, and his skin carried a yellow sheen from the single porch light. "Yeah, beautiful?" he whispered, his voice husky and his breath layered with alcohol.

I cringed away from him another step, but he followed me, one hand steadying him against the rough bark. "Micah, you're drunk. I'm going inside now, okay?"

"Come on, beautiful. The night's so beautiful." He chuckled, and his gleaming eyes revealed his amusement at his self-perceived creativity. But it was amazing how fast amusement turned to leering. I'd seen that look on him before, but it had never been this strong. My stomach clenched, and my posture stiffened warily.

His voice was dull, his eyes hard. His aura was growing redder with each passing breath. "You really tore Aaron up, you know that? But his reaction . . . it only made me more curious to see what you were capable of. To see what made him miss you that bad. I've always wanted to get to know you better, beautiful . . ."

I snapped my phone closed and wordlessly turned away from him, heading back to the house. I needed to check on Patrick, and I needed to get away from the wasted quarterback.

His hot fingers snaked around my wrist, jerking me to a stop. Something popped painfully, and a broken gasp escaped me. My hand suddenly throbbed, and I wondered if he'd sprained it with his iron grip.

I whirled around to face him, but I didn't try to tug my arm free—I was afraid of hurting my wrist even more. My eyes were slits, though, and I think he was a little taken aback by my angry expression. "Let go of me," I said, trying my best to sound threatening.

His momentary surprise passed, and something like excitement took over as his dominant emotion. His hold only tightened around my aching wrist, and his eyes were gloating. "Make me."

My breaths were coming faster now, and adrenaline coursed through my veins. I did the only thing I could think of doing: I employed the basic training that Patrick had tried to impart.

First, I forced my phone into my pocket, freeing up a hand. Micah watched me with fascination. The second my phone was safely tucked away he reached for my fingers.

I was faster. I straightened my hand and slammed it just below the crook of his elbow, hopefully sending a shock through the arm that was imprisoning my wrist. Then I twisted my caged hand fiercely, hissing through my teeth in pain as I jerked it through the weakest section of his fist—where his thumb and forefinger met.

I staggered back a step but stopped when I realized it had actually worked. I'd freed myself. From the big shot quarterback.

He looked as shocked as I was. After all, I was a lot smaller and not exactly the athletic type. But his already red aura turned livid, and I knew I'd insulted him in more ways than one.

"You shouldn't have done that, beautiful," he said heavily.

I glanced around, but the people in the yard were focused on other things. I wasn't going to get help from them. Besides, they were all buddies with the quarterback. It's not like they would have stood up to him.

So I turned and ran, darting for the house. I was sure that if I could get to the kitchen, Jaxon would talk some sense into the drunk football king. That's all I had to do—make it into the kitchen.

I felt a sickening yank on my hair before the excruciating pain registered on my scalp, deep in my head. Sure, the twins had pulled my hair all their lives, but this was totally different. I almost fell to my knees from the shock of it. I might have, if Micah hadn't yanked me back and wrapped an arm around my stomach, pinning me against his hard body. He was still pulling my hair, and I cried out without meaning to.

"That's better," he grunted. "Come on, beautiful. Show me what Aaron's missing . . ."

He bowed over me, and in that heart-stopping moment I realized that this was really happening. He was going to force me to kiss him.

And then we weren't alone anymore. Aaron grabbed my arm with one hand and with the other he shoved Micah's face back, not caring where his fingers landed. "What are you doing, man?" Aaron demanded hotly, shoving roughly. "Let go of her. Now!"

My eyes were burning from the pressure on my scalp. It felt like all my skin and hair was being ripped out. Quite suddenly I was released; Micah pushed away from me, desperate to escape Aaron's fingers that were sliding into his eyes.

I blinked rapidly, my heart pounding quickly. My breathing wasn't normal either, but at least the stinging in my eyes stopped there and didn't produce any tears. Aaron wrapped an arm around me, pulling me close up against his side even as he swiveled around to shield me from the enraged quarterback.

Micah was cursing loudly, cradling his face in his hands. "Dude, my eye!"

Aaron didn't back down, even though Micah was considerably bigger. "I don't care if you're drunk—you don't do that! Especially not to my girlfriend."

"She's not your girlfriend anymore," Micah said vehemently, his head finally coming up while his hands dropped. His one eye was extremely red and watering like Niagara Falls. I almost felt bad for him. But not really.

There was no remorse in Aaron's locked jaw. "Stay away from her. Or I'm going to give you the beating of your life. Got it?"

"Kate?"

His voice was small, even a little sluggish, but it was so close I wanted to cry in relief. Aaron let me go as I twisted around to make sure it really was Patrick. I watched as my Guardian stepped off the porch and quickly crossed the distance to us.

He face was still a sickly gray, and his eyes darted rapidly between me and Micah. I don't think he'd seen much—not as much as Aaron had, I was sure—but he must have pieced things together. His eyes still harbored twinging pain, but there was anger there too—and fear. Fear for me.

I took the last step into his arms, and he embraced me carefully, eyes still focused on the glaring football player. His body felt limp against mine, and I knew his violent sickness had taken its toll. "Patrick, are you all right?" I asked in a whisper.

"I'm fine," he muttered, for me only. His arms suddenly tensed around me. "What about you?"

"I'm fine," I copied him. "I think I'm ready to leave."

He nodded once, swallowed hard, and glanced to Aaron. "Thank you."

Aaron just jerked his head aside, dismissing the thanks. His aura was almost overwhelmed with anger and shame.

We had an audience now. Jaxon was on the porch, his girl right next to him, and all those people that had been kissing? Well, we had their attention now. Aaron's loud voice had done that.

Micah saw the scene that had been created, and he was flushed red. I didn't need to be a Seer to see that he was personally offended. He zeroed in on Patrick's sweat covered face, and he grunted. "So you don't fight your own battles, huh? You let someone else take the risks for you? Afraid you'll get knocked around in front of your girl?"

Patrick didn't say anything. But his whole body was coiled so tightly; I'd never felt him stand this rigidly.

"Knock it off, man," Aaron growled, eyes slicing like blades into Micah's body.

The quarterback didn't seem to notice. He was still centered on Patrick. "I've seen you, being all friendly with the retards every day. Do they make you feel important? You realize that that's not the real world, don't you? This is real, right here, right now. Just because a bunch of idiots worship you doesn't make you any better than them."

Patrick's hands were shaking—from anger or sickness I didn't know. But was he getting paler? Was it rage, or was he going to be sick again? A combination of both?

"Patrick," I whispered loudly, staring up at his stone face. "Let's go. Come on—you're sick." My voice broke on the last word, but at least that got him to look at me. He studied my face, saw the fear there, and misinterpreted it. I was afraid for *him*. What was happening to him?

He thought I was afraid of Micah.

Micah snorted loudly. "Oh no, *Patrick* isn't *feeling* well. I guess that excuses a guy from a fight now."

A couple of the football players gathered behind Micah chuckled. I wondered how they dared to take sides, since they obviously hadn't seen what had happened. I guess popularity really did count for something.

Aaron spoke through his teeth. "Micah. Knock. It. Off."

Micah grinned at Patrick's intense eyes, saw that he was so close to snapping . . . He lifted two fingers in demonstration, skin almost touching. "I got *this* close to her lips, man. And boy, was she tasting good."

Patrick's chest rose and fell; his eyes were locked on Micah's face over my head. "Patrick," I said firmly. But there was an unstoppable waver in my voice, something I couldn't control.

Normally I wouldn't have been worried about him in a fight. He'd been fighting Demons for centuries. He'd been in more dangerous situations than anyone else I knew. But he hadn't been sick back then. I didn't know what was wrong with him now, but I knew that I didn't want him fighting. Not with Micah, not with anybody.

He didn't seem to hear me, and he certainly wasn't looking at me. His arms pulled back from around me, his hands curling around my upper arms. He carefully forced me to step aside, causing a chain reaction of jeers from the gathered spectators.

Patrick released his hold on me, but I was grabbing his arm, holding him back despite my throbbing wrist. He still wasn't looking at me. He had eyes only for Micah.

"Patrick, stop it," I ordered. "Don't do this."

He looked at me at last, and something was burning in his eyes, something that I'd never seen there before and couldn't even begin to define. The sight of it startled me, and I released him unthinkingly, knowing that unidentifiable emotion would haunt me until I could learn what exactly had caused it to burn inside him like that.

Patrick turned back to face Micah, who was swinging his arms and twisting his neck to loosen up. Aaron hadn't backed down either—he and Patrick were now standing beside each other, both of them tensed for the oncoming fight. I stood helplessly on the sidelines—my mind racing with thousands of thoughts, my heart hammering with a thousand emotions.

And then Jaxon thrust himself between Micah and my protectors, his expression incredulous. "Come on, guys—really? We're totally not doing this."

"Pick a side or back off," Micah snarled, his aura overwhelmed with anger and excitement. He viewed this as a chance to prove himself, even though he was supposedly among friends. Egotistical males . . .

"You and Aaron are *not* duking it out in my backyard," Jaxon insisted, looking wildly between them. He must not have been as intoxicated as I'd first thought. His emotions were a lot clearer than the other football players in the yard.

Micah shrugged with impressive force. "Not after him. I want the cocky Irishman." His gaze fell on me, and his smile widened. "Then I want *her*."

The air seemed to change. Patrick and Aaron were already tightened to the point of breaking, so they couldn't visibly react to his words. Aaron's red aura practically made up for Patrick's lack of one. Jaxon looked completely floored, like he couldn't believe this was happening. They were all reacting to Micah's tone, his clear intentions . . .

But it was strange for me, because I could read his aura. I knew he had no feelings for me, that any attraction he'd felt was completely gone right now. He just wanted to use me to prove a point. Maybe if Patrick could have seen that, he would have acted differently. Maybe he wouldn't have. There was no way to know.

I blinked, and I almost missed it.

My Guardian's fist was planted in Micah's face, the space between them crossed in a single lunge. I think Patrick's speed took everyone by surprise, and as Micah groaned and clutched for his nose, doubling over in sudden pain, I almost thought that blindingly fast strike would be the end of the fight.

But after a half-second pause—a brief moment of shock—the backyard seemed to explode with sudden movement.

The four football players that had been hanging back behind Micah leaped forward, some offering theatrical yells. I might have laughed, if they weren't going after people I cared about. Two rushed for Patrick, and the remaining ones moved without hesitation for Aaron, who'd made his allegiance only too clear.

Jaxon was caught somewhere in the middle, but I was relieved to see him wrap his arms around one of the players swinging at Aaron. Aaron didn't seem to notice his friend's help—he was ducking a wildly thrown punch from one of his former teammates and then barreling headfirst into his bulky opponent's stomach.

I saw all of this from the corner of my eye, because my gaze was focused almost exclusively on Patrick. He saw the two players coming at him, and he crouched into a defensive position. I might have felt sorry for the unsuspecting bullies who'd pegged him for a weakling. But I was too worried about Patrick being overwhelmed to feel anything but mounting apprehension.

Patrick dodged the first punch easily, and then he lifted his leg in a powerful but fluid kick to one player's gut. The teenager gasped at the surprise impact and curled in over himself. Patrick returned to the defensive position in time to bat away a second thrust with a well-practiced arm, and then he brought in his free fist and slammed it into the other guy's face. Blood spurted, and he grabbed wildly for his injured nose, thoughts of punching Patrick gone in that moment.

By now Micah was recovered, and he came up behind Patrick, shoving himself on top of his unsuspecting back and pushing them both to the ground. They hit hard, and I instinctively stumbled back a step. Things were happening too fast—I didn't know what to do. I realized distantly that I wasn't even breathing.

Aaron's face was splattered with blood, his shoulder plowing into the football player attempting to tackle him. Jaxon was taking a punch, but already responding by head-butting his sudden enemy.

I felt completely helpless. Now I understood how all those girls in the movies felt. Fights happened too quickly—if you weren't an initial target, it was really hard to find something to do. Still, I didn't understand how those girls found the breath to scream.

Micah's knee was driven mercilessly into Patrick's back, pressing him more firmly against the ground. One palm crushed Patrick's skull deeper into the rocky earth. The quarterback was breathing heavily, shoving once more against the body beneath him before he called out curtly for someone to help hold the struggling Guardian down.

The two enraged guys that Patrick had already struck out at came forward, expressions terrifying. Their girlfriends were watching, and they were not willing to be played as fools again. They stepped closer, and the one that Patrick had kicked drew back his leg before throwing it into Patrick's undefended side with all his might. Patrick couldn't even draw up his legs and curl around the injury, because Micah was pinning him so effectively.

I couldn't see Patrick's face, because his head was forced away from me. But I heard his pained groan against the earth—saw his clenched hand shake in agony beside his turned head—and I suddenly had command of my body. I'd never done anything like this in my life, but it was surprisingly easy. Instinctual.

I ran at the guy who'd kicked Patrick, ran right at his back. Without actually telling myself what to do, my legs bent and lunged and I was jumping on the large football player. My arms latched tightly around his neck, pulling him back and choking him. My legs locked around him too, making it look like a strange variation of a piggyback ride. But I didn't care what it looked like—the only thing that mattered to me was stopping this guy from hurting Patrick again.

Was this how guys felt all the time? Did they have to constantly battle this drive for a fight? If so, I pitied them. I couldn't think clearly at all. I just wanted to hit something.

The football player I strangled staggered back a few steps, and his bruising fingers clawed at my arms, fighting for freedom. I only tightened my hold in response and gritted my teeth, ducking my head against his back when I felt us sway dangerously. I suddenly wondered what it would feel like to be crushed by a beefy football player.

I heard Aaron shout my name, but he might as well have been in China. I could feel us falling, and I knew that I was going to be the luckless one on the bottom. I swung my legs out, hoping that I could somehow land on my feet and balance us out.

Nope.

We hit hard. My head rebounded painfully against the unforgiving ground, and I gasped loudly, startled by the pounding sensation that swept through my entire body. I was being smothered, and I swear his elbow dug into my rib cage intentionally, driving out the rest of my air. My eyes watered, and my mouth hung open in shock.

Ow.

The guy rolled off of me in a short second, though it felt a whole lot longer than that. My pain hadn't even fully registered yet. There was just a throbbing ache everywhere and a sharper burn where his elbow had intruded forcefully.

And then his weight was gone, and I lay gasping on the ground. The football player whirled around to defend himself, realizing belatedly that I was a girl. I could see from his aura and his suddenly wide eyes that he was shocked at my gender, surprised to learn that he'd hurt me. He didn't have a chance to apologize, though, because Aaron was shoving into him, pushing him away from me.

"Kate!" Aaron yelled loudly, though he was leaning right over me now, crouched at my side.

I blinked quickly and struggled to sit up. Aaron grabbed my arm and helped pull me to my feet. I flinched in pain and wrapped a trembling arm around my stinging ribs. I felt a little unsteady, and I was grateful for Aaron's strong grip. And then I saw Patrick, slumped against the tree trunk that he'd been dragged against, blood pouring from his nose and mouth from his brutal pummeling.

Guardians weren't supposed to bleed like that. From my experience, they were healed almost as soon as the injury had been delivered.

They weren't supposed to be throwing up, either, but that didn't stop Patrick from gagging and doubling over, bile ripping out of his throat and pouring to the ground in a sudden torrent.

Micah jumped back to safety, letting his arm fall midswing. He was obviously grossed out, and staying that close to Patrick wasn't worth the satisfaction of delivering another punch.

The football player that had been holding Patrick's shoulder and shoving him against the rough tree also reeled back, and without that support, Patrick fell to his knees, his hands flashing out to catch his body before he could fall into his pile of vomit.

But while everyone else flinched back, I darted forward, pulling away from Aaron and wincing as my heavy footfalls jarred my aching body. I ran the few paces to his side and crouched down beside him, gripping his shoulder while his whole body heaved and shuddered.

I held on to him tightly, watching in mute horror as he continued to retch. *This isn't right! It's not right!* I cried internally.

I felt Aaron move to stand beside me, but before he could do or say anything, Patrick stopped throwing up. He breathed heavily for a moment, lifting shaking fingers to his mouth—wiping at his lips with the back of one cold, trembling hand.

"Patrick?" I breathed, my fingers tightening their grip. "Patrick, what's wrong?"

Slowly his head lifted, and he turned his bloody face to me. His eyes were haunted, his brow furrowed with intense pain, and his nose was still dripping blood. The cut on his lip looked especially painful, and I winced sympathetically. He pulled in a ragged but shallow breath, and as I looked into his crazed eyes, I knew that I wouldn't get an answer, no matter how hard and long I begged. Because he was as scared and clueless as I was. He couldn't give me an explanation, because he had none.

"I need to go," he whispered painfully. "Kate . . . I need to get out of here."

Aaron was instantly on his other side, and between the two of us we helped him gain his feet. Jaxon looked completely stunned, like he couldn't believe this had happened. I knew the feeling. One of his eyes was already swelling, but that only managed to make him look more dangerous. He rounded on Micah, who was still glaring at Patrick.

"Dude—party's over," Jaxon said loudly. "It's time for everyone to get lost."

Micah just went on glaring. He lifted a long finger at Patrick, his eyes darkly menacing. "This isn't over. Next time your girlfriend won't be around to save you. And, trust me, it'll be a lot worse."

Aaron grunted. "Back off, Micah. You've just kicked around a guy who's sick. Congratulations."

Patrick's eyes closed tightly, and I knew he was fighting another wave of pain and queasiness. He needed to get to a bed. I completely ignored Micah and the other people standing around, instead focusing on helping Patrick walk toward the open back door. Aaron followed my lead, and we silently made our way around the enraged quarterback, not even sparing him another glance. He wasn't worth it.

Before we got too far, Jaxon came up beside us, quietly pointing out a side gate. "It's better than going through the house," he said.

We changed our course, and he wordlessly offered to take my place as Patrick's support. I just shook my head, and Jaxon moved ahead of us to get the gate. No one moved or spoke behind us, and we slowly made our escape.

We were crossing the front yard when Patrick spoke levelly. "The keys are in my pocket, Aaron."

My ex-boyfriend reached into Patrick's wide pocket without hesitation, snagging the key ring and pulling it out easily. He pressed the unlock button, and all the doors hummed shortly in answer. Jaxon grabbed the passenger door and pulled it open, holding it while Aaron and I helped lower Patrick into the seat. He didn't take as much support as I thought he would—he seemed to be regaining his old strength. Not that it made me feel much better.

"Thank you," Patrick told Jaxon and Aaron meaningfully. For some reason, he didn't look at me. I had the feeling that he was concentrating very hard on anything but me.

Jaxon snorted. "Yeah—because we did *so* much. I'm sorry about Micah. He can be a jerk without the beer, and with it, well . . ."

Aaron was still seething, but his voice was surprisingly calm. "I'm sorry, Patrick. I had no idea he would do anything like that. I swear." He glanced my way, and his true sorrow leaked into his words. "Maybe he wouldn't have been in that mood if they'd won the game . . ." It was a lame excuse, and we all knew it.

But I wasn't going to torture him any more than he was already torturing himself. "It's okay, Aaron. Thanks for everything. And Jaxon . . . thanks."

Both boys nodded silently, and then Jaxon turned to Patrick.

"You want a bucket or something?"

Patrick shook his head. Carefully. "I'm feeling better already."

I wondered if I picked up on the lie because I knew him so well, or maybe I was just used to his easy deceptions now. But no one else seemed to read the lie, so I kept my mouth shut.

Jaxon prepared to close the door, but someone called out to him. "Wait, baby!"

We turned and watched Jaxon's date, the pretty girl with the dark skin come darting across the yard, carrying a glass of water. She rushed right up to the car and handed the tall glass to Patrick. "You'll feel better once your mouth is washed out," she promised sympathetically.

I was surprised by her compassion, and Jaxon noticed my look. While Patrick sipped at the water delicately, Jaxon introduced the girl. "This is Maria. She lives down the street. Moved in about . . . two weeks ago?"

"Close enough," she told him, before extending a warm hand. I shook it slowly, grateful for her small, reassuring smile. Seeing an aura surrounded by something other than red was also a relief.

"I'm Kate. Thanks for the water."

Maria nodded. "No problem, Kate." She dropped my hand and stooped to check on Patrick. "Do you want some Tylenol or something?"

"No, thank you." Patrick handed the glass back to her, only partially drained.

Her head bobbed again. "You get feeling better."

"Thank you," Patrick repeated dimly.

Jaxon closed the door as if on cue, and he took Maria's hand and stepped back. I faced Aaron, hesitated, and then gave in and embraced him quickly. "Thanks," I whispered deeply.

He pulled me close and then pushed back. He gave a shaky smile. "Anytime."

I returned a timid smile, he handed me the keys, and I moved around the hood of the car to the driver's seat. As soon as I was in the car, I turned it on, setting the heater on low. Patrick was shivering despite the warmth that still pervaded the air of the car. I switched on the headlights and shifted into reverse while he searched the glove box for something to staunch the meager flow of blood from his nose.

It was a little weird not driving a clutch, but I only reached for the nonexistent pedal a few times before I got the hang of it. Patrick silently used a small pack of Kleenex to wipe up some of the blood, and I tried not to give in to my queasy stomach.

We didn't speak at all until I'd pulled out of the small neighborhood streets and onto the main road. Only then did I glance over at him to find him carefully watching my face.

"Are you all right?" he asked, his eyes filled with pain. "I saw him fall on you."

My side still throbbed, but I wasn't going to bring it up. Not while he was covered in blood. "Patrick, what's going on? Why aren't you healing? Why did you . . . get sick?"

He swallowed with difficulty and leaned his head against the seat, his tired eyes still focused on me. "Kate . . . I need to ask you something. It may sound a little strange, but I need you to be entirely honest."

"What?"

He pinched his eyes closed, his words muted and quick. "When we went after the Guardian on Tuesday night . . . He was sleeping when I found him. I startled him and he tried to back away and tripped. I reached out without thinking, and when our hands brushed his skin, something . . . happened. It was like an itch, an irritation. It covered my fingers, climbed up my arm . . . by the time my whole body was covered, it was like a burn." He opened his eyes and met my worried stare. His lips pressed tightly together, then parted slowly. "And then it disappeared. The feeling was gone. I had other things to think about, I didn't consider the fact that he may have transferred something to me. Kate, I think . . . I think I have what he had. I think I might be . . . dying too."

My breath came out in a small, shuddering release, and my fingers around the steering wheel were extremely white. "That's not possible," I whispered, my eyes trained on the road.

His voice was barely a whisper in the still space beside me, but it was layered with determination. "Kate, you need to tell me . . . You've touched me. I . . . I've touched you. Kissed you . . ." His voice choked off, the question never fully formed, and I hurried to reassure him.

"No, Patrick, I haven't felt anything weird. Whatever this is . . . you haven't given it to me."

His eyes closed once more, in fervent relief, and a weary hand pressed against his forehead. "Thank heaven," he breathed shakily. "I couldn't have . . . Kate . . ."

How could he be so relieved? I didn't understand it. "You can't die, Patrick. That's not possible."

He opened his eyes, watched me warily. "I don't understand what's going on, Kate. But it's not normal. I've never heard of this happening. Something's wrong with me."

"Then we'll find some answers. But you're immortal. You can't get some . . . disease." That word had never sounded so terrible to me.

"Unless the infection targets immortals?" he asked, almost to himself. "What if . . ." His thoughts drifted, and there was a glaring silence between us.

At last he spoke. "I need to speak with Toni. I must have touched him at some point . . . he hasn't shown any signs, but . . . maybe I'm not contagious yet? That would explain your health, unless humans are simply immune."

I gritted my teeth, hating the way he was calmly discussing this.

He didn't seem to notice my reaction. He continued to wonder and plan aloud. "If Terence weren't coming tomorrow, I'd call him immediately. But until then . . . I need to stay isolated, just in case. If you can drive me to the warehouse, maybe you could take Toni home with you? He could sleep on the couch, and no one would know. Just tell your grandfather," he amended quickly. "He'd be a little surprised at seeing an invisible Guardian in his living room . . ."

"You've *got* to be insane if you think I'm leaving you alone like this," I said, overriding his murmuring, and he glanced up at me, his eyes on the side of my face as I swerved a bit too quickly through the traffic. I continued to try and reason with him, my voice too tight. "If you're worried Toni might get it . . . maybe you should be the one to sleep at my house."

He shook his head, peeling back the tissue to check his nose. It must have finally stopped bleeding because he balled up the bloody wad of Kleenex in his fist before answering. "Until I know if I'm dangerous, I'm staying away from your family. From you. I should have pieced this together days ago—known to keep my distance. That I might be a risk to you."

"Patrick, stop it."

"Kate, please. Don't. Just . . . don't."

I felt tears sliding down my face, heard him groan, but I couldn't stop the silent crying.

"Please . . . please don't cry." He implored powerlessly.

I didn't look away from the road. The lines were becoming hard to see through the fog my tears created. I blinked quickly, but if anything that seemed to make it worse.

"Pull over," he instructed a heartbeat later. "Kate. It's okay. I can drive."

"I'm fine," I snapped, regretting my tone instantly. It sounded so sharp.

He was quiet for a moment, and then his sensitive words made me hurt that much more. "I know how you're feeling. It's exactly how I felt, when I finally realized that I . . . And then I came outside and I saw you, saw that cretin, and . . . and I needed something to attack. Anything. I needed to protect you in the only way I know how, because I knew that I couldn't stop this thing inside of me. How can I fight something that kills from the inside?" His voice was so quiet—hardly audible.

"You're not dying," I whispered fiercely. "You can't die."

"Maybe we can," he breathed.

"You can't," I insisted stubbornly.

He didn't answer.

I didn't speak again.

Neither did he.

I drove straight to the warehouse, knowing that he was right—I couldn't expose my family to anything harmful. Well, more than I already had. But if I wasn't sick, then maybe Patrick was right. Maybe humans were immune to this infection. Or maybe he was crazy, and he didn't have the insane Guardian's sickness. Maybe this was just a Guardian flu or something . . .

It was too much to hope for, and I knew it.

I pulled into the dark alley, past the warehouse and toward their small shed. While I parked the car carefully, I wondered if everything that had happened tonight was real. It seemed so surreal. Dreamlike. Untrue. I wanted it to be untrue.

I shut off the car, and it clicked and cooled mutely in the enclosed space of the makeshift garage. From my peripheral vision I saw Patrick undo his seat belt and then silently settle back against the seat, waiting for me to make the next move. I left the key in the ignition and returned my hands to the wheel. I kept staring out the windshield, as if not looking at his pallid face and the bloodstains on his shirt would make them go away. But nothing could erase the image of him falling to his knees, retching on the ground.

I struggled to breathe, and he observed me silently. I could feel his eyes on me, but he wasn't saying anything. What could he have said?

I'd stopped crying at some point on the way. But now that we'd stopped and I had only my thoughts and fears, no traffic to distract me, tears started falling again. A single drop of moisture slipped down the curve of my cheek, and in the darkness I felt him hesitate, deliberate, and then finally overcome the internal struggle. He lifted his hand and a single finger stroked down my face, following that wet trail until it intercepted the tear at my chin.

"Don't cry," he whispered brokenly. "Please . . . anything but that."

I finally turned my head, and his hand fell as our eyes met, mine stinging so painfully it was almost hard to focus on any of my other injuries.

"You're jumping to conclusions," I argued thinly, meeting his worried gaze firmly. "There's something wrong. I know that. But that doesn't mean that you're . . ."

"Dying?"

My eyes closed against the nauseating word. "Yes."

"You're right," he allowed, but I had a feeling that he was just saying these words for my sake. "There are no guarantees. We'll consult with Terence tomorrow."

I opened my eyes slowly, and another tear escaped. He brushed tenderly at it, and his touch finally broke through whatever had been holding me back. I released my seat belt—his hand began to fall—but then I was leaning toward him, ignoring the minor obstructions that rested between our seats. He was hesitant at first—afraid of touching me too much, or maybe he was worried about rubbing the last traces of blood on me, but his need for contact was just as great as mine, and in a shaky second we were holding each other tightly.

He was weak—I could feel that—but his closed fists rubbed my aching back, his head pressed against mine, and he murmured soothing words in my ear, mostly just unintelligible sounds. My arms wrapped securely around his body, and I buried my face in his shoulder, intensifying the embrace. I raised my head and laid my lips against his clammy forehead. "I love you," I told him steadily, mouth brushing his skin.

His hands slipped to my arms, where they moved comfortingly up and down. "And I love you."

He pulled back a little, swallowing hard. "If it would make you feel better, Toni can stay with me tonight. If he's going to get it from me, it's probably already too late anyway."

"You'll call me in the morning?"

"Of course. And as soon as Terence comes, I'll let you know." He nodded to the keys, still hanging in the ignition. "Take this home."

"But what will you drive?"

"We won't need it overnight. There's nowhere I can go . . . you can bring it by tomorrow."

Somehow, I realized what he was trying to do—what he was trying to orchestrate. "You think Terence might . . . not let me come over?"

The corner of his mouth twitched. "I'm sure your safety will be his top priority. It's just how we Guardians think. If he believes I might be dangerous to you . . ." He didn't bother to complete the thought.

"You want me to have an excuse to come over," I finished for him.

He didn't have to answer me. It was clear in his solemn expression that I'd guessed right. His guilt was also extremely clear.

I reached for his hand, squeezing tightly to let him know that he shouldn't feel guilty. He didn't have to face this unknown alone.

I wouldn't let him.

I then noticed that his bottom lip—still coated in a bit of dry blood—was completely healed. Whatever caused his rapid regeneration had finally kicked in.

But why had it been late at all?

eighteen

Grandma, the early riser, saw his car first. She came storming into my bedroom, fully expecting to find more than just me. Her interruption of my sleep wasn't exactly unwanted, however. I'd been struggling all night to find some semblance of rest, but that was easier said than done. I couldn't stop thinking of Patrick, which I guess was understandable. But the more I pondered his situation, relived those tortured looks on his face, saw again those displays of sickness and vulnerability, the more I began to feel that there had to be some other explanation. To conclude that he was dying—just because a crazy Guardian had thought he was—was a nonsensical way to approach the situation.

Not that it made me sleep any easier. Picturing him in pain was pure torment, even if I'd almost completely assured myself that he wasn't dying.

Until I remembered Clyde, the Demon who'd heard a rumor . . . Guardians dying . . . Surely there were too many coincidences. There had to be some truth to what Clyde had said.

I wanted to know what Terence thought. Strange, how just yesterday morning I'd been more interested in asking Terence about my weird mind-reading moment with Grandma. Now, Patrick's health was all that mattered.

It took five minutes to explain to Grandma why my boyfriend's car was parked in our driveway. No, he wasn't here. Yes, it was his car. No, he hadn't been feeling well—he asked me to drive. Yes, I'd dropped him off at his house. Yes, I'd take it back sometime today . . .

Once she left, I settled back onto my bed and stared at the ceiling. It was far too early to call Patrick, and I knew that I'd be alone with my thoughts for another couple hours at least. Besides, if he was sleeping, I needed to let him get rest. Toni would call me if something happened, and if nothing else, Patrick had promised to call me in the morning.

I wasn't alone for long. Grandpa came in next, toothbrush in hand, face chagrined. "I saw his car out the window, Kate. Where is he? You better tell me that he isn't here . . ."

I sighed wearily and pushed myself back into a sitting position. "No, he's not here . . ."

I basically told him the same things I'd told Grandma. Only this time, I added a lot more truth. I told him a little bit about the party—leaving out all details of drunk football players and backyard brawls. I stuck to the important details. Like telling him about Patrick throwing up—twice within ten minutes. The story came pouring out at that point. How Patrick believed he was infected with some illness he'd contracted from the insane Guardian, and how I believed that it was the same sickness Clyde had heard about.

By the time it was finally all out—down to the part about me going over there as soon as Terence got in—Grandpa looked extremely worried. "Kate, Patrick is right. Maybe he's just not contagious yet. Until we know more, you need to keep your distance."

After everything I'd told him about Patrick, he was worried about *me*?

"Grandpa, don't you understand? We need to talk to Clyde. Follow up on this rumor. Maybe we can learn something helpful."

He was shaking his old head. "Kate, that's just not possible. He told us everything he knew. He always does. Clyde can't help us."

"Then what are we supposed to do?" I demanded.

He sighed. "I don't know. But until we learn more . . . I really feel that you should stay away from Patrick."

"I can't do that."

"Kate, don't be immature and melodramatic."

"I'm not."

"Yes, you are," he insisted.

"Considering all that's happened, I'd say I'm pretty calm and collected." I nodded to his toothbrush. "Go finish getting ready. I'm going to try and get a little more sleep, okay?"

He wanted to argue. That was clear in his overwhelmingly green aura. But for the moment he listened to me, giving up the fight for now. He left me alone, closing my door softly as he retreated to the hall.

I lay back down, stared up at the ceiling, and waited for Patrick to call.

At nine, I pushed my way out of bed, quickly dressed, and then finally, unable to stall any longer, I snatched up my phone.

Toni answered on the third ring. "Yo, Kate. I knew you'd be up. Patty told me last night to let you sleep, but . . . I'm betting you've been pacing around for a while now."

"How is he?" I asked tensely, hoping that my nerves would negate any edge that might be construed as rudeness.

Toni sighed deeply, sounding more serious than I'd ever heard him. "Not so good. He was throwing up half the night, but I think his stomach's finally empty. We should be past the worst of that now, because I've grounded him from food forever."

"Is he sleeping?"

"Yeah—for almost two hours straight now, a new record." He hesitated, but the delay was transient. "Kate, I'm not gonna lie. I'm freaking out."

"Have you heard from Terence?"

"Yeah, he checked in this morning. I didn't dare tell him about Patrick over the phone—we try not to talk about too many sensitive things—but I think he got the drift that we need to see him as soon as possible. He'll be here around five, but I suggest you come late. Unless you want to be chewed out for dismissing direct orders."

"I never got the orders, so technically . . ."

He laughed a little too much at the poor joke, but I didn't call him on it.

"Toni, I'm coming over."

"Um . . . Patrick would really appreciate it if you didn't. Besides, you can't do anything right now. Heck, none of us can."

"I can't just sit here all day, doing nothing."

"Sweep a floor or something."

My head suddenly bowed, my voice turning into a whisper. "Do you really think he's got some rare illness? Is he really in danger of . . . ?" I couldn't croak out the final word.

His voice was an unpretentious murmur. "Kate, you know I can't answer that."

"Just give me your opinion, please."

"I think that taking some precautions can't hurt. If he does have something, he hasn't given it to me. I'm pretty sure of that. Does my health ruin his theory? I don't think so." He sighed, and I could imagine an accompanying shrug. "Be prepared, as the saying goes . . ."

"How can you prepare for something that's supposed to be impossible?"

"Is that, like, a rhetorical question?" His voice became more firm and soothing. In an instant he changed from fellow worrier to protecting Guardian. "I got this, all right? You can't do anything for him, and you and I both know that he wouldn't rest with you here. So just chill with the fam, okay? I'll call you if anything changes, and I'll just plan on seeing you around five thirty."

"Toni . . ."

"I know. I'd kiss him for you, but it wouldn't be quite the same."

I didn't even acknowledge his attempt at humor. My voice was laced with worry. "Just . . . just please take care of him."

"I'm on it. I'll have him call you when he wakes up."

"Thanks, Toni."

"Sure. Buh-bye now."

A reluctant smile tugged at my lips. "Good-bye."

"I hear that grin . . ."

"You've got a gift."

"Darn straight I do . . . and Kate?"

"Yes?"

An infinitesimal pause. Then, "Don't just spend the day freaking out, okay? He wouldn't want that."

"Sure. Right. I'll just toss all the worry out the window . . ."

"We don't even know that . . . Okay, that was dumb. *Something's* wrong, obviously. But don't start planning for a flash flood when it could be a little cloud burst, all right?"

"Um, I think you should stick to jokes and steer away from the attempt at proverbs."

"Think so?"

"Yeah, I do."

"Sheesh. I can take a hint."

The banter was incredibly light, and though our voices still held tightly to our fears, the joking felt good. If only for a moment.

We said our good-byes once more and I released a long, pent-up sigh while I closed my phone.

It was going to be a long day.

❊

Patrick called around eleven. He spent the first full minute apologizing for calling so late and for causing me to worry unduly. I admit, I laughed at him for that one. But it was an insubstantial laugh, and he knew it.

We didn't talk long. He assured me that he was feeling better but that he was still tired. He planned on getting a bit more sleep before Terence's visit. I told him I loved him—he returned the words to me but as always with more feeling. I guess living for two centuries could really add depth to a person.

After Patrick ended the call, I took my book out on the front porch to read. I reclined back on the small, white bench, a pillow cushioning my back.

My bruised body actually didn't hurt all that bad, despite being slammed to the ground by a football player last night. My side still ached where his elbow had dug sharply against my ribs, but a gingerly conducted investigation assured me that nothing was horribly damaged. My wrist ached too where Micah had pulled it, but I was quite sure the injury wasn't serious.

Truthfully, the only reason I took an inventory in the first place was to distract myself from my obvious fears. It didn't work great but better than some things. Like trying to read on the front porch, for example.

Aaron called me at two, curious if Patrick was feeling better and to make sure I was okay. We ended up talking for almost an hour, for lack of anything better for me to do. And having a relatively normal conversation with Aaron, well . . . it felt nice. We talked about the party, but only in the beginning. The conversation shifted to school, Lee's Rainbow Days, and sketchy college plans. Nothing serious. It was a good distraction, and when I thanked him for calling, I'm sure my fervency leaked through.

After talking to Aaron, I went inside for a late lunch. Sundays were pretty relaxed around the house, and so I knew it would take only a well-placed lie or two to convince Grandma to let me visit Patrick. She sort of drew the conclusion that I was going to eat Sunday dinner with his parents, and I didn't bother to dissuade her from thinking that. Honestly, it was better than I could have come up with.

I took Toni's advice, though only heaven knows why. I waited until my bedroom clock said 5:20 before picking up my purse and the keys to the Altima and heading out the door. Jenna was at the piano, and she glanced up as I walked past. But that was all the resistance I met. My sister didn't even bother to mouth a good-bye. I was out the front door, in Patrick's car, heading down the street before anyone could have stopped me.

I drove a little too quickly to the warehouse, arriving just a couple minutes earlier than Toni had suggested. Close enough. I turned into the appropriate alley, but was momentarily surprised when I saw a silver Nissan Altima parked in the spot my car usually claimed. I guess some Guardian knew someone who dealt with Nissans. It was my best explanation for the general use of the same type of vehicle.

I pulled past the parked silver car, then turned around the corner and into the smaller alley, guiding the car quickly and carefully into the open garage. By the time I'd switched off the car and climbed out, I wasn't alone in the garage anymore.

Toni was just wandering inside, a weary smile on his face, his thumbs snagged in his pockets, leaving the rest of his fingers to dangle free. It was a lazy pose, but his tense shoulders ruined the facade. "Hey, you're a bit early."

"I feel late," I admitted, tossing the keys at him.

He lashed out a hand and caught them as they fell, bouncing them on his palm once before shoving them into his pocket. "You haven't missed much. Patrick's been sleeping on and off all day. Puking all night wore him out."

I grimaced unthinkingly, and he took the last step toward me, offering me a comforting hug.

I leaned against his strong chest, closed my eyes, and ordered myself to relax. His warm arms were soothing, and breathing became easier almost immediately.

He pulled back, and I smiled gratefully. "Thanks, Toni."

He nodded once, and by silent agreement, we began our brief walk to the side door of the warehouse. "Terence got here right on time," he informed me as calmly as if we were discussing the weather. "He knew something was off as soon as he saw Patrick on the couch, and the story came out pretty fast after that."

"Was he upset?"

"That we disobeyed him? Pretty much. But he feels worse than we do. He's giving Patrick a physical now."

"Terence is a doctor?"

"Not medical. He used to be some biologist, though, so if that counts . . ."

"I'm not sure that it does."

I wondered if Terence knew anything about the rumor Clyde had heard. Was he checking Patrick for certain signs? Did he know what was wrong with him? And more important, did he know what to do to make him better again?

Toni led the way up to their mock apartment, and I was a mere step behind the whole way. I'd heard so much about Terence, I felt like I already knew him somehow. But his appearance was still a mystery to me. I knew his voice because of his strange call that had happened so long ago. Had it really been only a week? So much had happened. Would the real Terence match the personality and image I'd created in my mind?

I was about to find out. We were at the second floor. Toni twisted the doorknob, and I stepped into the makeshift living room after him. The familiar room had two large differences that I noticed right away.

The older-looking man standing in front of the couch was new. He was wearing a nice gray suit, and his silver hair was combed over neatly. The silver aura marked him as a Guardian, and I knew this was Terence. Though I couldn't see his face initially, I already knew that he was different from what I'd been imagining. I don't know exactly what I'd thought a Terence should look like. Geeky with greasy brown hair? Maybe some acne scars? Certainly not a refined-looking business man, or possibly even a government official.

His back was to us, and though he must have heard us enter, he wasn't going to let that break his concentration.

He was crouched over the couch, partially blocking whatever he was doing. Or rather, the person sitting on the couch. This was the second thing I noticed, though it held my attention a lot more firmly than my first glimpse of Terence had.

Patrick wasn't wearing a shirt. His pajama bottoms were securely in place, but he had removed his shirt for Terence's rudimentary examination, and the sight of his pale and muscular chest almost had me blinking in surprise. It was so perfectly sculpted and toned—matching his long arms perfectly. I mean, I knew his body was hard with muscle. I'd felt that in every embrace. But to actually see it . . .

To view the evidence of his strength was a new experience for me.

Patrick's head was ducked, his longish light-brown hair falling into his eyes. He was struggling to breathe normally, and Terence was counting the beats of Patrick's heart with two fingers laid against the inside of Patrick's wrist. Patrick breathed; Terence counted each pulse, his spare hand gripping Patrick's bare shoulder in a secure but somehow comforting hold.

I hesitated just inside the room, and Toni closed the door behind me before stepping forward to stand at my side.

Patrick glanced up, finally reacting to the sound of our coming.

I tried not to look shocked by what I saw, but I don't know that I succeeded.

His eyes were rimmed by dark circles, and his skin was ashen. He was trembling minutely, as if the warm day still managed to chill him. His gaze focused on me easily, but holding it there was another battle, which he struggled to win.

His taut lips forced a thin smile, but I could see the intense emotions in his blue eyes—the emotions that registered my pain, and were tortured by it. He didn't want me feeling sorry for him and his suffering.

Fat chance, I wanted to tell him.

"Keep the breaths even," Terence cautioned him, still ignoring me and Toni. His voice was kind, but it was obvious he was worried. Patrick dragged his eyes away from mine, finding it easier to stare at the floor. But before his face dipped from my view, I saw the fear that he'd been trying so desperately to hide.

Still gauging Patrick's heartbeats, Terence spoke again. "When did the headache first show up?"

Patrick was slow to answer, as if this was the most important question in the world and it couldn't be rushed. "Wednesday morning. It's only increased in intensity since then."

"When did the vomiting begin?"

"Last night. I'd been feeling nauseated all day. I thought it was a by-product of the headache. I wasn't overly worried about it."

Terence nodded once to himself. Though I couldn't see his face, I could sense his disquiet from here, his apprehension.

No, I realized a second too late. Not apprehension, or even worry. Resignation? As if something he'd been fearing had just been affirmed?

Terence let his fingers fall, and he straightened. "You can put your shirt back on," he said, pulling off the latex gloves that coated his hands. While Patrick reached for the discarded shirt lying on the couch, Terence finally turned around to face us, and I got my first look at the supervising Guardian who oversaw the safety and effectiveness of all the Guardians in the area.

His face was surprisingly weathered, and I was once again confused by his age. Patrick had told me once that most Guardians were young, mostly because when older people died, they were more connected to other people. They'd formed relationships and were more loathe to part with friends and family and become Guardians. It made sense to me, but Terence must have been an exception.

He looked to be in his late fifties, early sixties. Younger than my grandpa, though not considerably. He looked stronger than my grandfather—more fit, more sturdy. His hair was mostly silver and white but had some remaining dark streaks that would never leave, now that he no longer aged. He looked refined, trustworthy. Someone who wouldn't steer you wrong. His eyes were a dark blue and set against his tan skin and white hair, the contrast was handsome in a debonair way, and I found myself wondering what could have possessed Patrick and the others to ignore his orders. Such a kind and compassionate man must have a reason for every command. Why hadn't they listened?

Boys.

His smile was warm when he saw me, despite the lingering uneasiness in his eyes. "Ah, you must be Kate. It's a pleasure to finally meet you." He stepped toward me, and soon enough we were shaking hands.

"Terence," I said, feeling a little weird using his first name. "It's good to meet you too. I've heard a lot about you."

I waited to see something in his eyes—anything that would betray the fact that we'd already spoken to each other on the phone. But if he was thinking about that, or our private meeting he was obviously saving for later, it didn't register in his expression. "I've heard a lot about you as well. You've had to deal with an unusual amount of Demon problems for being such a young Seer. You must be resourceful and brave to have withstood it all unscathed."

"I just have really great Guardians," I argued delicately.

His smile widened just a little, and he dropped my hand to view Toni. "So, Antonio, you still haven't learned to knock?"

Toni shrugged. "Force of habit, I guess. At least I've stopped using windows. Mostly."

"Don't worry about it. We were just finishing up," Patrick said, and we all turned to watch him stand slowly, tugging the hem of his shirt down as he did so. Once he was standing and fully clothed, he focused on our faces, and a small smile stretched his mouth. "You all look like you're staring at a ghost."

I was crossing the room before he'd finished speaking, and he stepped around the table to meet me. I slid my arms around his waist, and he pulled me close against his chest, tucking my head beneath his chin. His hands stroked my back, and though he tried to disguise weakness for gentleness, I could tell the difference.

"Thank you for coming," he whispered, low enough in my hair that I thought I was the only one who heard.

"I wouldn't be anywhere else," I returned seriously, twisting my head up so I was able to glimpse his wan face.

He responded by bending his lips to mine, and we kissed briefly, my hand skirting up his body to rest high against his neck. My fingers brushed against his cheek, along his jaw, and one of his hands rose to mirror my actions. Somehow his fingertips tingling across my skin seemed much more powerful. I closed my eyes fluidly, reveling in his sensitive touch, and then Toni cleared his throat awkwardly, ending the moment.

Patrick's breath stuttered in a thin laugh that bordered between embarrassment and annoyance, and then the warmth of his face retreated from mine, and we were only holding hands, both of us facing our audience.

Terence looked mildly shocked, but he hid it well enough that we could ignore it. We didn't have to explain our relationship. Yet.

Toni just rolled his eyes at us, but his usual joking manner wasn't present in the sarcastic action. I think it was his small way of keeping the tentative calm from shattering around us, and I was grateful for that.

"So," Toni said suddenly, realizing that we were all looking at him by now. "What's the verdict, Terence? Do you know what's wrong with Patrick?"

Terence's shoulders seemed to drop, but none of us missed it. We were watching him like his words would declare whether we lived or died. Which, I guess, was a pretty fair way of looking at things. "I think you should all sit down," he said. Famous earth-shattering words.

Patrick's fingers tightened around mine—as if it was his job to brace *me*—and he pulled me back toward the couch. Toni moved around the other side of the dinged-up coffee table, and in seconds the three of us were sitting on the lumpy cushions—me in the middle, a tense Guardian on each side.

Terence remained standing, the table between us. His dark-blue eyes were watching us closely, measuring our ability to digest the coming information.

This was going to be bad.

His eyes finally went to Patrick's alone, and the words came out deliberately so he wouldn't have to repeat a thing. "It isn't the Guardian way to keep secrets. But I've been keeping one for a while now. It's time that you knew."

Patrick's free hand shifted unconsciously, so my hand was cradled between both of his, balanced on my knee.

Terence breathed in deeply, then released his breath slowly. Finally, he spoke. "Your illness, Patrick—this isn't the first time I've seen it. Several Guardians along the West Coast have gotten sick as well. We were trying to keep it quiet because it seemed so isolated. You're the furthest case inland we've had. We didn't realize that you might be in danger."

Toni's voice was incredulous. "When you told us to stay away from that Guardian, did you know that he was infected?"

"No, of course not," Terence said quickly, looking wounded that Toni had even reached that conclusion. "If I'd have known, I would have warned you of the danger. As things were, I had enough reasons for you to keep your distance. It isn't good for morale to see fellow Guardians regret the course of their lives. I'm sure you understand." His eyes darted to each of ours, seeking silent forgiveness.

Patrick's voice was perfectly even, controlled. "Am I a danger to you? To Toni?"

Terence shook his head quickly. "Whatever this is, only some Guardians seem susceptible. Many of us appear to be immune, at least to this strain of the virus. I've been exposed repeatedly and never fallen ill." He nodded to Toni. "I think it's safe to assume that you are also immune."

Toni's head dipped once, and he hurried to ask the question I knew Patrick wanted answered, but was afraid to ask. "What about humans? What about Kate?"

The lead Guardian shook his head quickly. "It seems that humans are completely safe from whatever it is. They can't contract it. Seers included."

Patrick's head bowed gratefully, but I wasn't ready to relax. The most important question had yet to be addressed. "These other Guardians," I started haltingly. "You were able to help them, right?"

Terence didn't answer right away, and Patrick's head smoothly lifted until all three of us were staring hard. Terence spoke quietly. "The first infected Guardian we found . . . he'd gone missing a week before, but we thought little of it. There was no reason to suspect he'd been taken against his will, and I knew he had been struggling with depression lately." He looked to me, trying to explain. "Some

Guardians regret their choices, and it's not unheard of for them to disappear for a while. They like to be alone. He called me early one morning—he sounded terrible. He asked me to come pick him up at a gas station in Southern California. I went immediately. He couldn't tell me much. His memories of being imprisoned were hazy and dark. He remembered being injected with something by a beautiful Hispanic woman."

"Selena Avalos," Toni muttered.

Terence nodded lightly but didn't stop in his explanation. "We have since confirmed her involvement. I took him back with me to headquarters. He complained of headaches, he was tired and cold, and he deteriorated with every passing day. I called in everyone I could, but . . . we couldn't save him. By then we'd gotten calls from other Guardians, seeking help in their sickness. All had similar stories of kidnapping, shots, and cloudy memories of Ms. Avalos."

"So . . . this is a biological attack by the Demons?" Toni struggled to understand. "They've found a way to kill us?"

"They're still working to perfect it, or so it would seem. Statistically, I think most of us are immune." Terence paused, waiting to see if we had any more immediate questions. When none of us spoke, he continued grimly. "During the process of trying to help the sick Guardians, we learned that it can be transferred through touch. We learned that the hard way, of course. The virus seems to attack whatever cells cause our regeneration. In a literal way, it destroys our bodies so rapidly that our natural healing abilities can't keep up. The organs and tissues gradually give out after being fractionally healed again and again. The brain becomes overwhelmed. It's a painful way to go, I'm afraid."

"But you've been able to fashion a cure, right?" Toni asked. "I mean . . . you've found something, haven't you?"

Terence didn't answer right away.

He didn't have to answer at all.

Patrick and I had both stopped breathing.

Terence forced himself to say the words out loud. "No. We've found no cure. No way to halt the process. Once it has begun . . . I don't know if it's even possible to recover after what the body is put through. Of course we're still trying. Four sick Guardians, each in a different stage, are being monitored as we speak. We're doing everything we can. But though we have some of the top scientific minds at work . . . we're beginning to realize that the Demons must have someone better."

Patrick suddenly spoke, his voice quiet. "How long do I have?"

The lead Guardian hesitated. "It's hard to say. Some were dead in a matter of days, but they were the ones that the Demons personally injected. Most fought the illness for about a week. The longest survivor lasted just over two weeks, from the initial touch."

We all did the easy math in an eternal second.

Patrick had until next Tuesday, at the longest.

I felt like my entire body was being crushed. I couldn't breathe, and I think my heart actually stopped beating under the pressure. It was too much to take in, the implications too frightening to consider.

Terence's voice was quiet, but the words weren't lost to any of us. "Once the nosebleeds begin . . . it isn't long. They usually begin soon after the vomiting ends. It's the next sure marker. Once they start . . . it's down to mere days, sometimes hours. The destructive rate seems to vary with each Guardian, though. Sometimes a cough is involved, after the nosebleeds start."

Patrick repeated his question, the desperate edge he'd been struggling to hide permeating each syllable. "How long do I have, Terence? Your best guess?"

"I can't be sure, but . . . judging from your history, I wouldn't be surprised if the nosebleeds start in the next couple of days. You don't appear to have an accelerated strain, but you're not moving slowly either. You've already lasted almost a week. Based on my experience, most of your time is already up. You'll deteriorate more rapidly now." I knew the words were hard for him to say, but I don't know how he still managed to relay them so calmly.

I finally found my voice, though it was irresolute despite my best efforts. "But Guardians can't die," I protested, still clinging to that ridiculous truth. "Where would they go? Beings don't just cease to exist."

If Terence hadn't looked tired and slightly fearful before, he did now. "That has been one of my greatest concerns. From what I've been able to gather from our sources, they're not showing up in heaven."

"Sources?" I asked, confused. Guardians had access to heaven? That was certainly news to me.

Terence explained quickly. "When a person dies, they spend a brief time on the other plane—like a halfway house—on their way to heaven. If they choose to become a Guardian, they can bring back messages from the other side when they return to earth. These message carriers are our connection to heaven."

I nodded once, showing I'd understood.

Terence continued at once. "They don't appear to be given the choice again either, so I assumed that maybe they're like Seers—not given the choice at all. After all, it made sense to me. Guardians sacrifice so much; they shouldn't be required to give more, just like a Seer. But since they're not turning up in heaven, we really don't know what's happening to them."

"They just . . . disappear?" Toni demanded, askance.

"That's the theory for now," Terence admitted.

I wasn't breathing again. Because something Terence had said, it just didn't compute. Not initially, anyway. At first I thought some new fear for Patrick had triggered my reaction. But no. It was something else.

And then the words began to sink in, and the realization struck me like a flash of lightning.

Seers didn't get a choice when they died. They went straight to heaven. Even if Patrick wasn't dying . . . we would have been separated eventually.

It was true that I'd thought about the choice I would one day face—my family or a life with Patrick. I hadn't agonized over it too much, though, because it was in the distant future. It wasn't important right now.

Why hadn't he told me this?

Toni and Terence didn't seem to be aware of my body's sudden lockup. But Patrick was. I think he realized what Terence had just revealed at the same second I came to fully understand it.

His fingers pressed deeply against mine, and suddenly I became the focus of the room as Patrick twisted to face me, worried because I was so still. I felt the other Guardians watching us—watching *me*—but I kept my eyes downcast, not really looking at anything while my mind raced endlessly.

Patrick angled his body to me, lifting one bent leg onto the couch between us. He lifted a hand to cup the side of my face, effetely forcing me to meet his ardent gaze.

"Kate?"

Even now, when he'd just discovered that he was dying, he was more concerned about me.

I struggled to pull in a breath, for his sake more than mine. Surprisingly, I wasn't crying. Maybe I was in shock—I don't know. All I knew was that a choice I'd never had the chance to make was suddenly no longer mine.

I wet my bottom lip with a quick purse of my mouth, and my eyes flickered up to his at last. "I'm okay," I breathed.

His eyes narrowed, and I knew he didn't believe me. A muscle in his jaw twitched tightly. "I meant to tell you," he whispered breathlessly, his fingertips pressing tighter against my face, as if that extra show of strength would somehow help me understand. "I *wanted* to tell you. But you were so happy, and it seemed so inconsequential at the time . . ."

He looked so worried over this, a distant part of me wanted to laugh. He was agonizing over the possibility that he'd hurt my feelings, after we'd just learned that he had only days to live? It seemed so ridiculous. Yet here he was, unsure if he'd crossed some line or had upset me so badly that he was hesitant even to comfort me with an embrace.

I pulled in a deeper breath through my nose, and then I released it a bit unsteadily through my mouth. I lifted my free hand—the one Patrick wasn't gripping tightly—and brushed my fingers along the side of his firm face, stroked his concerned brow. My thumb rubbed delicately along the hollow beneath his eye, and I finally had enough control to speak, though my words were pressingly quiet. "It doesn't matter now. You're the one that matters."

I glanced over at Terence, who was watching us carefully. "What can we do?" I demanded, not unkindly. Just determined. Very, very determined.

Terence nodded once, accepting my silent offer to do anything necessary to ensure Patrick's recovery. Because I wasn't taking no for an answer. He was going to make it. He couldn't die. I'd already lost my parents. I wasn't losing the man I loved on top of that.

"I'll take him back with me, where he can receive the best medical attention possible. Our facilities have everything he'll need. We can isolate him and start running some tests."

I gave my own nod, though it was the hardest thing I'd ever had to agree too. Letting him go, even if it was for the best, wasn't going to be easy.

"Do you think there's hope then?" Toni asked the superior Guardian.

Terence wasn't about to lie. "We haven't been successful yet. But we think we're getting closer, and we only have to do one thing right to find the cure. With Patrick there, we'll have five Guardians we can study."

"I'm not going," Patrick broke in easily.

My hand almost slipped from his face. I stopped it before my fingers could fall from his jaw. We all turned to look at him, but I think I looked the most surprised.

What did he mean he wasn't going?

"Patrick," I stumbled out. "If they can help you, you have to go."

He shook his head easily, eyes on me though his words were for everyone. "They can't help me. We all know that. If I was the only test subject available, I would have a harder time refusing. But my presence there wouldn't help anyone. Not even me." He glanced up at Terence, daring him to disagree.

He didn't.

Patrick's eyes came back to me, his hand on my face exceedingly gentle. "Kate, if I'm not a hazard to you . . . I want to stay right here."

I couldn't believe what he was saying. He was giving up? Already? Before we'd even started to fight? How dare he give up! My breaths were coming faster. I swallowed hard, my eyes finally beginning to sting. But it was from anger. At least that's what I told myself.

"No. Patrick, you're not giving up. There has to be something— you're not just going to give up and die."

"Kate, please, try to understand," he urged. "This is my choice. I may not have a lot of them now, but . . . this is mine to make. I don't want to die alone."

"You're not going to die," I said through gritted teeth.

Why did he insist on making this the end? Why wasn't he fighting? Why was I the only one trying to talk some sense into him?

I knew the answer without looking to Toni or Terence.

I knew it just by glaring painfully into Patrick's resigned face.

They didn't speak because I was the last one still clinging to any hope of his recovery. In their minds, he was already dead.

And I knew they were right. That was the worst part of all.

nineteen

I stopped arguing with Patrick. I became pretty overall silent, actually. While the others pretended to discuss possible treatments, or ways to stall the progression of the virus, I became numb. I refused to dissolve into tears, and I knew they were only seconds away if I continued to feel and think. I needed to be strong. Even if I was losing hope as rapidly as the others, I couldn't let it show. I needed to be the positive one. The believing one. Patrick needed that. He needed me.

Terence didn't press Patrick to accompany him. He seemed to understand his reasoning perfectly, and it was clear that Patrick was grateful to him. Toni asked some questions about taking care of Patrick in the later stages, and I knew that was his way of telling us he wasn't going anywhere.

Patrick clung to my hand, but we were once again sitting side by side, no longer looking at each other. Whenever my hand began to tremble, my shield of numbness slipping momentarily, Patrick reflexively tightened his hold. His thumb drew endless circles on the back of my hand, soothing in their continuity but haunting once his skin had passed over mine, leaving only insubstantial trails behind. There, then gone. There, then gone. He was here now. But soon he would be gone.

Numb. Think numb.

Terence was sitting on the coffee table now, telling us how Patrick would start losing the ability to do the simplest things. Things like staying visible and hiding his aura. He would die invisible, wrapped in colors of pain. I cringed at the thought, and I received the almost customary squeeze from Patrick's cold fingers.

They talked for a long time. I listened to their voices but didn't pay attention until I realized Terence had asked me a question, and now everyone was looking at me, waiting for me to say something.

"Sorry. What was that?" I asked, too numb to blush at being caught.

Terence offered a small understanding smile. "I would like to speak with you alone, if that would be all right. It won't take long."

The meeting I'd been waiting for ever since his phone call—the conversation I'd been looking forward to since the incident with Grandma—it was the last thing I wanted to happen now. I didn't want to leave my Guardian. I looked to Patrick, but he only forced a smile and squeezed my hand. "I'll be right here," he promised softly.

I swallowed, then leaned in to touch my lips to his. But I didn't let myself linger over the kiss, because I didn't want to start crying. I pulled away and stood, Patrick's fingers slipping from mine as I followed after the lead Guardian.

As soon as we stepped into the hall, Terence closed the door and then gestured with one long arm toward the stairs. "We'll take a short walk around the building. This won't take long, Kate."

I walked with him without a word, and we remained in silence until we reached the bottom of the stairs on the main floor of the warehouse. Finally, he spoke, slowing his steps unconsciously. "I know this isn't an easy time for you. Patrick had mentioned that you were good friends, but . . . I gather that there may be something more between you?"

I just nodded. I wasn't going to cry. I wasn't.

Terence hesitated, wondering how to begin. "I assume you kept my phone call a secret?"

Again, I just nodded.

"Thank you for that. I just have a few questions—things that couldn't be discussed over the phone, and things that . . . for your own safety, should be kept secret from all others. Including your Guardians."

"Can you please just tell me what you're trying to say?" I asked suddenly, knowing it was rude to interrupt but sick of the useless waiting. We were wasting time, and time wasn't something I could afford to waste right now. Patrick didn't have any time to waste.

Because maybe he had given up. It certainly sounded like they'd all given up. But I hadn't. I wouldn't. Already I was trying to form a plan of action. A visit to Clyde, maybe call on Jack if it became necessary . . .

I was prepared to do anything, look anywhere for answers. The numbness was fading. It was time for action. Before I went crazy.

These thoughts happened in a split second. Terence bowed his head apologetically and held one of the double doors for me. I blinked heavily into the sudden sunlight, and Terence was squinting beside me. His silver car gleamed brightly in the falling sun, and we averted our eyes to the ground almost immediately.

Terence guided me to the right, and finally he began to speak while we paced in front of the abandoned structure. "Have you stopped to wonder why the Demon Lord would be interested in you, Kate? Have you wondered why he'd send Far Darrig after you? Why Romero and Avalos believed they could return to their king's good graces by hand-delivering you? Have you wondered what made you so special?"

I shrugged a single shoulder. "Patrick said that . . . maybe they're just really desperate for Seers."

Terence smiled kindly. "He doesn't really believe that."

"I know." I sighed and stole a glance at the old Guardian at my side. "He didn't want to admit it, though."

Terence nodded. "And he was wise to keep his ignorance from you. Seers—especially new Seers—depend greatly on the strength of their Guardians. If their protectors are anxious and unsure, those emotions simply transfer to the Seer and generally intensify." He paused, as if to take a breath, but didn't continue.

"It makes sense," I grunted, wondering if that's what he was waiting for.

"Yes, it does. But I believe I may know why the Demon Lord is after you. And why Far Darrig is stalking you—how they knew of you so soon."

"And?" I prompted, allowing some of my impatience to leak through.

We rounded the first corner, and Terence shot me a look. "What do auras look like to you, Kate? What do you see when you look at a person's emotions?"

It seemed like a weird question. I felt dumb answering it, saying the obvious out loud. "Well, um . . . I see a ribbon of light, surrounding the person. Gold if it's human, silver if it's a Guardian, and black if it's a Demon."

"And what of emotions?" Terence questioned.

"It gets complicated." I bit my bottom lip, considering the best way to explain. "Swirls of colors. Sometimes streaks, sometimes just small splotches. The colors are all jumbled, but I've learned to interpret them pretty well. It was harder in the beginning."

"You see multiple colors at once?" he clarified.

There was a hint of something in his voice I couldn't identify, but the hairs on the back of my neck rose in response. "Yeah. Why? Is that wrong?"

He gave me a reassuring smile, but the furrow between his eyebrows was deep, and not just because of the bright sun. "No, of course it's not wrong. But it's different. Rare."

I blinked in surprise. "You mean . . . most Seers don't . . . ?"

"Most Seers see only one color. One emotion at a time. The strongest, the most present. *You* see the underlying feelings that other Seers miss."

"And this is rare?" I kept thinking about the mind-reading experience. Grandpa had said that was rare too. Was it related?

"Quite rare, yes."

So I was a freak among freaks?

"What makes me see things differently?" I asked, still trying to figure out how I'd explain my experience to him. "Did I get . . . closer to dying or something?"

"My studies lead me to conclude that it has nothing to do with the actual near-death experience. Instead, it has to do with genetics." He shrugged. "At least, that's the best conclusion I've been able to draw. It could be something entirely different. But the few Seers who have family members that also become Seers, they all see things the same."

"So my grandpa is different too? Like me?" That made sense—he'd had the mind-reading thing happen to him.

Terence nodded, and we turned the next corner. There was less sun on this back side of the alley, and the other factory building was close; there was just enough room to have the couple dumpsters along the walls and still have what could manage to be a one-way street.

"Your grandfather was interviewed a long time ago, but yes, he sees multiple emotions as well."

"Is there a reason he didn't mention this to me?" Why wouldn't he have told me that even the way I—we—saw auras was different?

"He was sworn to secrecy, of course. As you will be."

"You mean, I can't talk about this—even to my own family?"

"For your safety, you'd better not. The fewer people who know, the better."

"Why? Why is it such a big deal, seeing multiple colors?"

"The Demon Lord has been hunting down every special Seer he can get his hands on for the past century or more. Surely your Guardians mentioned the other Seers taken by Far Darrig. The kidnappings seemed random, but they were anything but."

"So why does he want us? Why does he want me?"

"Because Seeing isn't the only thing you can do, Kate."

He was going for cryptic, but he didn't quite succeed, since I already knew what he was trying to wow me with. I surprised him by nodding. "I know. We can read minds."

He blinked rapidly, shocked by my response. "You can *what?*"

Now it was my turn to be surprised.

I frowned. "Some Seers can read minds."

"Could you explain that, please?" he asked, kindly, but still baffled.

I hurried to tell him everything, including my grandfather's explanation of events. Almost immediately his surprise vanished, and he was nodding. "I see why you'd reach that conclusion," he said after I was done speaking. "And I understand why your grandfather wouldn't tell you the truth. He was sworn to secrecy, after all."

I waited for his words to make sense of themselves.

They didn't.

"What do you mean?" I demanded, feeling apprehension for the first time. Grandpa had lied to me?

Terence slowed his step. "Let me explain, Kate. Most Seers only see the emotion of the moment. The strongest. The one color. But you can see everything; even the thoughts and feelings that are in the back of a person's mind. Our feelings are doorways to memories. Since you can access more . . . see emotions that aren't based in the present . . ."

I stopped walking. He stopped with me, and we stood facing each other. Slack jawed, I just stared at him.

Talk about one of the most overwhelming days of my life.

"Are you saying . . . ?" my voice drifted. "Are you saying I can access people's *memories?*"

He tipped his head once.

"I can . . . *see* their past experiences through their auras? Isn't that a fancy way of saying mind reader?"

"Not exactly," he said. "It's more comparable to . . . you can actually relive their past experiences with them."

"As in, I focus on one of their emotions, and I get to feel their memory with them?" It sounded exactly like what had happed in the front room. The vision had been real, overwhelming. It really had felt like I was there, standing in the room with my parents.

He smiled just a little. "No. That's not exactly how I'd describe it.

It's closer to actually *going* back and watching things unfold. As your own separate person—a living witness to events. Possibly an active participant of the moment, if you chose to interact."

I blinked. "Like . . . travel through *time*? Do you know how ridiculous that sounds?" My heart was racing with the sudden implications, even as my mind rebelled against the absurd idea. Why hadn't Grandpa told me this? Promise or no promise, why had he kept something this huge from me? I had been standing in the room with my parents. I'd actually been there, if only for a split second. I'd used Grandma's memory as a gateway, and . . . I'd somehow physically been there. My arms were aching, thinking that I'd been so close to them, and hadn't embraced them. Not that they would have known me, their yet-to-be-born-daughter.

"No more ridiculous than seeing emotions, I'd imagine." Terence's voice brought me back.

"No. Actually, it's a *lot* weirder. Are you saying that I could actually use a person's aura and take a stroll through their past?" If so, I could do it again—I could see, touch, and talk to my parents again whenever I wanted.

"Well, that's what you did with your grandmother, didn't you? Of course, you were there for only a moment—the shortest instance. I'd imagine that was because you didn't realize what was happening—you didn't know how to keep yourself grounded there. It's hard for us to understand, because we don't really know much about this power. And for the time being, the Guardian council has asked Seers to refrain from experimentation. There have been casualties in the past. Accidents."

"Casualties?" That got my attention.

He nodded solemnly. "I wasn't an overseer for the experiments, so my knowledge is somewhat limited. I only know the basic findings. I believe it was over a decade ago when the Guardian council put a stop to the research. As with all things, time travel has rules, and the penalties of nature can be severe. For one thing, you can't alter events in your own lifetime."

It was like he'd guessed all my thoughts. What better way to stop Patrick's illness than making sure it never happened? And then . . . the possibilities . . . not only could I visit my parents, but they didn't have to die in the first place. I could prevent the accident.

"Why not?" I demanded, distracted and more than a little upset that he'd shot my ideas down so quickly.

Surprising me, he shrugged. "I'm not sure what happens exactly. But any Seer that's ever tried disappears, only to return with their heart no longer beating. As if the act of changing their own past somehow takes their own life." He was suddenly apologetic. "It's not a clear science, Kate. There is so much we don't understand."

"So what use is changing the past if you can't improve your own present?" I asked rhetorically.

"Some gifts aren't meant to be used for our own gain. Perhaps this one shouldn't be used at all."

"Where could we use it, anyway? If we can't change the fates of anyone in our lives . . ." Understanding began to dawn, and I could feel it registering on my face.

His head bobbed as I pieced it together. "Yes. Any memory in your lifetime would be considered off-limits. But what of us who live forever? Those of us who have memories that date back hundreds, even thousands of years?"

Things were clinking into place, now. "The Demon Lord. Is that what he's trying to do? Rewrite the past?"

"It's pure speculation. But it would explain a lot of what's been happening. The ease of his rise to power."

"But . . . how did he know about me so soon? How I see things? I've only ever told Lee, and . . . oh."

He nodded grimly. "Your grandfather. The Demon Lord must have been after him initially. And then Far Darrig discovered you during his plotting to retrieve your grandfather, and plans changed. They wanted the younger Seer of the family."

"And they were sure I saw things the same way, because we're related," I finished for him.

"Quite right." He waved a hand, and I slowly forced myself to continue walking. But it was hard to concentrate on each step when my life was spinning out of control.

We walked in silence to the next corner, and started moving along the last full side of the building. The shed housing the midnight-blue car took up most of the alley, so we had to walk single file past it.

Once we were walking side by side again, I asked a tentative question. "So how does it work? How do I stay in a person's memory? How do I access the right emotion at will? Everything with my Grandma was so accidental . . ."

"Obviously I can only tell you what's been told to me. But it seems that the only thing necessary is to concentrate on one color, one feeling. The specific memory pulls you in, and your body is suddenly in two places at once—though you are decidedly unconscious in your real time. It exhausts you to stay long in the past—at least, that's what we've learned through experiments. The further back you go, the easier it is on your body. But as long as a Seer is traveling to a memory that predates the Seers's birth, the Seer returns alive. Extremely exhausted—usually unconscious—but alive."

"It would work the same if a Seer traveled into a Demon's past," I muttered. "So we're like tools to them."

It wasn't a question, but he answered me anyway. "Yes, or so it would seem. But this type of travel . . . the Seer has no control. The one with the memories is the one who does the guiding. A Seer can't pick and choose where to end up—what time to inhabit. As you can imagine, this ability doesn't do a Seer much good. What can they change? Nothing for their benefit."

I nodded once, my thoughts still running wild. Time travel. And I'd just been told that I shouldn't use it, and that there was no way it could benefit me. I felt incredibly gypped.

Terence slowed his steps, not ready yet to reach our last corner. "Kate, you must promise me that you won't experiment with this knowledge. You understand the dangers. If you tried to alter events in your life, you would die. Any year you've lived is strictly prohibited."

"I understand," I told him.

His eyes bored into mine. "You cannot use this to save Patrick. Your entire lifetime is off-limits, so any of the years he's lived during your lifespan are fatal to you. Is that clear?"

"Yes."

He watched my face carefully, but must have decided that I honestly understood. He continued, "You must also promise to keep this knowledge a secret. Not just for your sake, but for the sake of all other gifted Seers. Demons aren't the only ones that wish they could rewrite the past. Think of the Guardians that have regretted their choice. What if they could have a Seer go back and convince themselves to choose differently? We would lose so many . . . Please, Kate. You must promise me that this will not be discussed again."

"So, we can't even tell my Guardians why the Demons are after me?" I asked, completely incredulous.

"No matter how content Guardians may appear, they still have regrets. Every living thing makes mistakes, ponders the possibilities if they'd only chosen a different course. Guardians aren't exempt. *Your* Guardians are not exempt. Am I making myself clear?"

Again, I nodded.

He seemed to be convinced, and we rounded the front corner— we could see his parked car and the double doors that marked the end of our time together.

But I still had one question. "Terence, if the Demon Lord wants me this badly . . . then why did Far Darrig stop?"

The lead Guardian glanced at me, his wrinkled eyes squinted. "But he hasn't, Kate. He hasn't stopped. He probably never will."

twenty

Terence didn't linger. There wasn't much left to do or discuss. He took a few minutes to talk to Toni alone, and then Patrick. Last instructions? Good-byes? I tried not to think about what was happening behind the closed doors. Instead I sat on the couch and plotted.

Despite my concern for Patrick, I thought a lot about what Terence had told me. How could I not? To learn that time travel was possible—that I had the power to do it—was both awesome and terrifying. True, there were a lot of limitations, and it was the reason I'd been being hunted so relentlessly by the Demons. But still. It was cool. Intriguing. And no matter how much I thought about it, I couldn't find a good way to use it to remedy the current situation.

Why hadn't Grandpa told me? He'd probably known all along that this was why Far Darrig was after me. And he'd lied to me. He hadn't told me I saw things differently, and he'd let me write off my time-travel incident, like it didn't matter at all.

I tried to keep my anger in check. Quite frankly, I could worry about Grandpa's lies later. Right now, I needed to try to focus on Patrick.

What if I told Patrick everything and he could use his emotions to guide me to his past? If I could get to him before his death, before he made the choice to become a Guardian . . . the only problem with that, of course, was if he didn't become a Guardian, we would never meet. It was hard to wrap my mind around. Could that even work? And then, of course, I wouldn't ever know him. But if I was going to lose his love anyway . . . I'd keep it open as an option, something to think about, but it would be a last resort.

True, I'd made promises to Terence to keep this quiet. But what were a couple promises to a near stranger when I was dealing with Patrick's life? In the end, there would be no debate. I wouldn't be my grandpa; not if sharing the truth could help Patrick at all.

There had to be a way. I felt quite confident that I needed to start with Clyde. If I could question him . . . maybe get the name of his contact, hear the rumor from the actual source . . . maybe I could get on the trail of a cure. For the moment, it was my best thought.

Not that I had a lot of time to formulate this stuff.

Terence was soon leaving, and he offered to drive me home. Patrick was obviously tired, so I accepted the ride. I didn't want to leave him, but I knew staying here constantly wasn't an option. I had a Demon to meet up with.

Patrick and I murmured quiet good-byes on one side of the room while the other Guardians tried to pretend we weren't there.

He held me tightly. I ran my fingers through his hair, told him how much I loved him; I promised to come by tomorrow, and he smiled gratefully. "I'll be waiting," he breathed against my mouth. He planted an easy kiss on my lips, and then a second, more meek one against my forehead, smoothing the tension out of the muscles beneath my skin.

I closed my eyes and leaned into him, curling his thick brown locks behind his ear. "Call me if you need anything. Please?"

"I will," he promised, almost contritely. He pulled back, tapping a single finger against the tip of my nose. "Promise me you'll do the same."

"I don't want to disturb you," I protested.

He cut me off with a forced smile. "At least promise you'll call Toni. I won't get any rest if I think you're afraid to call."

I made a big show of my surrender, rolling my eyes and every-thing. "Fine. I promise."

"Thank you." He kissed me once more, but this wasn't a fast brush, like most of our kisses had been today. This one was con-trolled by the emotions he'd been struggling so hard to keep inside. Pain. Fear. Desperation. Worry. Love. Even anger was there. His lips moved slowly around mine, and I knew he was trying to be strong. It wasn't a fierce kiss, exactly. Just deep. Moving. It was everything. It was what we both needed.

It ended too soon. Patrick broke it, and at first I wasn't sure why. I opened my eyes, focused on his, and saw how brightly the clear blue was shining. He was biting back something, trying to push a grimace into a smile.

He was trying not to cry.

I swallowed hard, touched my hand to the side of his face, and he closed his eyes tightly. My fingers brushed against his skin, and I felt the tenseness gradually fade. He ducked his head, and my hand lowered with him.

His head suddenly twisted, and my hand shifted to rest over his parted lips. "I love you," he whispered into my palm. Every inch of my skin tingled, and I could feel my own tears building up, wanting to escape.

But by the time his eyes opened and he was looking at me, my emotions were under control. I gave him my most tender smile, and I embraced him a last time, breathing easily against his ear. "I love you, Patrick."

It was so hard to let go and leave him. Sitting in Terence's car, all I could feel was the emptiness. My fingers and hands were empty—there was nothing to cling to. My arms felt strangely weightless, because there was nothing to hold on to.

So I hugged my stomach tightly and prayed for inspiration. I wasn't going to live like this forever. I wasn't going to let him go.

❋

Terence dropped me off at the curb in front of my house, and we said quick good-byes. He told me to call if I had any further questions or concerns. I was having a hard time keeping it together, so I simply nodded and slipped out of the car. It was just after dinnertime, and though I hadn't eaten, I wasn't hungry. My emotions were frazzled; my brain was overloaded. I heard Terence's car pull swiftly away, and I was partway up the driveway before I saw the front door swing open. Grandpa stepped out onto the porch, his aura confused, his face unreadable.

I took a deep, trembling breath and clenched my hands into fists. I was still irrationally angry at him for lying to my face, and that anger spiked the moment I saw him standing there in his worn overalls.

He waited to speak until I was almost to the porch steps. "Kate, what's wrong?" He pulled the door closed as he spoke.

I didn't answer. I climbed the steps and tried to brush past him, but he grabbed my nearest elbow, halting me. "Kate? What's happened?"

I jerked away, backing up a step to face him. "I don't really feel like discussing it with you," I retorted sharply.

He looked like he'd been kicked in the face. His aura flashed with hurt and incomprehension. "Whose car was that?" he asked at last. "Where's Patrick?"

My lips pressed together as my hands shook. My eyes suddenly filled with tears—the tight lid I'd been keeping on my emotions for the past few hours ruptured in an instant. "He's dying, Grandpa. Patrick's really sick, just like Clyde said, and the Guardians can't help him. That was Terence, their supervisor, and he confirmed everything. The disease is real—Guardians are dying. And Patrick's infected. He's only got a few days to live." I bit off the last words, my throat too constricted to speak anymore.

Grandpa kept peeking at my aura, and I think what he saw there kept him from approaching me, even though it was obvious he wanted to take me into his arms. "What's the plan? How can I help?"

I half laughed through my sheen of tears. "Help? How can you help? Are you serious? Why didn't you help me by telling me the truth?"

His whole face twisted in confusion. "Tell you what?" he asked cautiously.

"You've known all along that Far Darrig wants me because I'm different. Why didn't you tell me? And why lie about what happened Friday? I went back in *time* but instead of telling me—warning me of the danger—you shrug it off, let me believe it would be a one-time thing—an accident?" I sucked in a breath and swiped my hand over my wet eyes.

He held out a peaceful hand. "Kate, I didn't mean to hurt you . . ."

His words faded as I shook my head ruefully. "You made a promise to them. I understand."

His eyes became hooded in an instant. "Do you think a promise to the Guardians would honestly keep me from protecting you?"

"That's what you did. Terence told me about the danger of traveling into my own lifetime. Weren't you worried I might end up having another 'accident,' and end up in one of Jenna's or Josie's memories?"

"It was improbable that it would happen again. Frankly, I was shocked you stumbled upon it accidentally at all."

"And you thought a lie would protect me?"

"Yes." His voice was fierce, but his face softened almost instantly. He blew out his breath and turned away from me. He lowered himself onto the cement steps and gazed out across the deserted street, his thin hair lifting gently in an unexpected breeze. I watched his profile as he spoke slowly, my anger evaporating as I saw the hurt in his aura overwhelm every other color. "There is a pain I've felt every day since losing your parents," he whispered. "A pain that none of you have had to feel—not your grandmother, not the twins, not even you." He shook his head. "I was just trying to keep you from bearing what I've had to struggle with since the accident. I'm sure it's something you've already considered now that you know the truth."

When I remained silent, he glanced up at me. "You want to save them. But you can't without sacrificing your own life."

He turned away again, shoulders dropping. "It was my first thought as we rushed to the emergency room. When I saw my son's lifeless body, and your mother's . . . when I saw you lying on that hospital bed, Kate. I nearly told your grandmother everything, then and there, so I could access her memory and change the events of the day. I was ready to sacrifice myself. I reconsider my decision every day."

Though my eyes still burned, I wiped the last tear off my face as he paused.

He snorted vaguely. "You're probably wondering why I didn't change things. I'm an old man. I've lived a long, good life. Why not give up my life for your parents? Why not save you from ever becoming a Seer?" He looked my way once more, his eyes blurry with moisture. "I'm a stubborn man, but there are a few things I've learned in life I'll never dispute. Destiny exists, Kate. I'm not talking about fate—the idea that every moment, every decision in your life is mapped out for you, and there's nothing you can do to change your design. I'm talking about the concept of destiny, that there is a purpose for everything, and every person has a purpose that can't be frustrated. Do you understand the difference?"

"I think so," I whispered, though I wasn't sure I did.

"We can change the past, Kate—Seers like us have that ability. But we can't change the destiny that guides a person's life experience. I could have saved your parents from that accident. But would they still be alive today? If their part on this world was over . . . if you were meant to become a Seer . . . my sacrifice would have done nothing to disrupt destiny."

"Nothing's ever one hundred percent," I said, pathetically stubborn.

He nodded. "And that's why every day I wonder if I made the right decision to let destiny take its course. And I assume I'll be second-guessing myself for the rest of my life. I just wanted to save you from that for as long as I could."

We were silent for a few long minutes, but eventually my anger was exhausted. I was too tired to remain so upset.

I moved to sit on the stair beside him, and in seconds his arm was wrapped firmly around my shoulders.

"I'm so sorry about Patrick," he said, wisely choosing to avoid the topic of my parents and our special abilities. "I don't know if Clyde can find out anything more, but I can ask him to start digging for information. He has some Demon contacts that might know something."

"Thank you," I mumbled.

His hand rubbed my arm. "I love you, Kate. We're not going to give up on Patrick."

❄

When Patrick came walking into American lit the next day, I could barely believe my eyes. He arrived just before the teacher did, so there wasn't much time to talk.

Aaron was still sitting across the circle from us, but he gave us both meaningful nods. I gave him an exaggerated wince when I saw his black eye and puffy lip. Just like any self-respecting male, he only grinned. I shook my head at him and then tried to pay attention to what Mr. Benson was trying to say.

But all I could really focus on was Patrick. Sitting so close but still impossibly far. There was no way we could get away with having a conversation, yet that was the only thing I wanted to do.

When class finally ended and I'd gathered my things, Patrick was already standing and waiting, backpack slung over one shoulder. "Good morning," he said. He looked tired. But his voice seemed almost perfectly normal. If I hadn't known he only had days to live, I wouldn't have ever thought he was even sick.

While I zipped up my bag, I glanced around to see that most of our fellow students had already managed to slip out. The rest were clustered near the door, talking loudly. They wouldn't hear a thing. "Patrick, what are you doing here? You can't come to school."

"Why not?" he asked, honestly confused.

Because you're sick. You're dying. "You know why not. Don't make me say it."

His eyes were sympathetic, but his tone remained falsely light. "Terence assured me that this is perfectly safe. I can't expose anyone else, so I may as well spend the day doing what I want."

"You want to spend the day here? At school?"

He shrugged a single shoulder; his eyes didn't waver from mine. "I want to spend my day with you, Kate. Wherever you go."

My heart reacted to his fervent words, but I kept my gaze disapproving. "You should be resting. Or at least have told me that you felt up to doing something. We could both ditch together."

"And why would we do that?" he asked, eyes dancing just a little. "Did you have something else in mind?"

"I could think of something to do with you. But you shouldn't spend your last . . ." My voice trailed off, and I was unable to finish.

He took a step toward me, reaching for my hand. "Kate, you can say it. It's okay."

"No," I whispered, staring at our joined hands. "It's not."

"I'm with you. Nothing else really matters for the moment." His head tilted obligingly to the side. "Well, except being late for second period," he allowed.

I snorted, but the sound was barely audible. "You're hopeless."

"I believe you've said that before."

"Yeah, well, you haven't changed yet."

We met up with Lee in second period, where Patrick was able to see her newest color in Rainbow Days—blue.

She went the whole nine yards, once again. Blue hair, blue makeup, blue clothes, blue jewelry, blue shoes, blue backpack. I had to admit, the darker shade was a lot easier on the eyes than orange.

Patrick reached the same conclusion, and he told her so. Lee practically beamed. "You like it, then?" she asked. "I'm curious to see what Rodney will think of it."

"If he could stand the orange, I think you're safe," Patrick joked.

Lee slapped his arm, then turned her attention to the teacher, who was calling us all to order. I was the only one who saw Patrick rubbing the spot Lee had hit, and I don't think he realized that I caught the flinch that twisted his face.

He was in more pain than he was letting on.

At lunch he paid more attention to the kids than ever before. He was careful to take a moment to focus on each individual, and I could see in their auras how much they adored him. How much they would miss him if I wasn't able to . . . I didn't want to consider that possibility.

He even took a couple minutes for Lee, asking her about how her date with Rodney had gone. She told him about the flat tire and about the movie they'd watched at his house. It was obvious in the way her face lit up that she was pretty happy about the new possibilities. He teased her lightly about Toni, who he had to pretend he'd never met.

I watched them interact, wondering if they'd get the chance again. Would he be able to push back the pain long enough to last another day in public? Or would the headache finally take over? Would his dying limbs finally give out and turn numb? Would he be invisible by tomorrow, unable to communicate with anyone but me and Toni?

I needed to stop this train of thought. I was making myself depressed, and in record time.

After school Patrick looked completely exhausted. While leaving the choir room, I worried aloud if he should be driving, but he was one step ahead of me.

"Toni dropped me off this morning, and he hasn't stopped texting me for the last ten minutes. He's waiting around the corner, so hopefully no one will see him."

"Do you want me to drop you off there? You shouldn't be walking."

"And let Lee see him?" He chuckled. "That would complicate her life in a hurry. I can walk. I'm not a complete invalid. Besides, I need to wear myself out so I can take a nap."

"I think you can check that one off the list," I muttered a bit ruefully. But the concern was there too, and I knew he'd pick up on it.

He squeezed my hand. "If you say so." His voice turned serious. "Will you come over later?"

"Of course. But it depends on how long you sleep—Jenna's piano recital is tonight."

His head tipped. "Right. I might just have to meet you there. It's at six, right?"

"Yeah. But don't force yourself out if—"

"I wouldn't miss it for anything." He grinned tiredly. "Can you imagine what she'd do to me?"

"Forgiveness wouldn't come for a while," I agreed.

We stepped outside and wandered to the sidewalk. Patrick tugged on my hand, pulling me to the side and out of the student traffic. Once out of the way, he turned to face me, cradling my face with both hands. His clear eyes stared into mine, as if he were trying to memorize every speck of color in them. He then swept his gaze over every plane and curve of my face, searing them into his memory.

After an intense moment of scrutiny and heart racing, he smiled. It was just a half-grin, but there was no denying that he thought he was the luckiest man on the planet. My knees felt far too weak.

"Who needs sleep?" he murmured teasingly, bending our heads together until our foreheads touched. His rough thumbs stroked my cheeks, and his other fingers brushed at the strands of hair that slipped down. "I don't want to waste a second on rest," he whispered seriously, the palm of one hand cupping my cheek perfectly. "I just want to be with you."

I pinched my eyes closed and pulled in a steadying breath. My own hands rested on his firm chest, rubbed up to his shoulders until my fingertips were stroking his prominent jaw line. "Don't be ridiculous. You need sleep. You need to keep strong."

I felt his whole body shift in his sudden exhale. His head lifted, but only so he could twist and place a kiss against my left temple. "I need *you*," he argued fluidly, the tip of his nose nuzzling my hairline.

My eyes scrunched tighter, and breathing steadily became increasingly difficult as his lips lingered on my skin. I wanted to give in. I wanted to stay with him. But I'd been counting on this time to start my investigation. Saving Patrick's life was more important than spending a few hours with him.

I needed to see Clyde. Grandpa had called him last night, and the Demon had promised to try and learn more about the strange Guardian illness. He hadn't told Clyde that the virus was real, and I didn't protest this lie. It seemed best to keep Patrick's condition a secret. Grandpa intended to take me to visit Clyde whenever the Demon contacted us, but after sitting in class all day, I needed to do something. I needed to go see Clyde myself.

"Please?" I breathed, pushing my mouth to Patrick's cheek. Who knew? Maybe I could use his own moves against him. I let my lips light gingerly against his cheek, then drew them slowly down to his jaw, one thin breath at a time.

I wondered if it was working, but I didn't have to wonder for long. I could feel the tremble in his fingers against my face, felt the shiver ripple through his body. His lips pressed against the curve of my neck, and then he groaned very lowly. It wasn't a groan of pain; it was the kind of groan that made my stomach flip.

"It's not fair," he whispered. "*You're* not fair."

"It's for your own good," I argued. Finally I slipped my mouth to his, and he kissed me deeply. His palms on my face were comforting, and I tried to offer him the same sensation by stroking my fingers through his hair. I pulled him closer and closer, suddenly desperate to keep this kiss from ending. His lips melted to mine, and I knew from the way his hands shook that he was as determined as I was to make this moment eternal.

It didn't matter that we were standing in front of the school, that people were walking all around us. For that moment, it was just us. My every thought was on him, and his only concern was strictly for me. There was no one else, nothing else.

His mouth lifted, but only subtly. He breathed my name, and I shivered down to my bones. I felt the pleased smile twist his lips, because they rested so completely against mine. "I can do it too," he confided, almost mockingly.

I could feel the tears behind my closed eyelids, burning, stinging, wanting to get free. No matter how hard or long he insisted on pretending that nothing was wrong, I wasn't going to believe him. Would it be worse if he were in constant mourning? Maybe. But this fake ease he was trying to achieve . . . it almost made me sick to my stomach.

But of course I couldn't tell him that. Whatever made this easier for him, I was willing to play along.

I forced a smile, ordered my tears to retreat. Then I opened my clear eyes and pulled back from him, letting him see that everything was fine. I could pretend too. "You need to go. We can't leave a bored Toni lying around—there's no telling what he'd do."

Patrick smiled, brushing his fingers a final time against my face before he dropped his hands. We remained standing very close together, my hands still on his shoulders. "You're right—we can't have that."

"I'll come pick you up for the recital," I said spontaneously. "You shouldn't be driving, and Toni probably shouldn't randomly show up."

He nodded once, accepting the plan. "I'll be waiting for you," he promised.

"I love you," I whispered. The words were quiet, but completely sincere.

He stooped in for a quick kiss, and then he took a step back and my hands slipped from his body. He forced a smile. "I love you, Kate. More than you can imagine."

It was a good thing he stepped around me then, because if he hadn't moved in that second, he might have seen the moisture once again gathering in my eyes. I turned to watch him walk away, more rapidly than he usually moved. His tense shoulders were slightly hunched, and I got the distinct feeling that he was running away from me. From the emotions he refused to show.

I took a deep breath and released it expansively. It was time to get to work.

Lee was a little surprised by my sudden desire to go shopping, but she told me that she was still hoping to find a purple necklace for next week, so she was all for it. I didn't mention that we were heading for a pawnshop, because the twins were still in the car, and I didn't want Grandpa to know I was going. That was the whole point of having Lee accompany me. He would never believe that I would do Seer stuff with my best friend, let alone go visit a Demon, even if he was "safe."

I dropped the twins off at the house and told Jenna that I'd be back around five. After we'd pulled out of my driveway, Lee asked if we could stop by her house so she could pick up some more cash. Though she probably wasn't going to need it, I pulled into her driveway anyway—next to Peter Keegan's car.

"Huh," Lee grunted as she took off her seat belt. "He's here pretty early. I doubt Mom's home yet." She suddenly threw me a look, when she realized I hadn't shut off the car or removed my own seat belt. "Uh, do you have something against my house? I don't want to be alone in there with him. You might as well come in and get a drink or something."

"We don't have a lot of time," I reminded her, glancing down at the clock. It was nearing four and fast.

She rolled her eyes. "Seriously, Kate? I don't think the store's going anywhere. It's hot. I need a drink. You coming or not?"

I hesitated, but gave in with a sigh. I twisted the key and reached for my seat belt. "Fine. But let's make it fast, all right?"

"Sure. It's called a pit stop for a reason, genius."

She opened her car door, and I was a split second behind her. I didn't bother to lock the doors because I knew we'd be fast. I followed Lee to the front door, which she hurried to unlock. I was mildly surprised that Lee's mom trusted her new boyfriend with a key to the house, but I guess it wasn't any of my business. Besides, Peter really was a pretty cool guy, and I guess they had been dating for quite a long time.

We stepped into the house, and I glanced around the living room, expecting to see Peter. He wasn't around, but there was a cell phone sitting on the otherwise immaculate coffee table, so I knew he was here somewhere.

I looked to Lee, but she only shrugged, obviously not worried. "Why don't you get us some water? I'll be right back."

Lee jogged up the stairs, and I moved to the back corner of the quiet house. I went right to the cupboard next to the sink, pulling out two clear glasses. I stepped up to the fridge and filled the first cup with ice, then moved it under the water dispenser. While it filled up, I pushed the second one under the ice.

The sounds were loud in the still house, and for no reason my arms were suddenly covered in goose bumps. I tried to shake off the feeling by concentrating on the glasses. Once both were ready, I carried them back out to the living room, sipping from one as I walked.

I wandered into the room, wishing that I could set the freezing glasses on the coffee table. My fingers were turning numb, but Lee's mom would kill me if I made rings on her wooden table. So I sat down on the couch instead and attempted to balance the cups on my knees—anything to try and relieve some of my fingers from the cold.

I was startled when Peter's phone suddenly began to vibrate in front of me. The dull whine rattled the whole table. I literally jumped, and tried to recover from the momentary scare by taking a deep breath. I glanced around the room, thinking that wherever Peter was in the house, he had to have heard that.

The phone continued to go off, but I heard no footsteps. "Peter?" I called out, albeit not loudly. It's hard to talk in a quiet house—it feels weird. Especially when it's not your own. "Mr. Keegan?"

He didn't seem to be coming. Unable to stop myself, I leaned over to read the caller ID, mindful of the full glasses I held. Maybe it was Lee's mom?

My heart—which had already been beating a little more irregularly since the phone first went off—stopped altogether when I saw who was calling.

Selena Avalos.

My lips parted in a wordless gape. The stinging cold against my fingers suddenly didn't matter as my confused brain tried to make sense of what this meant.

Selena Avalos, a Demon who wanted me, was calling Peter Keegan. She was one of his contacts, for crying out loud! And his car was in the driveway. He was in the house with me. With Lee. How could I have missed this in his aura? So he wasn't a Demon or a Guardian—but that didn't mean he was harmless. He was a Demon Seer.

He wasn't here by accident.

He was here for me.

It was a trap, one I'd fallen for completely.

"What are you doing?"

I gasped and jumped at the voice behind me. Water sloshed out of the glasses I held so tightly, and I whirled to stand and face the speaker.

It was Lee. I exhaled sharply in relief. "Oh my gosh! Don't *do* that to me!"

She raised a single eyebrow, and her blue lips drew apart in concern. "You weren't going to set those on the table, were you? My mom would kill you."

I just stared at her, the light blue couch between us. The phone was still vibrating loudly. The annoying sound spurred my next action. I turned back toward the phone, dismissing Lee's protests when I set the glasses on the table and reached for the phone.

I flipped it open and put it to my ear, watching Lee dance quickly around the couch to scoop up the glasses, casting me an annoyed look as she did so.

But I wasn't paying attention to her.

I was focused on the chillingly beautiful voice speaking impatiently into my ear. "Finally, Peter. Have you done it yet?" Such a cruel tone was unmistakable. It was her.

The phone slipped from my fingers, falling to the carpet with a muted thump. I could feel the sudden tension in all of my muscles, could feel the blood drain from my face.

Lee just looked at me like I'd lost my mind. "Kate, what the heck is wrong with you?" she demanded, glancing down at the still open phone lying at my feet.

Before I could decide if I should even *try* to answer her question, the sound of the back door opening cut through everything else. Loud footsteps announced Peter's return as well as any shout could have, and I knew I had to move fast.

I grabbed the nearest glass of water from out of Lee's hand and dumped it onto the phone. The ice cubes pelted it and scattered across the floor, and Lee's eyes popped extremely wide. "Kate, what the—!"

I grabbed her arm and jerked her toward the door. "Trust me!" I hissed. "We have to get out of here!"

She must have thought I'd lost my mind. But she followed me, her blue hair fluttering out behind us while we ran. I reached the front door first, and I was pulling it open when I heard the sound of Peter stepping into the living room. He must have seen the fallen glass and the ruined phone immediately.

"Lee?" he called out.

I pushed her out the door, not bothering to mute the sound as I slammed it closed behind us. "Get in the car!" I yelled at my best friend.

"What's going on?" she demanded, pausing at the base of the porch steps. She threw a glance over her shoulder, still clinging to the second glass of water.

I latched onto her arm and yanked, making her stumble with me toward the driveway. "Trust me!" I repeated loudly while we sprinted, digging in my pocket with my free hand for the keys.

We were just getting to the car when the front door was torn open, and Peter Keegan stepped onto the porch. His narrowed eyes went to us instantly, and his brown suit and blue tie flapped as he darted toward us—jumping off the porch in one surprisingly graceful lunge. Lee was in the car and slamming her door closed a second before me, and neither of us were thinking about seat belts as I shoved the ready key into the ignition and twisted it harshly. I shoved the gearshift into reverse and twisted in my seat to glare out the back window.

Lee screamed when Peter slammed into the hood of the car, and I punched the accelerator to the floor, too concentrated on getting away to think about the fact that a man had just thrown himself onto my car. Tires squealed and rubber burned, but I got up to the speed I needed. I peeled out to the street, and when I violently turned the wheel to the right, I heard the horrible sound of a body rolling on the hood.

By the time the car was in the street and I was looking up, Peter was falling off the front of my car, landing on the ground on the passenger's side.

I jerked into first gear, but I let up on the clutch too quickly, and the car stuttered and died.

"Kate!" Lee yelled suddenly, and I saw from my peripheral vision that Peter was coming to his feet. He looked dazed and a little bruised, but he was turning toward the car, focusing on Lee through the open window.

"Lock the door!" I screamed, brutally slamming the clutch and brake as far as they would go and twisting the key with a desperate shove.

Lee's hand crashed against the lock, and then she grabbed for the manual lever to roll the window back up. She turned it wildly, cranking it so fast that the glass shuddered on its way up. But she wasn't fast enough. Peter forced his arm through the gap and his hard fingers snagged her fast pumping wrist.

Lee's blue fingernails glinted against the glass of water she held—the glass of water she lifted and splashed defensively into Peter's face as he leaned in. He closed his eyes instinctively, spluttering as the cold water shocked his skin. The ice cubes glanced painfully against his face, and his grip loosened. Lee bashed his knuckles with the mostly empty glass, and the car roared in sudden life.

I floored it, and this time it didn't die. Lee yanked her hand free and we shot forward. Peter stumbled backwards, hands shoving the water out of his eyes. I shifted harshly to second, and then third. Lee was looking back out her window, and I was staring in the rearview mirror.

Peter was going for his car.

Lee was completely freaked out. "The psycho's getting in his car!" she gasped.

"Put on your seat belt!" I ordered firmly, reluctantly slowing for the stop sign in front of us—I didn't stop completely—a lady honked angrily as we drove right in front of her, but I wasn't about to feel bad.

"Kate, what the heck is happening?"

"It's a little complicated," I said through gritted teeth.

"My mom's boyfriend is chasing us!" Lee growled angrily. "He jumped on your freaking car while it was freaking *moving*! I want answers, *right freaking now*!"

I swerved around a slow-moving blue car, and Lee grabbed for the dash when I almost hit the new car in front of us. "Would you slow the freak down!" She gasped, fear mingled with the anger. "You're going to get us killed!"

"I can't slow down!" I yelled. "He's right behind us!"

Lee twisted around, and by her silence I knew she'd seen him. Somehow—though we'd had the head start—he was right on our tail. I nearly killed the engine again as I gunned it around the car that might as well have been parked, it was going so slow. I slipped in front of the blue car I'd just swerved around, and the driver flipped me off angrily.

"What's going on?" Lee muttered, sounding completely dazed. "This isn't happening."

I didn't answer her. I couldn't.

I focused on the traffic, trying to put as many cars between us as I could before we reached the light. I also needed to figure out where I was going. I couldn't lead him to Clyde, but I sure wasn't going to take him to Patrick either.

But I knew nothing of high-speed chases, except what I'd seen in the movies. How on earth was I supposed to lose him?

I managed to put some distance between us by driving like a maniac. I felt like the rush of adrenaline was going to give me a heart attack, but I managed to make it into the left-turn lane without getting so much as a dent on the car. I was forced to stop at the light—three cars were between us and Peter.

Lee had her window completely rolled up by now, and while I waited tensely for the green arrow to flash on so the car in front of us could go, I took a second to slip my seat belt on. I glanced at Lee, to see that she was clutching the door and facing straight ahead, absolutely motionless.

I felt bad for her, but there would be a time for comforting her later. Right now I needed to save us both. I quickly locked my own door before focusing back on her.

I took a deep breath, for some reason remembering something Terence had told me. If the leader is freaking out, the person following would just freak out that much more. And so I tried to be calm when I finally spoke.

"Lee, I need you to stay with me. Do you have your phone?"

"Wha—?" She turned to look at me, her eyebrows scrunched in confusion. At least she wasn't screaming anymore.

"Your phone. Do you have it?"

"Oh. Yeah, sure. I got it."

"Great," I interrupted her slow words easily. "I need you to call Toni."

"Toni? As in, *Toni*, Toni?" Surprise leaked through her otherwise placid tone.

"Yeah. Tell him what's going on."

"Sure. Why *wouldn't* we call Toni?" She reached into her pocket, and the light changed while she hit a couple buttons.

"He's on speed dial?" I asked as I shifted, somewhat surprised.

She nodded, the phone already at her ear.

"Oh. Cool."

I hated making the slow turn across the intersection, but at least I knew Peter was just as trapped. He couldn't gain on me yet.

Suddenly Lee spoke into the phone, sounding almost bored. "Hey, Toni. What's up?"

I switched lanes while he gave her a short answer, and then she chuckled feebly. "Yeah. That sounds like fun. So listen, um, Kate said to call you. We're in the car, being chased by my mom's demonic boyfriend."

I shot her a look. "No! He's not a Demon."

"Oh. My mistake. Kate says he's *not* a demon. But he's obviously possessed, because he jumped on the car. While it was *moving*." She paused. Then, "We just turned left out of the subdivision. We're heading toward Main . . ." She craned her neck around the seat. "He's coming up fast. He's just moving into our lane, and there's only one car between us."

"Ask him what I should do," I cut in.

She relayed my question, then answered hastily. "He says to come to the warehouse. He'll be outside waiting."

I shook my head. "No. I'm not leading the Demons to Patrick."

Lee repeated my words and unconsciously copied Toni's sigh. "He says that doesn't matter. You're going to get yourself killed if you keep driving like this. I happen to agree completely."

"Lee, I need to know how to lose Peter. Ask him."

There was a pause while Toni deliberated, then Lee spoke. "He says you could try getting pulled over. Peter shouldn't stop with a cop around. Also, he wants to know what Peter is, if he's not a Demon."

"I think he's a Seer. He's working for Selena."

Lee relayed everything as calmly as if she understood exactly what was going on. I hoped I hadn't overwhelmed her to the point of insanity. I think she was just in shock.

"Toni says that . . . wait . . ." She turned to me. "He's putting Patrick on. What's Patrick doing with Toni?" She focused back out the window.

The light turned yellow—I had every intention of slipping through. And we would have made it, if the car in front of me hadn't chickened out and slammed on the brakes. I almost hit his bumper. It was so close I felt my entire body break into a sweat. The seat belt kept me from hitting my head against the wheel, but the resulting welt hurt. It reminded me of the car accident. My dad hadn't been able to stop . . .

Lee was listening intently to the words being spoken into her ear. She glanced over at me, and her voice cracked a little when she answered Patrick's question. "We just stopped—really fast. Patrick, what's going on? . . . I don't know." Another worried glance in my direction. "I think she's losing it. She's shaking really bad."

I turned to face her, to assure her and Patrick that I was perfectly fine. From the corner of my eye I recognized the car right behind us. It was Peter. He was opening his door—climbing out of the still running car.

"Oh my *Oreos!*" Lee gasped, noticing Peter coming toward us the same second I did. "He's out of his car!" she yelled frantically into the phone, her earlier calm shattered. "Kate! The back door—!"

I hadn't told the twins to lock their doors. I hadn't thought of them until now.

Lee strained against her seat belt to reach the lock before Peter could open the door . . . too late. Peter slid into the backseat behind me, slamming the door closed. He looked angry—and more than a little winded, as if his heart had been pounding just as rapidly as ours.

Lee and I both cried out and fought against our seat belts. Peter leaned forward and grabbed Lee's hair, pulling her back against the seat.

"Don't even think about it," he hissed, eyes on me. "Don't you dare try getting out of this . . ." He saw the phone pressed against Lee's head. "Who are you talking to? Hang up! Right now!" He tugged on her hair, and Lee offered a yell.

But she didn't close the phone. "Patrick! Help us! *Please!*"

The light changed. The car in front of us rolled forward.

I didn't budge. The cars behind Peter's abandoned one began to honk angrily.

Peter tightened his hold on Lee's hair, and with his free hand he reached into his jacket pocket. He pulled out a small handgun and pressed the barrel against the side of my best friend's head. "Easy, Kate," he growled. "I don't want to hurt either of you, but I swear I will."

It was the longest second of my life. The urge to try and escape, the desire to disobey Peter, the necessity of saving my best friend.

I didn't have a choice. I knew that the second he'd pulled the gun. I stared at it, knowing that he was completely serious and there was only one thing to do.

I gave a daunted nod, surrendering to this man I'd imagined to be a friend.

My compliance gave Lee the courage she needed to close the phone, despite the loud protests I could hear from across the line. Patrick's distant voice was cut off, and our only lifeline was severed.

twenty-one

Patrick O'Donnell
New Mexico, United States

Dying isn't complicated. I'd learned that the first time around. Dying is as easy as falling. Easier than breathing in many ways. The actual act of dying—the seizing of the lungs, the stopping of the heart—is the least complicated thing in the world.

At the same time, it's the hardest thing a person ever has to do. Not the dying part, but the stopping of life part. The end of living. That's where the complications begin. That was where the real pain came in.

Knowing you're going to die is a weird way to live. Because it suddenly seems like there's no point to anything. Your time is fading fast, and there's nothing you can do to stop it. There's no use fighting, working, doing anything. Because it's all meaningless. It will all be over. You'll be gone, and your life will fade from memory—just another fatality in the unstoppable course of time.

Yet, at the same time, nothing had ever been as important as it was now. In these last hours, these final moments of life . . . nothing matters more than making the most of them. It's hard to find a balance. I don't know how I would have survived if I didn't have the perfect anchor, the perfect thing to tie me down and give me purpose in these last days.

Kate.

Without her, I would be completely lost. Unbearably unsure. Hopelessly fighting for something—anything—to cling to.

But as much as her presence in my life was necessary, it was also the most painful torture I suffered. Worse than the headaches, the roiling insides, the endless clenching of my dying muscles. Knowing I would lose her made every other torment I suffered inconsequential. The cold that sunk through my body, the insentient ache in my bones, the heavy throbbing of my heart—what did that matter when I was faced with the knowledge that I had only so much time to hold her hand, so many minutes to kiss her, so many seconds to tell her how completely I loved her . . . ?

The fact that some foreign substance was killing me from the inside out, repeatedly fighting to win by destroying every last part of me, meant nothing when I knew I was going to lose her.

It was unfair. How could I lose her after she'd just agreed to be mine? There was no justice to this fate. No sense in what was happening.

And there was nothing I could do. No matter how long I spent on my knees, crying out for something—anything—it would do no good. No matter how much I needed her, or how much she needed me, there was no way to stop the inevitable. No matter how tightly I held her, I wasn't going to be able to hold on. No matter how much I promised to love her, I couldn't stay with her. No matter how much I struggled, how hard I fought—I was going to lose.

I knew she thought I'd given up. And I had, in a sense. There would be no saving me. No cure, no hope. But I hadn't stopped fighting. Not completely. I was going to stay alive for as long as possible. I wouldn't let death be easy this time. I wasn't going to let death win without an adamant struggle. I would keep my lungs expanding, keep my heart beating, keep my eyes open until the ultimate end. I would be with her until my body gave out, hold her in my arms until it was totally impossible to do so any longer.

This was what I promised death. This was how I would fight. I would love her more in this abbreviated time than any other living thing had ever loved another. Death would have to drag me away from this earth, because I wasn't going willingly.

I knew as Toni and I drove silently back to the warehouse that I wouldn't be returning to school. This had been the day to say my good-byes, since spending time with Kate had become the priority, the reason for my holding on at all. I would force myself onto a new schedule, so I could be resting while she was at school. It would be the best way to ensure we had the most time together.

Toni didn't talk about the inevitable, for which I was grateful. I wasn't ready to say good-bye to my partner and friend. Not yet. He wasn't in his regular joking mood, but I was tired enough that I didn't care.

We got to the warehouse, and I was quick to open my door and shrug into my backpack. I didn't want him getting doors for me or offering to carry my bag. I needed to stay strong, and I think he understood and respected that.

I moved right for my bedroom, asking him to make sure I was up around five thirty.

He assured me that he would, and I shut my bedroom door and sank onto my bed. I pushed my backpack aside and let my head fall into my hands. I focused on my breathing, trying to ignore the crippling numbness in my fingers, the debilitating weakness in my arms. Though I hadn't eaten in days, my stomach still twisted uncomfortably, and the nausea had yet to fade completely. Toni had joked that maybe I should eat something just so I could throw up and feel better, but it didn't seem worth it to me.

I could feel my organs breaking down against the constant assault the virus was inflicting. I knew without Terence's warnings that time was short. It was obvious to my throbbing insides, and especially noticeable when the sharp stab of pain lanced through me, leaving me doubled over and gasping until my body managed to partially heal the newest hole inside of me. These stabbings had started last night, soon after Kate had left. Terence had told me they would start at any time now, but no amount of warnings could have braced me for the all-consuming torture of having your insides burned through; the sensation of having your guts torn apart—no matter how soon your body struggled to repair the damage—was pure agony.

The first time I experienced the piercing laceration, I thought it marked the end—I thought I was dead for sure. Surviving such excruciating anguish was inconceivable. The body was meant to die from this. I was supposed to die. My stomach was ripping, and I fell to my knees, my fingers grinding into the floor as the pain caused me to shake. It hurt so terribly that I wasn't even able to scream—I couldn't breathe. And soon I couldn't even see. But, though I was blinded by pain, I couldn't escape it. Time meant nothing during such suffering, but I know it must have lasted for minutes.

I wasn't even aware that Toni was gripping my shoulders until my regeneration finally kicked in and the unimaginable hurt slowly receded as the damage was painfully healed. But the organs and tissues were bruised after such a penetrating blow, and I knew that the hole would be reopened soon enough, and I'd feel the gut-wrenching, heart-stopping punch again.

Luckily, it hadn't happened again since last night. I waited for it to happen at school, constantly keeping tabs on every twinge of pain, every muscle spasm I felt, just in case I needed to get away from the crowds before the stabbing torture could return and take over.

Kate knew I suffered. But I didn't want her to see this. I didn't want anyone to see this. I hated that Toni had already been forced to witness my agony. I would be as careful as possible to be alone when it happened again. The only problem was, there really wasn't time to prepare. There was no sure warning.

I sat on my bed, the heels of my hands digging into my closed eyes as I fought the wave of hopelessness.

Kate. I needed to concentrate on her face. Her eyes. Her smile. Her touch. Her voice. Her love. It was the only relief available to me, and I groped for it like it was my only chance to survive the pain. Which, admittedly, it was.

After wallowing and clinging to thoughts of Kate for several minutes, I stretched out on the bed.

Now that I was lying here, sleep seemed unattainable. My body ached, and ignoring the heavy numbness pervading every limb was futile. I let my eyes wander the room, searching for something—any-thing—to distract me enough so I could find rest. I needed to sleep so I could be at my best for Kate and her family tonight. It might be the last time I saw the twins, her grandparents . . .

As if my eyes were being guided by some force, I found myself turning to look at my old leather book containing the sketches from my past life.

I hesitated only briefly before reaching for it. Since today was a day for good-byes . . .

I didn't sit up as I held the book and ran my fingers over the worn cover. It smelled of age, and the yellowed pages revealed the passage of time in a way that my skin never had. Slowly, I let my fingertips tuck around the edge, and I lifted the cover.

I was staring into the faded face of my brother. It wasn't a perfect portrayal of him. Far from it. The head was too round, the brow too long . . . but somehow, even though I'd failed at everything else, his smile was just right. More of a smirk, really. He knew some joke that I didn't, and his eyes—perfect copies of my own—shined in anticipa-tion of something. It was really quite horrible, as most drawings go. But it was all I had of him, and I found myself fingering the lines of his face.

When it became too much to stare at his youthful face, I turned the page over, finding my parents. The drawings were far from per-fect. My mother looked too wide, my father's eyes too slanted. But again it was something to hold, to remember . . . Just seeing these imperfect sketches had my heart burning, my memory stimulated and filling in the characteristics my drawings had cheated.

For the first time in over two hundred years, I looked at every page in that book. Many were unfinished. A raggedy, black stray dog, a single wildflower . . . Some I'd declared complete but were far from perfect. Sarah McKenna's smiling face, the landscape in front of our house . . .

I was overwhelming myself with memories, but strangely it didn't tear me up like it usually did. But that was because I was making peace. I was saying good-bye, knowing that soon enough I would leave another life unfinished, and they'd both cease to hurt me once I was gone, because I obviously didn't have heaven to look forward to. I would cease to exist . . .

The page turned—I was in the middle, nearing the end of the used pages—when suddenly an unexpected face was peering up at me.

I knew who it was immediately. There was no mistaking those eyes, that hair, that face . . . I'd traced that hair with my fingers less than an hour ago. I'd committed the curves of that beautiful face to memory, I'd been held captive by those eyes . . .

But though there was no mistaking the identity of this woman, lost in my memories of the past, putting a name to the face was difficult. Because it was absurd.

"Kate?" I breathed, alone in my room, my eyes riveted on the sketch I'd made two centuries ago.

It was her. It was impossible, but it was her. It was Kate.

How? My mind begged for understanding.

I tried to remember where I'd received my inspiration. I never drew anything unless I'd seen it, and even then sketching was still difficult for me . . .

The memory of that day came back incrementally. I was seventeen, thoughts of rebellion and war the furthest things from my mind. I'd dreamed of this face. I'd dreamed of this intriguing girl. She hadn't spoken a word but merely posed for me while I tried to keep the memory of her fresh in my mind. Because somehow capturing her on paper was so important. Vitally important.

I'd sat in one of my favorite thinking places, near the back fence of my family's property. I'd worked endlessly to capture the right emotion, to frame her lips into that perfect smile . . . What had begun as a merely pretty face became the most beautiful thing on earth.

Sean had seen it. He came to find me because . . . Sarah McKenna had come to visit. He was teasing me, and we laughed together. He looked at the sketch . . . he was troubled. He knew her face. He'd seen it.

Surely not in your dreams, he'd said.

But then . . . how?

How did I dream of a woman who wouldn't be born until centuries later? How did Sean recognize the face of the woman I would someday love?

I swallowed hard, unable to tear my eyes from Kate's face. It looked like I had captured her exactly as she was now—eighteen and impossibly beautiful.

Somehow I'd known Kate's face before we'd ever met—before she'd been born.

I groped wildly through my thoughts, trying to discover what had spurred my dream of her in the first place. Had I seen someone that resembled her? That seemed highly improbable. While my father entertained many guests, we lived in a small area, so unknown faces were quite rare. Besides, surely I would have remembered such a captivating young woman. I wouldn't have forgotten her eyes . . .

But if I hadn't seen her, why had I dreamed of her?

The thoughts were too overwhelming to keep to myself. I needed to talk to someone—just so I could work this out aloud.

Toni.

I pushed myself up into a sitting position, keeping my book open as I swung my legs out to the floor . . .

It hit me without warning. I doubled over and my book of drawings slipped through my unresponsive fingers to slap against the hard floor. My arms curled around my gaping stomach, but it didn't relieve the scorching agony.

There was a hole in my body—in a different place than the first one had broken through. The torturous feeling was worse than I'd remembered. My head felt like it would explode from the pain, and

I could swear that my heart actually stopped throbbing inside my chest.

I felt myself falling, but I couldn't catch myself. I crashed against the cement and I felt my forehead split open with a horrible gash. My bared teeth slammed into the concrete next, and it felt like a few might be loosened from the impact. Blood filled my mouth as I bit my tongue roughly all the way through.

But those pains were hardly noticeable compared to the ripping of my stomach. It felt like all my insides were being engulfed by flames, yet the stabbing pain pushed through all other hurts.

Curled there on the floor, rolling onto my back and choking on my blood, I wanted to die. Anything to escape the agony of this slow destruction.

My vision blurred and then went black. I could feel my body trying to repair the internal damage, and I wanted it to stop.

Give up! You can't win! Don't let it kill me again and again . . .

I heard Toni swear at my side, could feel his unyielding fingers forcing my head to the side so the blood from my mouth wouldn't clog my throat and fall to my ruined stomach.

"Patrick!" Toni yelled through the blackness and the fire. "Come on man, fight it! You can't lose yet. What about Kate? Come on!"

Kate . . . Kate would understand. She would understand that I needed to escape this . . .

. . . Kate . . . How had I dreamed of her? What did it mean?

"Patrick!"

I felt my eyes roll, and then suddenly I could see. The convulsions inside my stomach slowly ceased, and I knew that the hole was gone and the bleeding was stopping. I continued to tremble, and the lingering pain sent shock waves through my body, reminding me that it would be back. That I would feel that horrific torment again.

My heart pounded against my chest, another dull ache that hardly registered. My throbbing mouth tingled for a moment, and then my teeth and tongue were perfectly normal again. I felt the broken skin on my forehead sealing up, and at last I could breathe.

I gasped—gagged—then shuddered. My stomach was heaving, but nothing came up. My body had nothing else to give.

The pitiful cry of pain that I'd been unable to let out before escaped now, though it hardly expressed the suffering I'd gone through. It was too mild—it barely ripped my throat on the way out.

Toni's hand was crushing mine. He was on the ground with me, his other hand pressing against my head, keeping me from bashing against anything else while I thrashed. When I was able to lift my eyes to his, I saw a haunted pain there that I'd never seen before.

My body was still being racked with tremors, and my breaths were ragged and gulping. But now that I was conscious of the fact that Toni was genuinely distressed, I tried to rein my shaking in.

My heart gradually slowed, my panting became more level and less forced. My muscles relaxed, simply because they couldn't stand to be wrenched any longer. I stared up at Toni and swallowed hard, knowing that I needed to say something but worried about how hoarse I'd sound.

In the end, my voice just cracked a lot. "I can't feel my fingers," I whispered laboriously.

He released me immediately, afraid that he'd hurt me. I wanted to laugh. As if squeezing a hand too tightly was anything compared to having a hole burned through your body.

"Toni . . . I was—*kidding* . . ."

He blew out his breath, and it shook dangerously. "This is a sick time for you to get a sense of humor, man," he muttered ruefully.

I tried to smile. It was more like the most painful grimace I'd ever produced.

"Can you stand?" Toni asked. "Can I get you anything? You need to get back in bed . . ."

I shook my head, pinching my eyes closed. "The book, Toni . . . Look at the book . . . Kate . . ."

I heard his knees shift on the ground as he looked around, trying to make sense of my words. I heard the leather slide against the floor, get lifted up . . .

"Yeah. She looks great. You've got some talent."

I forced my eyes to open and met his anxious gaze. It was evident he'd given the drawing less than a passing glance.

"I drew that . . ." I stopped to suck in a deep breath.

He nodded quickly, eager to please. "Yeah. You did good. She's stunning, even if her nose is a little too long."

I shook my head impatiently—gasping when my head suddenly stabbed with pain, increasing the throbbing ache. "No," I hissed through gritted teeth. "Toni. I did that in . . ."

His eyes had wandered to the date at the bottom, and his eyebrows shot up. "May 1797. What the . . . ?"

"I dreamed of her." I winced deeply. "Back then, before I died . . . before she was ever born . . ."

"How the heck is that even possible?" he demanded.

"I don't know . . ." My voice trailed off as Toni's phone began to ring in his pocket. He cast me an apologetic look as he dug for his phone, and I rolled to stare up at the ceiling. *Concentrate on breathing . . . try to do it without causing any pain . . .*

Toni glanced at the caller ID and his face brightened a little, which was good. Toni didn't have a face meant for grimness. "Lee, hi," he said right away, and I lost a bit of my interest. Unless Kate was with her, of course . . .

He listened to her quick greeting, and he glanced down at me. "Yeah, not a whole lot right now. Just chilling at the dorm . . ."

His voice trailed off, and I forced myself into a sitting position. He reached out a hand to help me, but I shrugged him off. I could sit up without assistance. For now, anyway.

I could hear the distant hum of Lee's voice, but the words were unclear. I was ready to ignore them completely and go back to staring at the drawing of Kate, when suddenly Toni choked.

My eyes shot to his face, my hands flexing against the ground to steady me. He was completely pale. "What?" he asked, a new edge to his voice.

More talking from Lee—confusion on his face. He broke into

her rush of words. "Whoa, slow down. Where are you guys?"

He listened curtly, his expression darkening an alarming degree with each passing second.

"What is it?" I asked, one arm wrapping insecurely around my aching stomach. "Is it Kate?"

He waved an impatient hand at me, and I obediently shut up so he could concentrate on what Lee was saying. "Wait—how close is he?"

I was losing patience fast. I stared at him, as if desire alone could make me hear what he was hearing. *Kate . . .*

I didn't know what he knew, but that look on his face . . . that was the Guardian look. That determination and dedication only surfaced when a Seer or human was in danger—or both. Suddenly the drawing of Kate in my sketchbook wasn't important. My pain wasn't important. Only one thing mattered right now.

"Lee, what the heck . . ." he hesitated, then spit the words out to me quickly, while Lee was distracted. "I'm not sure of the threat yet, but they're in a freaking high-speed chase with her mother's boyfriend. He's right behind them."

"He's a Demon?" I asked in confusion, mentally forcing my pain away. Kate needed me. I might be dying, but I was still her Guardian.

"No, Kate said he's not but . . ." His voice fell and his eyes dropped. He was listening to Lee.

"Put it on speaker!" I hissed.

"Tell Kate to come to the warehouse," he told her, completely ignoring my request. "I'll be outside waiting."

A quick exchange happened on the other side of the line, and Toni rolled his eyes. "Oh for the love of—look, Patrick will be perfectly safe, I swear. She's not going to put us in danger. But Kate's not a freaking professional—she's going to get you guys killed if you keep this up."

"Toni," I fairly growled.

"You could try getting pulled over by the cops, for speeding or something. I saw that in a movie once. This loser won't stop with a cop there, especially if he's not a Demon. You could try that. Oh, and ask her what he is if he isn't a freaking Demon." The tense words were dripping from his lips, making the air in the room seem tighter.

Lee relayed Toni's words, and I silently fumed, my fingers itching to snatch the phone away but unwilling to keep Toni from learning something important.

Lee said something, and Toni's mouth fell open. "Is she serious? How did . . . never mind." His eyes bored into mine. "Kate thinks he's a Seer—for Selena."

I felt like I'd been punched in the gut, which was a lot more painful after having my insides burned only minutes before. I could easily imagine Kate in her car, driving too fast, breathing too quickly, chased by someone who worked for Selena. I guess I hadn't thought too much about the evil Demon because I'd been so focused on Kate and my own imminent death. I'd briefly thought about Far Darrig and what would happen to Kate when I was gone, but . . .

This was happening while I was *still here*. Only I couldn't do anything because I was here and she was somewhere else.

"All right, tell Kate that she needs to get to the warehouse— forget about losing him. We'll be ready for you guys . . ." I didn't realize his words were dying off because of the look on my face, until he told Lee he was putting me on. Then he handed me the phone.

I looked at it for a terse second, that small device my only connection to Kate when she needed me so badly. I took a steadying breath, hoping that I could sound strong for Lee's sake, then I put the phone to my ear.

"Lee, I need you guys to stay calm. I know you're probably really confused right now . . ." my words faded when I heard the sudden screech of brakes, Lee's sharp gasp.

My heart stopped beating. "Lee? What's going on? What happened?"

She was breathing heavily. "We just stopped—really fast. Patrick, what's going on?"

"Lee, there's no time to explain right now." I swallowed very hard. "Is Kate all right?"

"I don't know. I think she's losing it. She's shaking really bad . . ."

I closed my eyes tightly—trying not to picture it. But Kate's fearful face was all I could see. I hadn't known that there was a pain worse than anything I'd felt so far, but here I was, experiencing it. I was completely helpless.

Toni was suddenly standing, and he shot a hasty explanation as he fled from the room. "I'm gonna get the keys."

I gave him a nod, flinching when the pain in my head exploded once more. "Lee, I need you to keep her calm. She needs to concentrate on driving—"

"Oh my *Oreos!*" Lee gasped suddenly, breaking through my words. "He's getting out of his car!" she screamed to me, as if somehow I could do something to stop this from happening. All I could do was feel like throwing up.

And then suddenly she wasn't talking to me anymore. "Kate! The back door—!" I heard Lee's voice strain—heard a door open, then slam closed. I heard screams—Kate's was further from me but was definitely the clearest.

My face crumpled at the same time my body surged with adrenaline. I'd never felt so defeated and yet so suddenly energized.

Lee's cry grew sharper in pain, and I yelled her name through my torn throat. She didn't respond.

I heard a deep voice, a darker voice, but I could only make out a couple scattered words. "Don't . . . Dare . . . Try . . ." A slight pause. And then he must have raised his voice and leaned closer, because now every word was clear. "Who are you talking to? Hang up! Right now!"

"Lee, don't hang up!" I cried out at the same time she did. He was hurting her. This man that Kate had assured me was fine and good . . .

"Patrick!" Lee yelled desperately. "Help us! *Please!*"

Lee's gasps suddenly got very quiet, and I heard the man's

threatening voice again, and his words chilled me to the bone. "Easy, Kate. I don't want to hurt either of you, but I swear I will."

I only grew more desperate when I heard them stop screaming. "Lee, where are you? Give me something—a street sign, anything! Lee? Lee!" I heard the engine idling, could almost hear Kate silently give in to his demands.

I knew Lee was going to close the phone the second before she buckled under his threats. "Lee, please! Give me something! Kate!" I screamed.

The pain in that single word brought Toni rushing back inside, knife in hand.

And then there was nothing. The line was dead.

I felt completely empty. I couldn't make myself close the phone. I couldn't make myself breathe.

"Patrick?" Toni asked, apprehensively watching my face.

My words were hollow. "He's in the car with them. They stopped at a light . . . the back door was unlocked . . . Lee hung up. He was hurting them."

Toni's eyes narrowed, and he stepped closer, stooping to snatch the phone away from me. "Are you coming with me or not?" he asked tensely.

I couldn't focus on anything. I felt like I was drowning. "She wouldn't tell me where they are. I don't know the first place to look . . ."

"Well, I know where they were two minutes ago—heading toward Main, just outside the subdivision."

My eyes went to his, and life returned to my body.

He gave me a grim smile. "You up to this?"

I didn't even bother to answer.

twenty-two

Kate Bennett
New Mexico, United States

Peter Keegan didn't seem to care about our fear, or the fact that people were honking all around us. The light was still green, and I knew that we needed to move soon, or else someone might actually notice there was a guy in our backseat holding a weapon on us. The traffic beside us was moving, so I knew we couldn't expect help from any of them. And with Peter's car behind us, shielding us from view . . . We were on a busy street, completely alone.

He kept the gun trained on Lee, and his voice was horribly businesslike. He sounded nothing like a sixth-grade teacher or the guy who'd spent last Saturday with us at a soccer tournament. "Lee, get Kate's phone. And then you're coming with me. Now!" he snapped, when Lee didn't move right away.

Trembling, she took off her seat belt and leaned toward me. She reached in my tight pocket, gripping my cell phone with shaking fingers.

He shifted the gun to me, and I felt the cold metal press against my head. "Wait for the light to change again. You'll keep driving alone. Turn right at the next street, and let me pass you. You'll follow me exactly, or I'm going to have to do something we'll all regret. Understand?"

I nodded, but the motion was jerky. Having a gun pressed to my head made it hard to keep strong for Lee. My overwhelming fear had to be abundantly evident.

Peter tucked the gun in his jacket, but we were smart enough to realize that wouldn't save us if we tried to run. He'd just draw it again.

Lee and I shared a look, and then Peter ordered her to get out of the car. She followed his commands quickly but carefully. No erratic movements.

Peter exited the car behind me, and I was suddenly alone.

The light was still burning green, but I didn't roll forward. I was going to wait for the next change of the light, because that's what would keep Lee safe from that maniac.

I watched them in the rearview mirror. Peter looked very non-threatening out there as he waved to the people behind him, apologizing without words for the delay. Lee looked a little unsteady, but she climbed in the passenger's side without hesitation.

Her aura was terrified, confused.

Peter's aura was the most complex and confusing I'd ever seen. Did he do that on purpose?

The light turned yellow, then red.

I was seeing red.

This couldn't be happening. I needed to get to Clyde. I needed to find a cure for Patrick. Lee and I weren't supposed to be kidnapped.

Patrick . . .

The light changed back to green, and I obediently crossed the intersection. Peter followed directly behind me, shifting through the traffic to reach the right lane in time. I made the appropriate turn, glancing in the mirror repeatedly, trying to keep an eye on Lee.

I let him pass me. Then I followed him as he led us away from the busier streets, toward more residential areas. Within ten minutes we were pulling into a quiet park. Peter shut off his car, and I did the same. I'd parked on the passenger side so I was closest to Lee. She wasn't looking at me, so I couldn't read her expression. But her aura was the same mix of fear and pain as it had been the last time I'd seen her. I tried to be grateful that we were both still alive, but who knew how long that would last?

I unbuckled my seat belt but stayed in the car, waiting for further commands. I could see Peter getting out of his Mini Cooper, and he strolled around both our hoods. Lee stayed in his car, completely motionless.

He opened my passenger door and climbed inside. The gun was held at his waist, leveled at my stomach.

He stared at me for a terse moment, then shook his head fiercely. His aura was a confused jumble, but I was a little surprised to see so much green uneasiness. "Why'd you have to make this complicated?" he demanded roughly.

I blinked, disbelieving. *Seriously?* The disbelief mixed with my desperation, and somehow that combination pushed my fear down enough that I was able to find my voice. "I'm not the one holding the gun, so don't talk to me about complicating things."

His aura pulsed angrily. "You shouldn't have run away."

A part of me wondered if I'd lost my mind, but that didn't stop me from snapping back at him. "You work for Selena, for the Demons. You might as well be a Demon." The slight quiver following after my sharp words the only indication of my fear.

"Shut up!" he growled furiously. "You don't know anything!"

I swallowed hard, my unexpected surge of bravery gone in an instant.

I watched his eyes flicker to my aura, interpreting the change in my emotions. His own aura was seething as he stared at me. The sudden quiet in the car pounded in my ears, along with my heart.

He glanced out the windshield, and that's when I realized he was scrambling for something to say. I kept my mouth shut and just watched him struggle to find his voice. Again—like the green uneasiness in his aura—I found it odd that a man who'd just chased down two girls would be at a loss for words.

Finally, he spoke. "This isn't how I wanted this to happen." His words sounded almost like an apology, but the gun was still pointed at me, so I didn't really feel like pitying him. "But you didn't give me a choice, Kate." He turned back to me, and I tried to keep my eyes steady.

His voice was firm, unyielding. "You saw Selena's call. You answered it. What did she say?"

"So the ice water worked? Great." My courage hadn't all fled, apparently.

His jaw flexed in sudden fury. "Kate, you don't understand. I'm not one of them."

"One of Selena's dogs, you mean? Yeah, right. I'm not stupid, Peter."

His eyes were almost slits. "You don't understand *anything*. Not all of us were as lucky as you. Some of us didn't have the alternative."

"What are you talking about?"

"I don't want to do this!" he burst out. "But I don't have a choice. I have to, or she's going to kill me. And Jeanette, and Lee."

That got my attention. "Selena is going to kill Lee and her mom?"

His eyes pinched closed, and he blew out a powerful breath. "I don't have a choice," he repeated dully. The words came pouring out quickly now, and I tried to absorb every detail, any way to better understand what was going on. "If it weren't for Selena, I wouldn't be in this situation. I never got a Guardian, like you did. I've been a Seer for over a year, and yours was the first Guardian I've ever met. All I had was Selena."

Over a year? Had Selena really planted Peter into Jeanette's life— Lee's life—so long ago? Why? I hadn't even been a Seer at that point! It didn't make sense.

"Did Selena tell you to date Jeanette to get close to me?" I asked point-blank.

He glanced at me, unsure. But his aura was creeping with new colors—colors that revealed just how desperate he was. But not desperate to kill me, I realized. No, he was desperate for me to understand his actions. "No," he whispered. "I met Jeanette on my own. I fell in love with her . . . It wasn't until a few weeks ago that Selena found out who she was to you—who Lee was. She arranged every-thing, forced me to move out here, so I could get to you. She ordered me to move here, to start teaching your sisters."

"You're not even a teacher?" For some reason, that really both-ered me.

He rolled his eyes at my outraged tone. "Of course I am. I used to teach high school. But with a little Demon help, school districts don't ask a lot of questions."

"You expect me to believe that you actually care about Lee's mom?" I asked, incredulous.

"Yes." The truth in his aura was undeniable. The sudden burst of yellow and blue were undertones of that conviction. "And that's why I have to listen to Selena. If I don't . . . she's going to come after Jeanette and Lee."

I let that sink in, and suddenly the air was a lot heavier. Even without his aura, I knew from his eyes that he was telling the truth. He was being completely honest with me in this moment. He really didn't want to be doing this.

"Why? Why are you following Selena's orders? How does she have any hold on you?"

"Selena made me," he said simply.

"Made you do this?" I asked, confused.

"No. Well, yes . . . But she made me. Turned me into a Seer." He must have seen my incomprehension. He sighed deeply. "I was sailing with some friends, just over a year ago. A terrible storm came up out of nowhere. We were experienced sailors, but the lines ripped during the storm, and we overturned. I nearly died, Kate. All of us did. And then Selena was there, with some of her Demon friends. She saved us, pulled us from the water." He shook his handsome face, a snort punctuating the air. "She rigged the whole accident, of course. She wanted us to nearly die. She wanted us to be like this."

I could feel the horror on my face. "You mean . . . she intention-ally turned you into a Seer?"

He nodded once, and the gun quavered at his side. "She took us to a prison, locked us in cells. She explained our new world to us, and then she promised to kill us if we ever disobeyed her."

"You and your friends—you work for her?" I was still trying to grasp the fact that the Demons had created their own Seers. Maybe they were sick of fighting over the regular rabble, sick of dealing with the Guardians. It was a disturbing thought.

He laughed mirthlessly at my halted question. "Don't sound so accusing. I didn't have a couple Guardians looking out for me. It was help Selena or be killed. Devin—he learned that the hard way. Only three of us are left now. We have no other choice."

"That's not true. Of course you have a choice. All you had to do was find a Guardian, tell them what you've been through—"

"And have Selena come hunt us down?" He shook his head. "No. I can live without that experience."

"So you'd rather be her puppet?" I questioned stiffly. "Demons *kill* people."

"Yeah. I know." We both looked down at the gun directed at me. It was as steady as a rock.

I glanced out my window, saw that Lee was staring through her window at me. Her face was a calm mask, but her aura was terrified.

I pulled in a steadying breath and looked back to Peter, who was scowling out the front window. "What are you supposed to do?" I asked softly. "What are you going to do to me? To Lee?"

He avoided my questions. "What did Selena say on the phone?"

I decided resisting wouldn't do any good. "Not much. She was wondering if you'd done *it* yet."

Surprising me, he rolled his eyes in exasperation. "That woman needs to get a life . . ."

"What did she mean?" I dared ask. I was feeling a lot less threatened somehow. Maybe because I now understood where he was coming from—the terror he'd been living with, and the realization that he was trying to protect Lee and her mom. The gun seemed less like a threat and more like a formality. Neither of us wanted it there, but for the safety of those we loved, it needed to stay in place.

Peter sighed and then tried to explain. "She wanted me to corner you. I've been meaning to do it for days, but . . . I lost my nerve every time. I don't want to be this person, Kate. But I don't have another choice. Selena will kill us all."

"Peter, we can protect you. I promise."

"Like you protected your family? No offense, Kate, but Selena told me everything. She got your sisters easily enough. I'm not letting Jeanette and Lee get dragged into this."

"You've sort of already done that. You pulled a gun on her," I reminded him bluntly.

He sighed again, more heavily this time. "I know. But I couldn't let you get away—or get hurt. You were driving like an idiot."

"More like driving to avoid the idiot chasing me."

He smiled just a little, and I truly felt bad for him in that moment, despite everything he'd just put me and Lee through. "I've made a mess of things," he whispered, almost to himself. "Lee thinks I'm insane now, and when your Guardians find out what I've done . . . I'm a dead man either way."

I tried to distract him from thoughts of death and Selena's dreaded revenge, and help him toward making a decision—letting us go. "So you were supposed to corner me. Then what?"

"Pass along a message."

"Which is?"

He hesitated, but not for long. "'You have my number. Call me when you run out of ideas.'"

I blinked, shocked by the simplicity of the anticlimactic message. "She threatened all our lives, just for that? What sort of . . . ?" My words died as the full impact of her words hit me abruptly.

Patrick. She knew about Patrick. There was no other explanation. She knew that he was sick. Had she planned all of that too? Had she purposefully planted an infected Guardian in the area, knowing that Patrick would try to help him? It was the sickest thing I'd ever heard. Mostly because it had worked so effectively.

But how had she known he would contract the virus? Terence had made it clear that most Guardians seemed immune . . .

And then her message was suddenly so clear, and nothing else mattered.

She had the cure.

Of course she did. That was the whole point, after all. The Demons wanted me, and now they had the most tempting bait. They'd lure me in with the promise of saving Patrick's life. It was a perfect plan. A horribly perfect plan. Because just as she'd known that Patrick would go after the sick Guardian, she knew that I would do anything to keep him alive. Meeting with Clyde was no longer a priority. Not when Toni and I could work out a more definite course of action.

Peter was speaking, unconscious of the fact that I was undergoing one of the most overwhelming moments of my day so far—worse than being kidnapped by him was the knowledge that Selena had complete control of the situation. "I know—dumb. And message delivered. I'm supposed to threaten you into silence, so your friends and family don't find out. But obviously *that* cat's out of the bag. Your Guardians are probably searching for you already."

I nodded distractedly, forcing thoughts of what exactly Selena would want from me, aside from my freedom. What the Demon Lord could possibly want me for. "Yes," I answered his half-question distractedly. "And you need to let me call them."

"Kate, I can't let them find me. I have to stay here and do whatever Selena wants—or else Jeanette and Lee . . . I can't let your Guardians kill me or stop me from following Selena's every order."

"But I *can* protect you from her," I protested, trying to keep the impatience out of my voice. "In a way, we're all after the same thing—keeping people safe."

He shook his head. "I need to help her. Please, try to understand."

I glanced down at the gun he held and then spoke mildly. "So what now? You hold me at gunpoint the rest of our lives? How does that help anyone?"

His eyes became earnest. "I want a compromise. If you're willing."

What choice did I really have? I needed to get Lee out of this mess, and I needed to talk to Patrick and Toni. They needed to know that Selena held the cure for the virus.

"What are your terms?" I asked.

He looked relieved, and his words were rushed. "I want you to call your Guardians off. They can't touch me. I also want you—and them—to keep from interfering with any of my future orders."

I shook my head. "I can't just let you work for Selena. She's trying to hurt everyone I care about."

"Those are my terms. Agree to them, and I'll let you go." I knew he didn't want to draw these ultimatums—but I could sort of see his point too. He was just doing what he thought he had to do to keep the people he loved from getting hurt. I could understand that, even if I wished he could see my side.

"I won't stop you from helping Selena," I finally agreed. Before he could thank me, I continued firmly. "But I *will* try to keep her plans from succeeding."

He blew out his breath. "That seems like a bit of a gray area, but . . . I can live with it for now."

I held out my hand. "Give me a phone. I'll negotiate your terms with my Guardians."

A heartbeat later Peter was reaching into his pocket, drawing out my phone. He handed it to me, almost eagerly. "Don't tell them where we are," he warned as an afterthought. "Not until they agree to the terms."

I offered a quick nod and then took the phone. I thought about calling Toni, but then I realized I wouldn't be sparing Patrick from anything because he'd been the last one to talk to Lee. He probably wasn't taking a nap anymore.

I glanced out my window at Lee while the phone began to ring, and our eyes met briefly. She was obviously freaking out, but she was shockingly in control. At least on the outside. Her calm was enviable, and I don't think there was any way I would have been that confident looking if our places had been swapped. I offered her a timid smile, trying to reassure her that everything was going to be fine.

I think I heard Peter sigh regretfully at my side, but I didn't comment on it because Patrick was answering.

"Kate?" he gasped, his voice cracking.

"Patrick, it's all right," I soothed quickly, wincing sympathetically when I heard how terrified he sounded. "I'm all right, I promise."

"I heard you scream." His desperate voice broke on the last word.

"I'm fine. We both are."

"Where are you?" he demanded.

I hesitated, casting a quick glance to Peter's tense face. "He doesn't want me to tell you that yet."

There was a slight pause—the thrum of the engine the only sound coming from the other side of the phone—and then his voice was dangerously narrow, barely controlled. "I'm going to kill him. I swear I'm going to kill him . . ."

"Patrick, please calm down. You're going to make yourself sick."

"Nothing could make me feel worse than I do now," he assured me darkly. "Kate, I need you to give me something. A hint. Anything to help us find you."

"I can't do that."

"Why?" I heard him struggle to swallow. "He's threatening you." A statement of fact—no hint of question. "What has he done? Is Lee all right?"

"He wants to negotiate a compromise. A truce."

"What sort of truce?" He seethed impatiently, upset that I wasn't cooperating with him. Or maybe he was just infuriated that we had to have this conversation at all.

"I can tell you our location if you agree not to hurt him."

"I can't promise that," Patrick nearly growled. I could hear the pain he was trying to mask, and I knew that his condition had somehow worsened since I'd last seen him—a mere half hour ago. My stomach clenched in awful panic, and I wondered how long he had left. A day? Maybe two?

"Please," I whispered, hoping that the softness of my voice would somehow calm his pain and fury. "This isn't what it looks like. Peter was only doing what he had to do—to keep Lee and her mom safe. He's working for Selena, but only because he's being blackmailed."

"He took you away from me. No excuses can save him."

"Patrick, I know this sounds crazy, but . . . I won't let you hurt him."

I could feel Peter Keegan's shocked eyes on my face, knew that Patrick was probably sporting a similar expression, so I hurried to explain myself to the both of them. "He's already put himself in danger for Lee and her mom. He doesn't want to hurt me—he's just trying to protect the ones he loves. Is that so hard to understand?"

There was a long silence, then, "What are his terms?"

I sent Peter a fast look, daring him to argue my next words. "Just promise you won't hurt him. We can discuss the rest when you get here. He can explain things to you as long as you give him the chance."

"Kate . . ." I imagined him looking to Toni, desperate for some way around this impossible oath he knew he had to make. "I . . . I promise. I won't hurt him."

I gave Peter a nod, and he nervously dipped his head, allowing me to continue. "We're at Johnson's Park. Do you know where that is?"

His voice was curt. "We can find it."

"We're parked on the east side." I hesitated, knowing that he wouldn't want to hear what I was going to say next. "Patrick, I'm going to have to hang up."

"What? No. I need you to stay with me."

"Lee needs me right now. She's completely confused. Please, try to understand."

There was a long, icy silence. But when he finally spoke he seemed to be in control. "You're right. Of course. Just . . . just promise me that you'll be okay."

"Honestly, Patrick, I'm fine. He's not going to hurt us."

"I'll be there soon."

"I love you."

He swallowed. "I love you."

I pursed my lips, murmured a last good-bye, and then ended the call. I handed the phone back toward Peter, but he waved his free hand. "Keep it."

I nodded my thanks and slipped it into my pocket. I took a deep breath, then faced him fully. "You need to let me talk to Lee."

He shook his head, almost to himself. "I didn't want her to know about any of this. Demons, Seers . . . I didn't want her to know any of it."

"Well, you either let me explain things to her, or she's going to press charges. You know that. If you really want to stay here and protect them, Lee needs to understand what's going on. Or else she's going to tell her mom all of this, and you'll be lucky if you don't get arrested."

"I know," he whispered. "I just . . . I don't want her to be afraid of me."

"It's a little late for that," I told him, feeling slightly sorry for him but keeping my voice firm. "Let me go to her."

He considered for just a moment, then he surrendered with a nod. "Just stay where I can see you."

I opened the car door, glanced back at the gun, then stepped carefully outside. Lee watched me as I closed my door and reached to open hers. Once I was holding it, she threw a look over my shoulder, toward Peter.

"What's going on?" she asked lowly. "What's he doing?"

I laid my hand on her nearest arm, squeezing gently. "It's okay. He's not going to hurt us."

She grunted, still not looking at me. "Good. I mean, now that *that's* all cleared up, I'll just go buy him a thank-you card."

"Lee." The confidence in my voice finally caused her to move her stunned eyes to my face. My heart constricted a little, knowing that I'd put her through too much. "Lee, it's going to be okay. Patrick and Toni are on their way. You'll be home soon. I promise, everything's going to be fine."

"We were kidnapped, Kate. He had a gun—he pointed it at us. What does he want from us?"

"It's kind of complicated."

"You saw his aura. How did you miss his psychotic edge?"

I took a steadying breath, and then reached for her hand. "Walk with me. There's something I've been meaning to tell you . . ."

twenty-three

Lee's aura was pretty wild. Almost every emotion possible to feel, she *was* feeling. But despite my fears about how she'd react to my secrets, I was just relieved to finally be telling her everything.

And I told her everything. It was a rush of words, but once they were out I felt much better. I told her about Toni being the invisible man that had been haunting me in the beginning, told her about the Demons who had been after me; all about Patrick, Guardians, and Seers . . . She listened without speaking, her eyes occasionally widening. Like when she learned my grandpa used to fight Demons. Or when she learned that Toni was immortal.

"So . . . he's not a freshman in college?" Lee said, opening her mouth at last.

I smiled just a little. "Not even."

We were sitting on a strip of grass, under a large tree. I knew that Peter was watching us from the inside of my car, but we were far enough that I felt alone with Lee.

As my explanation came to an end, I saw Lee's aura lose a large portion of the fear and anxiety that had been plaguing her. Her tense shoulders were relaxed. Her eyes weren't as guarded.

I took a deep breath. "And that's pretty much everything. That's why Patrick and Toni were here in the first place—to help me. To protect me."

Lee shook her head slowly, her eyes on the ground. "Wow. I mean . . . wow."

"It's a lot to take in."

"And then some." She glanced up at me. "Why didn't you tell me this? We're best friends, Kate. Why would you keep something like this from me?"

I'd known this question would come. It was one of the reasons I'd worried about telling her everything in the first place. But now that she'd asked it, I had an answer for her.

"I didn't tell you because you *are* my best friend. I know that sounds messed up, but . . . Lee, I needed to keep some part of my life normal. And I entrusted that to you. Because you're one of the only constant, real things in my crazy life. I know I wasn't being fair to you, but . . ." The right words were suddenly lost to me, but I didn't need to continue. Lee was reaching for my hand, gripping my fingers.

"It's okay. I understand. Yeah, I feel a little left out. But friends do what they have to do—be what they have to be. And I'm glad that you knew I would be this for you."

I smiled gratefully. "Thank you. You're the best."

"I know, right?"

We hugged quickly, and when I pulled back Lee blew out her breath and slapped her hands on her knees. "Right. So what now?"

"It's tough to say . . ." I hesitated but knew the words had to be said. "You're going to have to keep all of this a secret."

Her head dipped easily. "Of course. I'm not going to tell anyone about Patrick and Toni. Why would I?"

"No. Not that. I mean, yes, no one else should know about them. But . . . I meant Peter. About everything he did today. You can't tell your mom."

Her aura darkened, and her expression was quick to match. "Kate. The psycho kidnapped us at gunpoint. There's no way I'm not telling my mom to dump him."

"Lee, he's done all this to protect you."

"He's one of the bad guys. Tell me you wouldn't complain about being stuck with him."

"He's not a bad guy, he's just . . . giving in to their demands." I wondered if these words would soon be spoken of me. Would I be Selena's puppet if it meant saving Patrick?

Lee interrupted my thoughts. "Yeah. And as touching as that is, I still don't want him around my mom."

"I can understand that. I just . . . If he doesn't follow Selena's orders, you and your mom are going to be targets."

"So share some of your Guardians with us."

"It's not that simple. Patrick . . . he's not exactly at his best right now."

Her brow furrowed, and I watched as she mentally connected the dots. His sickness, which had seemed so normal, but now after learning that he was immortal . . . "What's wrong with him?" she finally asked quietly.

I bit my lower lip but forced myself to stay detached and clinical. "He's sick. It's a virus the Demons have made, and somehow it manages to kill Guardians."

"Is Toni . . . ?"

"No. He seems immune. Most Guardians are, apparently."

"Patrick is dying?"

I swallowed hard, my voice a mere whisper. "Yes."

Lee reached for my hand once more, holding it tightly. Her eyes bored into mine, and I could see the sympathy in her face and her aura. "I'm so sorry, Kate. Is there anything we can do?"

I didn't answer right away, and in that slight pause she knew that there wasn't much hope. Before I had to see the pity register on her face, I spoke smoothly. "I'm not giving up."

Lee smiled quietly, and I was grateful for her understanding of what I needed. I guess it was just more evidence that one didn't need to see a person's aura to know what they were feeling—one just needed to pay attention.

We shared a quiet moment together, and I was glad for the

chance to contemplate my new plans. Now that I knew Selena had the cure—something I should have considered before, I guess—I knew that going to Clyde would no longer be necessary. I wouldn't have to track a rumor anymore. I could go right to the source. I don't know if that realization was frightening or just a major relief. I think it was a mixture of both.

I heard Lee take in a breath, prepare to speak, but the sound of a fast-moving car tore toward us, and we both twisted to look toward the small empty street.

A midnight-blue Altima came screaming around a nearby corner, sliding past the last couple houses and toward the line of parking spots. By the time I was coming to my feet, the new car was skidding in next to my car, where Peter was just opening the door—his aura a new blend of fear and apprehension.

The blue car jerked to a stop, the engine dying a split second after. Patrick was in the passenger seat, and his door was the first to be thrown open. He pushed out of the car, gripping the door tightly as his eyes scanned sharply around the park before falling on me. Instead of relaxing when he saw me, his shoulders abruptly stiffened. He slammed the door shut before walking briskly toward me, not even sparing a glance at Peter Keegan. Maybe he was worried that if he saw the Seer, then he wouldn't be able to keep his promise.

Lee was standing beside me now, but I was already moving, rushing to reach Patrick before he had to walk any further.

Though I was focused on his drawn face, I could see what was happening over his shoulder. Peter was standing next to my car now, the passenger door closed, stepping toward the back so he would be out of Toni's way. As soon as he was no longer blocking the driver's door, Toni forced it open and stood, turning to face Peter exclusively.

It wasn't until Toni was slamming him against the side of my car that I realized he wasn't going to honor the promise not to hurt the Demon Seer. Peter Keegan cried out in fear and pain, and Toni harshly twisted the gun out of his hand and jabbed it against the Seer's forehead. Toni was holding the gun sideways, and he looked like he seriously knew what he was doing. I hadn't expected that because I'd only seen him deal with knives. This seemed a lot worse, and I was sure he was going to pull the trigger any second.

"Toni, stop!" I burst out. I changed my direction thoughtlessly, intent on interfering, but before I'd taken two steps Patrick had reached me, and with a single arm he snagged me, dragging me back to his chest with surprising force.

"Kate." He crushed my back to him, keeping me firmly away from the gun. "It's okay. We're here now."

"No, you don't understand—I was telling the truth. I can't let you hurt him!" The last I yelled toward Toni, not that he was looking at me. "Toni! You promised!"

He didn't look up, but his voice projected well. "Nope, I sure didn't. Patrick did that all by himself."

"Toni, stop it!"

We all looked to Lee, who was coming up behind me and Patrick. She was glaring at Peter, but her words continued to be directed to his captor. "If Kate has a reason to keep him alive, I think we should listen to her. She's the All-Seeing One, right?"

She glanced to me, and I gave her a thankful look. She continued to walk toward Toni, but Patrick was holding me too tightly for me to follow after her. I twisted in the tense cage of his arms and stared up at his tight and colorless face.

"Patrick," I said. "It's okay. I'm all right."

"No. Nothing about this is all right."

I released my breath slowly and continued patiently—as if explaining something to a stubborn child. "I'm so sorry that you had to go through this. But it's over now. No harm done."

"Did he point that gun at you?" My silence was answer enough. He growled deep in his throat, and then—arms still surrounding me—we walked over to join the others.

Lee was standing near Toni and Peter, hesitating between the two hoods of our cars. We came up behind her, stopping on the side-walk. Toni was still pushing the barrel of the gun to Peter's head, and the school teacher was wincing in pain.

"Toni." I sighed, giving up on the forceful approach. "Does he look like that much of a threat?"

"If you'll recall," Toni said seriously, gazing firmly into Peter's fearful eyes, "you misread him once before."

"It's all right, Kate," Peter said quietly, unable to look away from the menacing Guardian before him. "There aren't any bullets in the gun."

Toni pulled the trigger, just to be sure.

"Toni!" I yelled. "What if he'd been lying?"

Toni just shrugged. "Would have taught him a good lesson about the benefits of honesty, I guess." He focused back on Peter. "I thought it was too light. Then I just thought you were a wimp—barely brave enough to take on two girls. Well, you picked on the wrong ones, pal—"

"Would you guys please just listen to him?" I begged. "Toni, let go of him already!"

Lee sighed and walked forward. She reached Toni and laid a hand on his arm. He stole a fast look at her, and she spoke calmly. "A guardian angel, huh? I knew there was something off about you."

He stared at her—adjusting to the fact that she knew every-thing—and then he sent me a mean look. "Seriously, Kate. Guardian angel? Real cute and mature."

I shrugged. "Don't look at me. I didn't say anything."

"Every stinking time," he muttered, rounding back on Peter. He let out his breath and then shoved Peter harshly back against the car before releasing him in disgust. He grabbed the barrel of the gun and pointed the handle back to the Demon Seer, returning the useless weapon. But he didn't step back. I guess he wanted to maintain a threatening presence.

It was working.

Peter fumbled to replace the gun into his brown jacket pocket, and then he looked to me for help to explain this mess.

Patrick's arms tightened around me, and I could feel his heart pounding through my back. It shouldn't be working that hard, should it? I didn't let myself dwell on his growing weakness—that could be addressed in a minute, after I was sure Peter would be safe.

"Peter isn't the enemy you think he is," I told them all. "Yes, he works for Selena. But not by choice. He's just trying to protect Lee and her mom from the Demons."

"I think we can take over the job," Toni grunted, narrowed eyes slicing into Peter, who flinched.

But he didn't back down. "I know you have every reason to distrust me, but Kate is telling the truth. I'm only here to keep them from getting hurt."

"But you're hurting Kate's family," Lee said, before either of my Guardians could speak. "And who knows who else. This woman you're working for—she kidnapped Jenna and Josie. I may not know all the details, but I know that helping that creep isn't protecting me and my mom. The twins are like sisters to me. You're not going to hurt them again."

"I don't want to. I wouldn't touch those girls."

"But you'd hurt Kate?" Patrick spoke at last, his voice barely controlled.

Peter shook his head quickly. "No. I couldn't do that. At first I thought I could, but . . ."

"Then you met us?" Toni said darkly.

Peter swallowed nervously. "No. I met Kate. Seeing how happy another Seer could be . . . it's given me hope."

"So we're supposed to feel sorry for you?" Toni asked sarcastically.

"No. But let me have a chance to change things."

"You'll stop working for Selena?" Patrick asked bluntly. Peter hesitated, and Patrick continued quickly. "No deal. Not if you're working for Demons."

"Selena has a message for me," I said suddenly.

That got everyone's attention. Patrick released me, only to wrap his taut fingers around my arms and twist me to face him. Wordlessly he waited for me to share the message, and the tension around us built until I finally spoke. I knew everyone was listening to me, but I directed my words to Patrick—the only person that mattered to me in this one moment.

"She has the cure, Patrick. She can save you."

He stared at me, and through his wide, clear eyes I could see the wheels in his mind turning, fighting to understand every implication my words gave birth to.

He suddenly looked grayer, felt a lot stiffer.

I couldn't blame him. I was feeling pretty much the same.

We finally reached an unsteady compromise. It was getting late, and we had to get ready for Jenna's piano recital. Toni stopped man-handling Peter Keegan, and Patrick stopped glaring at him. Actually, Patrick stopped doing a lot of things. He wasn't really looking at anyone now, and he'd released me so I could give Lee a good-bye hug.

Toni was going to take her home in the Altima, since my best friend seemed to have a few questions she was hoping to get answers to.

I was a little put out that no one else had gotten excited about Selena's revelation. Toni had been my strongest ally in the beginning, but a quick look from Patrick had silenced any of his possible comments. It seemed as if I was the only one who thought this track was worth pursuing. But just because everyone else thought it was a bad idea didn't mean I wasn't going to try reasoning with Patrick. Once I got him to come around to my way of thinking, I was sure that Toni would be all for it.

By unspoken agreement I was going to take Patrick back to the warehouse in my car so we could have a few minutes alone. Peter was already driving away in his red Mini Cooper, more than a little happy to escape my Guardians. I hoped I made the right choice in trusting him, but I was pretty sure that I had.

Then again, I'd once been pretty sure that he had nothing to do with Demons.

"Are you coming to the recital?" I asked Lee as we took a step back from each other.

She shrugged. "I'd been planning on it, but . . . now I'm kind of thinking I might be having a talk with Peter instead."

"You don't have to do anything with him," Toni insisted firmly.

She nodded once. "I know, but . . . I trust Kate. If she says he really cares about me and my mom, I've got to give him some sort of a chance, right?"

"Yeah, just . . . don't ever get in a car with him, okay?"

She smirked at the Hispanic Guardian. "You know, you're pretty cute when you're concerned."

Toni rolled his eyes but didn't deny anything. He moved to open the door for her, and Lee climbed into the passenger seat. He then gave us an offhand salute as he rounded the hood of the car, and then he was opening his own door and climbing inside.

In less than a minute, they had disappeared down the street, leaving Patrick and me alone on the sidewalk. I looked to him, but before I could ask him if he was ready to leave, he was shuffling to the car, moving to get my door for me. I pursed my lips and followed him, wondering how long this silence would last between us.

Once we were both in the car and I was backing up, Patrick finally made a sound. He released a shaky breath, and my eyes flickered over to him as I shifted into first.

"Patrick, you look awful," I said.

He cracked a thin smile that didn't lighten any part of his face. His eyes were focused out the windshield, his head pressed back against the headrest. "Yeah. I feel pretty awful."

I hesitated, but the words still came out. "I'm sorry this had to happen. Especially today, after everything . . . you must be exhausted."

He was quiet for an uneasy moment, and then his voice was incredibly fragmented. "Please don't apologize. I don't think I can listen to you making any more excuses for him."

I bit my lip, nodded once, and then turned my attention to the winding residential streets.

Patrick spoke again, his voice was stronger this time. "Kate, I know you're thinking about Selena. About . . . her message."

"I'm not alone in that." I glanced at him, and he nodded once, allowing that.

He looked to me for the first time, keeping his voice low but firm. "We can't contact her. We can't trust her."

"But she's got the cure. She could make you better."

"I know."

I shot him a look, a sudden feeling of betrayal sweeping through my body. "You thought she would have it. You made the connection before."

He glanced back out the front window. "They have the virus. It only makes sense that they have the cure, if there is one."

"So why didn't you mention this sooner? Why didn't Terence? We could have been working on a way to get it from her!"

He shook his head, still staring out the window and avoiding my quick looks as if they had the power to shake his firm resolve. "There would only be one way to get it from her. And that's not happening. She's not getting you."

"Patrick, you're going to die. I can't . . . I can't stand that."

The knob in his throat leaped as he tried to swallow. His voice was wavering, fragile. "You don't understand, Kate. We would still be separated. But you would lose everything—your freedom, your family, your home. Your life for mine . . . it's not even worth debating."

"If you die, that's it—there's no way to fix that. But if you're alive . . . you can come back for me."

"I'm not discussing this with you."

"Why won't you listen?"

His voice was growing stronger. "I've considered this option, Kate. For all of a minute. That's all the time it took for me to realize that it's not a viable alternative. The Demon Lord . . . he has too many followers. Too many bases of operation. There's a good chance I'd never find you again, no matter how hard I searched."

"I trust you."

"I don't trust me. Not with something like this. Not when I'm gambling your life with the devil himself."

I stopped trying to meet his gaze, because I knew he wasn't going to negotiate this. He wasn't even going to consider the words I was saying. Why even talk at all?

We continued on in silence, until roughly ten minutes later when we were pulling in front of the warehouse. I stopped in front of the double doors and turned to him at last. "You don't need to come tonight. Jenna will understand."

He gave me a tired smile. "I want to be there."

I nodded once, glancing out the front window. "I'll come pick you up, then."

He sighed, but I didn't look toward him. "Kate, please . . . please don't be upset with me."

"I'm not."

"Then why are you refusing to look at me?"

I pulled in a deep breath, then twisted back to face him. My eyes were stinging but I ignored that. "I don't want to see this, Patrick," I admitted, the pain making a sharp edge of my voice. "I don't want to see you die. Why can't you understand that? Why can't you help me try to save you? Why don't you fight?"

"Kate . . ."

I looked away again, because seeing how my words had cut him only succeeded in making me feel worse. How was that possible? "No." I blew out my breath in a forced and rapid burst. "It's okay. Forget I said that."

I heard him shift in his seat. "Kate. I want . . . I wish you could understand. Losing you . . . It's the hardest thing I'll ever have to do."

Then why aren't you fighting? I wanted to demand. But I couldn't. Not when his voice was so haggard, so pleading . . .

I did the only thing I could. I released my seat belt and reached for him, kissing him intently. His lips were cold, and I knew that time was running out. I ducked my head into his shoulder.

"I love you so much," I mumbled against him.

His lips pressed into my hair. "I love you, Kate Bennett."

Not enough, though, my mind taunted my heart.

twenty-four

Watching Patrick at the recital was difficult. He tried to put on a brave face, but even the twins seemed to pick up on his illness. They didn't drag on his arms like they usually did, and their voices weren't as loud and piercing as was typical. Grandma seemed concerned, but it was Grandpa I really watched. He knew *exactly* what was wrong, and I think it bothered him to see this mysterious illness up close.

Jenna finished her piece with a flourish, and when she bowed deeply on the stage, Patrick clapped loudly with the rest of us. But it was obviously taking too much effort. Once all the performers had had a chance to shine the recital was declared over, and we all filed out into the cool hallway. Patrick had brought his camera, and he snapped pictures of Jenna posing in her black dress, Josie pretending to lick one of the walls, and even one of my grandparents walking away hand in hand.

I was standing next to him, so I wasn't expecting the flash to brighten my own face. I turned instinctively, but he was already lowering the camera, the image of my profile captured in that second. He looked at the image, and I saw how serene and detached I looked. He sighed deeply, the sadness in my tilted chin disturbing him.

He glanced up at me. "Can I ask for a smile? Just one?"

My family was already filing out the front doors of the recital hall, out into the cool night air. I didn't want to force a smile. But I knew that I couldn't deny his gentle wish. So I turned to him, focused on how it had felt to kiss him for the first time. Surprisingly, it wasn't much of a struggle. The memory of the darkened entryway, my quiet house . . . I was suddenly surrounded by it.

The flash went off, Patrick viewed the snapshot, and a thin smile tugged at the corner of his mouth. He looked up from the display to meet my eyes, and the tender look he gave me made my knees want to give out.

"Thank you," he said simply. He reached for my hand, and we followed after my family.

My car was parked next to the van, where my family was standing and waiting for us to catch up. Jenna and Josie promptly began teasing Patrick and me about the possible reasons for our delay, eyebrows wiggling suggestively, but Patrick just smiled at their antics.

Grandma was saying something to Grandpa, but he wasn't really paying attention. He was staring at Patrick, looking at me only when he felt my heavy stare. Our eyes connected and his face melted into something sickeningly close to pity. I quickly looked away at that point, and Patrick—without turning his attention away from my sisters—squeezed my hand tightly.

"Henry?" Grandma huffed. "Did you hear a word I just said?"

Grandpa shot her a quick smile, his voice only a little edgier than usual. "Charlotte, I told you the night we were married that I'd always pay strict attention to your mouth."

She smacked his stomach with the back of her hand, but as she rolled her eyes I could see the hint of amusement she felt. "You old fool. Get in the car. I'm ready to go home." She raised her voice. "Jenna, Josie, come on." Before she'd finished speaking, Grandpa had taken her hand and was leading her around the front of the van so he could help her inside.

Jenna, standing closest to Patrick, was the first to react to Grandma's order, but she'd barely had time to turn before my Guardian was suddenly wrapping his arms around her thin form. My sister seemed a little shocked by his unexpected display of affection, but that didn't stop her from slipping her small arms around his waist, returning the hug.

"You did great tonight," Patrick told her seriously. "Keep it up, all right?"

Jenna snorted. "I don't think Grandma would let me quit."

He drew back with a small smile. "You're probably right."

Jenna rolled back on her heels and Patrick's hand fell from her shoulders. "See you tomorrow?"

The skin around his eyes tightened, but his voice remained calm. "Maybe."

Jenna nodded easily and moved for the van, sending an unconcerned wave in my direction on her way to the large sliding door.

Josie was standing nearby, curious as to why Patrick had suddenly embraced Jenna. She became even more bewildered when he turned to her and gave her a quick hug as well. "Take care of yourself, Josie," he said after a slight pause.

She eyed him suspiciously. "You planning on dying or something?"

I swallowed hard, but Patrick only shrugged at her accusing tone. "Doesn't everyone? We all have to go sometime."

"Yeah, well, save your words of love and wisdom, okay?" she patted his arm and wriggled out of his hold. She nodded to me. "See you at home—and don't plan on showering, 'cuz there won't be any hot water left."

She darted to the open door, and that's when I noticed that Grandpa was silently observing the scene near the front of the van. I felt Patrick sidle up next to me and slipped one arm around my waist. Grandpa was eyeing Patrick. I realized he was debating only when he took the couple steps toward us, hand extended.

"Thank you, Patrick," he said quietly as Patrick took his offered hand. "For all of your service to my family."

"It has been an honor, sir," Patrick returned indubitably—in no way could his sincerity be doubted.

I pursed my lips, fighting the urge to scream.

Grandpa's eyes darted to my face, and then he released Patrick's hand and stepped back. "I'll see you at home, Kate."

I nodded, unable to speak. My eyes were beginning to sting, and my head was throbbing with the sudden pressure. Patrick moved his palm up and down my side, trying to soothe me as we watched my Grandpa fit himself behind the wheel, start the van, flash on the headlights, ease out of the parking space, and roll toward the exit.

Patrick's words were too light to be considered a whisper—much more like a thin exhale. "I'm sorry. I needed to say good-bye . . ."

I forced my head to dip as I pulled away from him to unlock the passenger side door, the key slipping twice as my shaking fingers tried to fit it into the lock. After Patrick's door was open, I rounded the hood to the driver's side. Normally Patrick moved quickly enough, and he would have had my door unlocked by now. But not anymore. By the time I was inside and closing my door, Patrick was barely closing his.

I reached for my seat belt, but before I could jerk it across my body Patrick spoke.

"Kate, can I ask you something before we go?"

I pretended to glance out my window, hoping he wouldn't notice the tears in my voice. "Yeah, sure."

He didn't respond right away but took a moment to gather his thoughts. With my peripheral vision I could see him fiddling with the bracelet on his wrist, spinning it in endless circles. He continued to toy with it when his words finally came. "I told myself I wouldn't ask you this. I figured you'd tell me yourself, if you truly wanted me to know. But now that . . . that our time is so limited . . . There is something I would like to know."

I forced my eyes open, as wide as they'd go, hoping that would keep the tears from gathering. I was still looking out my window. "You can ask me anything," I told him honestly.

"Kate, can you look at me? It would be easier if I could see you."

I blinked quickly as I slowly turned toward him, still trying to halt the tears just beginning to fall. There was a street lamp not far from where we were parked, and the yellowish light just managed to illuminate the inside of the car. Patrick furrowed his brow with concern when he saw the tears on my face, but there was a new emotion in his eyes that distracted me. He looked afraid. That was definitely not a feeling I'd seen him express yet. I was instantly worried.

"Patrick, what is it?"

He hesitated, essentially squirmed in his seat. His words were dim. "I don't want to hurt you. But . . . I want you to tell me about the accident. I want to know what you went through. Of course I know the after-effects, but I want to know how it happened. What happened? Can you tell me?"

It was certainly the last thing I expected him to ask about, but that didn't stop my whole body from reacting to his request. My pulse quickened, my breathing spiked. My stomach clenched and my chest tightened.

"I haven't really talked about it," I whispered reflexively. "Ever."

"I know. I just . . ." He sighed, an edge of frustration in the sound. He quickly looked away. "I thought we'd have more time. This isn't how I wanted it to be. But I want to know what happened to you. To know what it was like for you."

I drew in a sharp breath and curled one hand over the steering wheel.

Patrick didn't move or say anything else. He was waiting for my decision.

How could I deny him? Haltingly, I began telling the story that had completely changed my life. A story I'd never had to speak aloud before. A story I didn't want to remember.

"It was a Saturday. Dad had made waffles for breakfast. He always made a mess whenever he was in the kitchen. There was batter all over the counter. He'd even smudged some on his glasses—the wire part that went over his nose." I cleared my dry throat and closed my eyes, lost in the memory of that morning. "Mom was wearing khaki shorts, and her hair was in a high ponytail. She saw the batter on his glasses but didn't say anything. He kept asking her why she was smiling so much, but she'd just shrug.

"I was watching the whole thing. I was trying to get some math homework done before we had to leave for Josie's soccer game. Jenna was playing something on the piano—something she'd written herself." I opened my eyes and let them flicker to catch Patrick's expression. His eyes were riveted on me, his face pale. He didn't even seem to be breathing. "I haven't heard her write her own stuff since that morning," I told him.

His head inclined ever so slightly, but he seemed reluctant to speak. He didn't want to distract me.

I bit my bottom lip and turned to stare out the windshield. "Dad was teasing Mom about her shoes. They were her favorite sandals, but they were falling apart. Mom just stuck her tongue out at him and flipped on the radio. She loved music. She couldn't do anything without music in the background." I shook my head a little. "I don't think I'll ever forget these images. I mean, it was just breakfast. A normal Saturday morning at the Bennett house. But . . .

"It happened on the way home from the game. Grandma and Grandpa had joined us at the field—they didn't live far away—and Jenna and Josie clamored to go home with them. Grandpa invited me to come along, but my stuff was in my parents' car. My dad told Grandma we'd see them back at the house. He had to swing by his office at the college. He had some summer term papers that needed to be graded by Monday. I climbed in the backseat. Dad started the car. Mom turned on the radio.

"He didn't notice the waffle batter on his glasses until he got back in the car, a stack of papers on his lap. Mom laughed—thought it was the funniest thing that he'd been walking around all morning like that. He pretended to be upset, but he could hardly hold back a laugh.

"He handed the papers to me. I put them on the seat next to me and glanced up from the book I'd been trying to finish all morning. The clock said it was 11:34, but it was always fast. Almost three minutes too fast."

My whole mouth was dry. My grip on the steering wheel was strangling. I couldn't feel my fingertips, but I couldn't make myself let go. My right hand lay on my leg, too heavy to move, unable to do anything.

"My dad pulled us out onto the street. We were accelerating. Mom turned up the volume, started to hum along to the song that was playing. And then she suddenly screamed. I looked up from my book. The clock said 11:37. Something white was skidding toward us from across the intersection. It rolled right into us. Smashed us. Glass was everywhere, and I was being crushed. I tried to scream, but I couldn't."

I was suddenly aware of Patrick's fingers around my right hand. He was gripping my fingers with all his strength. His face was drawn. He looked sick.

Somehow, I forced my left hand to uncurl from around the steering wheel, and I angled myself toward him. My voice was wooden as I rattled off the facts. "The light was green. We had the right of way. We were in the left lane, just entering the intersection when it happened. Someone came from the left side road, trying to turn in front of us, even though the light was red. A white SUV. It wasn't fast enough to make the turn but they were angled just right, and a moving truck in the oncoming traffic hit them head on and sent them rolling toward us. Dad tried to swerve, but it hit us anyway. Dad was killed instantly. Mom died just after the paramedics arrived on the scene."

I was crying. I only realized it because I couldn't breathe, so I couldn't keep talking. Patrick had lifted my hand to his face. He was pressing his lips against my knuckles, his eyes shut tight.

I swallowed back a sob. "I don't remember much after that. I was trapped. There was blood in my mouth. I couldn't see anything. I blacked out. I woke up in the hospital, with Grandma and Grandpa standing over me. Grandma was sobbing, and Grandpa's eyes were red. I had some broken ribs, but there was some serious internal bleeding. I was pretty cut up—I had a concussion. Grandma just kept saying over and over, 'We thought we'd lost you too.' That's when I realized my parents were gone."

Patrick's hand was shaking around mine, and the air in the car was tense. My body was shuddering as I tried to get control of my grief.

He didn't say anything. As the minutes passed and my cries were replaced by calmer weeping, I began to realize how weird that was. He was usually so quick to comfort me, and I'd never yet had this severe of a meltdown in front of him. I tried to gulp back my tears before turning to regard him, figure out why he was remaining silent.

He wasn't looking at me. He was staring out the front window, soundless tears curving down his cheeks and slowly dropping from his chin. The muscles in his jaw were flexing, and his whole body was rigid. He looked so tortured.

"Patrick," I fairly growled, not meaning to sound so fierce. I cleared my throat as his eyes swiveled to meet mine.

He must have sensed my question. His attempt to smile failed miserably. "I'm sorry, Kate. I shouldn't have asked you to relive that. I didn't—" he cut himself off, his face contorting in pain. He thrust his head abruptly away from me, keeping me from getting a better handle on his emotions. His chest heaved as he sucked in a deep breath. He tried again. "I had no idea that . . . That it . . ."

I leaned toward him, surprised at the intensity of his reaction. My own tears seemed to halt instinctively as I reached out my free hand to touch his knee.

He trembled at my touch, his gaze still locked on the passenger window so I couldn't see his expression. His voice was lined with a cross between pain and desperation. "Forgive me. My death . . . the experience was painful. Agonizing. Physically, but emotionally as well. Forced from this life, and my family . . . But I suppose I never managed to understand how hard it is to be the one that remains behind. And now . . . I'm causing you to go through that again."

The stinging was back in my eyes, but what could I say? Vent out my frustrations? Attack him with the ferocity of my anger at being abandoned yet again? I couldn't do that to him. I didn't have any desire to increase his misery. He was dying. I needed to try and make this easier for him, regardless of what I felt. What I would surely feel when he was gone. I couldn't focus on that now. I'd have the rest of my life to focus on the emptiness his absence would create.

"Patrick," I whispered, my voice cracking. He didn't visibly react. I decided to play the card he had earlier. "Patrick, can you please look at me?"

His head ducked. He took a heavy moment to compose himself, and then he carefully slid his wet eyes to meet mine.

I didn't even try to smile, because I knew I wouldn't succeed. I tried to keep my voice from fluctuating with emotion. "Patrick, you're what matters right now."

"But, Kate—"

"No. Or, if you can't accept that, fine. *We're* what matters." I applied pressure to his knee, where my hand still rested. "What's happening right here, right now, that's what we need to focus on. All right?"

His eyes narrowed and he bowed his head, considering my words. "All right," he echoed at last. I knew that he wasn't going to stop thinking about me—and I certainly wasn't going to stop thinking about him—but we were both prepared to put on a front for the sake of the other.

As I started the car and aimed for the warehouse, I couldn't stop reflecting on Patrick's words: *I never managed to understand how hard it is to be the one that remains behind.*

I hated being left behind.

When I dropped him off at the warehouse, he asked if I could come by after school tomorrow. I promised I would, and we shared a quick kiss. And then he was gone. I tried not to let his absence overwhelm me. I'd see him tomorrow.

If only that was enough to stop the tears that drizzled down my face.

❋

School passed slowly without Patrick. I tried to focus on

Lee—making sure she was still okay with everything that had happened and asking how things with Peter were going.

"I haven't really seen him much," she admitted. "We talked for a while, before Mom got home. And then they went out, and I haven't seen him this morning. I think he's afraid of freaking me out." She shrugged. "I worried it would be really weird, being alone with him, but it wasn't. I mean, no more awkward than it ever was before, surprisingly."

"Good. I'm glad."

She gave me a look, glanced around to be sure that none of the special-needs kids were listening, and asked softly, "How long does Patrick have? This sickness . . . is it moving fast?"

I nodded, unable to look at her. I focused on the tray of food I had yet to touch. "Very fast. The longest anyone lasted was two weeks. Today makes one week for him, but . . . I think it's down to a couple days."

She wasn't sure what to say, but that was okay. I wouldn't have known what to respond with. Because I couldn't lie to her—I wasn't okay with any of this.

When school got out, Lee told me that Rodney had asked to take her home. She offered that they could get the twins for me, an offer I was quick to accept. And so I was able to leave the school and head straight for the warehouse, hating that even those few extra minutes meant the world to me, because they were among his last.

While I drove I called Toni, who informed me that Patrick had been sleeping all day, and he had yet to wake up. I didn't change my direction, though.

"How's he doing?" I asked at last, afraid of what I might hear.

Toni blew out his breath, knowing that I wasn't just asking for a routine checkup. "Honestly? Not so good. Worse than he lets on, I'm sure. His nose hasn't started bleeding yet, so . . . we're still good for now." He hesitated and then continued, knowing that I'd want to know every detail. "Terence called while you guys were at the recital. I didn't tell Patrick, but . . . One of the Guardians they've been monitoring passed away last night. They don't expect one of the others to last the day."

Though I'd never met them, a piece of me mourned the poor Guardians. Hearing about these deaths only made Patrick's fate seem that much more real, and unavoidable. He really was going to die.

"Thanks for telling me," I whispered.

"Jack called this morning. He wants to come over, but . . . we don't know if he's susceptible or not. I told him to keep his distance for now."

"That's probably for the best." My voice was hollow.

"Yeah, that's what I thought." Toni decided to change the subject. "So . . . how was school?"

"Long." I sighed.

"How's Lee?"

"Learning the truth about everything hasn't stopped Rainbow Days, so I think she's okay."

He chuckled. "Wow, she's a really awesome chica."

I swallowed hard. "I'll be there in about five minutes, Toni."

"Sweet. I'll be right here."

We said good-bye, and I hung up. I took a few bracing breaths, focusing on my pounding heart. I needed to slow it down, keep it steady . . .

I expected Patrick to still be asleep when I got there, but when I walked into the living room he was sitting on the couch. The laptop was on the table, but it was obvious he wasn't really watching the beginning of *Peter Pan*.

He smiled up at me, his brown hair a messy pile on his head, hanging down around his ears and curling over his face.

"How are you feeling?" I asked, moving straight for him. He didn't stand up to meet me, so I knew that he was doing worse.

"I'm feeling good," he lied. "Refreshed."

My lips tugged into a thin smile. "Good. I'm glad." I sat on the edge of the couch and embraced him, holding him more tightly when

I realized his weak arms couldn't squeeze any more than they already were.

When I pulled away, he settled back against the couch and his eyes searched my face. "How was school?"

"The gang missed you. Especially Trent."

"I miss them. You told them hi for me?"

"Yeah. I did."

He nodded and glanced at the movie that was still quietly playing. "I've watched bits and pieces of this off and on all night and morning. I'd wake up sometimes, and I couldn't fall back asleep."

"I should bring over some other movies for you."

He shrugged. "I like this one. It reminds me of you."

I bit my lower lip and turned my eyes away from him. What was he trying to do? *Make* me lose it?

I saw a book lying on the coffee table, next to the computer. It was old, and the leather cover was shallowly cracked in places.

"What's that?" I asked, grateful for the subject change.

He followed my gaze, then laboriously stretched to reach it. "It was my sketchbook. It was far too expensive, but my parents were supportive of my talents."

"Oh my gosh. Why didn't you tell me you had this?"

He balanced the book on his flat palms, and he stared at the leather as if transfixed. "I hardly ever take it out myself. It holds too many memories for me. But it was a piece of myself I couldn't resist taking with me. I've never shown this to anyone else, for all these years . . ." he looked to me. "There was something I wanted to show you."

"Of course." I curled my legs up onto the couch, angling myself toward him. The movie continued to play, but it was a detached background accompaniment. While Patrick settled more comfortably beside me, I took a fast look around the large living space. "Where's Toni?"

"In his room. I think it's his way of giving us some privacy . . ."

"Huh. That's considerate of him."

"It makes me worry about what he wants from us," he joked lightly.

I might have made some quirky answer, but Patrick had just lifted the cover, and I was staring at a familiar face. "You?" I asked quickly, staring at the piercing eyes.

Patrick shook his head. "My brother. Sean."

"He looks so much like you . . ."

"He was always the better-looking one. This sketch doesn't do him justice."

"You have the same eyes."

Patrick swallowed hard and turned the page. Whatever he wanted to show me, it was further in the book.

Through the somewhat faded lines of his art, I met his parents and saw his old home in Ireland. Every line was beautiful. Not because he was a talented artist—because even though sketching was not his forte, he was indeed talented—but because he had tried to capture his family with such love. It was one of the most touching things I'd ever seen, and I was almost overwhelmed by the fact that he wanted me to view these very personal thoughts and memories.

The only drawing that made me a bit wary was of a beautiful young woman. She had flowing hair that curled naturally over her shoulders, and her perfectly sculpted face was stunning. I couldn't imagine how she must have looked in real life. Breathtaking was probably too inadequate a word. In addition to that, her lips twisted flirtatiously, not that I couldn't blame her for looking that way at the artist. Patrick was impossible to ignore. It made total sense that he'd had the affection of a beautiful girl. I wondered what had happened to her, if her eyes had remained that bright after his death.

What would I look like after losing him?

Though I was a little jealous of this attractive Irish woman, I found myself drawn to her. Because she'd gone through exactly what I was about to go through: losing Patrick.

To appease my more jealous thoughts, I assured myself that there was no way she could have loved him as much as I did.

demons

"Sarah McKenna," Patrick explained quietly. "We were good friends growing up, and she was a wonderful young woman. She was the first girl I believed myself to be in love with. My mother tried desperately to throw us together at every opportunity. I would have probably married her someday, but . . ."

"But then you died," I whispered.

He glanced my way. "No. I met you. And I realized that love is a lot stronger than I'd ever imagined."

How was it possible for my heart to be so warm and yet so cold at the same time?

He began to leaf more quickly through the pages, and we were nearly to the middle when he turned the stiff page that revealed an unexpected face.

My face.

Because though the rendition wasn't perfect, it was uncannily close.

"But . . . how . . . ?" My voice drifted, and my eyes were glued to the page.

Patrick was shaking his head slackly. "I don't know. I wish I did. But . . . Kate, I never could draw anything unless I'd seen it. And this drawing . . . all I can remember is that I saw your face in my dreams. But I must have seen you. Two hundred years ago, I dreamed about you. Perhaps even more baffling is the fact that my brother, Sean . . . I remember him looking at this, and he knew that he'd seen you too. I don't know how it's possible, but . . . There you are."

I stared at the curved lines of my face, staring up at me from the yellowed page. The shading that his practiced fingers had placed around my eyes, the way he had graciously sculpted my lips to look beautiful . . . and that's when I suddenly knew. That's when I understood.

Terence had told me that I had the ability to travel through emotions. That they acted as doorways to different memories, different times. But after learning that I could do nothing for Patrick, do nothing in my own time . . . well, what was the point in continually

295

thinking about it? I'd been so preoccupied with other alternatives for saving Patrick, the whole idea of time travel had sort of slipped my mind.

But this picture was evidence; it was the only explanation I needed. At some point, I was going to go back. I was going to travel through Patrick's emotions, and I was going to journey to the past. What other answer was there?

But if I did go back . . . why didn't I talk to him? Why didn't I imprint myself on his memory? Why was I only a dream to him? Just a picture in an old sketchbook? Why would I journey to his past and not approach him?

It made no sense.

Patrick's eyes were on my face. He was waiting for me to say something. I'd promised Terence that I wouldn't tell anyone. But if I didn't tell him . . . his time was running out. If I was going to travel back in time, it would have to be soon. Sometime this week, I would be in the 1700s.

It was ludicrous.

It was the only thing that made sense.

Was this picture proof that I broke my promise to Terence? Did I tell Patrick about my special Seer abilities? How else would he help guide me into his memories?

"Kate? Is something wrong?"

My thoughts were so focused, so intense, that I barely registered the sound of his voice.

Terence had been clear—I couldn't change anything in my own lifetime. But I could go back to before Patrick died—before he ever joined the United Irishmen. What if I saved him from ever making the choice? Then he would never get sick . . . because he'd never be here. I'd never meet him.

And if I never met him—if he was never *here* . . . How could I see the sketch that made me go back in the first place?

Something wasn't adding up. Was there another reason the sketch was important?

One question bothered me more than all the others. *If I didn't go back in time to see Patrick, why in the world would I ever go back at all?*

"Kate?"

I tore my eyes off the drawing, glancing up at his mildly worried expression. "I'm fine. It's just . . . weird."

He nodded once, relaxing a little when he realized I wasn't going into shock or anything. "I know. But I thought you should see it. Whatever it means . . ." His eyes suddenly squinted, focusing on a point near my left eyebrow.

"What?" I asked self-consciously.

His eyes darted back to the page, still narrowed. I looked at my image, tried to see what he was seeing . . .

I felt his eyes back on my face. "It's a pimple," he whispered.

I blushed a little, and my finger reached up for my eyebrow. Sure enough, near the bridge of my nose, I felt the small bump. It was in the early stages, hardly developed yet at all. "Yeah, it happens when I'm stressed. I break out . . ."

He shook his head. "No. It's a pimple." He pointed to the picture—a small spot near my eyebrow I hadn't noticed before, because it seemed to blend right in.

I felt my face twist in bewilderment. "You drew my pimple? . . . No one does that sort of detail. It borders on the compulsive—"

"Kate," he interrupted, his voice almost urgent. "This picture . . . It captured you *now*." He glanced back at my real eyebrow. I could tell from the way his face was knit up that he was trying to remember the dream that had inspired the drawing. He was trying to remember *exactly* what I'd looked like . . .

"It was bigger then," he finally decided. "I wouldn't have noticed it otherwise. But not much bigger. A day? Maybe two? . . . Kate, what's going on?"

I was completely baffled. But if my pimple still had a couple days to grow, it must mean that Patrick had to still be alive for those days. It was amazing how much relief I felt at that realization.

He was still waiting for me to speak, watching me closely, reading every emotion to cross my face. "Patrick, I . . ."

He saw my hesitation, and his forehead wrinkled in something like confusion. "If you know something about this, I need you to tell me. I'd nearly convinced myself that I had to have seen a look-alike—your twin in absolutely every way. But this, the pimple . . . there's no way this was a coincidence. That's *you*, Kate. How is this possible?"

I knew I couldn't keep this from him. He knew that I knew something—he'd seen the realization, then the relief . . .

He wasn't breathing.

I reached out and gripped his fingers tightly, our hands balanced on the picture. "Patrick, I'll tell you everything I know. But first I need you to breathe."

His hand was cold, his fingers stiff. That's when I realized his expression had changed. He wasn't looking into my eyes, searching for answers. He was staring past me, something like dread tightening his skin.

He wordlessly pulled his hand from mine to close the sketchbook, and he tossed it onto the table—and suddenly he was falling, doubling over as he crashed against the table.

The laptop shuddered at the impact, and I thought the table would snap under his sudden weight. But before any damage could be done he was rolling off, crumpling to the floor.

"Patrick!" I screamed, a second before a horrible cry ripped out of his body and tore through his throat.

It sounded like he was being burned alive.

I pushed off the couch, kneeling beside him in the thin space. He continued to scream in agony as I groped along his thrashing body, trying to reach his contorted face.

I heard a door open, and we weren't alone anymore. Toni crouched beside Patrick, struggling to hold his jerking head still in an effort to keep him from damaging his straining neck.

"Toni!" I gasped, unable to tear my eyes away from Patrick's indescribable pain. "What's happening?"

In answer Toni swore darkly, his eyes blazing with many different heartrending emotions as he saw his friend writhe on the floor. "It's killing him!" he shouted at last.

"What do we do?" I cried, tears practically pouring down my face. I grabbed Patrick's hand, where his taut fingers were curled into claws. I couldn't stop shaking. My stomach felt completely turned inside out, and I could barely breathe.

"Nothing," Toni growled. "There's nothing we can do . . ."

While Patrick was tortured, I clung to his hand. I tried to hold him, but he just ended up jerking away. As if somehow—even in the depths of this horrible inferno—he knew that he didn't want me to witness this. Toni protected his head, keeping it firmly in place. His shrieks rent my soul and made me feel as if there would be nothing worse than this pain of watching him slowly die.

But he wasn't dying. Toni's vicious undercurrent of mutterings assured me of that. Even as the virus tried so hard to annihilate him, Patrick's tormented body worked feverishly to repair the damage, tried to heal despite the fatal wounding.

Most of Toni's words were in Spanish, and I didn't know enough to follow the fervently uttered words. A prayer? Probably not, I realized, as a heated expletive I understood perfectly punctuated his breathless monologue.

I wanted to swear with him, but I didn't have the breath.

Patrick's hand crushed my fingers. It was the wrist that had been strained by Micah's pull, so long ago at Jaxon's party. Before I'd known that he was dying . . .

Had there ever been a time I hadn't felt this terrible burning in my chest? It seemed like so long . . . When would it stop?

His cries choked off slowly—and then he was simply gasping. His eyes stopped rolling, his arching back pressed limply to the floor. His panting was short, sharp, and shallow. He was covered in sweat, and I could feel his whole body trembling in the wake of that awful onslaught. His tensed muscles spasmed, and slowly his eyes drifted down to me, where I sat at his side—the coffee table pressed painfully into my back.

He stared at me and slowly uncurled his fingers, taking the intense pressure away from my throbbing hand. "I'm sorry," his voice cracked.

"Why didn't Terence mention this?" I asked hollowly, still clutching his sagging fingers. "Why didn't you tell me this was happening?"

"I didn't want you . . . to worry . . ."

I looked to Toni. "How long has this been happening?"

Patrick groaned. "Toni . . ."

He ignored Patrick's pleading, his eyes on me. "The first time happened soon after Terence left. It *was* happening about once a day, but it's becoming more frequent. This is the third time since the recital."

My gaze fell to Patrick's face, but he was squeezing his eyes closed, trying to force away all the pain. As if he could simply will all of this to stop happening. I swallowed hard, barely believing that he could have survived this torture so many times . . . even an immortal could only endure so much.

Patrick's blue eyes opened, and he focused on me. "This doesn't matter," he whispered finally, his voice wavering as his body fought to recover. "The drawing. Show Toni the pimple."

Toni's eyebrows drew together. "The pimple? Have you lost your mind?"

Patrick chuckled partially. "Maybe." He swallowed. "Kate. Please."

I didn't release his hand, but I twisted around and snatched up the book. I handed it over to Toni, who took it and flipped open almost immediately to the right page. So he'd already seen it before.

I watched Patrick's drawn face as he hurried to explain everything to Toni. The pimple, what it meant as far as a timeline went, and then they turned to look at me—both waiting for an explanation.

I was definitely too tired to fight them.

"I know how I got there," I whispered slowly. "I just don't know why."

Toni shook his head, not understanding the distinction between my words. "You know how you got into Patrick's dreams, but you don't know why you were there? Aren't they the same thing?"

"No. Not exactly." I took a deep breath, unable to look at Patrick without losing my voice. So I focused on Toni. "When Terence took me outside, he told me some things . . . things I wasn't supposed to tell anyone. Not even you guys."

"What things?" Toni demanded.

"He confirmed the mind reading?" Patrick asked, obviously not caring if Toni learned he'd been kept in the dark.

"Sort of," I told him, even as Toni started shaking his head.

"Wow, what are you talking about?" he asked. "Mind reading? Would someone please start making sense?"

"I'm not normal," I said. "Not even by Seer standards." As I briefly brought Toni up to date on the incident with my grandma, we both helped Patrick get resituated on the couch, where he'd be more comfortable. He sagged gratefully against the cushion, clinging to my fingers as I took my place beside him. Toni remained standing, arms folded across his chest as he listened deliberately to my every word.

"So you can read minds? Geez, no one tells me anything any more," he whined.

"It's not really mind reading—that's just what I thought in the beginning."

Patrick had eyes only for me. "What did Terence tell you?" he asked thinly, roughness still lingering in his voice.

I squeezed his hand. Even now, he was intent on being my Guardian—he wanted to protect me, even while he was dying. I closed my eyes, trying to organize my chaotic thoughts. "I See things differently than most Seers. I see Demons and Guardians, and I see emotions. But I See more than one emotion at a time. Normal Seers See only one emotion at any given time, the most prominent, whereas I can See everything a person is feeling—*everything*, even the subconscious stuff."

Toni nodded slowly. "Okay. That's not so weird. It doesn't explain your little jaunt into mind reading over the weekend, or—" He caught sight of my opening mouth and quickly amended. "*Excuse* me, what you *thought* was mind reading. It also doesn't explain what you were doing in Patrick's head two hundred years ago."

"But it does." My eyes met Patrick's intense stare without my consent, but then I couldn't pull away. "I can use emotions to travel through time. Terence said that emotions are gateways to memories, and if I can See the memory, I can travel to that memory. I can literally go back in time. I didn't just See what my Grandma was thinking—I was actually living inside her memory."

Patrick's face was unreadable.

Toni was undeniably awed. "Wow." He whistled lowly. "You can . . . wow . . . Kate, I think you're my new best friend—no offence Patrick. Have you tried it yet?" Envy was burning in every eager word. "Oh my gosh, Kate, the possibilities!"

"It's unnatural," I argued. "Not cool."

"How can you even say that?"

"There are limits," I told him.

The eager light that had been lifting his face faltered just a little. "Like?"

"Well, for one thing, I can't alter anything in my own lifetime. Any year I've lived in is completely off-limits."

"Ew. That stinks."

Patrick spoke at last, his voice heavy. "Traveling . . . is it dangerous for you?"

I shrugged. "I don't know all the risks. Terence said that the Guardians were experimenting with the ability, but things were kept pretty quiet. And then there were some casualties, and the Guardian Council shut things down."

"Casualties?"

I tightened my hold on his tense hand. "Apparently if I try to change anything in a year I've lived, I'll die. Traveling in time before my lifetime is safe, according to Terence. When you get back, you're a little tired—sometimes you pass out, or feel nauseated. The further back you go, the better."

"A little tired," Toni muttered. "Kate, do you realize what you could do with this? Heck, you could still positively change your own future. Go back and get your ancestors to invest in some choice stock, and when you come back to this time, you'll be rich!"

I shook my head. "I can't pick and choose where to go. Remember, other people's emotions are the doorways. I can only go where they would take me."

Patrick's fingers tightened around mine, thoughts racing. "I take you back to 1797. Why?"

"I don't know. I thought that maybe I go back to save you some-how—convince you not to join the rebellion or something. But then—"

"I would have remembered that, right?" he muttered.

"Remembered it? You wouldn't even be here," Toni pointed out. "You wouldn't have died when you did, and you never would have become a Guardian to save your brother. Poof, we'd never have known you existed."

"You wouldn't have drawn the picture either," I told him. "At least, I don't think so . . ."

"The time loop wouldn't make sense," Toni agreed with me. "You were there, but you never met him. He might have seen you—*must* have seen you—but you didn't even say 'hi' . . ."

"But why would I do that? Why go back if not to interfere?" I asked, frustrated that this was an endless circle with no answers.

Patrick shook his head slowly. "I don't know. But one thing is clear—you do go back. And you do it soon."

There was a deep pause, and that's when I saw the drop of red slowly slide out from Patrick's nose. My whole body seemed to freeze as the liquid bead slid lower, coming toward his lip . . . A second drop—falling faster than the first—dripped from his other nostril and splattered down on his shirt.

Patrick realized he was bleeding a second before Toni did, and then I wasn't the center of attention anymore.

Patrick ran a single finger under his nose, and it came away with a streak of blood. He stared at the glistening color, no emotion on his face.

No one was breathing, and no one had to say anything. We all knew what this meant.

Patrick was nearing the end. This was the last sure marker before death would stiffen his body, and then he would never breathe again.

twenty-five

Patrick's nose didn't bleed for long. Just enough to show us that the end was coming, and then it stopped—his body trying to erase the damage before it could become permanent. But we all knew it would be back.

Patrick was exhausted, so Toni and I helped him into his room. Once he was laid out on his bed, I leaned over and kissed him faintly; his response was disturbingly weak.

"I love you," he murmured with underlying fervor, revealing the depth of emotion his feeble kiss hadn't managed to convey.

My fingertips stroked his hair, his forehead, and his eyes fell closed instinctively. "I love *you*," I whispered. I heard Toni exit the room behind me and I lowered myself onto the edge of the bed.

Patrick's eyes quivered open, his smile frail. "I look that bad, huh?"

"Do you mind if I stay?" I asked, my words virtually faded, my fingers still moving attentively over his face. "Just until you fall asleep?"

His eyes closed once more, his body relaxing as his lungs emptied slowly. I got the impression that he was debating between what he wanted, and what he thought was best for me. "No," he breathed at last. "I don't mind. Actually . . . I'd like that. Very much."

He had one hand resting on his chest and I slipped my free hand beneath his loose fingers. "Then I'll be right here."

"Thank you, Kate." He hesitated, and then his eyes peeled back again. "I know this is impossibly hard for you, but I'm grateful for your being here."

"Patrick, just rest. You need it."

But he wouldn't be so easily swayed. "There's something I want to do first. I'm . . . I'm going fast." I glanced away, unable to watch his open face. "We both know it," he whispered carefully. "And . . . soon I'm not even going to be able to stay visible. But before that happens . . ." My eyes returned to him, and he smiled dimly. "Close your eyes."

"What?"

His smile widened slightly. "Just trust me. Close your eyes."

I gave him a strange look, but I obediently pushed my eyes closed. I didn't know what I was waiting for—I didn't know what he could possibly think of doing.

After a short minute of silence he whispered very softly. "You can open your eyes now."

I did, slowly. And I gasped at what I saw.

Patrick was still lying on the bed—he hadn't moved an inch. But he was different. Or rather, his aura was different. It was no longer hidden from me. The familiar silver outline was there, but then there were colors . . . so many strong colors.

A dull cloud of brown pain and distant traces of gray. They were so muted in this moment that I wondered if he even registered the depression, or if it was just on a subconscious level. There was red too—more than I thought there would be. He was angry—angry at the Demons, at his own self-destructing body, at the entire situation. But I knew that these weren't the emotions he wanted me to linger on. They weren't the ones he wanted me to see.

It was the blue of contentment—far deeper than I'd expected to see in a dying man—and the yellow. So much yellow . . .

It was as if he could read my thoughts. His voice was nearly silent. "I wanted you to See what you made possible, Kate. Before you, I doubted my choice to become a Guardian. I feared that I'd lost my only chance for happiness the day I lost my family. But then

I found you. You changed everything. I just . . . I wanted to show you this while I still had control. I wanted it to be my choice."

There were tears in my eyes, but for the first time in a long time they were not tears of sadness. I squeezed his fingers delicately. "Patrick, I . . . Thank you." I took a last look at the yellow clouds, then I leaned down and kissed him warmly. From the corner of my eye I could see the yellow in his aura expand, and I knew that I'd never loved him more than I did right now.

"I love you so much," I breathed against his lips.

"And I will always love you, Kate. No matter where I am. I want you to remember that."

"I will. I promise."

His tired eyes closed, and his smile relaxed as he finally gave in to his exhaustion. But his aura stayed visible to me, and I watched it while he slept. Watched as it changed. It was easy to see when he slipped into unconsciousness, because the brown pain grew and expanded, slowly driving the other colors back. He wasn't awake to keep them away; I watched as he was almost overwhelmed by the colors of suffering and death.

When it became too painful to watch anymore, I looked up to his desk. The silver camera was sitting on the edge, and with my free hand I reached for it. I balanced it on my palm and my thumb pressed the few necessary buttons to access the memory card. I glanced at every picture he'd managed to take so far. There were more than I expected, but far too few. He couldn't cease to exist—not when so much was left for him to see. It couldn't be his destiny to die.

I skipped rapidly to the first pictures he'd taken, the day of his mock birthday party. Our camera war was surprisingly painful . . . seeing those snatches of his face, that half-grin that still managed to take my breath away and cause my heart to pound . . . I skimmed past the pictures of me quickly, and then suddenly I was looking at the picture Toni had stolen in a surprise flash. The one with Patrick's lips on the top of my head, my eyes closed peacefully, our arms around each other . . .

Something inside me snapped. Quietly but conclusively.

I wasn't going to let this happen. No matter what anyone else thought. Even Patrick. I wasn't going to be left behind. Not when I could stop this from happening. I may not have a lot of power over my past, but I could still change my future.

I turned the camera off and replaced it on the desk. I looked hastily to his face, saw the slight cringe twist his lips, and stood. I slipped my hand out from under his, moving quietly out of the room.

I told Toni good-bye, asking him to call me when Patrick woke up—no matter the time. I didn't bother trying to discuss my plans with him, because I knew he wasn't going to approve of them.

I waited to pull out my phone until I was sitting in my hot car. I scrolled through my contacts, finding the number I'd saved just so I'd know to avoid it. I took a deep breath before I hit send, and I waited impatiently while it rang flatly in my ear.

Someone answered, sounding far too happy.

My voice was more controlled than I thought it would be. "Selena. We need to talk."

✳

The plan was simple. So easy. I wondered what had taken me so long to get to this point, because now that I was here things seemed so uncomplicated.

As soon as I was done talking to Selena, I started the car and pulled away from the warehouse. But I didn't head for home. Instead I made my way to a small pawnshop, knowing that Clyde was the only one I could trust with this information.

I got there just before closing time. I pushed open the glass door and stepped onto the faded orange carpet. I moved right to the counter, where the Demon was just looking up after hearing the bell clang. He'd been writing in a logbook of some kind, and he seemed preoccupied. Still, when he saw me he smiled and removed the cigarette from his mouth. "Welcome to Clyde's Pawnshop. What can I interest you in?"

I stopped at the counter, placing my hands on the glass. "Clyde, it's me—Kate Bennett."

He hurried to crush the cigarette out into the nearby ashtray and then gave me a wider smile. "Of course—I knew you looked familiar. Your grandfather outside?"

"No. I came alone."

"Huh. No offense, miss, but this is a pretty edgy part of town. Probably shouldn't come around here alone."

"I need your help."

He seemed to notice for the first time that my tone was even and businesslike. He straightened behind the counter, closing the book he'd been scribbling in. His eyes came to me, and he matched my serious expression. "Right. What can I do for ya?"

"You mentioned that rumor—the one about Guardians getting sick and dying."

He seemed to relax a little. "Yeah. Yeah, I did. But it's just a rumor. You can't take them seriously—"

"It's real. One of my Guardians is sick."

His eyes widened in momentary surprise, and then he blew out his breath. "Blimey. It was true. This changes everything. The balance between the Guardians and Demons . . . They've evened the playing field. This war just got serious."

While he rambled, I reached into my pocket and pulled out a fifty-dollar bill. The sight of the cash closed his mouth immediately. "I need your help to save my Guardian," I said, placing the money between us.

"Now, wait just a minute. I heard the rumor by word of mouth. I don't know anything else. I can't help you—"

"I know," I interrupted. "I'm not asking you to help me find a cure—I've already done that. I need you to deliver a message to my grandfather when he comes here looking for me."

"What?" He continued to eye the wrinkled bill, though.

"You're the only one I can trust with this. If I told anyone else, they'd try to stop me."

"Why? What are you planning on doing?"

"I'm going to the Demon Lord."

He blinked. Then his mouth opened, but no sound came out. His lips crushed back together, and he gave me a disapproving look.

I wasn't moved by the worried display. I was too decided on my course to have second thoughts. Not yet, anyway. "There isn't any other way. He has the cure, and I'm going to get it from him."

"You can't just . . . I mean, *really*. Your grandfather is going to kill you. Oy! He's going to kill *me* for not talking you out of this madness!"

"Please calm down. Your job is going to be simple. I don't intend to just sacrifice myself to the Demons. I need you to let my friends know where I've gone so they can follow."

"Which is?"

"Las Vegas. There's a casino—"

"The Illusion Hotel and Casino, yeah. I know it."

"You do?"

He grunted. "Don't sound so surprised. I've managed to stay alive as long as I have by keeping tabs on all the Demon Lord's hot spots. Whenever he's out west, he's either in Hollywood or at the Illusion. Sometimes he visits San Diego. He likes Sea World."

I shook my head. "Look, that's not important. I just need you to help let them know where I've gone."

He still looked uncomfortable with my idea, but he was going to cooperate. That's why I'd decided to come to him in the first place. I handed him the bill without a word, and he easily slipped it into his apron pocket. "When exactly were you planning on leaving?" he asked.

"Tomorrow. I'll get a good head start, because they won't be looking for me until after school."

His eyes tightened. "You're really going there all by yourself? Do you realize how stupid that is?"

I nodded. "Yeah. But I won't be alone . . ."

❋

After I'd dropped the twins off at the elementary school, I told Lee of my plans to skip my classes for the day. She understood that I needed to spend time with Patrick, so she didn't argue. She offered to get a ride home with Rodney again, but I assured her I'd be back to pick her up—even though I felt terrible for the lie. "I'll need to get away for a few minutes," I told her. "It gets hard, watching him . . ."

She understood.

"Besides," I added easily. "I want to take you somewhere after, if that's all right. There's this really cool pawnshop my grandpa took me to . . ."

She nodded, down for whatever I wanted. I knew that when I didn't show up after school, the planted message would reach my grandfather. He would go to Clyde, and then everyone would know what I'd done.

So far, everything was going according to plan. I dropped Lee off and then headed to the warehouse. While I drove, I couldn't help but wonder if I'd made a mistake in not telling my family better good-byes. I hadn't wanted to draw attention to myself, and I certainly didn't want to admit on any level that I might not ever see them again. But I couldn't stop thinking of how Josie had looked after her soccer tournament, and I wondered if I was about to do something that would crush my sisters all over again.

I got to the warehouse and shut off my car before grabbing up my backpack. I hoped that Toni wouldn't find it odd that I brought it along with me, and I really hoped he wouldn't notice that it was filled with anything *but* school supplies.

I climbed up to the second floor quickly. I knocked lightly once on the door before I opened it and stepped into Toni and Patrick's living space.

Toni looked up from the laptop that was balanced on his knees. He shifted on the couch, trying to sit up straighter. "Oh hey—aren't you supposed to be in school or something?"

"Aren't you?" I shot back easily, knowing full well that this "college student" had never stepped onto a campus in his life.

He rolled his eyes, but I was already moving onto my next question. "How is he?"

Toni's eyes tightened. "Not good. But he doesn't complain much."

"Is he asleep?"

"Yeah. Just barely, though. He was talking to Terence just a few minutes ago."

"How are the other Guardians?" I asked, unable to stop the somewhat-morbid question.

"The second one passed away last night—the third one started getting nosebleeds two days ago. The last Guardian—he seems to be moving more slowly than the others."

Two down, two to go . . .

I looked to Patrick's closed door, tightening my hold on the strap over my shoulder in an effort to steady my mostly full backpack. "How long does Patrick have? Did Terence have a better guess?"

Toni nodded, but he was staring at the screen—unable to look at me. "Yeah. Terence gives him two days. Counting today, of course . . . possibly an extra day after that if he keeps fighting."

I tried to keep my breathing even, but it was hard. Even knowing that I was going to do everything I could for him . . . it was impossible not to worry.

Toni glanced up at me, and seeing my pale face he spoke quietly. "You can go in. I'm sure he won't mind."

I cast him a thin but grateful smile. "Thanks, Toni. For everything."

"Yeah, yeah—don't get all mushy on me, chica." But he was smiling back at me, and I knew he appreciated the thanks. He just didn't realize all the connotations the simple *thank-you* held. Not yet, anyway.

I stepped quietly into Patrick's darkened room. Toni had covered the windows with pieces of flimsy cardboard, some old sheets . . . anything to block out the bright New Mexico sun. Patrick was lying on his side, rolled tightly in a cocoon of blankets. Despite the warm morning, he was shivering dimly, unable to stay warm as his body haltingly collapsed.

I closed the door behind me and then stepped slowly over to his bed. I crossed the small space and slipped my bag to the floor before lowering myself on to the bed's edge, beside him. He hadn't bothered to hide his aura, so I was free to watch the pain mingle through every other emotion he was feeling while he dreamed. His face was tight, even in sleep, and his pallid lips trembled in a silent whimper.

I couldn't resist touching his tangled hair, gently combing down the stray locks with my fingers. I didn't want to wake him up, but we didn't have long. We needed to get moving.

I swallowed hard for strength and let my fingertips stroke against the upturned side of his face. His skin was chill to the touch, but I didn't pull away. I bent down closer to him, leaning against his bunched up blankets in an effort to transfer some of my heat to him. "Patrick?" I whispered, hand still against his face.

I repeated his name, a quiet call, and he responded hesitantly. His face twisted in a grimace as he pulled himself out of his uneasy sleep, and I breathed his name once more, my tone trying to reassure him that everything was going to be all right.

His eyes blinked reluctantly open, and then they squinted in momentary confusion. He hadn't expected to see my face mere inches from his, but he didn't seem to mind my unexpected presence. "Kate?" he groaned thinly.

I forced a smile and pushed some of his hair back behind his ear. "Yeah. I'm sorry to wake you up."

He swallowed, blinked some more, then cleared his throat before speaking again. "No. It's fine. What time is it?" he craned his neck, lifting his head to look at the digital clock on his desk.

I realized that he was worried he'd slept all through school, and I hurried to calm him. "It's just after eight. I decided school wasn't worth it today."

His head relaxed back against his pillow, and he glanced up at me. "I should be upset that you're skipping out, but I'm not." He struggled to push himself up on his elbow, and I wordlessly helped him adjust to a sitting position. He leaned heavily against the wall, and a quick shudder ran through him when his blankets slipped down to his lap. His muscular arms were suddenly covered in goose bumps, and I knew that his thin gray T-shirt wasn't enough to keep his dying body warm.

My hand had fallen from his face, but he was taking it up with his stiff fingers now, balancing it on the lump of blankets that was his leg.

My voice was muted but apologetic. "I shouldn't have disturbed you, but I was wondering if you felt up to going somewhere with me."

He blew out a shaky breath, his eyes not quite as clear and piercing as usual. "I don't know if that's such a good idea, my being in public . . ."

"You don't have to get out of the car," I whispered reassuringly. "I just want to take you on a drive."

I knew he didn't want to go. He obviously wasn't up to traveling, and though I hated to force him, I knew he would give in. No matter what he wanted, he would do whatever I asked. I felt terrible using that advantage, but I would do anything to keep him alive, even if that meant manipulation.

"Please?" I murmured. My voice cracked a little—it wasn't intentional, but I know that's what did it for him. That's what made him cave. Seeing my pain—even just a glimpse—had him willing to do anything.

He squeezed my fingers. "All right. Just let me get dressed first."

"You may want to try taming that hair too," I teased.

He smiled just a little. "I don't know if that's going to be possible."

I got Toni to come inside and help Patrick into their small bathroom, where he attempted to get himself ready to go. I knew I didn't have long, so I was quick to pack just the bare essentials for him. A pair of pajamas, a change of clothes . . . I'd already gotten most of our supplies at my house, including toothbrushes, a first aid kit, a blanket, one of my dad's old hoodies, and some money—anything I could think of that we might need.

I'd just finished stashing a couple pairs of socks into the full backpack by the time I heard the bathroom door open into the living area. I zipped the bag closed, pushed it up onto one shoulder, and walked out to join them.

Patrick was wearing his usual blue button-up shirt and some light-colored jeans. The sleeves weren't rolled up to the elbows, though, and his skin was ashy. The purple bruising under his eyes made him look haunted, but he was smiling at me.

"That's the best it's going to be," he told me, waving a hand toward his hair.

Toni was holding Patrick's arm, steadying him almost unconsciously. He snorted at Patrick's words, intentionally ignoring how weak his voice had been. "Yeah. You look beautiful, Prince Charming."

I moved to his side and took his free hand. "You look great," I told him.

He tugged his arm free of Toni so he could tap a finger to the tip of my nose. "You liar," he said simply.

The corner of my mouth twitched, then I wrapped both hands around his nearest arm. I looked to Toni. "We'll be back soon," I lied smoothly.

He nodded. "Don't hurry back. I could use a little good, old-fashioned Toni time . . ."

Toni offered to help us out to the car, but we both assured him we'd be fine. Patrick was slightly unsteady, but with my help we made it down the wide staircase and across the main factory floor. He winced when we emerged out of the building, the bright sun forcing him to squint. Our steps slowed, but the car wasn't far now. I opened the passenger door and helped him down into the low seat. I bent and pulled on the seat belt, but his sigh stopped me from continuing.

"What?" I asked quickly, wondering what I'd done wrong.

He shook his head at me. "I'm not that pathetic-looking, am I?"

I pressed my lips together, but I relinquished the seat belt to him. "Sorry. I didn't . . ."

"It's okay. Don't worry about it." I could hear the undercurrent of frustration that he fought to hide, but I didn't comment on it. I stepped around the car, letting him close his own door too. By the time I'd pushed the backpack into the backseat and my own seat belt was clicked into place, he was ready to go. I started the car, and we backed away from the old warehouse.

"Can I ask where we're going?" he questioned suddenly.

I focused out the front window, knowing that would make lying easier. "It's a surprise. You can try to sleep, though—I'll wake you up when we get there."

twenty-six

Patrick was asleep almost instantly. The combination of the warm sun through his window and the lulling movement of the car had him asleep before I was on the highway. The radio was on , but I wasn't listening to the subtle music. I was thinking about everything Selena and I had discussed yesterday.

I hadn't wanted to bring Patrick along. Taking him to the Demons seemed like such a stupid move on my part. But after Selena had learned how far along the virus had progressed . . . bringing Patrick with me was the only way to ensure he could get the cure in time.

I knew I was putting a lot of trust in Selena, and though it wasn't something I wanted to do, I had little choice. If I helped them, they would save Patrick—that was what I needed to focus on. In the end, that was the only thing I had to trust. I sort of wished I knew exactly what they wanted from me, though . . .

I'd printed out a map off the Internet, and it told me that the drive to Las Vegas would be just over nine hours, nonstop. I knew that would be too much for Patrick, and so I'd already planned out a few pit stops. I hoped we could make it as far as Kingman, Arizona, today. It would take approximately seven hours—and that was driving straight, which I knew wasn't going to happen. My bet was that it would take us more like eight or nine.

Patrick woke up around nine thirty—we'd been driving for just over an hour. He glanced out at the flat and fast-moving landscape around us, obviously trying to figure out where we were. It was more than apparent that he'd been expecting houses and buildings, not the open and dry desert landscapes that surrounded us.

I took in a steadying breath and my fingers flexed over the steering wheel. "We're in Arizona," I told him, keeping my voice light.

He blinked at the sun and turned to regard me, his face showing that he thought he'd misheard. "What?"

"Arizona. The sunny state. You know—Arizona." My throat was beginning to constrict, so I stopped talking.

His forehead wrinkled, and his voice was scratchy with disuse. "I know Arizona. What are we *doing* in Arizona?"

I finally dared to meet his gaze, even though it was hard. My heart was pounding, and I hoped I could keep my words steady. "I called Selena," I informed him, immediately focusing back on the road. The traffic was light, but I tried to pretend like it was taking all my concentration.

He didn't speak for a long minute, but when he did his voice was wooden. "You kidnapped me."

I pushed my aching shoulders back against the seat, stretching the tired muscles without slowing the speed of the car. "You didn't really give me a choice."

"Kate, this is insane," he insisted lowly.

I couldn't quite meet his eyes, but I sent him a fast look. "I can't watch you die, Patrick. Maybe you can let go, but I can't. Please try to understand that."

With my peripheral vision, I watched as he leaned back against the seat, turned his head so he was angled away from me. He gazed silently out his window for a long time, and finally I couldn't take the quiet any more.

"Please, Patrick, say something."

"Like what?" he whispered dully, still centered on the window. "There's nothing I can say to change your mind. Nothing I can do to make you go back."

I stole a few fast glances at his aura, and I was surprised by how present the red was. It made my insides curl, and I wondered for a brief moment if I'd done the right thing.

I swallowed painfully, and my voice was pinched and quiet. "You're so angry. I'm sorry. I didn't think you'd . . ."

He didn't turn, but his body stiffened at my words. "I'm not angry with you," he muttered to the glass. "I'm angry with myself. With Selena, with . . . everything. Not you."

His aura suddenly disappeared, and I knew that even though it took him more effort than usual, he was going to try and hide his emotions from me. I felt a little sting, but I could live with whatever made him more comfortable.

We drove in silence for a good fifteen more miles before his head twisted around, coming back to face me. "Where are we going?" he asked, his voice quiet but controlled. Resigned.

"Las Vegas," I said quickly; now that he was no longer in the dark, I wanted him to know every detail. "The Demon Lord owns a casino there called the Illusion Hotel. That's where Selena will be waiting."

"And the Demon Lord?"

I nodded, still looking at the road. "He'll be there too." A sigh escaped without my command, making my next words sound more regretful than they would have otherwise been. "I didn't want to make you come with me, but you need the antidote as soon as possible. I'm sorry I had to trick you like this."

"So that's it?" he asked, his even voice beginning to waver. "You just won't come home from school? Your sisters will never see you again . . . and you're okay with that?"

"Going to the Demons is a necessary risk—"

"No, it's not. It doesn't even make sense."

His words cut me, but I tried not to show it. "Patrick, I took every precaution I could. Trust me, this was the only way. Toni would have stopped me—my grandpa would have locked me in my room."

"So you're going to sacrifice yourself, just like that?"

"Of course not." I shot him a quick glance. "I'm not playing the martyr. I left a way for them to find us. I just needed the head start."

"What do you mean?"

I quickly explained about Clyde, and the directions I'd left with him. He didn't seem as surprised by the existence of my grandfather's Demon friend, but I guess he had bigger concerns on his mind, like how their eventual presence in Las Vegas would do any good.

"Kate, if the Demon Lord is there, then that whole city is going to be crawling with Demons." He shook his head gingerly, reminding me that he still had a throbbing headache. "Even if Toni called Jack, there's no way they could do anything. Not against so many enemies."

"Toni's resourceful—so is Jack. They'll figure something out."

"That's not good enough, Kate."

"Well, it was the best I could come up with." My voice was sharper than I'd wanted it to be, and I knew I'd stung him when he twisted away from me again.

Staring back out the window, I barely heard what he said next. "Why do you have to be so self-sacrificing?" Or something close to that.

I straightened at the wheel, more ruffled by his tone than I should have been. "I think I learned it from you," I muttered finally.

He didn't say anything, but I knew he heard.

We stopped for an early lunch at about 11:30, in a small town just off the highway. Or rather, we both stopped so I could eat. Patrick wasn't interested in food—only some water for his dry throat.

It was our second stop in the two hours since Patrick had woken up, and I knew he was more worn out than he let on. At our first stop, after filling up with gas, I'd helped him walk around and stretch his legs. I also bought some road food to help keep me more alert. I wanted to just have him walk around the gas station parking lot, but he moved so slowly that by the time we were back to the car we'd already been off the road for a half hour. If the rest of my pit stops went this slowly . . . It would be more like ten hours until we reached

Kingman. Three additional hours to what the map had originally laid out.

Before we started driving again, I dug out the blanket I'd packed for him, and he took it without a word. He wasn't speaking much at all, actually, but I think that was mostly because he was so tired. Yeah, he was still upset with me, but he wasn't giving me the silent treatment, per se.

I didn't dare leave him alone while I walked into a place to get food, but I wasn't going to make him go into public either. So I found a familiar looking fast-food place and decided to use the drive-thru. I ordered some food through the speaker, and then—before proceeding to pay—I suggested he go invisible. He looked sickly, and I didn't want any questions.

I of course couldn't tell if he was no longer visible, but at a quick nod from him I continued forward.

The young woman who took the money from me never glanced at him, and she didn't seem to find it strange that I ordered two waters. It was a hot day, after all.

I didn't want to eat and drive, and I knew Patrick's muscles were straining to get out of his cramped position. So I drove around until I found a small city park, and I decided to make lunch a longer stop. I helped Patrick out of the car and took him to a nearby bench where he could sit for a moment in the sun. I hoped it would warm him up, because even in the hot car without any air blowing through his vents, he was still trembling. I left him to go back for the food and drinks, and then we were sitting side by side at the wooden table.

He slipped the straw between his lips and sipped deliberately while I ate my hamburger, and we listened to the shrieking laughter of small children playing on the nearby playground. We'd been quiet for so long that the sudden sound of his voice almost caused me to jump.

"I know I'm being ungrateful," he said slowly, one hand gripping the large paper cup on the table, the other fingering his straw. He watched his fingers as he pulled the straw out and then pushed it back in, scattering the ice with each new thrust. He continued, his voice not quite so rough now that he'd had a drink. "I'm grateful—more than grateful—that you'd do this for me. I just . . . Having you give up so much for me—your Guardian—it just feels criminal to me." His piercing eyes met mine firmly, his voice intensely serious. "I can't protect you there, Kate. And that kills me."

I reached for his hand, and he let go of the straw so he could squeeze my willing fingers. "It's okay," I told him thinly. "I know this isn't easy. But everything's going to be all right. I know it is."

It was a lie, of course. I knew no such thing. But it was a lie worth telling to see his thin smile.

He didn't drink much before he slid out from the bench to lie on the dying patch of rocky grass nearby. He was only going to stretch out for a few minutes while I finished my food, but soon he was sleeping soundly.

I finished eating before stealing away quickly to the car. I brought back the blanket and draped it over him. Then I sat on the ground beside him, unable to make myself wake him up just yet.

I got a little lost in my thoughts, thinking how unreal all of this seemed. On the run with my immortal boyfriend, rushing to save his life—turning to his natural enemies for help while leaving our friends in the dark.

I also couldn't help wondering what the Demon Lord would want from me. Selena hadn't given me any clue—just that he "had plans for me," whatever that meant. She said I could learn the details once I got there, and then—after proving myself—Patrick would be injected with the antidote.

But what on earth would the Demon Lord expect me, an inexperienced Seer, to do? I was pretty darn sure it had to be related to the whole traveling-through-emotions thing. Still, that conclusion didn't exactly give me a job description. Who knew what I would be asked to do.

But would I do it? Yes. No matter what it was. What other choice did I have?

I was broken out of my thoughts by Patrick suddenly moving beside me, and I turned to see one hand against his nose, attempting to stop the flow of blood that had woken him. I hadn't thrown away the napkins from lunch, so I was able to use those to help staunch the bleeding before his shirt could get more than a few red drops on it.

This bloody nose lasted longer than the first one had—his body was taking longer to repair itself. By the time he was done washing off the remaining blood on his face in the park's dirty bathroom, I was also ready to go. We headed back to the car, but before climbing inside, I dug around in my backpack until I found the small square box of Kleenex I'd brought and my dad's old hoodie. Patrick took the black sweatshirt gladly, and while he shrugged into it, I checked my phone.

It was twelve thirty now. We'd been stopped longer than I thought. But at least I didn't have any messages. That meant that no one knew we were gone yet. I was a little surprised that Toni hadn't called—surely we'd been gone longer than he'd expected by now . . .

We got back on the highway, and Patrick had almost fallen back asleep when my phone started to ring. I knew without checking the ID that it would be Toni. Who else? I scooped up the small device, saw that it was indeed my Guardian, and then promptly shut off the sound.

Patrick was watching me, and I could see in his eyes that he knew exactly who was trying to call me. But he didn't argue with me about ignoring Toni. The acceptance, that resignation, was back in the stone set of his jaw, and I knew he was done arguing with me.

I passed a slow-moving semi, and Patrick drifted to sleep in the seat beside me.

❀

I tried to keep our stops to a minimum, but here it was, five o'clock and we still had a good three hours before we'd reach the motel I'd been shooting for in Kingman. Some of the stops had been my fault. My Elantra got exceptionally good gas mileage, but still, stopping to refuel had been necessary. The stop that had taken the longest was when Patrick suddenly doubled over against his seat belt, screaming as his insides were torn apart. The sound of his shrieks in the close confines of the car were deafening, and my whole body shivered as I struggled to pull over onto the shoulder of the road.

The instant I got the car to stop, I killed the engine and threw my seat belt off, kneeling awkwardly on my seat so I could wrap my arms around him. I don't know what help or comfort it offered—honestly, I don't think he was even aware of my existence for most of it—but when the heart-wrenching torture finally ceased, he could barely lift his eyes to look at me, he was so wiped out. Drenched in sweat, he lowered his head onto my shoulder, where he struggled to control his breathing. My fingers twisted in his hair, and I rubbed his shoulder, his back. "It'll all be over tomorrow," I whispered finally, pulling him impossibly closer as the tears rolled deftly down my face. "I promise. I'll fix this."

He didn't say anything. I don't know that his torn throat could support words.

I held him for a few minutes, until he stopped shaking and gasping. Only then did I allow him to pull away from my embrace, let him lean heavily against the seat. I searched in my bag for a bottle of water, which I helped him support so he could get a drink. He didn't drink much—a couple swallows.

I didn't start driving until he gave me an impartial nod, quietly assuring me that he was all right. He wasn't, and we both knew it. But I restarted the car, and we merged back onto the highway.

And now at five o'clock he was nursing his latest nosebleed while I ate another fast-food meal. We didn't bother looking for a park this time—we just stayed in the car at the restaurant's parking lot. I knew he was exhausted, and I didn't want to push him. But if we stayed here in Flagstaff . . . it would take that much longer to reach Las Vegas tomorrow. It felt too early to call it quits for the day. He must have felt the same way, because when I asked him if he felt like going on to Kingman, he told me that he did.

After a fast dinner, we were back on the road. Patrick slept most of this last stretch, and though my car was getting low on gas, I didn't stop until we reached Kingman, at 8:00 p.m. on the dot. There were quite a few cheap but respectable motels to choose from, and I finally settled on a Motel 6 just a couple blocks off the highway. The money was coming out of my college fund, but I figured it could take the hit. I mean, seriously, if things didn't work out, I wouldn't be going to college anyway.

Patrick was startled awake when I parked the car underneath the tall blue sign for the motel, and he seemed momentarily lost as he struggled to make sense of the dimly lit sky and the stopped car. He squinted at the familiar sign and then glanced over his shoulder to the white building behind us, and that's when I realized that his aura was visible to me again. I wasn't planning on mentioning it, just in case that made him want to hide it again, but he saw my eyes flicker to his aura and mumbled a soft explanation. "I can't control it anymore. It's like that ability is just . . . gone." He hesitated and then added more quietly, "I'm invisible too. I have been since before dinner."

I tried not to let these revelations bother me—but they did. He was already disappearing from the world. Humans could no longer see him. Soon, I would lose him too.

I forced a smile. "Thanks for the warning. I'll stop talking to you in public now. I don't need anymore of a claim on the crazy corner."

He cracked his own smile, but the colors of pain swimming around his body reminded me that every muscle he moved took effort.

I left him in the car, doors locked, while I went to pay for a room. That done, I returned to get him and my bag. I was still a few steps away from the car when I realized he was trying to stop yet another nosebleed. We were running out of time, but there was no way either of us could keep driving. We'd been traveling for ten hours—we needed to get some rest before tomorrow. The last stretch of the journey would be the hardest in many ways, because I had a feeling that those two hours or so would pass by quickly. And then we'd be at the mercy of the Demons.

I tried to act nonchalant about his nosebleed, and I knew from his aura that he appreciated that. He finished tending to the blood before he got out of the car, and I made sure everything was locked up before throwing the backpack over one shoulder. I took his hand, not caring how it must look to twine an invisible person's fingers with my own, and we walked toward our room, which was located on the second floor. I quickly found our room and was soon pushing through the mint-green door.

Patrick's look was priceless when I pulled out a pair of his pajamas. It was a mix of surprise and reluctant appreciation. My attention to detail had him wanting to congratulate me, but his still-lingering disapproval wouldn't let him say more than a quiet, "Thank you."

Within ten minutes, he was changed into something more comfortable and was curling up on one of the beds. He kept the hoodie on, and that seemed to keep him from needing to wrap himself quite so tightly in the blankets.

By the time I came out of the bathroom in my shorts and tank top, he was sleeping soundly.

The light was already turned off, so all I had to do was climb into the second bed and wait for sleep to come. I silently searched through my missed calls and messages—and there were a hundred, almost literally. Some from my grandma, who had no idea what was going on. Several from Lee, wondering if I was going to come and pick her up at school and where I could be, and threatening to call Patrick— the subtle worries went on and on, until she finally realized I wasn't coming back.

Missed calls from Grandpa, Toni, Jack—even Jason, his Seer.

None of these I dared answer. Because if I spoke to them, heard their arguments, I might just allow myself to hesitate. And Patrick didn't have time for second thoughts. He needed help *now*.

I knew that by now Lee had helped Grandpa make the connection with Clyde. They knew where we'd gone, and there was a chance they were already following us. That's why we'd need an early start tomorrow. True, they'd have no idea where we'd stopped for the night. But if they drove straight—if they'd left around five, when I imagined they'd probably put everything together—there was a good chance they were well on their way.

Not that going straight to Las Vegas would do them any good. It's not like they could stop us by showing up at the Demon Lord's casino first. No, I was pretty sure that they'd turn their attention to trying to locate us. Jason would try to pinpoint our possible position, using his Internet savvy, and they'd probably search most of the motels located just off the freeway. But a daunting job like that would keep them busy all night, and I was sure there was no way they'd find us.

Seeing that I hadn't missed any calls from Selena, I shut my phone and set it on the small bedside table. Then I curled into a tight ball on my side, rolling under the crisp sheets so my back was to Patrick.

It was a little weird, trying to fall asleep in the dark room, knowing that Patrick was four feet away from me. This was the first time I'd slept in the same room with a guy, and though the weirdness lingered, it didn't feel wrong or awkward. I mean, we were in separate beds; it wasn't anything like *that*. Still, I wondered what my parents would have thought about the situation—what my grandparents would do if they knew I was spending the night in a motel with my boyfriend.

Actually, having him nearby was comforting. Listening to his shallow but regular breaths helped my heart to slow to an even throb, and soon I was sleeping too—lulled into dreaming by the mere constancy of his even breathing.

twenty-seven

It was midnight when his breathing stopped.

I didn't realize it at first. All I knew was that suddenly my eyes popped open and I was no longer asleep. The room was dark, and I couldn't figure out what had made me awaken so suddenly. I could hear the cars outside, a dog barking nearby . . . that's when I noticed the absence of sound in the room. The rhythmic breathing that had helped me drift to sleep was gone.

I jerked up at once, clawing at my blankets as I fought to scramble free. I was still kicking haphazardly at the last of the tangled sheets by the time my body was twisted around, and my panicked eyes finally found him.

I expected to see his eyes open, his mouth gaping in death. I almost wonder if that would have been better than what I saw instead.

He was being tortured again—the attacking virus working to destroy every part of him. He'd balled up a fistful of blankets and shoved them into his mouth, attempting to smother every scream, every gasp. In the process, he was smothering himself. His nostrils flared wildly, but he still wasn't getting the necessary air.

I pushed off my bed, yanking the majority of the bed sheets to the floor as I stood too quickly, losing my balance in one awful second that made my stomach drop. I nearly fell over, but grabbing the nightstand kept me from toppling to the floor.

A second later, I was kneeling on the bed next to him, pushing him onto his back so I could pull the makeshift gag out of his mouth. Meeting his wide and agonized gaze—even just that transiently—let me know that he was still in the beginning stages of this torment. He wasn't oblivious to me yet—he was still trying not to buckle under the excruciating pain. I knew the gag was for my benefit. He was invisible to humans now, so no one in the motel would have heard him.

Had he really thought I could sleep through this?

His whole body jerked suddenly in a horrific spasm, and his eyes rolled back into his head. His thrashing became more intense, and his fingers curled into taut claws. He released his hold on the blankets, and I hurried to jerk them out of his mouth. He gasped wildly, pitiful whimpers accompanying every desperate exhale. I tried to hold his hand, but he was burying the hard fingers into the bed beside him. I gave up on that and instead wrapped my arms around his head, trying to cradle him against the torture.

He didn't scream much, until he neared the end. But the screams were so earsplitting, so gut-wrenching, that their arrival was no comfort. Tears were sliding down my cheeks, but I was hardly aware of them. I tried to hold him still, despite the tremors and convulsions that had him writhing on the bed. I pulled him closer and closer, as if the pressure of my embrace could steady him. If nothing else, maybe if I got close enough I could take some of his pain.

Suddenly his arms were around me, crushing me impossibly closer. I gasped sharply at the painful force, but I didn't try to squirm away.

"Patrick," I panted hoarsely into his hair, against his shoulder. "It's going to be okay. It's almost over. I promise."

His arms flexed around me—I think he was trying to let go—but his muscles wouldn't obey. He shrieked my name, and the raw emotion in that horrible plea had me shaking almost as badly as he was.

"I'm so sorry," I sobbed. "I'm so, so sorry . . ."

This was the end. It had to be. He couldn't survive this. He was going to die, here in my arms. And there was nothing I could do but cry over his torn body.

The uncontrollable writhing finally died down, and he sucked in air through his nose. His eyes were pinched closed, and his arms around my shoulders were quivering as his tortured muscles continued to tick and vibrate. I was half kneeling, half lying over him. My hands shook, and my body rocked with my tears. I'd buried my face in the crook of his neck and shoulder, and both of our touching cheeks were wet. I didn't know what was his sweat and what were my tears.

His body shuddered beneath mine, and I knew he was trying to gather the air to speak. His soft hands dragged languidly over my back, and I realized he was trying to soothe me.

"Shh . . ." he finally croaked, his words and breaths faltering. "Don't cry . . ."

"What can I do?" I gasped, tightening my arms around his neck. I blinked rapidly against my stinging tears, but that only succeeded in making them fall faster. "Please," I panted brokenly. "Please, just tell me what I can do."

He swallowed hard—it was a painful convulsion. "Stay," he begged hoarsely. "Just stay . . ." His breath hitched suddenly, and he flinched deeply—I could feel the horrible twist against my face. "No." He gasped heavily, shaking both of us as his chest expanded violently. "Oh, please no . . ."

Before I could ask what was happening, his back was arching, and his taut body was pushing mine back. His muscles strained against me, and he cried out sharply before slamming back to the bed. I was hovering over him now, and I hurried to stroke his face with wavering fingers. "Patrick? Patrick!"

His eyes rolled as the acute pain escalated, and his screams choked off to horrible gulps for air. And then he wasn't breathing at all.

I knew that the impossible had occurred—the torture was back for a second round, seconds after ending the first. It had returned to finish the job.

I stroked at his hair, as if that would somehow help him remember how to breathe.

When he finally started to inhale again—to howl under the incomprehensible torment—I sunk back against him, my closed eyes buried in his straining neck. I held him and cried and waited for this to be over.

It felt like this stretch of time would never pass. That he would never escape this, and that we would be like this forever—eternally trapped in this awful moment.

His nose started to bleed just before his body managed to stop the horrible invasion. I pulled the blankets away from his face while he gasped for air, trying to recover after such a harrowing experience. I leaned over to the nightstand, snatching out three tissues from the nearby box. He was powerless, unable to lift his arms, so I attended to the bloody nose while he struggled to breathe. Honestly, I didn't think he even knew who I was.

Once the bleeding stopped, it was almost one in the morning. He was exhausted, but as I pulled the bloody tissues away he managed to wrap his fingers around my retreating wrist. "Please don't leave me," he whispered faintly, voice breaking painfully. "Please stay with me . . ."

I knew he was already on the verge of being asleep again—he couldn't keep his eyes open after living through that unspeakable horror. But I spoke to him anyway, bending down to cover his taut face with wan kisses. "I won't leave you. Ever."

I waited until he was breathing more evenly and I was sure he was asleep, then I leaned away to toss the used tissues onto the night-stand. And then—exhausted and unwilling to break my promise—I lay down on the bed next to him. I stayed on top of the blankets, not caring that my legs were a little too cool for comfort. I didn't want to let go of his hand or look away from his face . . .

I clutched his limp fingers, curled up beside his limp body, and watched his face as he found a timid refuge in sleep.

❊

I didn't think I'd be able to fall asleep after everything that had happened, but I woke up around seven, one of Patrick's arms draped over my waist, his warm breath on my face. We were close, but the blankets still separated us.

I realized belatedly that his eyes were open, and he was staring at me, unsmiling. He was propped up casually with one elbow, so he was hovering partially over me.

I twisted around beneath his arm so I could unbend one of my arms and set my fingers against the side of his face. My thumb rubbed beneath one of his tired eyes, and then I finally spoke. "How are you feeling?"

He didn't answer right away, just continued to gaze down at me. Then his lips parted, and his croaking voice formed precise, unassuming words. "You are so beautiful, Kate."

I didn't know how to react at first. The words were unexpected, so out of place . . . I said the only thing that came to mind. "I think your brain was damaged."

A horribly thin smile twisted his lips. "I love you," he whispered calmly, his forehead tipping toward mine.

Before our noses could brush, I cringed back. "I have morning breath," I informed him.

"I don't think I care," he breathed, still coming closer despite my leaning away.

I moved my hand from his face to his chest, holding him back in his slow but maddening advance. "Trust me—one whiff and you'd care. A lot."

His neck bent, and I couldn't back up any more without slipping off the bed. But instead of moving to put his lips on my mouth, he set them to my forehead.

It was amazing how much that small, seemingly unexciting kiss left me reeling.

His easy lilting voice was a measured murmur. "You've packed pretty much everything else—what about a toothbrush?"

My eyes were closed—I couldn't seem to keep them open when his lips were on my skin. "Yeah, I did. But we need to concentrate on getting to Vegas."

He sighed deeply and pulled back slightly. I opened my eyes to watch him regard me with something like regret on his face. "This is definitely the worst side effect."

"Huh?" I questioned, completely lost.

He leveled a stern look at me, though I knew from his aura and his shining eyes that he was teasing. Mostly. "I collapse a couple times, and now my girlfriend's afraid to kiss me."

I rolled my eyes, a part of me uneasy with his joking, the greater portion of me loving this flirtatious side that had been missing for far too long. "I am *not* afraid of kissing you. I'm afraid—"

"I admit your lips are overpowering," he said, breaking through my explanation. "But I promise I won't faint." He actually winked, and I had to really work to keep my expression firm.

"I'm not afraid of hurting you," I lied. "I'm afraid of scaring you off with my morning breath. There's a big difference."

"Either way, you refuse to kiss me. So what's the notable difference?"

"You're hopeless."

"You say that a lot," he mused. "But you never actually give up on me. I wonder why that is."

I moved quickly, placing my lips against his before he could really react—or breathe, I hoped—and then I settled back against the pillow, a smirk on my face. "It's because I love you," I said.

I didn't expect that small kiss to affect him so much, but he swallowed hard before forcing a tremulous smile. "And how I love you." He shifted his weight around me; the arm that had been resting over my stomach moved up until he pushed his hand into the bed, in the narrow space between my arm and my body. And then his mouth descended, and he was tentatively brushing his lips against mine.

He kissed me so tenderly, and yet so deeply. I knew his arms were weak, but he was able to support himself while he tried to convey his love and appreciation. It was one of the most meaningful kisses we'd ever shared, and though our bodies were barely touching, I felt warm all over.

In a perfect world, we would have kept right on kissing all

morning. But Patrick was pulling back already, a light in his clear blue eyes that hadn't been there for days. He smiled widely, and his whispering voice was punctuated by a discreet, rippling laugh that wanted to break free.

"You really do have bad breath, Kate."

I slapped his arm playfully, and that was all it took to set off his low chuckling. He pulled away from me, sitting up on his side of the bed while thrusting a hand through his messy hair.

I sat up a second later, and I couldn't keep myself from speaking the words. "You seem . . . different. More like you."

He looked at me over his shoulder, his feet already on the floor. "I feel a little better. Maybe my body knows it's nearing the end, either way . . ."

I didn't want the conversation to get serious, even though I knew it would have to eventually. Still, I wasn't sure what to say—how to comfort him.

He shrugged. "Or maybe your morning breath scared the virus away. You were breathing on me all night, after all . . ."

I grunted. "Real mature, Patrick."

We got ready calmly, not bothering to rush. We knew time was of the essence, but for some reason we seemed untouchable here. After all these stressful days, and the horrible trials of last night . . . It just felt good to be able to tease each other lightly. He was still hurting, his energy still depleted from last night—that was obvious—but he hid it well. He was trying to do the same thing I was—live in the moment. Forget everything that had brought us here, and disregard everything that we were going to have to face today.

I checked us out of the motel, and Patrick walked with me to the desk. Not that anyone else could see him. He stood directly at my side, leaning in to blow a tickling stream of air on my exposed neck. I wanted to smack him, but I couldn't very well do that in front of the clerk without looking like an idiot.

The parking lot was more crowded this morning than it had been in the evening, so I didn't dare hold his hand. We walked slowly together to the car, and when we'd almost reached it my phone started to vibrate.

Patrick and I both looked to my pocket, and I pulled the thin device out.

"It's Toni," I whispered after seeing the display, not that anyone was close enough to pay any attention to a girl talking with herself.

"You should answer it," Patrick suggested. "That way we can better coordinate our rescue."

"*Our* rescue? The Demons wouldn't dare keep you a prisoner, would they?"

He shrugged a single shoulder, as if my question was immaterial. "I'm not leaving you there alone," he said. He gestured to the phone with his chin. "Answer it."

I let out a sigh—this went against my better instincts. I flipped it open. "Hey, Toni."

There was a strained laugh. "Hey, Toni?" he repeated. "You can't pull a crazy stunt like this and start out by saying, 'Hey, Toni.'"

"Um . . . Sorry, Toni?"

"Better. You two, running off to Vegas . . . Freak dang, girl, haven't we had the talk about shotgun weddings?" His voice dimmed suddenly, and I could imagine him speaking to the entire car. "Yeah, I think she's okay. She doesn't sound very repentant, though." He focused back on me. "How's Patrick? Is he tied up in the trunk?"

"Of course not." We stopped at the passenger door, and I pulled out my keys with my free hand, passing them off to Patrick. "He's doing better this morning."

"So . . . your grandpa wants to know where the heck you are. Actually, he didn't say heck. And I edited out a couple more bleeps. Man, you can tell the guy's been in some serious wars . . ."

"I don't think you guys need to know where we are," I said cautiously. "You know where we're going. Isn't that enough?" Patrick had his door open, and he climbed inside and reached to unlock mine. I moved around the hood, the phone still pressed tightly to my ear while I shrugged out of my backpack.

"According to Jason—who calculated the best places to spend the night, plus your estimated travel time—you stopped for gas twice? That was your grandpa's guess—anyway, we pegged you to be somewhere between Flagstaff and Kingman. And since there's not a lot in between there and we didn't find you guys in Flagstaff . . ."

"Wow. You guys *are* pretty good."

"Thanks," he muttered sarcastically. To the rest of the car, "They're in Kingman." Then back to me, "We'll be there in about an hour. Wait for us."

I already had my door open, and I slung my bag inside before sinking into the seat behind the wheel. "I can't do that. We need to keep going."

"Kate, do you *want* to give your grandfather a heart attack?"

"Who's with you?"

"The usual group. Me, your grandpa, Jack, Jason, and Lee."

My eyes widened. "What!" I gasped. Patrick cast me a worried look. My eyes narrowed, and my voice turned extremely dangerous. "Toni, if you dragged my best friend into all this . . ."

"Whoa! Watch those accusations. You're the one that started *all this* . . . Besides, she threatened to hate me forever if I didn't let her come along. What was I supposed to do?"

"Tell her no!"

"A little late for that. So are you going to wait for us or not?"

"And let you drag me back? I don't think so." I didn't even say good-bye—I just handed the phone off to Patrick, so I could start driving.

Patrick interrupted Toni's string of words. "Toni, it's me. How many are with you?" He listened to the short answer while I backed out of our parking spot, and then he was shaking his head. "That's not good enough. You're going to have to think of something else. You're just going to put yourselves in danger and get the humans killed . . . No, I'm fine. Don't worry about me . . . Yeah, I know. But I can't stop her. I've tried every logical argument . . . That's not a good idea—tell

Jack . . . No. We'll have to think of something else." He hesitated. "Hold on—I'll ask."

He turned to face me. "If Selena does intend to give me the anti-dote, do you know a timeline? When she'll do it?"

I shook my head, focusing on the traffic. "I'm not sure. She said once I've proven myself, they'll help you. Whatever that means."

"Today, maybe?"

I nodded. "I think so. If they're going to do it at all. They're not exactly patient people, and you . . . She knows you don't have a lot of time—that's why she told me to bring you along."

He bobbed his head slowly, before speaking to Toni again. "Whatever you're going to try, you should wait until this evening, if at all possible; just in case they're serious about the antidote . . . I understand Henry's concerns—believe me. But if the Guardians can get their hands on the antivirus, we might all stand a chance . . . No. I don't think so. We'll probably be there about . . ." He glanced at the clock on the stereo. "Ten. Call if you come up with something more concrete. If not . . . Yes, of course. And thanks, Toni. For everything." He paused, then pulled the phone from his ear, putting it on speaker.

Suddenly Lee's voice filled the car. "Kate Bennett, you are the dumbest person I know! Why would you do something like this without enlisting me first?"

I spoke a little louder than normal, to be heard over the humming sounds of the car. "It looks like you enlisted yourself."

"Yeah. But I'd rather be with you. I mean, what is this? Kidnapping?"

"He's pretty willing at the moment."

"Yeah, after dragging him five hundred miles from his home. I mean seriously, what choice does he have now?"

"She's got a point," Patrick mumbled.

I ignored him. "Lee, you have to promise me that you'll stay out of this, okay? Drive the getaway car or something, but just swear you won't go after any Demons."

"What's that?" She pretended that our signal was breaking up.

"Oh my Oreos, I can't hear you anymore! Here's your Grandpa."

"Kate?" His voice was extra gruff. "Honey, are you all right?"

I sighed. "Yeah. I'm fine."

"What the heck were you thinking? I don't care how brave you are, do you realize how insane you were to run off with him? And you better report that he's too weak to lift his hands, or you *better* have slept in separate rooms, young lady . . ."

"Um, Grandpa?" I blushed. "You're on speaker."

"I don't care—let him hear. Patrick? I know she's your girlfriend, but she's your Seer too. Hands off during a mission, or you'll cloud your judgment—and hers."

"Yes, sir," Patrick said obediently, casting me a small smile. "I understand."

"Good. Now Kate, I'm not going to lecture you anymore right now, because I need to say something else—it's more important, considering what you're about to go into . . . I love you. So does Grandma and Josie, and Jenna."

It was suddenly hard for me to swallow. "What did you tell them?"

"The only thing I could. I told your Grandma you ran away, leaving a note with Lee. The twins, well . . . they think you and Lee left on an uncondoned road trip."

"Not too far from the truth on that one."

"No. Not really." He blew out his breath. "I'm going to get you back, honey. Until then, I need you to promise that you'll do everything they say. Keep yourself safe, no matter what—I don't care what you have to do. Got it?"

"Yeah. And Grandpa . . . I love you. No matter what happens, please tell Grandma and the twins that I love them too."

"You'll do that yourself—after your Grandma grounds you for a year."

If that was the worst that would happen, I'd take it in a heartbeat.

But I was pretty sure that things weren't going to be that simple. They never were when you were dealing with Demons.

twenty-eight

I'd been to Las Vegas once before, on a family vacation. The trip had been an interesting one, since both my parents thought gambling was not only dumb but also a sin. "Wasting your intelligence on something like that should be a crime," my dad had said more than once. There were other things to do in Vegas, of course, but it was weird feeling as if we were the only ones in the city *not* gambling.

Still, coming here once had given me an idea of the city's layout, and the map I'd found online did the rest. The Illusion Hotel and Casino wasn't any bigger than any of the other large casinos on the Strip, but it had more of an elegant look to it. Fewer flashing lights, more architectural detail. Like only the very rich and famous would even bother to step inside. The building was made of white stone that gleamed in the desert sun, and a huge fountain sprayed water almost as high as the tallest palm trees. Since I was concentrating on the road, I didn't give it an in-depth look at the moment. But even that one glimpse made me feel colder and decidedly smaller.

The map I'd printed took me right to the parking lot Selena had directed me to find. It was located behind the Illusion, and I knew as soon as we pulled inside that this was it. There was no turning back now.

Patrick was quieter than he had been this morning. But he hadn't gone through any serious pain, so that was good enough for me. He'd had one bloody nose, thirty miles back, but it hadn't lasted long. The joking mood we'd been fighting to keep had died at the gas station we'd stopped at about an hour ago, so we were both feeling pretty tense and subdued.

Once we were parked and the car was turned off, Patrick placed a last call to Toni and the others. It was fast, because there wasn't much to say. From what I gathered on Patrick's side of the conversation, no firm plans had been made yet. But they weren't going to abandon us—that was the only surety. Patrick gave them a general idea of where we'd parked, in case that could somehow help them, and then ended the call.

He moved to hand the phone to me, but I just shook my head. "They're going to take it away—might as well leave it in the glove box."

He didn't argue. He stowed the phone away and took off his seat belt. I followed suit, but before I could reach for my door, he was reaching for my hand, gripping my fingers with surprising strength.

His eyes burned into mine, and his voice throbbed with intensity. "I'm not going to leave your side. Not for a second."

I tried not to let him see how much that promise meant to me, because I didn't want him to see how worried I was. This was my brilliant plan, after all.

I gave him a simple but grateful smile and then twisted around and opened my door. I didn't dare speak and nothing was really left to say. It was time to do this.

I heard him stiffly remove himself from the car, and by the time my door was closed and I was walking around the back of the car to gain his side, I saw them.

More specifically, I saw *her*. Selena was impossible to miss, even though she had four threatening men walking around her—all Demons except for one human, who I supposed was a Seer. He didn't look any less dangerous, though.

She was wearing an alluring dark-red evening gown, though it wasn't even noon yet. It stretched down to her manicured feet, revealing perfect toes and matching red stiletto heels. Her glowing brown skin was as exotic and beautiful as ever, especially her rounded shoulders and slender arms, which were left uncovered. Her luscious smile would have been inviting, if not for the coldness in her large, brown eyes. Her thick, chocolate hair billowed voluminously around her head, falling past her shoulders in large and generous curls. Her hips swayed while she walked, her long silk skirt skintight across that general area. It flared around her knees so the expensive material could shift and swell with every measured step.

I suddenly felt inadequate in my white top and faded blue jeans. My worn black Converses had never screamed this loudly, and my face cursed me for not even bothering with some mascara.

I reached Patrick's side and slipped my hands around one of his arms, but he was hardly paying attention to me. He was focused on the Demons, who were almost upon us.

Selena's makeup was as perfect as everything else about her. She applied it liberally, but it worked for her. Her eye shadow was mesmerizing, and her clear and unblemished skin made me want to avoid mirrors for the rest of my life. I knew she could read my thoughts, because her dark wet lips suddenly parted in a taunting smile, revealing her perfect white teeth.

Patrick took a strong step forward, pulling me along with him so we were standing at the hood of my car together.

When the Demons were only two cars away from us, Selena spoke, her voice husky without even trying. "Why, Patrick, you look simply awful. A little ill, are we? Your Seer isn't taking proper care of you."

My skin prickled angrily, but I'd already told myself I wasn't going to take her bait.

Patrick seemed to have a similar goal, but his voice was a little too dark to be completely innocent. "Selena, the outfit's a little eccentric for the morning hours, don't you think?"

She gave him an enticing wink, her lips twisting seductively. "You should see the rest of my wardrobe, Patrick. This is anything but . . . eccentric."

The words were out before I could think to stop them. "One might think you're trying a little too hard, Selena. Are you feeling your age today?"

The Demons were in front of the car parked next to us, and Selena stopped her advance. Her retinue paused with her, and she gave me an icy smile. "Hmm, the dog still lacks training, I see. Oh well—I love breaking in new pets."

She suddenly gestured to the Hispanic Demon standing directly beside her, her flair for dramatics far from flagging. "You know Jose, of course. You met just a few weeks ago."

She waved at the Demons on her other side—two thickly built men, both with blond hair. They looked almost identical, and I don't know if I would have been able to tell them apart but for their hair—the first had a long ponytail at the back of his head; the other had a short and spiky cut. They looked to be in their early thirties, their faces hard and decidedly terrorist-looking. "This is Viktor, and Yuri—the Dmitriev brothers."

Selena then tossed a nod to the last man, the one with the colorful aura. Actually, it wasn't all that colorful. It was the most grayish-blue thing I'd ever seen. He was in his late twenties, Asian, and he had knife scars all over his face—shallow and deep alike. "And this is Takao Kiyota. He is the Demon Lord's personal Seer. His favorite."

She focused back on Patrick, her cold eyes shining. "Well, we shouldn't keep the Demon Lord waiting. He's been expecting you all morning." She stretched out a hand. "Need any help, love? You look a little tipsy."

"I'll manage, thank you," Patrick said flatly, not even sparing a single glance on her perfectly sculpted hand.

Her arm sank and she smiled. "Very well. But first things first— Viktor, would you please shake the Seer's hand?"

The Russian with the ponytail stepped forward, unhurried, holding out a large hand toward me. I wondered how many bones those iron fingers had crushed before, but that didn't stop me from lifting my own hand to deliver the first touch.

Though a handshake wasn't necessary, since I'd already broken the shield that was designed to protect humans from a Demon's touch, Viktor still pressed our palms together. I got the distinct impression that he was measuring me up with a single handclasp, as if that could tell him everything about me. My strength, my fears, my tolerance for pain . . . everything he would need to know.

After a few tense seconds he released me, and as he stepped back I knew he was satisfied I wasn't a threat.

Without beckoning, Yuri stepped forward next, his light spiky hair glowing in the sunlight. His eyes were calculating, and his muscles were like steel cords running all through his body. He was wearing an expensive suit, like his brother, and I imagined they made quite the intimidating hotel security.

When Yuri shook my hand, I didn't get the feeling that he was searching me for weaknesses. No, it was more like he was trying to assert his authority over me. It was working. I was duly humbled by the time he dropped my limp fingers.

Jose and Selena had already broken the shield around me on our last meeting, so it wasn't necessary for me to touch them. Takao Kiyota was mostly human, so he didn't have to shake my hand either—but he stepped forward anyway. He didn't reach for my fingers, though; only came to stand right in front of me. His dark, shaggy hair fell over his face, covering large sections of his heavily scarred skin. He was also wearing a suit, which didn't seem to fit him well. It was obvious that he would rather be in street clothes. He stared at me through veiled eyes, and I realized distantly that we were about the same height— I might have been slightly taller. That didn't make me feel any less intimidated, though.

"I See your fear," he whispered at last, breaking the tense silence. His voice was airy—a wheeze, essentially. I found my eyes darting to his throat, where sure enough there was a ragged scar. His windpipe must have been badly damaged during a knife fight. The injury didn't make him appear impaired—it made him terrifying.

"You worry that you've made a wrong choice in coming." He

continued, before pausing cryptically to looked up at Patrick's drawn face. His eyes tightened at whatever he saw there, and then he turned back to me. "And indeed you have."

Selena chuckled as Takao stepped back, and I realized belatedly that she was laughing at me. "Don't feel bad. Takao does that to everyone."

She then clapped her hands sharply together. "Well then! I hope you don't think us rude, but I think it would be best to take you in through the back. No offense, dear, but we *do* set a certain standard here at the Illusion—one you just don't reach." She leaned in closer, and I could smell her heavy perfume. She cringed at my face, primarily the pimple near my eyebrow. "Oh dear. I could recommend something for that, if you'd like. And I know an excellent moisturizer, not that I suffer from such trivial things anymore."

She turned suddenly on her heel—Jose sticking to her side as if he were chained there—and they started to walk back toward the huge hotel.

I knew without waiting for an invitation that Patrick and I were supposed to go next. I held onto his arm tightly, and though he moved stiffly, his head was held high. The Dmitriev brothers fell into step behind us—following a little too closely for me to relax—and Takao came up behind them.

We crossed the parking lot, none of us speaking. I tried to pay attention to Patrick's breathing, since it had worked so well on me last night. But I wasn't calming down. My heart continued to pound, and I hated the fact that Takao would be able to read my every rush of fear and doubt.

Patrick reached over with his free hand and laid it over one of my own, trying to offer silent comfort. It helped, but only a little.

We followed a sidewalk to a side entrance, which was guarded by a bulky Demon. Selena didn't even acknowledge the guard, who used a key-card to unlock the door before he pulled it open and held it for us. We all filed into the building, the interior looking very dim compared to the sunlight outside.

I pushed closer to Patrick as we both stepped through the doorway together, and I couldn't help but wonder if either of us were going to see the sun again.

✷

The Illusion Hotel and Casino was spectacular. There really wasn't another word for it. Even here, in a remote corridor, everything was immaculate and undeniably expensive. The carpet, the heavily detailed paneling, the chandeliers and other decor—the effect was breathtaking. The Demon Lord had excellent taste, not that I was going to admit it out loud.

As our eyes gradually adjusted to the change in lighting, Selena tossed us a look over her shoulder. Still walking, she addressed Patrick. "I didn't bother to check, because I know you weren't foolish enough to bring weapons. But I'm afraid the Demon Lord does have certain rules. Before we reach his suite, you will both be searched." Her eyes narrowed, making them appear smoldering and innocent at the same time. I don't know how she did it, but I was sure that many women would kill for such a gift. "If you'd like," she whispered flirtatiously. "I could search you myself. I promise to be *very* thorough."

My voice was even and surprisingly strong. "Getting a little bored after you killed your last boyfriend?"

She blinked and cast me a pitying look. "Dear, dear. Have I made you feel jealous? Don't worry, pet—I have that effect on most women." She turned back around, and the conversation ended.

We didn't run into anyone else—a few maids, who didn't even bother to look at us. I had a feeling that they'd seen this sort of thing before and that they knew better than to comment or draw attention to themselves. There were a few doors, but mostly the hallway just stretched to an elevator waiting at the end.

Jose pushed the up arrow, but before the doors could chime open, a Demon wearing the uniform and tag marking him as the hotel manager emerged from one of the rooms. He was just closing his phone, and he stepped right up to Selena—completely ignoring the rest of us.

"Miss Avalos, the senator would like you to come to his rooms for a private luncheon."

The elevator dinged, and the doors slid open. Selena sighed deeply. "Very well. Tell him I'll be right up."

The Demon manager nodded and then moved to turn.

Her fast words made him hesitate. "Derek, when does he checkout?"

"This afternoon, I believe."

She cursed. "Fine. But I hate to miss this . . ." She turned to Patrick. "You behave, now. And don't do anything too exciting while I'm gone. I'll hurry back. But, obviously, I can't keep a senator waiting."

Just what our government needed. More Demon influence.

Selena turned us over to Jose, who motioned us to enter the elevator. Patrick and I stepped inside, moving to the back corner while the other Demons silently followed us. Takao Kiyota was the last to enter. He pressed the button for the penthouse, and as the elevator doors slid closed, he turned and focused his dark eyes on me. I felt my body tense under his open gaze, but I was sure my aura revealed the full force of my anxiety. The spike in my emotions seemed to please him, and he slowly grinned, the scars on his face stretching luridly.

Patrick must have felt my grip on his right arm tighten, because he glanced away from the menacing Dmitriev brothers and caught sight of Takao staring at me with his triumphant smile. Patrick's body stiffened, and he shifted protectively. But before he could get fully in between us, Yuri was stepping forward, latching onto Patrick's left shoulder.

Even though he was weak, hopelessly outnumbered and had no logical reason to resist, Patrick attempted to shrug out of Yuri's bracing hold. When that didn't work, Patrick tore his arm free of my grip and slammed his fist into Yuri's gut. I was surprised at the sudden jump in his strength and desire to resist, but Yuri didn't even grimace at the blow. The giant Russian merely snatched Patrick's retreating wrist and—in a move too fast for me to fully understand—he'd twisted Patrick's right arm behind his back and jerked his solid knee into Patrick's unprotected stomach, using his leverage on Patrick's shoulder to drive in the greatest pain possible.

Choking and shaking, Patrick crumpled to the floor as soon as Yuri dropped his supporting knee.

"Stop it!" I gasped too late, tearfully sinking to my knees in an attempt to reach Patrick's side. Takao caught my descending elbow, though, and jerked me stumblingly toward him. His arm snagged around my waist, and he dragged me up against his body, my back tight against his chest.

Yuri stooped over Patrick (who was curling up on his side in anguish) and grabbed his throat, pinching off his ragged breathing while lifting Patrick's squirming body with one massive arm.

Viktor and Jose hung back as silent observers.

"Stop it!" I repeated desperately, straining against Takao's hold as Patrick was slammed into the back wall of the leisurely gliding elevator, feet twitching inches above the carpet. Patrick's eyes were bulging, his nose was bleeding, and his hands tugged uselessly against Yuri's fingers. Strangely, his aura had never looked brighter than now as he was being suffocated.

"No—let him down—please!" My cries had no effect on Patrick's captive, but Takao's aura blossomed with contentment at the sound. Before I could reopen my mouth, a switchblade was pressed to my throat, just below the left side of my jaw. I stopped wriggling abruptly, instantly chilled by the horrible sensation.

Viktor spoke in a deep voice from the sidelines. "Guardian, would you like to see Takao's art? He's very talented with that blade—lots of experience . . ."

Patrick's aura seemed to be rippling with adrenaline, and his face was turning blue. I didn't think he'd even heard Viktor's words, but then his wide eyes rolled, and he saw me over Yuri's shoulder. His kicks became impossibly more frantic and wild.

Viktor chuckled, amused.

Jose's voice was clipped. "Enough. Yuri, just search him already. Kiyota, put that away. The king will be upset if you damage her."

Yuri took orders well. He obediently lowered Patrick back onto trembling legs, removing his stranglehold only when his other hand was securely wrapped around one of Patrick's arms. Once freed, his head ducked, and terrible rasping filled the confined space. He instinctively reached to soothe the bright-red handprint around his neck with one quivering hand, even as he strained to look up at me around Yuri's hulking shoulder.

Takao obviously didn't appreciate Jose taking command. The knife remained against my skin, making me terrified to even breathe. My heart was pounding erratically, and tears stung my eyes.

Patrick swayed dangerously on his feet, but rage-filled eyes focused past me, on Takao. He struggled to speak but couldn't form the words because he'd dissolved to further coughing.

Takao's wheezing voice was just behind my ear. "No, no, no. After Yuri's done with you, Guardian. Let's see how long she can stand on her toes, hey?" The knife pressed carefully against my jaw, and I had no choice but to rise with it, leg muscles flexing tightly. "Be good and quick," Takao taunted. "The clock's ticking."

Patrick was seething, his aura a tumultuous tangle of anger, pain, and fear. He swiped his sleeve over his slowly bleeding nose, but he obeyed Takao without further hesitation, holding his arms out to his sides, prepared to be searched for weapons he didn't have.

Yuri took his time patting Patrick down, brushing his hands over each arm, over his chest, and down his sides. My toes were aching when the elevator skimmed to a stop, and the doors opened. But Yuri wasn't finished. He forced Patrick to turn around, and, though he was reluctant to look away from me, Patrick was still quick to respond and lay his palms against the wall—anything to get this over with. Yuri kicked Patrick's legs further apart, hands sliding rigorously over his shoulders and back, eventually sinking to search the back of his legs, down to his ankles.

By the time he'd finished, Patrick's breathing was low and

measured, if a little shallow. Yuri stepped back and Patrick twisted around, his eyes leveled warningly at Takao.

My legs wavered, and it was a good thing Takao's arm was around me, offering some semblance of balance. I could practically feel Takao's grin behind me.

Patrick opened his mouth, aura flashing, but Jose's words came faster.

"Enough, Kiyota. Put it away."

I felt the ghostly pressure of the knife disappear, and I pinched my eyes closed with relief as my feet fell flat against the floor.

"Viktor, search her," Jose commanded impatiently.

Takao released me, and Viktor grasped my elbow, pulling me aside. I offered no resistance as Viktor pushed my arms up and proceeded to pat me down, just like his brother had done to Patrick—only he moved more swiftly.

It was uncomfortable and invasive. His hard fingers were bruising—but despite the discomfort, I definitely preferred this to Takao's knife.

Patrick stood behind Viktor with his arms dangling at his sides, Yuri's hand possessively on his shoulder. Patrick wouldn't meet my gaze. He was watching Victor closely, the colors in his aura squirming heatedly.

I was really beginning to second-guess the brilliance of my plan.

Jose and Takao stepped out of the elevator calmly, as if nothing had happened, and as soon as Viktor was done, he prodded me forcefully after them, Yuri pushing Patrick similarly. I got the feeling they preferred this hands-on approach over the lofty, ostentatious way Selena handled things.

The top floor of the hotel was more homey-looking than the downstairs hallway had been. This corridor was more like an inviting entryway, the carpet ivory colored with bits of gold stitching. There were some plush couches and expensive wooden tables. The flower arrangements were exotic and bright. I realized this served as a lobby of sorts; aside from the elevator behind us, there was only one other place to go.

A pair of white double doors stood across from us, and they seemed to dominate the small lobby area. That might have been partially because of the four guards who stood shoulder to shoulder in front of them.

Two guards were Demons—a large African American man and a thin but dangerous-looking Chinese woman. Just looking at her exquisite posture and severe face had me sure she knew kung fu. Standing on either side of them were two human-looking thugs, but I was pretty sure they were Seers. They were all wearing black suits, except for the woman—she was wearing long, gray dress pants and a loose off-white blouse. She had raven-black hair gathered into a thick braid that trailed down her back.

Jose stepped up to the woman. "Selena had to tend to other business. I am to present this Seer and her Guardian to the Demon Lord."

The Chinese woman glanced over at us, looking bored. "I will see if he's ready for them. Wait here." She turned, opened one of the thick white doors, and disappeared inside, closing the door after her.

They obviously didn't think she was going to be gone long, because no one took a seat. Yuri pushed Patrick to stand beside me, but we couldn't touch—the Dmitriev twins were standing directly behind us, fists wrapped tightly around each of our arms, keeping us rooted in place. Takao was standing behind us, which made my skin crawl. I could hear him pulling at his sleeves, trying to straighten them I guess.

Jose stood in front of us, waiting straight-backed for the woman to return.

It wasn't a long wait.

The door opened, and the Demon woman focused on Jose. "You will take my post." He bowed humbly, but she was already looking past him. "Yuri, Viktor—bring them. Takao, you may join us."

She waited until the Dmitriev brothers started to push us forward, and then she turned and led us into the Demon Lord's rooms.

It wasn't what I'd expected. At all.

His living room was as big as a ballroom—there were marble columns lining the gaping, spacious room. The ivory carpet lasted only a few steps into the enormous room, and then it gave way to polished stone, the color a grayish white.

The room was almost blindingly bright—not the dank, depressing lair I'd been imagining to find. The whole left wall was covered in floor-to-ceiling windows, letting in an overabundance of light. A huge, ornate fireplace was set against the back of the room, and low white couches stretched along virtually every wall. The right side of the room was decorated with large mirrors, more couches, and a couple bookcases. There were also more sets of double doors, leading to who knew where.

In the center of the spacious room was a cluster of people—Demons, mostly—all crowded around the same thing. Some were laughing quietly, and most were sipping champagne from tall glasses. Graceful strains of classical music drifted from invisible speakers, filling the huge room with light background noise to accompany the conversation. It sounded like Mozart, but I couldn't have named the familiar song right now.

I was so taken aback by this unexpected place that I know I was gaping. I couldn't help myself. The bright, open space was so un-Demon-like.

Our shoes tapped against the stone floor, and the group of standing Demons finally noticed our presence. The laughter died, though amused murmuring continued. I felt like we were walking in on some sort of celebration among diplomats, and seeing all the well-dressed people around us made me feel as if I were a bum off the street.

The crowd of Demons parted as we approached, and I finally saw what they had been gathered around.

Or rather, *who.*

The Demon Lord was almost as out of place in my mind as his lair was. He had a kind smile, for one thing, and he was extremely good-looking. Tall, dark, and handsome, he was the epitome of debonair. He had tanned skin, but it was a healthy compliment to his vivid green eyes. He looked like a prince from a foreign country or a famous movie star. And he was a lot younger than I expected him to be. He was probably only forty—he couldn't have been older, but I might have believed he was younger. He had light crinkles around his eyes, as if he laughed a lot, and his square jaw was perfectly sculpted.

He was wearing a white button-up shirt and black slacks. A dark-blue tie was loosened around his neck, and he was holding his wine-glass in one hand. His posture was perfect, his presence commanding.

But his good looks and unexpected youth were not what had me unable to look away in this moment. No, it was his aura that had me completely speechless—entirely disbelieving. Even though I knew this was the Demon Lord, his aura wasn't right. Because he wasn't a Demon. He wasn't surrounded in a thread of blackness. He wasn't even a Guardian. He was outlined in gold, and colors swirled obviously around him.

The Demon Lord was human.

twenty-nine

I didn't realize that he was looking right at me until those thick lips parted and he spoke my name. "Kate Bennett, we've been expecting you. How was your drive? Uneventful, I hope."

I just stared at him, unable to find my voice.

The Demon Lord gave me a kind smile, as if he understood—as if he was used to this reaction from every new Seer he met—and so he turned his bright eyes to my Guardian. "And you must be Patrick O'Donnell. You look younger than I imagined you'd be."

I was finally able to tear my eyes away from the Demon Lord so I could see Patrick's reaction. Obviously he couldn't see auras, but he still looked surprised by the Demon Lord's appearance.

I opened my mouth to tell Patrick the startling truth about the Demon Lord but couldn't force any words out.

The Demon Lord chuckled lightly, both slender hands fingering his tall glass of champagne. "Oh dear. I am sorry, Patrick. I seem to have stunned your Seer. It happens frequently, I assure you . . ."

Patrick's head twisted away from the Demon Lord so he could face me. His aura grew worried when he saw the astounded look on my face. "Kate?" he asked, voice fragile. "What's wrong?"

I couldn't answer him, only stare at the self-declared king of the Demons.

The Demon Lord started to move in our direction, his dress shoes clapping loudly against the floor. "Please, Patrick, allow me to explain. Your aura tells me that you need to calm down—you're going to overwhelm yourself . . ."

Patrick glanced at the Demon Lord, not realizing the significance of his words in the first few seconds. His eyes widened suddenly as understanding dawned. "You're . . . a Seer?" he breathed dimly.

The Demon Lord smiled, a concerned edge to the action. "Yes. I admit, it generally thrills me when people put it together for the first time, but . . ." he tilted his head to the side to better take in our expressions. "Patrick, you look absolutely awful. I hardly take any pleasure in your amazement. Can I get you a tissue?"

Patrick didn't answer, didn't move. Traces of blood remained on his face, and his sleeve was stained, but the actual bleeding had stopped back in the elevator.

The Demon Lord fretted by clicking his tongue. "I'm sure we can find you a new shirt once we're done here." He nodded suddenly to the two Dmitriev brothers. "Viktor, Yuri, our guests look a little tired. Would you please bring them some chairs?"

The Russians released us, but we didn't move—not even closer to each other. We were both staring at the Demon Lord, who was glancing over his shoulder at all his Demon friends. "If you would excuse us, please. We have things to discuss."

They all responded to the dismissal immediately, except for the Chinese woman and the other Demons that had brought us here.

One older woman—a Demon who looked to be in her seventies—held out her wrinkled hand to the Demon Lord, who graciously took it up and laid a light kiss against her skin. "Thank you, Lady Rovella. I hope you will join me for dinner this evening?"

"Of course, my lord," the woman returned, her voice stronger than I expected for an old lady.

He murmured an attentive good-bye and politely called out a few more direct farewells to the already retreating figures.

Soon all the well-dressed Demons and their accompanying Seers were gone, and the Demon Lord focused back on us. "Would you like something to drink? We have more champagne. We were celebrating a new alliance with the powerful Demon, Lady Rovella. She will be a great asset to the cause."

I finally managed to form words, but they weren't very loud. "You can't be the Demon Lord. You're not even a Demon."

"Ah, but you're jumping to conclusions." He nodded to something behind us, and we both turned to see the Dmitriev brothers, each setting down an old-style cushioned chair. "Please, have a seat," the Demon Lord urged.

He waited for us to lower ourselves onto the hard chairs, and then he continued in his velvety voice. "I'm not a Demon, Kate, but I am *Lord* of the Demons. If you think about it, the title still works quite nicely."

Patrick's voice was strained. "But if you're the Demon Lord . . . and you're human . . . how have you been building power and fear for the past couple hundred years?"

The Demon Lord took a generous sip of the bubbly drink and gave me an easy smile. "I believe Kate could explain that to you."

I nodded slowly, successively putting the pieces together. "You're a Special Seer. Like me. You've been going back in time."

He gazed at me like a proud parent. "Exactly right. I've lived for years in the past, if one added up all the time—not that it aged me here, of course." He glanced at Patrick, looking slightly regretful. "You don't seem too surprised by all this."

Patrick was staring at some point past the Demon Lord, his mind trying to grasp this rapid change of balance. "Kate has mentioned this ability before. I never imagined that you . . ."

The Demon Lord was back to smiling. He reveled in our shock. "I know. Dastardly, isn't it? But we Seers are more capable than you Guardians—or the Demons—ever dreamed. And much more powerful." He shot Takao a look, and the Japanese Seer hurried to find his master a chair.

"This doesn't make sense," I mumbled, almost to myself. "If you're a Special Seer . . . what do you need *me* for? What do you need *any* of us for?" Terence's theory that the Demon Lord was gathering special

Seers for traveling through time seemed a little redundant now. He could do that on his own. He *had* done it on his own.

The Demon Lord answered my question easily. "Really, it's not that difficult a concept. The more Special Seers I can get my hands on, the more of a force I can build. Demons are handy—imperative, actually—but I need Seers that can help me keep time in order. I can't effectively be in two places at once, and when I return to the present I'm unconscious for hours after traveling. It gets a little annoying."

Patrick's next words were touched with fear. "That's how you can be so manipulative. So powerful. You change the past. Or you threaten to change it. That's why Demons follow you."

He tipped his head and motioned for Takao to place the chair in front of us. He sat down, and Takao and the Chinese Demon took up positions around him. The Dmitriev brothers were hovering behind us, but they were easy to ignore during such mind-boggling revelations.

"The one who can manipulate time is the one who will reign," he said simply. "It's an easy enough concept. I've been able to create some of my best Demons by going back—some of my best Seers too. Like Takao Kiyota here and Mei Li." The Chinese woman gave me a slitted look, and I made a mental note not to ever make her angry.

The Demon Lord shrugged and leaned back in his chair, completely at ease. "I've even changed the fates of a few of my . . . how shall I put it? . . . my least favorite Guardians."

Patrick swallowed hard, receiving the thinly veiled threat.

I was getting over my shock—I was getting angry. "But you aren't a Demon—why do you want to *do* any of this?"

"What a rudimentary question." He laughed, and the sound echoed around the room. "I crave the power, obviously. Darwin knew what he was talking about. The survival of the fittest. The strongest beings always rise to the top. They command fear and respect. The Special Seers . . . we're the master race, Kate. Surely you can see that."

"When did you become a Seer?" I asked, curious despite my feelings of disgust.

He blew out his breath and tapped his fingertips against his glass. "Oh heavens, it was . . . almost twenty-eight years ago now. I was seven years old." He paused, but when I didn't lift my stare he sighed. "You want the story in its entirety? Very well. There's not much to it, really. I was shot on Christmas Eve by my mother's new boyfriend. This was in Chicago in 1971. My mother and my little sister—they were both killed during his drunken rage, but he didn't realize that the bullet hadn't pierced my heart. I waited until he passed out, and then I managed to call the police. I was barely alive when the ambulance came, but after a long surgery and an even longer recovery, I managed to heal. And of course I saw strange colors, though no one believed me then."

He spoke so calmly, it was hard to imagine he was telling his own tragic life story. His aura was a myriad of colors—I couldn't begin to guess what he was really feeling.

"I was placed in an orphanage—I had no remaining family. My new Sight alienated me from the other children, and no potential parent was interested in me." For the first time, his handsome smile was forced. "And then the Guardians found me. There were two of them, but their names are unimportant to the story. At first I was thrilled. Finally my new Sight made sense. I had a place to go. I was nearly ten at this time, but I felt much older. I wanted to help fight the Demons, because in my mind they were everything my mother's boyfriend had been. But the Guardians were reluctant to let me do anything. They raised me but kept me in the background. When I finally learned that I was special, I couldn't wait to test my abilities. I received special permission from the Guardian Council, and I was soon their most knowledgeable Seer. I recruited other Special Seers, and together we pressed our limits, continuing our research to understand how our gifts were used. Through our experiments, my partner and best friend helped me reach a marvelous conclusion: we could use time traveling as a weapon. We could destroy our enemies before they had a chance to become Demons.

"But the Guardian Council didn't like our reasoning. They

thought it wrong and dangerous. I was about sixteen when they shut down our research. I began to fulfill other Seer duties—the regular ones. The Guardians ordered me to abandon my special abilities, but I knew that I was right. Utilizing these powers would be the only way to stop the Demons from corrupting the humans.

"My friend agreed with me but came to enhance my thinking. Why should we be slaves to the Guardians *or* the Demons? Why should it be our design to help the humans? They were all inferior to us—no match for our special talents.

"The Guardians tried to have us killed, of course. Anything to keep us quiet. But we eluded them, and together we began to build this glorious empire. The Demons help me willingly, and together we will crush the Guardians. We, the Seers, will rule with complete power with Demons as our effectual slaves."

It was probably the longest monologue I'd ever heard in my life. It was certainly the most chilling. I felt I was in the presence of a madman, yet he sounded completely sane. That was the worst part of all. He truly believed in what he was saying—what he was doing.

Patrick was silent beside me, but I knew he was thinking something similar.

The Demon Lord suddenly straightened in his chair, a grin twisting his face. "Enough about that. We have so many other things to discuss. First of all, Kate, I need to explain to you why you're here."

"I'm special, I get it," I snapped, wishing he'd stop smiling and Mozart would stop playing. Both were getting on my nerves.

Mei Li, the kung fu expert, glared at me, but the Demon Lord just tilted his head, allowing my tone. "Yes, Kate. You are special. But more so than you realize. It's true that I've been gathering every Special Seer I could—in many different times, for many similar reasons—but you are even more unique than you know."

He took another sip of champagne, then continued quickly—deftly changing the subject. "Patrick, I assume you are also aware that—in addition to the ability to travel through emotions—Special Seers See more colors than regular Seers."

My Guardian nodded once, stiffly.

The Demon Lord took yet another sip. I wondered if he was nervous but decided he was probably more excited than anything else. But excited about what? "Well, I mentioned my Seer friend before, the one who shared my vision. Sadly, he passed away, back in the past. It was an accident, but he managed to share a bit of his research with me before he died. We'd long known that auras—or rather, *emotions*—held great power. My friend was a scientist, a biochemist. He'd searched long and hard to find a flaw in the Guardians—a way to kill them. But the only imperfection he could find was that many suffered from depression. Some cases were quite severe, actually. But what good would that do us?"

Another sip, the pause longer this time. Then his green eyes focused on me. "And then he pieced everything together. You've heard the saying that a happy person is a healthy person? Well, his research was centered around this adage, and he soon learned that the proverb was quite correct. Our emotions act as a sort of immune system. The happier we are, the healthier we are—quite literally. We learned through trial and error that the Guardians are not exempt from this. The darker a Guardian's aura is, the more susceptible he is to depression, which leads to a darker aura, which in turn weakens him. Some simple chemistry that I don't care to bore you with solved the rest, and suddenly we had a virus that could kill a Guardian. Only a depressed one, but it's a work in progress. All the sickness needs is the smallest cloud of a second thought, a small seed of a regret, and . . . poof."

He smiled at Patrick. "I sent Takao here to be sure you would be susceptible before I had Far Darrig put that infected Guardian in your path. I hope there are no hard feelings, of course, but all this was necessary to get Kate here."

"Why?" I fairly whispered. "Why would you do all of this? Just for me? How did you even know about me in the first place?"

"We didn't, originally," he admitted. "I'd sent Far Darrig to go after your grandfather, actually. I knew he was a Special Seer, because

I was so involved with the research the Guardians had conducted that I knew almost every name they had at the time. All Special Seers were put on a list back then, for tracking reasons. He was a little older than I wanted to enlist, but Special Seers are rare, and Guardians are struggling to protect them more and more."

"So you didn't even know I was a Seer? Let alone special?"

"I didn't know you even existed, Kate. I sent Far Darrig, as I always do for these special cases. And while he scouted out the area, he discovered you." I tried to ignore the tingle that ran up my spine, but it was difficult. His words were just so ominous.

"He realized you were a Seer. Far Darrig has always had a sense for that. Since the gene that makes Seers special is passed down through family, it only made sense to change our attentions to you—the younger, healthier option. And then he realized something."

The Demon Lord paused, taking another sip of champagne to build up the excitement. Then his eyes bored into mine, and for really the first time he seemed dangerous.

"He knew you. He recognized your face."

Every muscle in my body tensed, and my breathing became sharper.

I knew we were coming to a climax—I could feel it in the air, see it in his messed up aura. We were coming to that moment when our stomachs would drop. Our lives would spin out of control, and things would never be the same again.

Knowing this didn't keep my heart from pounding painfully against my chest while I waited for his words. Even though I already knew what he was going to say, I needed to hear him confirm my growing fear.

Finally he said, smooth and deep, "He knew your face, for he'd seen it before. Long ago, yes—but memories are funny things. Sometimes the mind clings to the most trivial moments and images. He'd seen you once before—briefly. But it was your drawing that lingered in his mind. The drawing done by his brother."

Patrick was no longer breathing beside me. He was staring at the Demon Lord, utterly pale and completely unperceiving.

I heard a door open from across the room, and I turned to face the sound; tearing my eyes off Patrick's silent face to see our newest enemy who was coming out, right on cue.

I watched the figure emerge from one of the back rooms, from a single door set in the wall near the gigantic fireplace. His face was partially in shadow because he walked with his head ducked. I seemed to take in everything at once. His black aura, his light-brown hair that fell across his cheekbones. He was tall and muscular. He wasn't wearing a suit, like most every other Demon here. Just dark blue jeans—a little baggy—and a black button-up shirt, sleeves rolled to the elbows.

His hands were deep in his pockets, and he walked fluidly toward us. He came to stand behind the Demon Lord, and finally he looked up. His face was hard, and he was probably in his early thirties. Younger than the Demon Lord, not that he looked it. He'd had a hard life—the evidence was there in the grim set of his mouth, the harsh way he held himself.

But it was the eyes that made me stare. The eyes that made me gape. The eyes that made my stomach clench.

Because I knew those eyes. I'd stared into them so many times . . .

I had to jerk my eyes away so I could look to Patrick, to try and understand how this was possible. But I found no answers there. Patrick was as bewildered as I was—more so, even.

The Demon Lord spoke happily, instinctively knowing when the new arrival was standing directly behind him, ready to be introduced. "Meet my most loyal servant: Far Darrig."

Patrick gazed at Far Darrig's darkened face, unable to utter more than a single word—a simple name. "Sean."

thirty

Far Darrig didn't say anything. He didn't react to his brother's voice. At first.

And then his lips parted, and his deep voice filled the quiet room. "Patrick."

From the corner of my eye, I saw Patrick's face twist in pain, and I knew that he knew the voice. It was really him. It was Sean.

Patrick's younger brother didn't say anything else. He just continued to stare at him, deadly serious.

It was strange for me, seeing the two brothers. I'd seen the sketch of Sean, but I could hardly believe this man was the same person. There was no laughter here. No love of life. Only suffering. And hate. I didn't need to see his aura to know this Demon felt so much hate. If it weren't for the eyes, I wouldn't have known he was related to my Guardian.

Patrick stared at his younger brother—who in physical appearance looked over a decade older than he was—but he couldn't do or say anything. He was in shock. His hands were gripping the arms of his chair, his fingers were trembling. I wanted to hold his hand, but I couldn't move. All I could do was watch his face as he struggled to realize that his brother was a Demon. His little brother was Far Darrig.

I heard the Demon Lord's low chuckle, and my eyes slowly moved to narrow on his handsome face. He was watching Patrick's face—watching his aura as new waves of pain, depression, and heart-ache threatened to drive him to his knees.

That smug face—that happy face—I couldn't stand seeing it. I probably did one of the stupidest things in my whole life. I lunged for the Demon Lord, my fingers curled into claws as I went for his sickly, delighted face. I didn't care what I did—I just needed to erase that smile, wreck this moment before it killed Patrick faster than the virus burning inside him.

My chair pushed back when I jumped, hopefully driving into one of the Dmitriev brothers. I felt Patrick's eyes shift to follow my unexpected maneuver, but there was no way he'd be able to stop me. I sensed more than saw everyone in the room tense—except maybe for Far Darrig, who seemed as immovable as a statue—but I was focused on my target. On those green eyes as they swiveled to me and realized what I was about to do. They widened in momentary fear.

I threw the center of my weight forward. There would be no pulling back. I was almost falling toward him now. The only thought running through my mind: what a shame that I'd bitten my nails so much this past week.

I got close—close enough that he jerked back, spilling cham-pagne all over himself. And then Mei Li's small form wavered with movement.

Her leg leaped up in the blink of an eye, and her foot slammed into my side, knocking me off course and causing me to sprawl out onto the unforgiving granite floor. The air was forced out of my lungs on the harsh impact, and my ribs throbbed where I'd been ninja-kicked. Before anyone else could move—she was *that* fast—Mei Li had jumped lithely to my side, and a second kick placed right in my gut sent me skidding further across the floor. The momen-tum of that powerful and perfectly trained kick could have sent me across the entire room, except that one of those obnoxious pillars got in the way.

My shoulder crushed against the resilient column, and my head cracked painfully against the floor. I was too breathless to cry out, and I was seeing black spots. And they weren't Seer related.

"Mei Li!" the Demon Lord reprimanded loudly, calling her back before she could kick me out of the state. Probably three more would have done the job.

Through the black dots, I could see Patrick being shoved back into his chair by Takao. I could also see Mei Li straightening out of her defensive crouch. Her long braid was still swinging, but the rest of her body had total control. She was so still, it was amazing that she'd moved at all.

The Demon Lord sighed loudly. "Takao, let him up. He can do no harm."

The Asian Seer stepped back immediately, but his heavily scarred face kept a firm eye on my Guardian. Patrick pushed up from the hard chair, his arms quivering, his expression breaking with animosity. He quickly crossed the floor to my side, shooting Mei Li an especially angry look before he reached me. He knelt laboriously beside me, one hand moving right to my arm, which I'd already managed to wrap around my throbbing ribs. He tenderly checked the area, his other hand slipping under my head, which I was struggling to lift off the floor.

"Ow," I croaked.

"Hold still," he muttered, not quite meeting my eyes. He shook his head at me. "What were you thinking?"

It was sort of a rhetorical question, but I found myself answering anyway. "I don't think I *was* thinking," I mumbled, pinching my eyes closed tightly.

His examining fingers pressed against a particularly painful spot, and I cringed sharply.

The Demon Lord's amiable voice filled the room, overriding the classical music that still played cheerfully in the background. "I'm very sorry, Kate. But Mei Li takes her job seriously. All my bodyguards do. I'm afraid your actions were a bit unwise. How are you feeling?"

I opened my eyes and blinked up at Patrick's stunned, bleak face. He was swallowing hard and repeatedly. He was staring at the pillar, and I knew without studying his aura that he felt as if his world was falling apart. "Hey," I whispered. His head moved slowly, neck bending mechanically to look down at me. My eyebrows drew tightly together, and my voice hitched with worry. "Are you okay?"

I sort of expected him to lie. Instead, he mutely shook his head. I thought I saw tears gathering in his eyes, but then he dropped his gaze and tried to help pull me to my feet. I was a little unsteady, but I could see clearly again. Patrick kept an arm wrapped around me, and we leaned against each other for support.

The Demon Lord was standing. Champagne had sloshed over his shirt and pants, and the glass was no longer in his hands. He took the first steps toward us, with Mei Li and Takao close behind. Far Darrig kept his position behind the chair; he couldn't stop looking at Patrick.

The Dmitriev brothers were circling around behind us—as if we would dare to run. Where would we go? Patrick still needed the cure.

It was time to stop beating around the bush. I forced my voice to sound commanding, and my words stopped the Demons' forward advance.

"What is it you want me to do? Why am I unique? Selena said that Patrick would get the antidote if I proved myself. What do you want me to do?"

The Demon Lord's smile was back, but it was less appealing to me now. "So many questions, and all so integrated. First of all, you're quite right. Patrick needs the antivirus. And he'll get it after you complete your first mission for me."

"Mission? Patrick doesn't have time for me to complete a mission. He needs the antidote now!"

"Kate," Patrick murmured beside me, warning me to watch my tone.

The Demon Lord chuckled. "Funny that you should bring up time."

I felt myself go whiter, and a bit of my bravery disappeared. Though he could still see how unsettled I was through my aura, I managed to keep my voice firm. "You want me to change something in the past?"

The Demon Lord squinted one eye and rocked his head back and forth, debating the accuracy of my description. "Not exactly. More like, make sure things go according to plan." He glanced over his shoulder at Far Darrig, who reacted to the silent command by stepping around the deserted chair and walking forward to join our tense circle.

I knew Patrick was watching his brother closely, still trying to prove to himself that this silent Demon was indeed Sean.

The Demon Lord's voice turned decidedly businesslike, and I focused back on him. "When Far Darrig realized that he'd seen you in the past, he called me immediately. Since you were just a vague drawing to Patrick, we both knew that your eventual journey to the past would have nothing to do with your Guardian. So who else could your trip be for? Far Darrig? But you never approached him— he couldn't even remember where he'd seen you at first. But obviously your visit would have to concern one of them—the Demon or the Guardian. But which one? Eventually we figured the little puzzle out."

He shrugged, as if it was a simple answer to an even simpler riddle. "You were there for *both* of them. But not directly . . . You're the one who convinces their father—Pastor O'Donnell, the silent patriot—to join the United Irishman. You're the one that will make him force his sons into the battle, where Patrick will die a hero, and Sean will go on to become my greatest servant."

"What?" I choked. The idea was ridiculous. Patrick was gripping my arm tightly, trying to make sense of the words.

It was me. I was the one responsible for Patrick's death. For his brother becoming a Demon. For a mother and a father losing first one child and eventually the other.

It was a lot to take in.

The Demon Lord continued to speak as if he liked punctuating the mounting tension with his polished voice. "Now you see why I needed you—and only you. You are unique, Kate, because without you, I never get Far Darrig. I need you to journey back through Far Darrig's memory to that moment when you unwittingly built my greatest weapon."

"And if I don't?" I suddenly ground out. "Patrick would never get sick—never be here. You couldn't kill him."

"No, I couldn't." The Demon Lord took a step toward me and his bodyguards mimicked his steps on either side. His voice became a strange mix of apathy and persuasion, and I couldn't take my eyes off his luminous green ones. "And I wouldn't have Far Darrig, it's true. But you would have never met Patrick." He sighed languidly. "If I were you, I wouldn't fight this, Kate."

"Why not?" I asked, my voice shaking with a timidity I didn't want to feel. Patrick squeezed my arm comfortingly.

The Demon Lord nodded to Patrick. "Because you already made this choice before, obviously. You went back. Or you will. Because he drew your picture. You were there, in the past. If you don't go back, you change history, which can have an assortment of terrible repercussions. And you don't want that, do you?"

I didn't answer because I knew he was right.

Whether I liked the idea or not, I was going back in time.

❊

Patrick would get the antivirus as soon as I returned from the past. Once that part of the deal was settled, the Demon Lord gave me all the instructions I needed. He taught me the basics of how to travel and how to return to the present when I was done. It was a crash course, but it would have to do. Patrick's nose was bleeding again, and I knew there wasn't any time to waste.

I tried to act brave, for Patrick's sake, but I think everyone in the room could sense my apprehension as I sat facing Far Darrig. We were sitting in comfy chairs across from each other, and I was trying to relax like the Demon Lord had instructed me. But that was hard because I was just so close to Far Darrig. Our knees were almost brushing, and I could have easily stretched out my hand and touched him.

I didn't, though. I was concentrating on his aura, trying to figure out which color was the right one. Which emotion would lead me to the right memory, the right time . . .

His aura was as chaotic as the Demon Lord's. Only Sean's was more resigned—more defeated. But that wasn't quite the right word, because it was almost like he was content with his own misery. His dark emotions confused me, but I tried to find the one that he was attempting to draw out for me. I knew he didn't like exposing his emotions like this—it was obvious. But it had to be done, and he wasn't about to complain.

Patrick was standing beside me, his hand on my shoulder. He hadn't said a word since I'd agreed to go back, and I wondered what he was thinking. Was he hating me for making this choice? For making his brother a Demon, for ensuring his own death? It would be completely understandable if he was upset with me. But I honestly felt like I didn't have a choice. The sketch he'd made of me proved that I'd done this once before. So there must be a reason . . .

Just like the Demon Lord had promised, I knew the memory Sean was trying to summon the moment I caught sight of it. It was a blue tendril of color that was lazily growing wider around his body. I squinted, watched it grow and grow, until I felt dizzy looking into it. And still the color seemed to get wider, hypnotic, much like Grandma's memory had been . . .

Far Darrig really spoke for the first time, his voice oddly distant. "I see you on the hill. Walk toward me. Ask for Pastor O'Donnell . . ."

I wanted to look up at his face, but I couldn't take my eyes off the soothing blue color that was now dominating my vision. I took a deep breath, and I tried to ignore the growing dizziness . . .

I felt a tug on my stomach—was distantly aware of Patrick's fingers digging into my arm—and then I was blinded by a flash of light.

I was standing on the top of a grassy knoll. I was still wearing my white top and faded jeans, but I was surrounded by green, and the blue sky was streaked with white clouds. A breeze fingered the loose hairs that had pulled free of my ponytail, and I could hear the distant sound of a dog barking.

I heard something else—a sound I'd only ever heard in the movies. Someone was chopping wood.

I turned around in a full circle, taking in the panoramic view.

This was most certainly not the desert.

I know, a stupid first thought. But all this green was just so alien to me. Large trees dotted the landscape, and I could see slightly crooked fences surrounding what had to be pastures. Everything was so open. I could see some distant buildings, further down a dirt road. Farms? Cottages? A low stone wall ran along one side of this knoll, and my eyes followed it until I saw a modest-looking structure I recognized from Patrick's sketches—it was his home.

Behind the gray and brown house, across an empty pasture rested a small one-room church. It was white and stark and hard to ignore when everything else was covered in green.

I started walking down the hill, following the stone fence. I wasn't sure if I was heading for the house or the church yet—I just knew I wanted to get closer to both.

I realized belatedly that I was moving toward the sound of chopping wood, and sure enough, at the base of the hill, I could see a young man swinging an ax, his baggy white sleeves fluttering in the wind with each mighty stroke. Seeing his brown pants and suspenders, I was suddenly conscious of my modern apparel.

Before I could worry about it too much, the young man was looking up at me, leaning on the handle of his ax, the position leisurely. He squinted through the several yards between us, but he was already smiling brightly. His aura matched him perfectly—completely different from the aura I'd just traveled through.

He spoke pleasantly, but his words were incomprehensible—his language absolutely foreign to me. He finished his quick greeting, his expression kind and helpful.

I think it was my blank stare more than my lack of immediate response that gave me away.

Understanding dawned in his eyes, and he hurried to repeat himself in lilting English. "Hello. May I help you?"

It was Sean. A much younger version of him, but there was no doubt that this was Far Darrig.

I could barely believe it. The sunny grin, the handsome face, the clear blue eyes. And in that one second I hesitated. How could I turn him into Far Darrig? This boy—fifteen, maybe sixteen—how could I be the one to set his horrible future into motion?

He was still looking at me, waiting for an answer. His eyes had dashed across my body, but if he found my clothes odd he didn't draw attention to the fact. I guess it made sense. He'd been brought up by a religious father, so his manners were probably immaculate—especially if he was anything like his older brother.

I was speaking before I could make myself regret the decision. "Yes. I'm looking for Pastor O'Donnell."

Sean nodded, his light brown hair shifting with the motion. "Sure. He'll be in the church about now, running through some wordy sermons most likely."

"Thank you," I said automatically.

He bowed his head respectfully. "My honor to help you." His pleasant voice bordered on flirtatious, and his smile really was quite dazzling. He looked a lot like Patrick. His face was younger, a little more rounded, and open.

I thanked him again and continued walking past him, toward the church. Once he was behind me and I heard the resumed sound of blade slamming against wood, I threw a last look at him over my shoulder. He was absorbed in his work, possibly used to strange people asking for his father. He would forget me, until Patrick sketched the picture tomorrow, and then Sean would struggle to remember where he'd seen my face. It would restart the whole cycle.

But did I want that on my conscience?

I left the question unanswered and instead moved along the stone fence, heading toward the church.

thirty-one

Kate Bennett
May 9, 1797
Wexford County, Ireland

Rolling hills covered this entire valley. It was one of the most beautiful places I'd ever seen, and I couldn't imagine growing up here. My artistic side was going wild. My fingers itched to capture everything, even though such a feat would be impossible. Surrounded by such beauty and peace, my body slowly relaxed, in spite of everything. It was so much easier to breathe here, compared to the room I'd so recently left. As unreal as my presence here was, there was something so tangible about this place. So real. I felt more alive here than in the present. But maybe that's because I had some measure of control here. I didn't have Demons breathing down my neck. I didn't have to watch Patrick's pain and confusion. I didn't have to worry about being killed any second.

The slow walk through the pasture and toward the church was calming yet invigorating. I felt it was a necessary break from the insanity that was my life. The fresh air, the gentle sun . . . They kept me from losing my mind.

On one of the distant hills, a herd of sheep grazed lazily in the field. I was walking with my back to the stone and wood house, my eyes on the church. I may have been calmer now, but I still had a mission. And I had no idea if I was going to actually go through with it yet.

The ground was surprisingly rocky for appearing so smooth. The long grass swallowed my feet, and the rippling wind created the illusion of waving water.

I found the dirt path that served as a small road up to the church, and I stepped out of the long grass. The church was taller than I first thought, now that I was getting close. It was whitewashed and plain, but there was something serene and beautiful about it. There was a tall steeple set on the roof, and beneath it was a front door. Three wide steps led up to the closed door, and the foundation was made of gray stone. On the right side of the church stretched a small cemetery, peaceful and quiet.

A man was kneeling on the ground beside the steps, digging in a small flower garden. He wasn't wearing a fancy robe or anything to mark him as the church's proprietor. In fact, he wore the same style of clothes I'd already seen on his son—brown wool trousers, suspenders, and a plain white shirt with generous sleeves.

His aura was almost shining, it was so peaceful and happy. Blue contentment and yellow pleasure swam gracefully around his body. There were a few strands of gray, and the couple clouds of green uneasiness let me know that he was quite aware of the uncertain times in which he lived. But he was still content, happy with his life, his family, his faith.

I was walking quietly, not wanting to disturb him and his peaceful work. But the sound of my shoes scraping on the dirt had him peering over his shoulder. His eyes were similar to his sons'. Not quite so penetrating but still extremely clear. His face was weathered with age, a pleasant sort of wear. His hair was beginning to thin, although his brown hair had retained its color.

"Um, hi," I said anti-climactically.

His smile was wide and friendly as he pushed himself up off his knees.

I continued quickly, while he slapped his hands over his pants to dislodge clinging bits of dirt. "I'm sorry to interrupt your work."

His English was strongly accented when he spoke. "Oh, don't be. The flowers can wait."

I reached out to clasp the hand he was already extending. It was warm and rough and slightly dirtied. "I hope you'll forgive my appearance. I wasn't expecting anyone to come strolling by this afternoon." His head tipped to the side, considering. "Your accent . . . you are American?"

I nodded once, the motion somewhat jerky. "Yeah. I mean, yes."

He let my hand slip through his fingers, and then he squinted up at the sun. It didn't seem bright to me, with all those clouds, but I'd never been to Ireland. For all I knew, it was unseasonably warm. "We don't get too many Americans in Wexford County," he mused. "Most stay around the area of Dublin. If we get any at all these days . . ."

"But you recognized it?"

"Yes. I've met with many different missionaries from many different countries." He looked back at his house, and his expression grew puzzled. "Surely you do not travel alone? Are your companions at the house?"

I shook my head. "No—I came straight here. I have . . . something I need to talk about. With you."

His eyes were confused. "Have you traveled far?"

I let a breathless sort of laugh escape. "Yes. Very far."

He nodded once—not comprehending, but willing to listen. He looked toward the door of the church. "Well, my child, you look tired. Would you like to sit inside?"

I bobbed my head, and Patrick's father led the short walk to the steps. He opened the door and I trailed after him into the church.

Simple windows on both walls let the light stream inside, brightening the simple church. There wasn't a center aisle, just narrow pathways along each wall. Several rows of pews rested in the middle of the room, facing the back of the church, where a modest pulpit sat. Everything was wooden and humble. There was something ethereal and calming about the modest room, and my heart that had been constricted for so long finally began to loosen.

A large wooden cross—the most glamorous ornament the church had—was nailed to the wall behind the pulpit, and it was the obvious centerpiece of the small building. My eyes went to it immediately and lingered there while I walked behind Pastor O'Donnell. The floor creaked beneath our feet, but it was a comforting sound.

We crossed down the left-hand aisle, and in seconds we were standing before the pulpit. We stopped moving, and Pastor O'Donnell followed my gaze to the cross.

"Humbling, isn't it?" He spoke lowly, his older voice a perfect match for this comforting place. "I've walked into this church a thousand times and more, but my eyes never cease to be drawn to that simple piece of wood."

"It's beautiful," I whispered honestly.

He gave me a small smile, obviously enjoying my reaction. "Yes. It is." He gestured toward the pew behind us, and we both sat on the hard wooden bench. He twisted toward me, our legs nearly touching. "Now then. What is it that troubles you?"

My eyes fell from his, and I watched as my nervous fingers fiddled together in my lap. "It's complicated. It's not . . . easy to say. I'm not sure where to begin."

He reached out to pat my unsteady hands. His large palm on my anxious fingers was soothing, and I lifted my face to view his. His eyes were serious, but his smile was still extremely patient and kind. "Many things in life aren't easy." He nodded at the cross. "But with His help, all things are possible." He returned his attention to me, his voice incredibly understanding. "Perhaps you would like to join me in prayer first? I've found that prayer makes many complicated things easier to face."

I was biting my lip, but I found myself nodding, grateful for the distraction and delay a prayer would give me. "Yes. I think I would like that."

He took my hands in his and bowed his head. I mirrored the

action a second after, and then he began to pray.

I honestly couldn't concentrate on the words he said. I found myself focusing on the feelings he inspired inside me instead. The amazing comfort that suddenly seeped into me was like nothing I'd ever felt before. He spoke so confidently yet so respectfully. He never hesitated. The words seemed to pour out on their own accord, and though I can't remember any of the specifics, I knew that they were words I needed to hear.

Before I'd entered this church, I was still unsure. How could I go through with this mission? How could I doom so many to so awful a fate?

But now, feeling wrapped in a warm cloud by his heartfelt prayer, I knew what I had to do. What I needed to say.

He ended the personal prayer, and though I hadn't stepped foot inside a church since my parents' deaths, I murmured my own thankful *amen.*

He continued to hold my hands, but I felt his eyes on my face. I took a deep breath and raised my chin until I was looking at him. Though he'd been attentive and kind before, there was more caring in his eyes now. His aura was even more at ease than before, and there was a strange new light brightening his face, as if the prayer had had an unexpectedly powerful effect on him too, not that he quite understood why yet.

He waited for me to speak, and finally I did. I trusted my calmly beating heart to pick the right words, grateful for the warmth that lingered in the room. It helped me decide to tell him everything—I was sick of keeping secrets, depending on lies.

"I'm not from this time, " I began, watching his expression carefully. "I've come from the future. I was forced to come here. I'm supposed to put something into motion. Something that will bring you great pain."

He stared at me, his eyes tightening just a little. Would he think I was crazy? Would he throw me out of his church?

Despite my many worries, the surprising calm remained. I simply waited for his reaction, assured that somehow everything would be all right.

When it was apparent I wasn't going to continue right away, he spoke slowly. "I have been feeling uneasy of late," he fairly whispered. "Worry for my family, my country . . . it has taken me to my knees many times. Yet my answers have been fractured. Distant." He glanced over at the cross on the wall, and his shoulders fell. "He answers in His own time, but . . . I began to fear that I was somehow unworthy. And then, three nights ago, I had a dream.

"It wasn't a visual dream. It was just . . . a feeling. A feeling of intense peace. That all would be well again, despite the growing fear . . ."

He turned back to me, and his fingers squeezed mine. "It was the same feeling that I feel now, that I felt while we prayed. I think I am supposed to listen to you, supposed to help you. Somehow, you are the one that will make everything right again."

His words were a little overwhelming, but I took the responsibility with a thin smile. "I hope you're right."

His eyes scanned my face, tried to memorize it. "What is your name?"

"Kate. Kate Bennett."

"Kate Bennett." He gave a tentative smile. "Tell me of the future."

I took a deep breath and shifted on the hard bench so I was looking straight at him. I decided to speak quickly, so I could just get everything out. "I know this is going to sound really insane, but . . . in the future, I'm in love with your son—Patrick. The only thing is, he's . . . immortal where I come from."

"Immortal?" Despite his previous statement of faith—faith in me—he sounded a bit unsure of that word used to describe his son.

I pursed my lips, trying to salvage the peace I'd just barely experienced. "Yes. He's my Guardian. Like . . . Like an angel, sent to protect me."

He blinked, and his voice was unsure. "The place you come from . . . it is the distant future?"

I nodded once. "A good two hundred years in the future."

His eyes widened, but to his credit he managed to keep his mouth from falling open. "I see."

I sighed, frustrated with myself. "I'm sorry—I'm not explaining this well . . . When a person dies, they're given a choice. To go on to heaven or to remain here on earth as a Guardian. Once a person chooses, there is no going back. Each place is separate and eternal—different planes of existence."

"And Patrick . . . he chose to be an immortal Guardian?" There was pain in his voice, but he was fighting to conceal it.

"Yes. The choice wasn't easy for him, but . . . he did it for Sean. To protect him."

"Protect him from what?" A defensive edge was entering his accented voice.

I tried to keep my words as calm and considerate as possible. "Patrick and Sean . . . they join the United Irishman. Patrick will die in one of his first battles, but Sean will survive. Patrick will make the choice to become a Guardian, so he can watch over Sean and keep him safe."

Their father swallowed with difficulty, his eyes wandering back to the cross. "Patrick will give up heaven for his brother. He will give up forever with his family . . . to save Sean's life?"

I tightened my grip on his hands. "I know this is hard, but . . . he made a promise to Sean. That he would get him home alive. He couldn't bear to break that promise, no matter the cost."

He turned back to look at me, his face guarded. "My sons . . . they are good boys. Patriotic boys. But joining a rebellion, the war . . . that is not like them. Why would they do such a thing?"

This was the hard part. I took a deep breath before starting. "You force them into the rebellion. From what I understand, you give them an ultimatum, and they choose to fight rather than dishonor you."

His face crumpled. Pain, disgust, anger, doubt . . . "Why?" he rasped. "Why would I do such a thing?"

I swallowed hard. "I think I make you do it. I think . . . I think it's the right thing to do."

"When? When does this happen?"

"Patrick never gave me an exact date. He just told me that he dies in the year 1798."

The pastor struggled to breathe. "That's in a year," he gasped. "Just next year . . ." He looked to the wooden cross, searching for comfort.

"I'm so sorry," I whispered, my voice wavering with sincerity.

I let him stare at the cross in peace for a few long minutes. Watched as he came to terms with the realization that his firstborn would soon meet his death. And not only that, but also that Patrick would be forever separated from his family, because of a single choice.

I waited until he finally looked back to me, tears glistening in his eyes. "But he is alive. In your time, he still lives. You know him. You . . . love him. Does he love you?"

My stomach clenched. "Yes. Yes, he does. He tells me every day."

The corner of his mouth quavered into a slight smile. "I am glad of that. Is he . . . happy, then?"

"Yes, I think so. He misses you, but . . ."

He nodded once. "Patrick was always special. I knew he was meant for something great. He has such a unique spirit . . ." His voice faded to nothing, and then he straightened his shoulders. "You are asking much of me. You wish me to force my son onto a path that will lead to his death."

"I know." I hesitated, wondering if I should tell him about Sean— about Far Darrig.

The same warm feeling that had been prompting my words so far gave me an almost imperceptible nudge, and the words came with surprising ease.

"You need to know that Patrick isn't the only one affected, if you agree to do this. Sean . . . something will happen to him."

Pastor O'Donnell looked to me, concern wrinkling his brow. "But you said that Patrick protects him."

"Yes. And he will. Sean survives being a rebel. I don't know every detail—and you probably don't need to know everything. But eventually, Sean will change."

"This change is for the worse?" he looked decidedly wary.

"Yeah, it is. By the time Sean dies, he won't have the choice to go to heaven. He will have a corrupt heart, and he will become a Demon—an immortal being that is an enemy to Guardians and humans."

"A Demon? Sean?" A disbelieving, frightened laugh burst out. "That's not possible. His heart is pure. He would never become a monster."

"I'm sorry." It was the only thing I could think to say.

Pastor O'Donnell suddenly stood, his hands pulling away from me as he walked toward the closest window. I stayed on the bench, knowing that he needed some space. He stood at the window, shoulders tensed as he gazed through the small panes of glass.

He bowed his head, and though he didn't utter any words aloud, I knew he was praying. I closed my eyes and bowed my own head, offering a silent, wordless prayer for his sake.

I don't know how long we stayed like that, but his voice pulled me from my thoughts. "I do not want to help you. It goes against every instinct I have." I looked to him, but his back was still to me, and I couldn't see his face. His aura was surprisingly calm, leading me to believe that his prayer had been heard and answered.

His body shifted, and he stood facing me, his eyes fierce. "I do not see the wisdom in this. But I cannot shake the feeling that it is right. Impossible as it seems, this course . . . it *is* right. You are a stranger to me, Kate Bennett. But this feeling I trust. I know that if I place my faith in you, all will be well. I trust the lives of my sons to you, because you will be the force that saves them both."

His words gave me strength, but they still seemed incredible. Maybe I could take care of Patrick. But Sean? What could I possibly do to save Far Darrig? Wasn't he about as lost as a soul could get?

I probably should have said something reassuring, like *Yeah, no problem. I've got it covered!* But I was feeling too honest in this moment to tell a lie.

So I let out a shaky breath. "I wish I could share your faith. In my world . . . things are pretty hopeless right now."

"Where love is, hope is never lost."

He paced away from the window, coming to stand in front of the pew. He extended a steady hand, and I reached out to take it. He pulled me gently to my feet, and suddenly I was throwing my arms around him. It was a little spontaneous of me, but I needed the contact. I felt a connection to this man I'd never met before this moment, and I think he felt it too. Because it wasn't a one-sided embrace by any means. In fact, Pastor O'Donnell gave a huge bear hug that made it hard to breathe. It felt wonderful.

"You are special, Kate," he whispered. "Patrick . . ." His voice faltered, and then he patted my back firmly. "He is blessed to have you, I think."

We pulled apart mutually, and he cleared the emotion from his throat. "So. What will you do now?" He pushed his hands into his pockets, and I smiled at the familiar posture.

"I guess I go back. I try to do what you said—save Patrick and Sean."

His head bowed. "And I will do as you have instructed. Trusting that both of my sons are in good and capable hands."

The door to the church suddenly burst open, and we both turned quickly to face the newcomer.

My heart virtually stopped. It was Patrick.

He looked faintly younger than the Patrick I knew, and his cheeks were flushed from running. He held a familiar leather book clutched tightly in one hand and his brown hair was windblown. His smile was wide, but it faltered when he saw me. The door was open, the bright sunlight framing his tall form. He stood just inside the church, and he looked so healthy. Not at all what I was used to now.

And his aura. There was no pain or regret. Only happiness and excitement. He was so carefree. I think that more than anything made him appear so young to me. He wasn't burdened with the cares and hardships of two hundred years. Not yet, anyway.

He was breathless and at once apologetic. "I'm sorry, Da. I didn't realize you were occupied."

Pastor O'Donnell forced a smile. "Not at all, Patrick. I will be done soon, if you can wait."

"Of course." He nodded politely to each of us, his eyes lingering over my face in a familiar sort of way. From that one look, he would dream of me—be inspired to sketch my face.

He gave me a last respectful bow, his blue eyes shining brightly, and took a step back and pulled the door closed.

We stood staring at the place he had been, and I knew that my work here was done. I'd finished everything I was supposed to do. Yet I was reluctant to leave.

Pastor O'Donnell spoke quietly beside me. "When you go back . . . you will tell him of my love? You will apologize for the things I am about to do—the things I did?"

"I will," I promised.

He gave one stiff nod. "Someday I will tell my wife these things, so that she will know a measure of peace. I will tell her of you, and she will be glad. And Sean . . . I will try my hardest to keep him from his folly."

I smiled just a little. "Maybe say a few of those magic prayers with him. You're really good at that."

He chuckled, but his eyes were serious. "That magic is available to everyone, Kate."

I nodded, because I knew that's what he wanted, but I had a feeling that I would never be able to pray like he did.

He smiled at me, and I think he could read my thoughts. But he didn't pressure me. He just reached out and shook my hand one last time. "Good luck, Kate. May God be with you."

He was ready for me to go. And it was time. I could feel the tug on my stomach, letting me know that my body was more than ready to go back to its rightful time.

"Thank you, Pastor O'Donnell. Thank you for everything."

"No. Thank *you*, Kate." A mischievous smile suddenly twisted his lips, and my cheeks warmed at his next words. "You and Patrick . . . I may be ignorant about what things are like in the future, but I raised my son on certain principles. Will you be my daughter one day?"

I was blushing deeply now. "Um . . . I'm not sure. We haven't really talked about anything like that."

His grin widened. "Well . . . I suppose I shall add a little something extra to my prayers . . ."

I didn't make a comment, but I don't think he was expecting any.

We said our last farewells, and then I took a deep breath and focused on the Demon Lord's instructions on how to return.

I closed my eyes to block out distractions, concentrating on the place I wanted to be. Back to the moment I'd left behind. I pictured Patrick's face, since he was my strongest pull. I struggled to remember exactly what his hand on my arm had felt like, and slowly the rest of the details came back to me. Far Darrig's serious expression, the Demon Lord's bright eyes . . .

I felt the tug in my gut, and suddenly the wooden smell of the church was gone. I knew without opening my eyes that Pastor O'Donnell was gone too.

I could feel myself sitting on the chair, felt Patrick's fingers tighten on my arm as I sagged forward.

"Kate!" Patrick's voice was distant, but the worry was evident.

I heard the Demon Lord's pleased voice. "Excellent."

And then I wasn't aware of anything.

thirty-two

Kate Bennett
Present Day
Nevada, United States

Someone was holding my hand. The air was cool, and I was lying on a comfortable bed. My eyes were closed, but I knew instinctively that the room was only dimly lit. Every muscle ached, and I had a slight headache. My limbs felt extremely heavy, but other than that I felt okay. I was alive, anyway.

Fingers lay against my smooth forehead, and then Patrick's murmuring voice warmed the room. "Kate? Are you really awake this time?"

"Hmm . . ." It was a cross between a sigh and a grunt.

His fingertips brushed at some of my loose hairs, and his other fingers squeezed my hand comfortingly. "It's all right. You can keep sleeping. Take your time . . ."

As nice as that sounded, I didn't want to drift away from him again. I forced my reluctant eyelids to lift, and I was instantly captured by his clear blue eyes. There were so many emotions there that I hardly knew what to focus on first. The most present was relief, and that made me feel better. At least he wasn't disgusted by the sight of me, despite everything I'd done to him and his family.

My peripheral vision told me that we were in a bedroom, easily double to triple the size of my room back home. The space was comfortingly dark, until I realized there weren't any windows. There wasn't a lot in the spacious room—an open door that led to a small bathroom, a closet, a couple of plush chairs, and some dressers. The decor was muted and purple in color, a pale lavender that seemed to make breathing easier. A lamp in the corner was on dimly, but that was the only light to fill the large space.

Patrick was sitting beside me on the bed, and though everything around him was in shadow, his face was clearly illuminated. I noticed easily that the Demon Lord hadn't been lying about replacing Patrick's shirt—he was wearing a crisp white long-sleeved shirt. The time was impossible to guess, but my internal clock told me that I'd spent hours unconscious; much different from the first time I'd traveled through a memory.

We stared at each other for a silent moment, and then I pressed my palm more firmly against his. "Your aura. It's gone."

He nodded once. "As soon as you returned, I was injected with the antidote."

"They kept their word."

"You sound surprised."

"Honestly, I guess I am. How are you feeling? You look a lot better."

"I feel better. Just tired." His eyes tightened. "Are *you* all right? One moment you were staring at him, and the next . . . you were falling."

"Really? It was instantaneous for you?"

He swallowed roughly. "Yes. An eternal second, but . . . the Demon Lord assured me that you'd completed the job. I don't know how he knew. They carried you in here, and I refused to leave you alone, though they offered me a room. Selena came in once to check on us, but I haven't seen anyone else."

"What time is it?"

He glanced over my body at the clock on the far nightstand.

"Almost six. You've come close to waking several times."

"Wow." I closed my eyes, trying to come to grips with everything that had happened—all the time that had passed, and the time that hadn't. "I can't believe that was one second for you. I was there for . . . a good twenty minutes or more."

"In the past."

I opened my eyes. "Yes. I saw Sean."

Patrick nodded, but didn't—or couldn't—reply.

"He looked so different," I whispered, almost to myself. "So happy. He was chopping wood. I think he was flirting with me."

"He did that frequently."

My eyes trailed down from his taut face to look at our joined hands at my side. "I saw your father, the church, and your house. It was so beautiful there. So peaceful. I didn't want to leave."

He exhaled heavily through his nose, and I looked up to his tightly flexed jaw. For one crazy minute, I thought he was angry with me. But then he spoke softly, looking at the headboard behind me. "Sometimes I think I remember every detail of that place. And sometimes . . . I struggle to remember anything."

My voice was a reverent whisper. "Everything was so green. I've never seen anything like it."

Patrick's voice was steady and even. "What did you say to him? My father?"

"I couldn't say anything at first," I admitted. "And then he took me into the church, right up on the front row. And then he held my hands and he prayed for me."

Patrick's lips tugged into a smile, and he lowered his eyes to my face. "The cross. I'll bet he kept looking at the cross."

I nodded, a thin laugh escaping my twisting mouth. "Yes." I hesitated, then released his hand so I could push myself up into a sitting position. My back rested heavily against the headboard, and I set my hand on his nearest knee. "I told him everything. About you and Sean. The Guardians, the Demons . . . everything."

He stared at my fingers on his leg, and his voice was wooden.

"You told him that both his sons would never reach heaven. I'm sure he's never been so disappointed."

I shook my head delicately. "He was heartbroken about losing you. But he wasn't disappointed in you, Patrick." I took a deep breath and reached for his hand.

He surrendered it belatedly, but soon I was cradling his fingers in both of my hands. I waited until he met my intense gaze before I continued seriously. "He kept telling me what a wonderful son you are. He told me to tell you that he was sorry for everything he did to you—everything he ever said. He loves you so much, Patrick. He always has, and he always will."

When my words died, his eyes fell, peering silently at our folded hands.

I couldn't have guessed his exact thoughts, but I knew he was putting this new information to the memories he had. That whatever his father had eventually said, he hadn't meant the words . . . It would have been a lot to come to terms with.

Finally he raised his head and forced a smile. "I'm glad you were able to meet him." It was all he could manage to say, but it said enough.

"I saw you," I added lowly.

He nodded once, his eyes a little brighter than before. "I walked in on you in the church. I wanted to show him the sketch I'd finally finished. I was so proud of it. I was sure it was my best work."

"You remember?"

"Vaguely. Most of my past memories are like that, though. Cloudy, until I place a few solid details."

I squeezed his hand and took a deep breath. "What are we going to do, Patrick? How are we supposed to get out of this?"

He gathered me in his arms, and I leaned gratefully against him. "This was your brilliant idea," he mumbled into my hair, but I knew he wasn't being completely serious.

"I know. I didn't think this far ahead. In all honesty, I thought we'd both be dead by now."

His arms flexed around my shoulders. "Isn't it a good thing we're not?"

I sighed into his chest. "Yeah."

"Then why do you sound depressed?"

"Because now I'm not sure what to expect from them."

His lips pressed against the top of my head, then he leaned back so he could meet my eyes. One hand lay against the side of my face, and his fingertips stroked comfortingly at my temples. "I don't know what's going to happen. Maybe Toni can get us out of here, maybe he can't. But I'm not leaving you. No matter what happens."

I swallowed hard, my emotions dangerously near the surface.

Before I could think of a good reply the doors pushed open without warning, and we were no longer alone. Patrick's position didn't change, but he seemed to freeze around me—his hand on my face fell to my shoulder only because I moved to follow his gaze to the open doors across the room.

The first person to step inside wasn't a Demon. Her aura was definitely human, but in this place there was every chance she was a Seer. She was dressed in a maid's outfit, and she was pushing one of those room service carts. It was piled with food, and the mouth-watering smells reminded me instantly that I hadn't eaten anything since breakfast.

She looked to be about sixteen. Way too young to be working for the Demon Lord. She had dark-brown hair, gathered into a service-able ponytail at the back of her head. It swished when she walked, but I was trying to focus on her aura—to see how much of a threat she was.

I was immediately confused by what I saw. There was obvious fear and some depression, but there was intense happiness too. Excitement? Great. She *liked* serving the Demon Lord.

Someday soon I might be in her shoes, but I promised myself that I would never be happy about it.

Following closely behind her was Far Darrig. After seeing Sean in the past, the differences between who he had been and who he was now seemed completely unfeasible. Yet the eyes didn't lie. Those beautiful, pristine blue eyes were the same. This was definitely Sean. But instead of flirting, those eyes were searing with a barely controlled, depthless anger.

I don't think Patrick even noticed the girl. He had eyes only for his brother, who was trying to ignore him in return. Far Darrig stood just inside the doorway, keeping an eye on the maid while she wheeled the cart to the foot of the huge bed.

She smiled at me and waved her tanned hand generously over the many dishes. "Dinner is served! The Demon Lord doesn't like his Special Seers to get sick, so you should eat as much as you can. Traveling takes a lot out of you, I know." She kept staring right at me, her smile too wide to be natural. It was kind of freaking me out. That, and her bright Texas accent was a bit annoying.

"Um, thank you," I finally said, when no one else opted to break the awkward pause.

She offered a slight curtsy. "No problem. If y'all need anything else, just call for room service. Ask for Maddy, and I'll be up in a jiff. The Demon Lord likes you to have anything you desire, and all your orders are on the house."

Far Darrig made an impatient sound in his throat, and Maddy pulled a face at us. "Sorry. I guess I talk too much. Anyhow, y'all just give a ring if you think of anything else you need. I get off at ten, though, so—"

"Enough," Far Darrig growled. "Get back to work."

Maddy gave us a last bow and then straightened her small white apron as she turned and walked back toward the doors.

She was almost to the Demon's side when she suddenly laughed and shook her head. "Oh my—I've forgotten the Oreos." She turned back to us, pulling out a small blue package from one of her apron pockets. Before Far Darrig could complain, she came rushing back to the bed. She stepped past her cart and came right up to us.

She was still smiling too wide, and her eyes were right on mine as she handed the individually wrapped cookies to me. "You can't forget the Oreos," she told me, her Southern drawl friendly but her eyes tight and layered with meaning. "You need the extra sugar, trust me."

And then it hit me—I don't know why it took me that long in the first place. Oreos. *Oh my Oreos.* It was a message from Lee. It had to be! Somehow Lee and Toni and the others knew Maddy. They were using her to send us a message. We could trust her.

Maddy saw the dawn of understanding taking place in my eyes, and she gave me a slight nod and a quick wink before turning and fairly skipping out of the room. I don't think Patrick caught any of this—he was still focused on his brother.

Far Darrig seemed clueless about the exchange as well. It was obvious he didn't care for Maddy's lingering or her happy attitude, but he didn't think she was an enemy spy.

I was abruptly filled with hope. I couldn't wait for him to leave, so I could let Patrick know that everything was going to be okay. Or at the very least, that we stood a chance.

Maddy stepped out of view and Far Darrig was turning to follow her when Patrick finally found his voice. "Sean. Wait."

Far Darrig stopped moving, his back firmly to us.

Patrick's words were pleading. "Please, Sean. Just tell me how. Tell me why."

Far Darrig moved slowly—almost imperceptibly—but finally he was facing the bed, his piercing eyes digging into Patrick's. "What's done is done," he said, his voice low and dangerous. "There's no reason to talk."

Patrick was shaking his head, eyes still glued to his brother's dark face. "No, Sean. I have to hear you say the words, or I'm not going to believe it. I'm not going to believe you're this person."

"I nearly killed you. Isn't that proof enough?"

Patrick swallowed hard. "No. Because I didn't see it."

Far Darrig grunted. "For such a creative mind, you lack a great deal of imagination."

"What happened? That's all I want to know."

"Time passed. Things changed. That's what happened."

"That's not good enough."

Far Darrig moved quickly. Patrick barely had time to push me away before his brother was crashing on top of him, hands clutching around his throat. "How about this?" Sean growled, tightening his fingers around the tender skin and shoving Patrick deeper against the unyielding headboard. "Is *this* good enough?"

Patrick's eyes watered, and he couldn't even choke because Sean was strangling him so completely.

"Stop it!" I yelled sharply, scrambling off my side so I could scratch Far Darrig's tightly flexed arms, push uselessly against his stone shoulder.

Far Darrig gave Patrick's bulging eyes an evil smile. "Or do I have to do *this*?" One of his hands peeled away from crushing Patrick's windpipe, and then I was backhanded so swiftly, so harshly that I fell back against the bed, completely stunned.

Patrick's gasp for breath was more like a growl, and then he was kicking Sean off of him, and they both fell grappling to the floor. I could hear them rolling around—a few grunts, a punch—and then Sean went skidding across the floor from a strong kick.

By the time they were both back to their feet and crouched defensively, eyeing each other calculatingly, I was back to a sitting position. My ears were ringing, but my vision was surprisingly clear.

I saw Patrick's back shake, and reluctantly he straightened out of his crouch, lowering his guard even while his brother continued to glare.

"Come on!" Sean rasped, drawing in shallow breaths too rapidly. "I'm not letting you get off that easily!"

Patrick shook his head seriously, breathing hard but somehow looking completely relaxed. "I don't want to fight you. I won't, Sean."

"Stop calling me that!" Far Darrig fairly yelled. "Stop acting like you don't hate me!"

"I don't hate you, Sean."

"Well, I hate you." He sneered, and I knew his words tore Patrick's heart.

"Why? Why do you hate me so much?"

Far Darrig actually laughed, but the sound was chilling and hard. "You left me." He spat mirthlessly. "You left me with a life that was falling apart. I was alone in every battle, and whenever I bled, I cried for you. When the rebellion fell, not even home was safe. We had to leave everything. Do you know what that did to Mother? The old woman was driven to the brink of insanity when she lost you, her beloved son. Losing her home was the breaking point. You left me with a broken mother and a ruined father. Him and his precious church, his precious patriotism. He constantly told me, 'all will be well,' but they were the mutterings of a madman! I had to build us all a new life in France. We starved, Patrick. Mother got sick. Father followed soon after. But were their last words for me? No. They were for you. Always for you. The wonderful brother. The talented brother. The dead brother. The worthless brother that didn't work day and night for them. I worked in factories until my fingers bled, I stole for them, I *killed* for them. But when I wanted to die, was that allowed? No. Because I had my debts to pay. Their debts to pay. *Your* debts, Patrick. I worked for the worst kind of filth, but it was never enough for them. Never. And when my death finally came, I learned I couldn't even come after you in the afterlife because I was a living Demon, forever barred from heaven."

Patrick had grown still long ago. His hands were trembling in the most intense pain, and I wished I could see his face. But I didn't even dare move to wrap my arms around him. I just knelt on the bed, wishing this moment would end.

Far Darrig laughed at the expression on Patrick's face. "You feel sorry for me? You pity your poor brother? I disgust you?"

"Sean . . ."

"Don't try. I get it. You don't even deserve their love, because you didn't choose them. You didn't choose us. You chose to become a *Guardian*." He chuckled, but his eyes were too filled with pain to be considered uncaring. "That was the first time I wanted to kill you myself. When I saw you for the first time. Alive. A Guardian.

Maybe you remember—it was 1915. I could hardly believe it when I saw you walking so calmly down the street. Walking around Germany like you were supposed to be there. Why would Patrick—the cherished son—give up heaven? I might have hated Mother and Father by the time I died, but I wasn't beyond feeling. What a horrible arrangement for them—to have heaven, but not precious Patrick?"

"You stupid fool!" Patrick broke in, voice cracked and shaking. "I did it for *you*. I chose all of this for *you*!"

"You've done nothing for me. I have the memories to prove it."

Patrick's words throbbed with emotion, and he took an unconscious step toward his brother. "I became a Guardian for you, Sean. So I could keep you safe. Like I promised."

Far Darrig laughed again. "You did a great job too . . ."

"I got you through the war. I got you home—I followed you to France!"

"What does that matter? You didn't *do* anything."

"I couldn't—there are rules—"

"Did you watch Mother starve? Did you watch father lose his mind?"

"I watched you forget me!" For the first time, Patrick's voice was sharp, but Far Darrig remained unaffected.

"Did I hurt your feelings?" he asked mockingly.

Patrick's jaw was locked. "If I'd known what you resorted to after I left . . . I never would have gone."

"Right. Because you're the *perfect* one."

"This isn't you, Sean," Patrick said desperately. "I know this isn't you. Please . . ."

Far Darrig finally moved out from his defensive crouch. He gave a full bow to his brother, his grin terrifying me. "I'm glad I could disappoint you. For now, that's enough." He straightened, turned on his heel, and moved for the door.

"Sean!" Patrick shouted, his body turning and shifting so he could keep an eye on his retreating brother. "Sean, come back here!"

But this time Far Darrig didn't turn. Not even to catch the doors. He pulled them closed without breaking stride, and we heard the solid click of a lock.

Patrick remained standing beside the bed, his shoulders rigid and his eyes on the closed doors. He didn't move for a long time, and I couldn't think of a single thing to say.

thirty-three

It was nearly ten o'clock. We hadn't had any other visitors, but I think that was in our best interest. I was especially glad that Far Darrig hadn't made another appearance. If I'd had doubts before on how my ability could somehow help Sean, I was now pretty sure that I didn't stand a chance.

When Patrick finally broke his stare and turned to look at me, I knew he didn't want to discuss what had just happened. He asked me listlessly, distractedly, about my stinging cheek, but I just shook my head, assuring him that I was fine.

I really wasn't. I was worried about Patrick. He wasn't handling this well, and I knew that Sean was ripping a hole in his chest. A hole that I wouldn't be able to fix.

He joined me on the bed, and I showed him the Oreos and shared my theory that Maddy was an ally. He wordlessly nodded—agreeing with me—and then I relayed the rest I'd figured out.

"She wants us to call before ten—but close to it. That's when they're going to try breaking us out. I know it."

"Good," he'd said, voice hollow despite his best efforts. "We need to get you back to your family."

And so we waited for time to pass, with me eating roughly the entire feast Maddy had brought. She was right—I was literally starving. Patrick nibbled a little. Not that he needed the food, but he wanted the distraction. When we finished, we sat holding each other on the bed. We waited for the clock to finally reach the glowing numbers we needed.

At 9:46 p.m., I couldn't wait anymore. With a nod from Patrick, I reached for the bedside phone. I'd already figured out that it was pretty useless as phones go. It was a direct line to room service—it wasn't able to call outside the hotel, which made me pretty confident that this room had been used as a prison before.

By the time the phone was against my ear, a happy voice was answering. "Miss Bennett, what can I get for you?"

I was more than unsettled by the unexpected use of my name, but I hurried to speak. "I'd like some vanilla ice cream, with some Oreos on the side. A lot of Oreos."

"Will that be all?" the cheerful voice asked.

"Yeah, I think so."

"Your order should be up in about five minutes."

"Thank you." I hung up and met Patrick's eyes. "Five minutes," I told him.

He nodded again, leaned in impulsively, and kissed me deeply. Before I could effectively melt into the kiss, he pulled his lips away from mine, setting our foreheads lightly together. "I'm sorry I've been so quiet. I know you need me. I just . . ."

I set my hands against his face, pulled his mouth back to mine. When I finally released his lips, we were both breathing hard. "It's going to be okay," I told him in a comforting whisper. "Your father told me that everything's going to be okay. He felt it. And I trust him." I decided not to add the part that I was supposed to be the one to make all this happy ending stuff possible. It seemed a lot more believable if fate were in charge of things, and not me.

Patrick didn't answer, but he didn't have to. I knew he trusted his father too.

Five minutes passed. Maddy's voice was energetic, even through the thick doors; we could hear her as she addressed whoever was guarding us, and a second later, one of the doors was unlocked and pushed open.

Maddy smiled brightly at us as she rolled the cart inside, and she parked it next to the first. She winked at me, then pushed the first cart over, spilling the dirty dishes and remains all over the carpet.

"Oh crap!" she cried.

The guard was already running inside at the loud sound—it was the big black guy who'd been guarding this floor with Mei Li when we'd first arrived. When he saw that it was only a clumsy mess and not an attack, he ordered her to clean it up. He gave Patrick a warning look before he moved back into the hall, pulling the door closed as he went.

As soon as the door clicked shut, Maddy's voice dropped to a whisper. "Howdy. Y'all okay?"

"Toni and Lee—where are they?" I asked, instead of answering.

Maddy raised an assuring palm. "They're safe. Lee's actually posing as my good friend. She's filling in for someone who didn't show up tonight. Trust me. You don't want the details."

"Lee's a maid?" I griped. "She can't be here!"

"I don't make the plans, honey. I just follow the orders."

"You know Terence?" Patrick interjected.

"Sure do. He put my Guardian in charge of infiltrating the Illusion months ago. I've been pretending to work for the Demon Lord ever since. I'm not a Special Seer, but he still likes having a few of us normal Seers around. Security, you know, so Guardians can't slip in." She threw me a nod. "Call room service—ask for Kellee to come help with this cleanup."

"I can't bring my best friend up here," I argued. "There's a huge hit man outside!"

Maddy gave me a stern look. Even if she was barely sixteen, she had a good one. "Look, hon, she's got the cleaning cart—which has a rather irritated Toni cramped inside. You want out of here or not?"

Patrick reached for my hand and squeezed. "She's the only one who can do this. We're all in danger if we don't get out now."

Maddy nodded, agreeing with that. "The Demon Lord is planning to take you away tomorrow, to Belgium, for training. As soon as you're gone, they're going to reinject your Guardian with a different strain of the virus. They only cured him in the first place so you'd trust them when they promise to let him go in return for your full cooperation."

I didn't like the corner I was in, but I was backed in pretty good. I sighed with frustration and reached for the phone.

When I was assured Kellee was on her way up, I put the phone down and turned back to regard Maddy. "How did Toni get in contact with you?"

"Through Terence. I guess they got smart and decided to ask if there was any additional help in the area. When Terence learned you were here . . . well, you can't stay undercover forever, I guess. Still, my Guardian isn't entirely happy with you. She doesn't want to rush things, but we need to move before you're lost forever, so I guess the Demon Lord's getting assassinated tonight."

"So Terence knew that the Demon Lord is a Seer?" Patrick asked, looking hurt. I understood what he was feeling, because I felt pretty much the same.

Maddy's eyes grew solemn. "Yes. But it's a secret worth keeping. If every Guardian and Seer learned of his abilities . . . there would be panic. That's why we infiltrated this hotel in the first place. So that when he came visiting, we might have a chance to assassinate him and end this twisted, Seer-Demon rebellion."

She threw a look over her shoulder, toward the door. Then she focused back on us. "I couldn't sneak any weapons in here. Toni's got some, though."

"What's the plan?" I asked. "Even with Lee and Toni, what are we supposed to be able to do?"

"Your grandfather and the Seer Jason are on the floor below us, making a scene. It's protocol for the nearest Seer to tend to things, to make sure that the trouble is created by mere humans. The closest Seer is a man called Martin, here on this floor. He'll leave his post after Lee's slipped past, and then my Guardian—Claire—will come up with the Guardian Jack. We'll be out of the hotel before anyone realizes you're gone."

It sounded too good to be true, but I tried to believe it was possible.

The wait for Lee wasn't a long one. Her voice through the door wasn't as bouncy and loud as Maddy's had been, but I knew it was her. I moved to get off the bed, but Patrick held me back. I realized why, when the door opened and the black guy stepped in as well, holding the door for Lee's large cart. She pushed it inside, keeping her eyes away from me as she moved toward the mess.

"Hurry," the Demon ordered gruffly. As soon as he'd closed the door, I jumped off the bed to embrace my best friend.

Lee caught me fiercely, near the end corner of the bed. We squeezed the breath out of each other until Lee gasped in my ear, "I know what you're thinking. But don't say a *word* about the outfit."

A breathless laugh escaped me, and I pulled back so I could look her over. She was pale, but seemed otherwise unharmed. Her maid uniform was very un-Lee-like, and the white and gray montage looked anything but Rainbow Days worthy. But I wasn't interested in teasing her at the moment. "You were completely insane to come after me. What on earth have you told your mom?"

"Yeah, well, I haven't actually told her anything yet."

Before I could reprimand her, we heard Toni's low grunt. We turned to face the cleaning cart, where Patrick was struggling to lever Toni out from the built-in garbage can. It was big, as garbage cans go, but Toni was wedged in pretty tight.

"Oh, for the love of—" Toni pulled free, nearly collapsing in Patrick's steady arms. Maddy grabbed the cart, keeping it from sailing into the wall and creating unnecessary noise.

Patrick let go of Toni's shoulders, but only so he could flip him around and pull him into a quick hug. "Thank you, Toni," he said fervently.

Toni patted Patrick's back. "Sure, man. And now, for my next trick . . ." He leaned back so he could pull out a slew of hidden knives from around his legs, his arms, even one in his shoe. By the time he straightened, his hands held almost more knives than fingers.

Patrick took three immediately, tucking one carefully into his waistband, keeping the other two out. I scowled at Lee when she took one. I couldn't really reprimand her, since I took one as well. Maddy also helped herself, and Toni stashed away the rest, looking confident that he'd use them later.

He opened his mouth to say something, but before he could, I wrapped my arms around him, embracing him gratefully. "Thanks, Toni. You're the best."

He squeezed me briefly. "Yeah, I am. Now if you'll allow me to perform my next amazing feat . . ." I released him, and he motioned for Lee to join Maddy, who was starting to clean the mess on the floor. Patrick followed Toni to the doors, and they each stood behind one. I was unsure of my role at the moment, so I just stood by the cleaning cart.

Maddy let out a sudden yell, and the doors pushed open.

"What now?" The dark man demanded angrily, striding into the room. My Guardians slammed the doors closed, and by the time the Demon was wheeling around, Patrick was lunging for him. They slammed onto the floor, and Toni followed right behind them. Patrick rolled off the Demon, and Toni moved in—their motions so synchronized that this tactic must have been used many times before. The guard had Toni's blade buried in his heart before he could call out an alarm.

My Guardians stood, each offering a hand to the girls on the floor.

After Toni pulled Lee up, she let out an admiring "Wow."

Maddy looked similarly awed.

Toni grinned—very un-humbly—and turned to Patrick. "The others should be here at any time now. Once we get the word, we'll slip out while they continue on to the Demon Lord's room. They're pretty sure some alarm is going to be tripped, so we'll have to move fast once things are clear."

Patrick nodded, understanding.

I moved to stand by Lee, and we wordlessly joined hands while we waited with growing tension for the word to move out.

Just before I thought something must have gone wrong, one of the doors pushed open.

My Guardians tensed for a fight, but I could see right away that this newcomer was a Guardian. It was also one we all recognized. It was Jack Williams, the Australian hero himself.

He gave us a salute as he strode in, a blade spinning around his other fingers lazily. "G'day, mates. Just another corker day in the figurative Outback, eh?"

More people were filing in behind him: a few humans—Seers, I assumed—and a handful of Guardians. At first I couldn't focus on any of them. They were coming in too fast, too many faces. Then I saw her. The silver aura was somehow brighter on her than on any other Guardian I'd ever seen, and I was completely spellbound by her appearance.

She was beautiful. That was the first word that came to mind. Her skin was white and flawless. She was small—probably barely five feet, if that—and all of her features were miniature. Her nose, her chin, her mouth. Her face seemed so tiny. Pixie-like. She had golden-blonde hair gathered into a large messy bun on the back of her head, but it was easy to imagine that it was long. She was wearing a white dress that ended just above the knee, leaving her legs free but making a good disguise. It was a simple dress, but obviously expensive. She definitely looked like she belonged at the Illusion.

The only thing out of character was the huge knife she held in one hand and the ready handgun in the other.

She was the last to come into the room, but she stepped right up to us while the others hurried to close the doors.

She glanced at Patrick and the others, and then at me. "So. You are Kate, the Special Seer." Her French accent was thick but flowing.

I nodded, but decided not to extend a hand. Both of hers were already occupied with a mini arsenal. "Yes. And you are . . . ?"

"I am Claire," she said, her voice slightly aloof. She glanced to

Maddy. "I want you to leave with them. I will find you after this is over."

Maddy wanted to argue, it was obvious. But she didn't. She merely nodded. "Yes, Claire."

Toni stared at the beautiful Guardian, a small smile playing one his lips.

Lee rolled her eyes beside me, but Claire was now turning to Patrick. "I cannot promise you a lot of time. Your other friends—Henry and Jason—they are to meet you outside. Maddy knows the place."

Patrick's head bowed appreciatively. "Thank you for your assistance, Claire. I don't know how to thank you."

"Pray that we succeed in killing the Demon Lord," she suggested. Then she turned on her heel and marched to the closed doors, her small army behind her.

Jack hesitated between the two groups, but in the end he remained with us. I know it was a hard decision for him, but I was thankful. I just wanted us to get out of here. *All* of us.

The Australian Guardian tossed a hand toward the door. "Shall we?" he asked expansively.

Toni moved immediately to his side, the two of them forming our front line of defense. Lee and Maddy came behind, and Patrick and I took up the rear. He gave me a look, and I knew he didn't want me to walk right beside him—he wanted me closer to Lee, more sheltered. But he saw the determination in my eyes, and he decided not to say anything.

Jack and Toni led us out into a wide, empty hall. The evenly spaced lights on the walls were bright compared to the shadowed light we'd had in the bedroom. Claire and her followers had gone right—we went left. I was completely turned around, but I trusted that Jack knew where he was going.

We passed several sets of closed doors, until we reached the end of the hall. Jack hesitated, silently letting us know he couldn't be sure of what waited on the other side. And then he nodded to

Toni, who cautiously pulled one of the doors open.

Even though I could only see a thin crack of the brightly lit room beyond, I knew it was the spacious ballroom. My heart started to pound. We were almost out. Closer than I'd thought. Jack poked his head through the gingerly opened door and quickly scanned the huge room. A second later, he slipped through, and Toni was quick to follow. We filed into the empty ballroom, but at every footfall I cringed. We weren't overly loud, but the echo alone was enough to alert someone, wasn't it? The soft strains of Mozart that had drifted across the room earlier were now gone, replaced by Tchaikovsky's *Swan Lake*. I couldn't wait to get out of this wrongly beautiful place.

Jack was to the outer doors, and we were right behind him. He pulled it open—not pausing this time—and I nearly had a heart attack when he ran into someone.

"Henry!" Jack gasped breathlessly. "You bloody old man! You're supposed to wait outside!"

"Kate?" Grandpa struggled to push past his Guardian, who was shoving him back.

"We can swap the drum later," Jack complained quietly. "Can we all bail out first?"

"Grandpa, I'm fine," I assured him, stepping up next to Lee so he could see me clearly.

He grabbed my hand, Jack still between us. "Are you sure you're all right? If you ever do anything like this again, young lady, I swear—"

"Give her the gobful later, Henry."

"I agree with the Aussie," Toni said acutely.

Grandpa released a tense breath before dragging me forward by the hand until I was being crushed in his embrace. "Later," he agreed, while the others pushed past us so we could all be in the lobby area, the ballroom safely behind us.

I leaned against him, suddenly realizing that this nightmare really was almost over. Once we were out of here . . . I felt the need to apologize. "Grandpa, I'm sorry. I really am. But I had to do this."

He nodded and pulled back. "I know. I love you."

I smiled, and for some reason tears were in my eyes. "Thanks, Grandpa. I love you too."

Patrick closed the door on the ballroom, and Jack rolled his eyes at Jason, who stood holding an arm in the elevator for us.

"You too?" Jack whined.

Jason just waved us toward the elevator. "We need to hurry—two big guys were right behind us."

"Russians?" Patrick asked, putting a hand on my back to help urge me forward. Grandpa continued to hold my arm while we moved for the elevator.

Jason nodded. "Yeah."

Jack grunted. "Just what we need. The commies."

Once crowded into the elevator, Maddy pushed for the second floor. At Patrick's strange look she shrugged. "Claire suggested we stop on second and use the stairs to get down the rest of the way. It'll be easier to get out of the hotel that way. They won't expect it."

Lee was watching the glowing numbers as we steadily climbed down. "Now we just hope no one needs this elevator . . ."

Her words felt like a jinx, but we didn't stop until we reached the second floor. The doors slid open and several paces away stood two security guards—one a Demon, the other presumably a Seer. Both looked dangerous, and the Seer was talking into a shoulder radio. "We've got them! Floor two!"

Maddy reached instinctively for the first-floor button, hoping to get the doors closed, but Grandpa dropped my hand to stop her. Toni and Patrick were already diving toward the security guards, Jack and Jason a short step behind them. The evil Seer saw Jason and quickly drew out his gun to shoot the vulnerable opponent. But before they could even take aim, the guards were both dead on the carpet.

Toni gestured with his bloody knife for us to get out of the elevator. "Come on, come on. Maddy, where do we go?"

"The end of the hall—there's a door leading to the stairwell." Her voice hardly shook despite the adrenaline rush she must have been feeling.

Patrick grabbed my hand as soon as I was close, and I tried not to look at the blood on his knife. We started to run, but we weren't fast enough.

The elevator we'd ridden in was the middle of the three. There was another elevator on either side. Both seemed to ding open at the same time, as security from nearby floors flocked to respond to the call. I counted at least eight—most Demons, some Seers.

Halfway down the long hall, we looked over our shoulders and saw them giving chase and pulling out their guns.

Patrick shoved me in front of him, so he was shielding my back with his body. "Go, go, *go!*" He yelled to all of us, primarily the mortals. Jack and Toni fell back, behind the others, but it wasn't like their immortal bodies were the best or most effective shields.

Gunshots exploded behind us, ringing in the hall despite the silencers used on the guns. Lee screamed, but it wasn't a cry of pain—she hadn't been shot.

Jack let out a yelp and grabbed for his arm. But in a split second, it was pumping madly again, so I knew the wound had been superficial, or the bullet had gone straight through.

"Don't shoot!" someone screamed behind us. Without looking, I was pretty sure it was Yuri Dmitriev.

Viktor finished his brother's harsh thought. "She must be taken alive!"

Grandpa was puffing loudly, beginning to lag behind. Toni kept prodding him, urging him steadily forward with frequent pushes. Lee was a good runner. Better than I was. She burst ahead of us, able to reach the heavy door and drag it open so the rest of us didn't have to hesitate.

Patrick shoved me into the stairwell, and Toni snatched hold of Lee's arm, hauling her in with him. The large metal door slammed closed, and a whitish light exposed the deep stairwell.

There was nothing to bar the door with. Jack stepped forward, as if thinking he could somehow hold it. Then he came back to his senses and barked, "Move it!"

Maddy led the way, Jason at her side. Lee and I followed with Grandpa in tow while the three Guardians took up the rear. We didn't bother to try and muffle our footsteps. Speed was the object now, not stealth. Maddy stumbled and would have fallen if Jason hadn't grabbed her swinging arm. We had four flights of stairs to get down before we'd reach the first floor. We'd rounded the first flight and started on the second by the time the door above us crashed open, our enemies in hot pursuit. There were grunts and gasps—some muted shouts—but no more words. They had their orders. We tried to move faster.

Patrick was suddenly running at my other side, clinging to my arm and throwing me around the next corner to the third staircase. I felt like I was in one of those dreams where, no matter how hard you run or how fast your heart beats, you can't get away.

Lee panted evenly beside me, and Grandpa was wheezing behind us.

Maddy and Jason stepped onto the first-floor landing at the same time. But while Maddy ran for the door, Jason turned around to look back up the stairs. I realized belatedly that he held a small pistol with both hands—he was taking aim somewhere above our heads. His eyes behind his glasses were wide open and his gun was steady, but I had to wonder if he'd ever pulled a trigger before—excluding on Nintendo's *Duck Hunt*. He certainly didn't look the type.

He fired off a few rounds, aiming high and picking targets with care—probably just the Seers. There were cries of pain, so I knew he was hitting something. Patrick released his hold on me so Lee and I could dash through the door Maddy held open. But he was right behind us, and that was a good thing. Because this thin hall wasn't empty.

"Patrick!" I yelled needlessly, as the three Demon security guards lunged for us. Lee pushed into me in an effort to clear the doorway, knocking us both to the floor. I could feel more than hear Patrick dart past us toward the Demons. While he stabbed at the nearest one—missing the Demon's heart by a mere half inch—another Demon drew out a gun and aimed it at Patrick's head. It wouldn't kill him, but it would hurt him, slow him down.

I wriggled out from under Lee, desperate to do something. But before I could gather the breath to warn him about the gun, Jack was there, squeezing the trigger on his own small handgun. The Demon with the gun was blown back, momentarily dazed while Jack jumped on the last Demon, who was turning for me.

While Patrick grappled with the first Demon—both of them trying to sink a knife into the other—Grandpa and Toni reached for me and Lee, pulling us to our feet. Maddy was holding a fistful of Jason's shirt, drawing him back while he still fired his gun. The door to the stairwell banged closed, and Maddy shouted for us to go right.

Lee and I were pushed in that direction, past Patrick and Jack. Toni darted around us, thinking that it would probably be a good idea for one of the Guardians to be in front. Lee tripped over her feet, and Grandpa grabbed her arm to keep her from falling.

I heard Jack yell for Jason to keep going. I knew he had a point— these three Demons were nothing compared to those still chasing us. They had to be almost here. Two flights to go? One?

Jason and Maddy were right behind me, and though I trusted Jack, something made me slowly start turning, to make sure he and Patrick were really okay.

Things didn't move in slow motion, like in the movies. Rather, my ability to take things in sharpened, and I was able to perceive every detail at once.

Jason and Maddy continued to jog past me. She was still holding his shirt, and they both gave me a questioning look. But they didn't stop. They kept running after the others. I was glad; I didn't want my grandpa stopping for me.

I saw Patrick, a bloody gash just healing on his face from where the Demon knife had swiped painfully. Patrick was obviously winning the fight, though, because the Demon was the one forced up against the wall, and Patrick was just pushing closer. I didn't have to see the knife to know that Patrick wasn't going to miss this time.

Behind them I could see Jack on the floor beneath his opponent. The knife was in his hand though, and that hand was coming up fast. I knew that Demon was as good as finished.

It was the third Demon—the one Jack had shot—that concerned me. He was just pushing up from the floor, and he was holding something—a small spray bottle that could have been perfume. Instinct—and the look he was sending Patrick—assured me it wasn't.

I don't know that I actually put it together right then, when I started running for him, but by the time I was jumping in front of him I knew it was the virus. I didn't make a sound as I swept behind Patrick, who was just letting the Demon he'd stabbed slump to the floor.

I blindsided the Demon with the virus so he didn't notice me until I was in his face. He stumbled back a step, surprised, but I knew that wouldn't last.

I took advantage of the moment by grabbing his thick wrist, and my snatching fingers scrabbled for the bottle. It was a desperate game of tug of war; neither of us were willing to lose. He knew that if he didn't use the virus, the Guardians would kill him. They probably still would. At least this way he had a chance. I knew that if I lost, Patrick would get sick again. And that wasn't going to happen.

I sensed Jack standing behind us, close to the stairwell door. He saw me, saw the Demon I was wrestling with. "Kate!" he cried in alarm, stumbling a little, off-balance as he tried to reach me.

His shout had Patrick turning behind me. He must have seen the bottle. I don't know if he realized what it was or not, but he moved to help me anyway.

"Patrick, no!" I grunted sharply.

The Demon saw Patrick's face behind me, and he knew time was up. He jerked his hands upward, trying to aim over my shoulder. I managed to cling to his stiff fingers, despite his last harsh pull. His thumb touched the top of the spray bottle, depressing the button.

I screamed as the misting substance settled all over my face—burned into my eyes. I pinched them closed, but I didn't relinquish my hold on the Demon's hands.

And then suddenly the Demon was gone. His hands ripped from mine. The bottle fell to the floor, mostly empty. My eyes were closed, but somehow—despite the horrible pain erupting in my eyes—I knew that Jack had slammed into the Demon, knocking him away. It was the only thing that made sense, because Patrick's fingers were biting into my arms, and his frightened voice was right in front of me.

"Kate!" he choked.

"Patrick!" Jack yelled urgently. "They're coming!"

I knew what Jack meant. Any second now that stairwell door was going to burst open.

"I'm fine!" I yelled, my voice cracking in pain. "Patrick, it's the virus!" It was meant to be a warning for him. I could feel the wet substance on my face. It was already evaporating, or sinking into my skin. I wasn't worried about that—Terence had assured us that Seers and humans were immune. But was I contagious? I definitely didn't want to find out. He couldn't touch my skin.

He didn't let go of me, though. In fact, he pulled me closer, wrapping an arm around my waist. "We have to run," he told me, sounding furious. "Trust me!"

It went without saying that I did.

He pulled me forward, and soon we were running down the hall, my eyes shut tight against the violent sting.

I could hear Jack in front of us, pushing forward to keep the others moving. They'd halted at the end of the corridor, but with Jack's urging they pushed through the door.

I gasped aloud when Patrick pulled me out of the building and a wave of warm air slammed over us. "It's okay," he said, panting thinly. "We're outside." But I already knew that. Even without the burst of air, I could have figured it out by the change of ground. No more carpet. We were running on hot cement.

"To the left!" Jason yelled suddenly.

"I'll drive Kate's!" Toni shouted.

My car. Had they moved it, or were we parked in the same spot? Where was Jack's car?

I reluctantly tried to pry my eyes open, despite the stinging. I blinked heavily, trying to make sense of what I saw. Everything was a blur. It was dark, but all the flashing lights of the city gave an illusion of day. We were in the parking lot, and though I couldn't see my car or Jack's, I had a feeling that we were close.

It became too hard to keep my eyes open. I pinched them closed, hoping that would relieve the strain. I couldn't keep the pathetic whimper of pain from escaping.

Patrick's arm tightened around me. "It's okay," he murmured breathlessly. "Please Kate, it's going to be okay . . ."

"It's just my eyes," I told him sharply, knowing that he was fearing the worst. "Some of it got on them."

"We're almost there. Just a little further . . ."

I forced my eyes open again—yes, I could see them now. The cars were parked side by side. Jack's black Altima, my maroon Hyundai. Toni already had my keys; Jack was drawing his out.

And then Far Darrig stepped out from behind the large blue pickup parked next to mine, pistol in hand.

He hadn't come chasing after us like the others, because he knew where we'd eventually end up. It made horrible, chilling sense. Almost as horrible and chilling as his triumphant grin.

Lee screamed at his sudden appearance, and I wanted to scream in frustration. We were so close—Toni could have touched the hood of my car.

Far Darrig fired a subdued shot—not as silent as I would have imagined a silenced gun to sound—and Toni fell to the ground in response, a cloudy spray of blood coming off his chest where the bullet had ripped inside. Jason shoved Maddy between our two cars, pushing her to the ground with his own body.

Lee dropped to Toni's side, but Far Darrig had already squeezed the trigger, intending to make her the next victim. The bullet was already discharged, and it was forced to hit another target.

The person who'd been standing right behind her.

Through blurry eyes I watched the deadly bullet pound into my grandfather's chest, the fierce impact spinning him around. He fell onto the rough pavement, and I knew he was dead before he hit the ground. His aura was gone. Just gone.

"NO!" I screamed, ears ringing from the sound of his fall.

Patrick was shaking around me. And suddenly I had no support. I fell to my knees as Patrick dove into his brother. The gun fired harmlessly into the air—a bullet possibly meant for me, next in line. The weapon clattered to the ground as Patrick slammed Far Darrig into the front of the truck's grill again and again.

I stared at my grandpa's unmoving body, the scuffed brown shoe on his closest foot. I couldn't breathe. Tears streamed from my searing eyes, and my insides felt like they were going to implode. This couldn't be happening. It wasn't possible. He couldn't be dead. What would I tell Grandma? The twins?

This wasn't happening. I would deny it forever if that could somehow change the awful truth.

Jack had tossed Jason the keys. The Seer was opening the driver's door of the Altima, and Maddy was scrambling into the back. The Australian Guardian was on the ground now, grabbing his old Seer's wrist, searching for a pulse that wasn't there, would never be there again.

Toni and Lee were stumbling to their feet, clinging to each other. Toni looked gray, but the bullet must have gone all the way through him—he was recovering from the wound. Toni saw Patrick, slamming a clenched fist into Far Darrig's already bloody face, and then he saw Grandpa's body and Jack quickly shaking his head.

Across the parking lot, far behind us, I could hear voices. The Demons were coming, yelling, getting closer. Still chasing us. Why were they still chasing us?

Jack slung Grandpa's limp body over one shoulder, the motion hurried but strangely graceful. Toni threw the keys to Lee. She glanced to me, and then followed Toni's clipped orders and moved to get behind the wheel.

I watched Jack as he jogged behind his car. Jason had already popped the trunk. Jack dumped my grandfather inside and then slammed the lid down. He looked to Toni, who was on the ground, picking up the gun Far Darrig had dropped. He aimed, yelled something to Patrick, and fired the weapon.

Patrick had thrown himself back at the last possible second. Far Darrig's face shattered with color, and he crumpled to the ground in shrieking agony. Knowing that he'd be healed in mere seconds didn't make the sight any less gruesome. Yet, more disturbing than the graphic sight was the fact that I didn't react to seeing it—I only blinked.

As soon as Far Darrig hit the ground, Toni stepped closer, his extended arm taut and ready to shoot him again when he recovered.

Patrick darted for me, his eyes unreadable, his face pale and drawn. He crouched before me, glancing over my shoulder at the approaching Demons. "Kate," he said, his voice surprisingly clear. "We need to go."

I just stared at him through narrow, watering eyes, completely in shock.

He swallowed hard at the sight of me.

Toni fired the gun again behind us, growled for Patrick to just pick me up, for heaven's sake . . .

"I'm so sorry," Patrick breathed. And then his arms were around me and he hefted us both to our feet. When I swayed, he scooped me up bride-style, my knees too weak to protest, and then he turned for the car Lee had revved and running.

The black Altima was already backed up, rolling forward, and fighting to reach the nearest exit.

I wanted to help Patrick. I didn't want to be carried, but I had no control over my body. I was detached, and I think I was grateful. The less aware I was of my pain, the better.

Patrick pulled open the back door. He dumped me inside, then pushed me across the backseat, making room for himself.

Toni shot a last bullet at Far Darrig, and then he jerked his angled arm closer to his body and ran toward us, actually sliding over the hood to reach the passenger side. Before he'd even closed the door, he was ordering Lee to drive.

She wasn't great with a stick, but I'd taught her enough that she didn't kill it. We backed away from Far Darrig's fallen body, away from the chasing Demons that were nearly upon us. Then she shifted to first and we stuttered curtly before shooting after Jack's car, out of the parking lot, away from the Illusion, and onto the Strip.

The Demons followed us in cars, but only for a little while. Eventually they gave up. I think that happened when we were suddenly surrounded by eight Nissan Altimas of various colors. After that, the Demons backed off. We were in Guardian territory now.

Patrick held me tightly, but I kept my face away from him. When he tried to touch my skin, make me face him, I finally spoke. My voice was dull and cracking. "I don't know if I'm contagious. You shouldn't be anywhere near me."

He stopped trying to touch my face. But he didn't move away. My back was against his body, and he kept pulling me closer as if that would somehow stop my world from spinning apart.

I didn't cry, even when he started whispering how sorry he was. So, so sorry . . .

I didn't acknowledge the words, because that would make them true. And they couldn't be true. He couldn't be dead. Not that quickly. Not like that. Murdered by the Demon I was supposed to have the power to save . . .

My vision was still blurry, but Lee was obediently pulling up to a large house. A mansion. We weren't in the heart of Vegas anymore. I don't know how long we'd been driving. I wasn't really aware of anything. Even Patrick's desperate whispers for me to hang on meant little, if anything, to me.

The car was shut off. Toni leaned over to hug Lee, who was shaking terribly. Patrick was opening his door, pulling me with him as he slid out. "Terence," he said loudly. "Kate needs a doctor. . ."

His words died off to me. Because Jack was looking in his trunk, asking one of the newly arrived Guardians to bring out a body bag.

My eyes rolled. I felt Patrick clutch my sagging waist just before I lost consciousness.

thirty-four

"Patrick, I need you to calm down." A voice, warm and calm.

"Is it the virus? You said it wouldn't affect her." A voice, frantic and worn.

"Patrick, breathe. She's going to be fine. The virus isn't causing this." It was the warm voice again, soothing in its familiarity.

A new voice, colder to my ears. Clinical. "Terence is right. She's just had an emotional overload. I rinsed her eyes and scrubbed her skin, but I'm confident she's not in danger. And since the virus couldn't take hold on her cells, it's not incubating. She's not contagious, and she's not in any danger."

Patrick's worn voice—a deteriorated whisper—was almost disbelieving. "She's going to be okay?"

"Yes," Terence answered mildly, tone a little less warm and a little more rough. "She'll be fine. As I promised. But, Patrick, we need to check you."

"I didn't get any on me. She took it all."

"No, not for the virus. You've been given the antidote. A sample of your blood can give us an idea of what we need to do to construct a cure. We could make our own antidote. I have five new Guardians here, all of them infected."

"Can you do that here? I don't want to leave her . . ."

The new voice sighed. "Very well. I'll be right back."

Footsteps trailed away, and I faded too.

When I resurfaced I was more aware of my surroundings. I didn't open my eyes, but I could feel things now, not just hear them. I was lying on an uncomfortable bed. I'd been in one of these before, so I knew exactly what it was: a hospital bed.

A muted monitor was beeping steadily. Someone was holding my hand.

There were voices again.

It was Lee. She was answering a question. "She'll be here soon. She just boarded the jet you sent." She sighed loudly, obviously worried. "Shouldn't we take her to a real hospital?"

If she received an answer, I didn't hear it.

"What are we going to tell the police?" Toni asked timidly. "We have to tell them something. Fabricate some story."

Terence sighed. "A mugging gone wrong, perhaps? He was following a teenage runaway. It's a believable story . . ."

"You can't put that kind of pressure on Kate," Patrick argued thinly, his voice the closest to me. The fingers around my hand flexed. "Even if it's just a story, she'll have to live with it."

"Because it's so close to the truth, you mean?" a new voice asked. The French accent was familiar, though.

The hand around mine vibrated with barely restrained emotion, but before anything could erupt, Terence was speaking warningly. "Claire . . . Patrick . . . Both of you must understand that this night has been a terrible ordeal for each of you. Try to show some compassion . . ."

I drifted again. I couldn't think of a reason to stay there, when oblivion was so much better.

I came close to surfacing once, when I felt moist lips on my face, his familiar mouth pressing enticingly against my unresponsive skin. "I love you, Kate," he whispered to an otherwise empty room. "Please, please come back . . . I need you to wake up . . . I need you, Kate. Please . . . please don't blame me. I'm so sorry . . ."

Blame him? For what? And then I remembered. My Grandpa

was dead. I slipped away again, even though of course I didn't blame Patrick. *I don't blame you . . .*

And then I heard the voice that could summon me back. The one that didn't make sense for me to hear, because I knew that I hadn't been moved, and she couldn't be here.

"Kate? Kate Bennett, you wake up this second. You're scaring us all to death."

I peeled my eyes back, wincing against the bright light. I stared up at my grandma's face, seeing that it was stiffer than usual. Her aura was darker than usual too, but her eyes managed to stay the same. Both loving and scolding. Grateful and grieved.

"I'm sorry, Grandma," I whispered, my voice cracking from disuse. "I'm so sorry."

"You stop that, girl," her voice was firm. "What happened to Henry—to your grandpa—it wasn't your fault. You hear me? It wasn't your fault."

It wasn't until she forgave me that I realized I *had* been blaming myself. That's why I hadn't allowed myself to wake up. I didn't deserve to wake up.

It was amazing how those words spoken in her uniquely husky voice had the power to release me, even though I knew a small part of myself would blame me forever.

I sniffed loudly as the tears began to fall, and then I reached for her. She leaned closer, wrapped her arms around me as I put my arms around her neck. I held her tightly—felt her tremble—and I knew she needed to hold me as much as I needed to be held by her.

It wasn't until she finally pulled back that I realized we weren't alone. That Patrick was still sitting faithfully at my side, watching me with hallow eyes. Toni and Lee were standing near the door to the small hospital room, and Jack was by the monitor that was keeping track of my every heartbeat.

"Where are we?" I asked.

My grandmother squeezed my hands while Toni cleared his throat. "We're still in Vegas, if that's what you mean. Only barely, though. This is a Guardian facility, one of Terence's bases. He's got one here, one in Oregon, and one in Cali—"

"Remember the mansion?" Lee interrupted. I nodded. "That's where we are," she told me, casting Toni a disapproving look.

Jack spoke next. "You gave us a scare, though. Holy dooley, girl . . ." He just shook his head.

"How long have I been out?"

Patrick answered that one, his voice meager and a little too abrupt. "Nearly six hours. We were getting worried."

"Getting?" Toni laughed once, without humor. "Patrick was ready to start punching through some walls."

"I'm sorry." I shot my Guardian a contrite look over my arm, but that seemed to bother him more than anything else.

That's when it suddenly hit me that my grandma was here, in Vegas, with a bunch of Guardians standing all around her.

Grandma seemed to read my thoughts. She patted my hand. "Yes, dear. No more secrets. I know everything."

"But . . . how?"

"Lee called a few hours ago. She told me something had happened here in Vegas. That you were in a hospital and you were going to be fine, but your grandpa was . . . he'd been shot. She told me that her mother had connections with a private plane agency, and that a plane was waiting for me at the airport. I'm a little worried that I believed her lie so easily—I've half a mind to warn her mother." She cast a quick look to Lee, who only shrugged in reply. Grandma focused back on me. "I left the twins with Mrs. Collins, and then I packed."

I looked to Lee, confused. If Lee hadn't told her about the Guardians . . .

Grandma hurried to continue. "A long time ago, your grandpa suggested we write letters to each other, in case something sudden like this ever happened. It would contain our last words." Her eyes glistened with unshed tears, but she tried to smile. "I used to tease him that his was so much longer than mine. His letter explained everything. An appended section told me about you, how special you are." She shrugged. "I called Lee back, told her I knew everything. I got the real story about what happened, and then I got on the plane and came straight here."

I struggled with my emotions, but I was clearly losing. "Are you mad? That he never told you?"

"Hmm," she considered briefly, but it was more teasing than anything else. "At first, maybe. But now I see the wisdom in it. I *am* upset that you didn't tell me anything, though. You're not supposed to keep secrets from your grandmother."

I swallowed hard. My words still had to fight to get out. "So what now?"

She squeezed my hand. "We mourn. We go home. We cry some more. And slowly we heal. What else can we do?"

I knew she was right. Partly because I knew from experience that she spoke the truth. But mostly I trusted her because she was my grandma, and she was the one person in this room suffering more than I was right now.

❀

Jason needed to fly back home for a calculus test, so the jet my grandmother had arrived in was being prepped for the flight back home. Terence and some Guardian doctor woman with a no-nonsense voice cleared me for travel. Grandma wanted to get back to the twins, who had yet to learn about Grandpa's death, as soon as possible. Lee also needed to get home before her mother grounded her for eternity. (She was out in the hall, trying to calm her down now. Funny, how the words *I'm in Vegas* hadn't done the trick.) Patrick would be coming back with us on the plane, leaving Jack and Toni on car duty.

While my grandmother made final plans for Grandpa's body and the fabricated story of his murder, Claire—the French Guardian—popped into my room to check up on me.

She still looked beautiful, but there was an anger in her eyes too.

I guessed that her assassination attempt had failed, but I didn't dare ask her for details. I didn't want her to bite my head off.

After learning that I was just fine, she straightened her shoulders and spoke firmly. She kept casting looks to Patrick, to see how he'd react to her words. "Terence has asked me to become your third Guardian. Such security is usually never offered to a single Seer, but as you are the Demon Lord's latest project, the more protection you can get, the better your chances of survival will be."

Patrick didn't seem thrilled with the idea. These two Guardians rubbed each other wrong, it was obvious. But Toni—who couldn't take his eyes off her—looked pleased.

I gave a grateful nod. "Thank you. I would appreciate your help."

She bowed her head. "It's that or relocate you—which would perhaps be the better alternative. But Terence assured me that you would be reluctant to relocate."

"Yes, I would be."

She shrugged. "It's probably for the best. According to Terence, we'd end up relocating half your city, you have so many friends the Demon Lord could torture."

"Um . . . thanks."

She gave a last bow and turned quickly to see Toni still staring. She actually grunted at him. "Don't even think about it. I'm too old for you."

Toni grinned. "I'm older than I look," he assured her with a wink.

She stepped right up to him and said moderately, "I was born in 1430. I dare you to beat that."

Toni looked a little shocked, but he overcame it quickly. "I've always liked older women."

She gave him a last look, then moved out of the room without another word.

Jack rolled his eyes and stepped around the bed. He stooped in to give me a quick hug. "I'll be in touch," he promised. "I'm staying with the body, until things with the authorities get cleared up."

"Thank you, Jack," I whispered into his shoulder. "For everything."

"No worries, Kate. No worries." He patted my arm, then shook Patrick's hand before he was gone too.

Toni stood around for a second, but then he wordlessly scooted out to give us some privacy.

As soon as the door fell closed, Patrick looked up at me, taking my hand easily. "Are you sure you feel up to flying?"

I squeezed his fingers. "I'm sure. I just want to get home. I need to be with Jenna and Josie."

He nodded once, and the despair he'd been fighting against won. His head fell slowly onto my nearest leg, his forehead pressing firmly against the textured blanket. "I'm so sorry, Kate," he whispered brokenly. "If I'd moved faster . . ."

I continued to hold his hand, but my free fingers sank into his hair, trying to soothe him. My voice was surprisingly calm. "Patrick, you aren't responsible for what happened. You didn't kill him. Far Darrig did that."

"He's my brother. I should have stopped him. I should have stopped him from becoming this."

"You aren't responsible for him. For what he's done. We each have a life to live. Our own choices to make . . ." My voice drifted, and then I spoke haltingly—fear leaking into my voice. "The Demon Lord isn't going to be happy with me, is he?"

Patrick finally looked up, his eyes hard. "He's not going to get to you, Kate. I promise."

I nodded. Not that I entirely believed him. But I loved him. And in the end, that was all that really mattered.

❄

Grandpa's funeral was that weekend. To say that it was a hard day would be a terrible understatement. I couldn't imagine what it would have been like if I hadn't had Grandma. She was so strong and dignified. Even when she cried, she was someone to look up to.

The twins were still in shock. They cried, but it had been so sudden. His death hardly seemed real. The story was horribly simple—he'd been killed during an attempted robbery while coming to fetch me and Lee. The twins didn't doubt the story, and surprisingly they didn't seem to blame me. But maybe that was just because they hadn't fully realized he was gone yet.

It wasn't until we'd left the church and we were at the graveside service. That's when it hit them. It wasn't when his casket was lowered into the ground. It wasn't when a soldier began to play "Taps" in the distance. It wasn't until Grandma accepted the carefully folded flag that Josie finally burst into tears. I was already holding Jenna, who'd started to cry with the music, and Grandma was clearly occupied with her own sorrow. But Patrick was there, sitting on the front row at Grandma's insistence. He gathered Josie into his arms, and when he looked to me, I saw so many emotions in his wet eyes. He was feeling our heartache—that much was obvious. He felt guilty that he was sitting with our family, when it had been his brother that had pulled the trigger. He was remembering his own losses. He wanted to hold me.

I gave him a thin smile, and he swallowed before giving me a nod. I don't know if he understood my silent message of love, but I watched as he tenderly whispered in my sister's ear, trying to calm her.

Jack was sitting behind us, and I could hear his sniffling, though he tried to hide it. He kept putting his hand on Grandma's shoulder. They'd become close over the past few days, planning the funeral, sorting things out with the police. I had to wonder how often he'd been through losing Seers. How many friends he'd lost and mourned. Immortality had a terrible price.

Toni was there too. And Lee and her mother. Peter Keegan came with them, but he looked uneasy. He didn't feel right being here—Toni's dark looks weren't helping anything. I gave him a small, thankful smile, and his aura slowly lost the nervous edge. Aaron was there, with his entire family, and standing in the back was Clyde, the Demon. Everyone my grandpa had cared about was there. Even Terence had flown in for the funeral, though he hadn't been able to stay for the graveside service. With Patrick's blood, he and the Guardian scientists were hard at work, trying to create a cure that could save the other infected Guardians. They were confident they were close, which was an unexpected comfort to me.

When the graveside was finished, everyone wanted a chance to hug the family members. Though most of our neighbors hadn't come to the cemetery, it was still a long line. Each hug was special to me. Lee—wearing a deep-blue, Rainbow Days dress at my urging—held me especially tight.

Toni, Jack, Clyde; and then Aaron was crushing me, and that's when I really started to cry. The whole funeral had been a giant dose of déjà vu for me. But Aaron's hug was especially poignant. He'd embraced me this exact same way in this same cemetery, in essentially the very same spot, not long ago.

"I love you, Kate," he whispered into my hair. "I always will, okay? I'll always be here for you. I promise. Whatever you need, whenever you need it—I'm there, all right?"

"Thank you, Aaron. Thank you so much . . ."

I finished hugging everyone else, and we all wandered back toward our cars. I didn't feel like going back in the limo. I knew Grandma was trying to talk to the twins in there, and offer more comfort. I needed to have just a moment's break from their horrible grief. Their auras more than their tears made me feel hollow inside.

Patrick came up beside me, scooping up my hand while I walked. "Do you want to ride with me?" he asked quietly, sensing my thoughts.

I nodded. "That would be nice."

We walked for a few steps in silence before I spoke, my voice soft. "I hate knowing I can't do anything." His eyes darted to my face, prompting me to continue. I shrugged a single shoulder. "It's ridiculous. I can go back hundreds, even thousands of years. But I can't go back and change this. I can't bring him back." I shook my head. "I keep thinking about what he told me. About destiny. I guess I'm trying to understand how this could possibly be a part of some bigger plan."

Patrick's voice was thin and compassionate—but once again, his eyes held a million other emotions. "You'll see him again, Kate."

I sighed. "I know."

"That has to ease some of the pain . . ."

"It does." And I guess he was right.

But that same thing that made it possible to see my grandfather again was the thing that would keep me from Patrick forever.

I'd once heard that it would be impossible to be unhappy in heaven. But if I didn't have Patrick, how could the afterlife be heaven to me?

I guess I would have to trust in the words of Pastor O'Donnell, and my grandpa. That everything would be all right in the end, and that things happened for a reason; no matter how impossible that seemed right now.

I held Patrick's hand and we walked to his car, neither of us saying a word. Words weren't necessary in that moment.

epilogue

Patrick O'Donnell
New Mexico, United States

I was in bed, trying to find sleep. I hadn't enjoyed much of that lately, and after the long day, the funeral . . . I just wanted to be unconscious.

Toni was in the other room. Claire had moved in the day before, on the floor above us. She'd brought her Seer, Maddy, along who was an orphan that knew only this lifestyle. Honestly, I didn't really have a strong opinion about them. I didn't especially like the French Guardian, but I wasn't going to complain about her presence. It meant more protection for Kate, after all. Even now, Claire was keeping watch over Kate's house, invisible to all of them except for Kate, obviously. The overzealous protection detail had begun.

Kate would need it, I knew. I was reluctant to burden her mind any more than it already was, but she wasn't out of danger. And she knew that, on some level. But I was confident that she didn't realize just how precarious her situation was.

Terence was quite sure that the Demon Lord would take his time with her, knowing that she'd be heavily guarded now. Now that she'd secured Far Darrig's existence, she was just another Special Seer. Rare, but not of immediate importance. He would wait.

But I could wait too. Because he wasn't getting near her ever again. Neither was Sean. I'd already irrefutably sworn that to myself. I would no longer be weak. I could have killed him in Las Vegas, after he'd shot Kate's grandfather. I could have killed him easily.

But I hadn't.

I wouldn't make the same mistake twice. I would be strong next time. Because I'd been right all along. Sean was dead. Only the monster Far Darrig remained. And I would kill him. It was my destiny. A way to put my brother's soul to rest.

The Demon deserved death after everything he'd done.

I closed my eyes tightly, as if that would make sleep come faster.

And then I heard a gasp at the foot of my bed.

I wasn't alone anymore.

I threw off my sheets, not understanding how someone could have gotten inside. I would have heard the door.

"Who's there?" I hissed, snatching up the knife on my bedside table.

There was no solid answer, just a short cry of pained anguish. The room was dark, but the filtered moonlight outlined the room. I stood, pushing the bedsheets aside as I moved for the foot of my bed. I don't know what I expected to find lying on the hard floor as I rounded the short corner, but it surely wasn't the sight that met my eyes.

It was Kate. She was staring up at me, eyes unfocused and already glazing softly in death. And she was covered in blood. Her whole stomach and chest—she was covered in the horrible color. "Patrick," she gasped painfully.

The dagger fell from my frozen fingers. I fell an instant behind it, slamming to my knees beside her. My eyes flashed over her wounds, though I already knew they were fatal gunshots—I wasn't sure how many. I grabbed her limp hand and searched her sallow, tortured face, my free hand stroking her hair back from her face.

My words ground out through gritted teeth. "Kate. What happened? What's going on? How'd you get in here?"

She swallowed hard, her unclear eyes focused on mine. "What day is it?" she choked urgently.

"What day . . . ?" And then it hit me.

This wasn't my Kate.

At least, not yet. Someday she would be—in the future. This Kate had come back in time. But that would mean . . . "Kate, you can't be here." My eyes revealed the words I couldn't speak. If she was here, in her own past, she was risking her life. She was going to die.

She almost laughed, though it was faint and stuttering. "I think I was already pretty done for." She saw the pain on my face, and she tried to squeeze my fingers. The attempt was pitifully frail. "I'm sorry, Patrick. I know this is hard. But I need you to listen. I need you to change what happens. But to do that, I need to know what day it is."

I fought for my voice. I couldn't stop my eyes from wandering back to all the blood on her ruined body. I wanted to hold her, cradle her in my arms, but I didn't dare move her. I didn't know how to save her. I forced myself to answer her question. "The funeral. It was the funeral today."

Her lips pressed tightly together, and she closed her eyes. "Not far enough," she mourned to herself. "I wanted to save . . ." Her eyes opened, and new determination was there. "Patrick, I don't have much time. I'm being pulled back. But you need to promise me something."

"What? Anything!"

She half smiled. But it was a sad smile. A heartbroken smile. A smile that said good-bye. I wanted to throw up. "I need you to promise that you won't try to stop me. That you'll let me do what I need to do. That you'll save the twins instead. Keep them safe, no matter what. Because you can't save me, Patrick. Not anymore. Not when I've gone back . . ."

"Kate, you have to tell me what happened—what happens. Who did this to you?"

"It doesn't matter."

I struggled to breathe. "Doesn't matter?" She was dying in my arms—how could that not matter? And I was helpless. Completely helpless. "Kate, please," I begged raggedly. "Give me anything . . ."

And then I remembered Toni. He could get a first aid kit, an ambulance—something. "Toni!" I yelled.

She winced at the intrusive sound, and then her eyes were back on me. "I know this is weird for you, but my Patrick isn't here. With me in the future, I mean, so if it's all right . . . If I can tell you, that . . . I love you, Patrick. I love you so much. No matter what, I'll always love you. No matter where I am. Please promise me you'll remember that?"

My bedroom door was thrown open. Toni literally cried out at the sight of her and all her blood. But I ignored him—I was trapped by her eyes. "I promise," I croaked. "I'll always remember."

She forced a smile, like my useless promise somehow possessed the power to comfort her. "Save the twins. When everything goes wrong . . . when everything we do fails . . . just take care of . . . of the twins." Her breath caught in a strangled choke. She fought to continue. "And please . . . please, Toni . . . tell Toni . . . he . . ."

She was gurgling, low in her throat, unable to form the desperate warning because of the unstoppable advance of her own death. She tried squeezing my hand again. And though she was impossibly weaker than before, I could actually feel the faint flex of her muscles this time. And then the light in her open eyes vanished, and her body grew still—a second before she disappeared.

My hand held only air. The blood on the floor was the only evidence that she'd been here at all.

Tears were lying stagnant on my cheeks. I hadn't even realized I'd started crying. I looked to Toni, my empty hand burning.

His eyes were wide, and his face was blanched.

I couldn't breathe.

I'd just seen a glimpse of the future. I'd just watched Kate die.

The only question was, how long until this nightmare future became my reality?

The Story Concludes in Book Three: *Guardians*

acknowledgments

Ican still hardly believe that I'm writing thank-yous for my second published book. It's so exciting! Dreams most obviously come true. There are so many people to thank, I'm sure to miss someone. But I'm going to start with the most important: my Heavenly Father, for blessing me with an imagination and putting me in a home where that imagination was allowed to flourish.

Mom, your help in the writing, editing, and encouraging departments is simply amazing. You're the most considerate slave-driver ever born. Dad, you've helped me with so much of the technical stuff, and I really appreciate the faith you have in me. I love you both so much!

I would also like to thank each of my siblings: Richard (best big brother, even if you tease me for my career choice—and everything else), Kevin (best Texan salesman and movie quoter—you rock, Elder!), Kimberly (best listener, period—your help is invaluable); Joseph (best comic relief—Toni's got nothing on you); Samuel (best supporter and an encouraging fan to boot); Emma (best teenage perspective of Patrick—and a great masseuse); Lilly (best little sister and fellow Disney princess fanatic); Matthew (best *Doctor Who* marathon buddy—don't blink!), and Jacob (best inspiration—thanks for everything). Growing up with you guys has been awesome—let's all stay young forever, okay?

A special thanks to my beloved beta readers, who helped in all the different stages of the writing process! Jill, Crystal, Rebecca, Yvonne, Craig, Ashley, Katelin, Alyssa, and the beautiful Townhouse Girls.

Brian, thanks for your endless help with the website—I truly appreciate all you do.

A special thanks to all my wonderful friends that continue to not only put up with me but also support me in every way possible. You know who you are—thank you! Also, a very special thank you to Emily and Landen.

And, of course, thanks again to my first unofficial fan club: James, Rex, Kent, Rich. You're all awesome! Thanks for your continued support.

The great people at Cedar Fort deserve a huge thanks, especially Shersta, for believing in me; Melissa, for helping me make sense; Erica, for an amazing cover; and Laura, for all the support.

And a HUGE thank-you to my dedicated readers! This wouldn't be possible without you. Thanks for reading!